To M

Read this and think
of me. I have courage
from the character

lots of love

JANE x.

Tales of Roumanhi

Volume 1

Homequest:
LIBERATION

JE Browning

authorHOUSE®

AuthorHouse™ UK Ltd.
500 Avebury Boulevard
Central Milton Keynes, MK9 2BE
www.authorhouse.co.uk
Phone: 08001974150

First published by AuthorHouse 7/6/2010

ISBN: 978-1-4490-9363-1 (sc)

This book is printed on acid-free paper.

www.homequest-liberation.com

Firstly, I would like to thank Despina Simeonidou, who encouraged my enormous hand written first draft back in 1992 when I was teaching in Greece.

Thanks also to my mum for passing on her love of writing, and to my dad for inspiring my love of fantasy and science fiction.

And finally, *lu'ari makash* to Natalie Cottrell whose insatiable appetite for my work not only inspired me to return to writing after a long absence, but also resulted in my desire to finally publish the first book in the series.

I hope you enjoy the following adventure as much as I enjoyed bringing the Tales of Roumanhi series to life.

Caelcáladrim dakrit louis!

CONTENTS

1   The inquisition 1

2   Clanmeet 16

3   Slythe 39

4   In trust there is hope 66

5   Parting of the ways 88

6   Strange revelations 109

7   Analysis 140

8   Gilgarad 168

9   Confrontations 196

10 Tragedy and transformation 222

11 Family reunion 244

12 It's all in the genes 269

13 The horn of Camaldriss 290

14 The Arena 310

15 Discoveries 343

16 Kylian 373

17 The Coronation 400

The Land of Roumanhi

Saxskotnak Lands

Blackwood

Youl

Kurkadin
Mnts

Roumanhi

Coronation
Feld

The Great
Desert

Ahrakha
City

Harouk
Lands

Idlbach

Vinewood

Bramwood

Mistenwood

El Greezma

Poppydom

Harvest on
Toman

N

Kalkass

Kalkass Gap

Denashika Keep

Kalkass
Sea

ONE

The inquisition

T'skya began to stir. Her sun damaged face, raw and soiled, contorted into a scowl, aging her otherwise youthful brow. Images of harsh impact and tortuous heat, desperate incapacitating thirst and terror swirled around her head like a vortex, threatening to engulf her. She struggled and clawed through schizophrenic nightmares towards the safety of consciousness, aided by a sudden stabbing pain in the centre of her chest. Her eyes sprang open and she quailed.

Three tall, cloaked and hooded figures, each brandishing an archaic weapon stood before her. A long flint-tipped spear was pinning her painfully against the gnarled and knotted bark of an ancient tree.

T'skya stared up wide eyed not daring to move, desperately trying to master her fear; desperately trying to comprehend. None of it made sense! She was meant to be in the sprawling city across the mountains but her recollections ended in the furnace of a hostile desert; her ship destroyed and all hopes gone, then falling, darkness, nothing. How in the hell had she come to be sitting in a cold, damp forest with a spear in her flesh?

T'skya fervently wished she had stayed on board the

Mothership. It was not fair! She was just an environmental analyst and had only recently passed her atmospheric entry examinations. But the situation on board was dire and she was duly expendable, and now it seemed her life was in jeopardy before she had accomplished anything.

She was trembling in spite of herself. T'skya did not want to die, not here and now, not by a stranger's hand, not by anyone's hand, and try as she might she could not discern who or what her captors were. Their cloaks were long and peculiarly camouflaged and their hoods hung low, casting long shadows upon their faces; scarves covered their mouths as if warding them from the cold, or concealing ugly alien features that she scarcely dared to imagine.

Glancing cautiously about her, T'skya realised she was surrounded. The beings' garments blended so perfectly with the bark of the trees and the forest hues that it was not until they moved that she could perceive their presence. The cloth seemed to alter its shades as a chameleon becomes dappled green amongst the flora or mottled hues of brown upon baked soil. In all she counted five in the group but could not swear others would not materialise from the forest like incorporeal spirits, and it did nothing to calm her.

Nobody spoke but their attention was firmly upon her. T'skya, unsure of their intent, remained silent, not wishing to provoke them; not wishing to become a host for their offspring or food for their tables. Observing their weapons, she imagined them somewhat primitive, perhaps no more advanced than her ancestors from millennia before; yet paradoxically their cloaks were of unparalleled craftsmanship and design - perhaps they could be reasoned with.

Turning her eyes upwards, T'skya bravely gazed at the aggressive shadow-masked figure. The response was not as she had hoped and she quickly averted her eyes, wincing as the spear tip pressed deeper, pricking the surface of her skin. Someone raised a hand and the pressure was grudgingly eased.

T'skya stole a glance assuming the figure to be the leader, but the being remained silent and motionless, tension shining through their posture like a beacon.

Uncertain what to do, T'skya raised a hesitant smile and ventured a couple of words in the softest, non-hostile voice she could muster, although certain they would not understand her. It was not the introduction she had expected or hoped for and the words sounded trite to her ears.

There were murmurs of derision. The spear bearer snorted and spat on the ground. T'skya's smile quickly faded and her mien became apprehensive. She had no idea what to do; the lack of communication was unnerving. She was burned, cold, tired, aching all over and was getting progressively wetter in the drizzle, which gave the forest an oppressive atmosphere and caused clouds of mist to rise from the vegetation. Her teeth began to chatter, half from the chill of the day and half through growing dread.

Coughing slightly to clear her throat, she attempted a few more words of greeting but was instantly silenced by an outburst. '*Loua tru trilákha oui,*' hissed the inimical figure gesturing towards T'skya.

She was surprised to hear a woman's voice and although she could not understand the language, it did not take T'skya's genius to realise the female wished her harm. T'skya ardently prayed to her lucky boots that the leader would be more merciful.

'*Dokh louas simih setih,*' he replied in a softer, more musical voice which told of forbearance.

'*Ala ys ben on tanai. Libiat oui yolli!*' the woman insisted, motioning her spear towards T'skya's head.

'*Ys raoun,*' someone seemed to agree, and others murmured their concurrence.

The leader gestured for silence and was immediately obeyed. Turning to each of his people, he asked in supplication; '*Da lasa se sepih, setih loua trilákha rel el korou on trilakhál? Cel, dokh louas railiki leo tanai!*'

The figures bowed their heads, considering his words as if vaguely ashamed. Only the woman showed no reaction. She stood with her head held high and T'skya could almost sense the menace penetrating her.

'*Lee ity loua taverio meh oui?*' she demanded.

The leader paused, fingering his bow with well sculpted hands. 'What we do with her remains to be seen.' Then he asked T'skya slowly; 'How came you here?'

T'skya's mouth dropped open, her amazement belaying her fears. It was impossible! 'You...you speak my language!'

'I know it well. I ask again. How came you here?'

T'skya knew instinctively her answer was imperative, but she had no knowledge of her coming and did not even know where 'here' was. One minute she was stumbling across swathes of desert sand and the next she was sprawled in the damp vegetation of an ancient forest.

She considered her options carefully. She doubted these obviously simple people would credit her story, even though their knowledge of her language ludicrously suggested previous contact of some kind. It was inconceivable; T'skya knew without question she was the first of her kind to journey to that region of space.

'I honestly don't know,' she answered, shaking her head. 'I had an accident and was walking in the desert trying to make it to the forest to stay alive and I think I fell. Now I'm here. I can't tell you any more, I'm sorry. I don't understand it myself.' She glanced around nervously as murmurs of disbelief began amongst the people. The leader again motioned for silence.

'Why were you seeking this place?' he asked solemnly.

T'skya grimaced inside. The directives from her Commander were absolutely clear. She paused for a moment trying to gather her manically wayward thoughts and replied softly; 'To learn about the people and the land.'

'To spy and betray!' came the woman's contemptuous riposte.

'At least that we can believe.'

'No,' T'skya insisted quickly. 'I'm not your enemy.'

'You are all our enemies!' she snapped, stamping her foot.

T'skya wondered what she meant by 'all'. Everyone who was not part of their group? Everyone from a different region? And how *did* they know her language...?

'Peace!' the man admonished gently. 'We must let her speak.'

'And listen to more lies?' the woman snarled.

'Perhaps; perhaps not.' He considered for a moment. 'Guard her,' he ordered before gathering the others about him. The group talked out of earshot for some minutes but T'skya could hear the occasional raised voice and sensed the undertones of disquiet as they argued over her fate.

Her heart was playing timpani and despite the chilly dampness T'skya broke into a nervous sweat. She had never felt comfortable in situations outside her control and was used to obeying orders. Now there was no-one to guide her and she only had her instincts and training, such as it was, to rely on. Doubts and insecurities sprang from every fibre of her being and tears began to well behind her eyes. She fought them off with what little strength she could muster and attempted to control her rapid breathing. She had minimally avoided hyperventilating when the situation appeared to take a turn for the worst.

With two swift commands the leader had her hands bound behind her back and a blindfold placed over her eyes. She resisted the temptation to struggle with difficulty until he did her the dour courtesy of explaining. 'Fear not, Kházakh woman. Your life is not yet forfeit. You shall be taken elsewhere for questioning. As you know, it is not safe for us to remain here.'

T'skya briefly wondered what a 'Kházakh' was. It did not sound pleasant the way he said it and her anxiety levels rose as she imagined what might endanger the armed and camouflaged.

And why on earth should she know it was unsafe?

'I'll fall if I can't see!' she objected.

'You shall not fall,' the woman replied sternly. T'skya was surprised and disgruntled by the firmness of grip as the woman seized her arm. She was sure to have marks afterwards but did not dare to complain.

T'skya could barely hear the footfalls of her captors as they made their way through the rapidly thickening undergrowth. She sounded like a blundering elephant crunching her way over twigs and twisted tree roots, but then they could pick their path whereas she was blind and reliant on guidance. At intervals she would be stopped and spun until completely disorientated. Although constantly afraid of falling, the woman guided T'skya so well that she rarely even stumbled.

They marched for what seemed like many hours, although it was scarcely more than two, before halting to rest. T'skya was certain it was for her benefit since she was breathing heavily and becoming a burden to lead. The air was thinner and the gravity slightly higher than she was used to and she needed time to acclimatise; assuming she lived that long.

Her arm was aching and throbbing from where the woman's vice-like fingers cruelly gripped her and it was a relief to have the pressure released. Her respite was short, however, and she grimaced as steel fingers were once more clamped around her.

The second march was briefer and they halted in a small glade. The drizzle had long since stopped and T'skya could feel the dim warmth of the sun on her face. She was manoeuvred to a tree and made to sit. Her hands remained tied but to her relief the blindfold was removed. T'skya blinked against the dappled light and looked cautiously around her.

The glade was little more than a small circle bedded with mosses and lichen. Delicate wood-sorrel and sunny celandines swayed gently in the breeze and dog-violets poked their tiny purple faces through the greenery. One or two brightly coloured birds were hopping about looking for beetles, unconcerned by their presence. The surrounding trees dripped with moisture, their leaves whispering lightly to each other. T'skya was intrigued to see that some of the trees were just coming into bud, whilst trees the image of maples had already turned golden-red brown and were beginning to shed their leaves. Still others, oak and beech, were in full foliage and yet more had clusters of pink and orange blossoms. It seemed that all seasons existed in that small area bar winter, for none of the trees was completely bare. She stared at the trees unable to contemplate how nature had managed to replicate those of her home world - the statistical chances that evolution would follow the same path were infinitely remote, but apart from a few minor deviations much of the woodland around her was familiar.

She shook her head in disbelief and then watched in wonder as a bird came to rest upon the fingers of one of the hooded figures as he called softly to it in words she could not understand. It seemed so contrary to her image of these people who had taken her captive and threatened her.

T'skya half expected them to begin their inquisition immediately but they appeared in no obvious hurry. Aside from the woman standing guard over her, no-one else seemed to be paying her attention. One was gathering berries from a nearby bush whilst a couple had ventured into the undergrowth keeping watch. The leader, as she assumed him to be, was standing, hands on hips, gazing down a narrow path that disappeared into the forest.

T'skya wished they would get the questions over and done with. Under the stern and unceasing watch of her guard and with the knowledge that her answers to the impending inquisition would decide her fate, she was anxious to begin.

She was startled out of her thoughts by a loud, shrill whistle; an excellent imitation of a bird cry she recalled from the march. The whistle was answered by a fainter double call, repeated and each time the reply grew louder. Those seated leapt to their feet and stared towards the path.

Presently four similarly dressed figures carrying bulging packs under their cloaks appeared from the shadows. The two leaders met and embraced, clasping each other's hands to their foreheads. There was warmth in their voices and after some hasty discussion, their attention turned to T'skya.

She shrank back as they approached her feeling like an animal trapped and examined by faceless people. She wished that she could see what they looked like, even if they were hideous and alien. It all seemed so absurdly impersonal.

The new arrival was some inches taller than the first and broader in the shoulders, although he held himself with less authority. Even as he stood in front of T'skya, his posture was one of relaxed unconcern, whilst the other stood erect, rigid and watchful.

The taller one, his scarf pulled down, bent his face towards her and she could just make out a strong jaw and the glitter of his eyes beneath the hood. She was immensely relieved that he appeared human; not a tentacle to be seen. He looked at her damp, straggling hair, much of which had come loose from its braid. He studied her burnt, scratched and dirty face. He observed her tattered and soiled clothing and the way she cowered against the tree and suddenly burst out laughing, tossing his head back in his humour. As he did so the hood slipped and T'skya caught a glimpse of his face, allaying some of her fears.

He was a remarkably handsome man with shaggy, dark brown hair and warm hazel eyes. His laugh had been one of boyish glee, although he looked to be in his thirties, and his whole appearance and demeanour was one of roguish merriment. Here was a man she was sure she would like, given different circumstances.

'Is this what you are so concerned about?' he asked using her tongue and opening his arms in bemusement. 'She is nothing but a frightened child.'

'Looks may be deceptive,' the other replied. 'Perhaps she was chosen to lower our guard.'

'What could they hope to achieve by sending a lone female? Their women do not possess the strength or skills of our warriors,' he said, smiling towards T'skya's guard.

'We do not know that she was alone.'

'Saw you others?'

'No, but that does not mean there were none.'

T'skya was confused by their conversation. They seemed to think she was part of some conspiracy. She also resented being talked about as if she were not there. With unaccustomed bravery she took a deep breath and ventured; 'I am alone.' And so she was. Despite being surrounded, she had never felt lonelier or more wretched.

At the sound of her voice, the men turned back towards her. 'If that be true will you answer our questions?' the first one asked her.

'I will try,' she replied tentatively.

The tempestuous woman interrupted, fiercely jabbing her spear into the ground. 'You cannot trust a Kházakh!'

The first sighed. It was clear that he did not like the situation and the burden of responsibility it placed upon him. He muttered a few words to the bigger man who, shaking his head regretfully, procured a small vial from his belt. T'skya eyed the vial suspiciously as it was unwillingly and silently passed over. T'skya could sense the strong disapproval of the one and the reluctant determination of the other.

'What is that?' she asked nervously.

'It is called *voule*,' he replied. 'It is a plant extract and causes no lasting harm to those who do not resist its power.'

T'skya did not like the sound of that. 'I don't understand,' she said glancing from one man to the other.

The taller began to explain. 'If you tell the truth then you will suffer no ill. If you lie, the pain will be great, but you will suffer no lasting harm.'

The first opened the top of the vial and stepped nearer. 'The initial effects are not pleasant. You will feel pain and disorientation. For this we are sorry but there is no other way to learn if you speak truth or falsehood.' He poured a small measure into the cap and crouching held it out. T'skya hesitated, fearful of the consequences, but knowing she had little choice compliantly opened her mouth.

The liquid was bitter and fiery on her tongue and she had difficulty swallowing. It burnt its way down to her stomach and she gagged. Within seconds her body was racked by convulsions; she twitched and jerked violently, her head exploding in agony. T'skya cried out pitiably and sank to her side.

Gradually the initial pain subsided and she lay panting, her eyes glazed and her skin a pallid white. The woman grabbed T'skya by the arm and roughly sat her up again.

T'skya was helpless, oblivious of her surroundings and empty of thought. It was as if nothing existed. Through the fog came a voice; a voice she could not resist. It beckoned her and prompted her and she had no choice but to respond.

'Who are you and from whence do you come?' it said.

'My name is T'skya. I come from a distant planet.'

'Why came you here, T'skya?' it asked.

'To explore and learn. To find a home for my people,' she said in a voice devoid of feeling.

'Who sent you here?' it probed.

'My Commanding Officer.'

Overtones of disapproval and 'I told you so' swept through the clearing but T'skya was scarcely aware of them. They were the voices of ghosts, surreal and undefined. The questions were repeated with insistence for clarification and gradually T'skya's head began to clear. She became aware of where she was and her subconscious warned her to withhold.

'Who is your Commanding Officer?' the voice said.

'I...I can't tell you,' she said with effort.

The voice repeated the question more forcibly. T'skya shook her head, feebly trying to resist, but the pain was insistent. 'Commander Talmana of the Homequest,' she replied through clenched teeth.

The pain stopped.

'When must you report back?'

'In twelve lunar months,' she answered.

Gasps of surprise and disbelief came from her captors. 'She lies,' one said.

'No,' the second replied confidently. 'She shows no sign of pain.'

'Where is your Commander?' the first continued.

'On the Homequest.'

'Where is the Homequest?'

'I don't know,' she replied truthfully.

'Do you not come from the Kházakha city?' the first asked in bewilderment.

'I know of no place by that name.'

Her interrogators turned to one another, whispering; 'How can she not know of the city? She is one of them,' said one.

'Do you think she is from another flying machine like the ones they say the Kházakha arrived in?' inquired another.

'If so, there could be others!' said a third.

'She said she was alone.'

'Other machines in other places?'

'It is possible,' the first agreed. He peered into her glazed eyes. 'Came you in a flying machine?'

T'skya tried to lie but could not. 'Yes,' she replied weakly.

'Came others?' he demanded sharply.

'Yes, but not here.'

'Where?'

'In other lands,' she said hesitantly. She urgently wanted to resist their questioning but had neither the strength nor the courage. Every attempt to hide the truth resulted in agonizing bursts of fire in her mind and she was already too weakened to fight.

'Are you a spy?' she was asked.

'No.'

'Do you wish us harm?'

'No.'

'How crossed you the desert?'

'I don't know.'

'Tell me!'

'I don't know.'

'Tell me!'

'For pity's sake, I do not know!' she sobbed with tears streaming down her face.

The first opened his mouth to ask again but the second laid a restraining hand upon his arm. 'No more,' he said. 'She can take no more.'

The first, nodding his head, relented. 'Forgive me. I was forgetting myself.' He reached out to T'skya, who was sitting with head bowed, sobbing to herself. Taking her chin in his hand, he raised her head and for the first time their eyes met. Through the blur of tears she saw a concerned and pitying pair of dark, elfin eyes regarding her intently. She blinked, trying to clear her vision, but by the time she could see he had concealed his face. 'Sleep now,' he said softly. 'There will be no more questions yet awhile.'

He ordered her untied. The female guardian neither believed nor trusted T'skya and considered it folly to leave her unbound. When the leader turned away she leant down and whispered threateningly into T'skya's ear: 'If you run, I will kill you!'

For once T'skya was unconcerned. She had no intention of running. Even fit she doubted she could outmatch these people in their own domain and she was far too tired.

Seeing that she was soundly asleep, the tension dissipated a fraction. The leader formed the group into a circle upon the mossy floor, having left one guard by T'skya's side and four scouts on the lookout for trouble. The woman protested mildly but was determined to have her say in the following discussion. She would ensure her opinion was recognised if not accepted.

Speaking in his native tongue, the first said: 'I believe our prisoner has spoken truly, though I do not understand all she said.'

'I, too, believe her words. But what are we to do with her now?' the second asked.

'Whether she spoke true or not she is a danger to us,' insisted the woman.

'I think not,' the first replied. 'She claims she is alone and I do not think she was sent from the city nor knows of its existence.'

'Then you think she is from the sky?'

'Probably. She may be a scout. The Kházakha invaded us once; a second time would mean our battle is over and our fate grim. But perchance there is another reason for her presence here. And now it seems that we must decide her fate.' He faced the woman, directing his words to her. 'I do not want her blood on my hands. We are a peaceful race and should not take the life of one who is perhaps by chance amongst us.'

'What then do you suggest?' she asked disdainfully.

'There is much we have yet to learn. She could be of aid to us.'

'You think that we should hold her with us?' someone inquired sounding less than convinced.

The first was sincere in his answer. 'I think we should tend to her and learn from her.'

'I agree with my brother,' the hazel eyed man said. 'Our aim has never been to destroy but to educate. Perhaps if we show her our ways, she will aid us and, if she is one of them, there are many secrets we could learn. I do not think she is a danger to us; she is too small and weak. A warrior would not have allowed herself to have been taken so easily. Surely *you* do not fear one woman?' he asked the female.

'I fear nothing but your foolish pity!' she growled.

He laughed. 'You have a sharp tongue, my lady. You are indeed a warrior in battle and in words.'

'Aye, and I need to be both when surrounded by men who are ruled by their hearts and not by their heads!'

'Enough, my friends,' said the first, smiling despite himself. 'This is not the time to be fighting amongst ourselves!' He knew that if given the chance the two would bandy words and forget all else, as was their almost daily ritual. 'Let us vote on it,' he added. 'Those who wish clemency cast your stones.'

The group, all with a non-descript stone in hand, placed their fists in the centre of the circle. When the stones were counted it was evident only one had disfavoured the idea and it did not take a genius to work out whom.

'It is decided then,' said the first approvingly.

The woman clenched her jaws but held her peace. The vote had been cast and there was nothing she could do to change matters. Silently, she vowed to watch every move that the Kházakh made until she could prove her a traitor.

T'skya had not stirred; the effects of the *voule* still upon her, rendering her unconscious to the world.

'The day will be half gone before she awakes and we cannot risk remaining here; we have already tarried too long,' the first said, looking across at her thoughtfully. She was a burden he had not wished for; a possible key to success or the catalyst to their destruction. Yet, as he studied her small bedraggled form, curled up foetus-like upon the ground, he was filled with compassion and a curious sense of peace. He could see no ill in her; no cruelty or hatred, no malice, no real seeds of deceit, and yet she held many mysteries for him; mysteries that only time would reveal.

'How shall we transport her? It is a long path to the enclave.'

'I shall carry her,' the second said, gently scooping T'skya up.

TWO

Clanmeet

T'skya awoke on a soft bed of leaves and down. She was housed in a sparsely furnished room with walls made from supple saplings trained to grow so that their uppermost branches curved inwards to create a thick, impenetrable canopy. Streaks of sunshine filtered through tiny gaps in the twisted wooden walls and the leafy growth-like shutters on a window. The heavy portiere had been pulled aside with vine ropes to leave an open space through which the air could circulate and additional light shine.

She sat up with a start and looked about her, half expecting to see the warrior woman snarling at her bedside or the leader to be there with another dose of that vile *voule*. She was surprised to see neither, but instead an old woman seated on a cushioned tree stump, dozing peacefully with her chin on her chest. In one hand she was holding T'skya's flight suit and in the other a tiny bone needle with which she had been meticulously darning the tears.

On seeing her uniform T'skya noticed that she had been dressed in a simple, pale green gown. It was short sleeved and came almost to her ankles and the fabric, although not fine, was soft to the touch. It was tied about her waist with a belt of beautifully woven russet brown reeds and her feet were adorned with woollen slippers soled with a strong, flexible substance T'skya did not recognise.

As she moved, the rustling of the bedding stirred the woman and T'skya came face to face with a pair of kindly golden eyes. 'You have been long in sleeping,' the woman said, her voice soft but containing a hint of disapproval.

'Please,' asked T'skya, stretching her hand imploringly towards the old woman who, despite her better nature, could not help recoiling, 'tell me what's happening. I don't understand any of this. I don't know who you are, or what you are, or what you think I am. Nobody has explained!'

'It is enough for you to know that you are safe and that you have been tended to as best we could. For that be grateful.' Her voice was chastising, as if she were scolding a naughty child. 'I have repaired your clothes, though I am unhappy with my skill. My thread is not suited to this strange cloth; I have never seen a fabric quite like it. You may exchange them again if the touch of our garments discomforts you.' With that she placed the suit upon the bed and went towards the door. T'skya turned to speak but could find nothing fitting to say except a mumbled thank you. The woman nodded briefly and left her alone.

For some moments she felt too overwhelmed to do anything and sat staring at the doorway. T'skya stretched her hand out to the neatly folded flight suit and fingered it thoughtfully. She would feel more secure in her familiar uniform and it was a shame to waste the woman's repairs, yet something in the tone of voice alerted T'skya that it would not only be an insult to their hospitality but also a slight to their culture. T'skya remained in the gown.

She was surprised by how well she felt physically. T'skya touched her face and felt no sign of tenderness from where the sun had burnt her. Her cuts had almost healed and her joints no longer felt stiff or painful and this had been accomplished in the middle of nowhere, by a people who used bones for needles and flint tips for weapons, yet had mysterious skills and knowledge for which T'skya, as yet, had no answer.

She then realised the homing beacon was missing from her wrist. Panic gripped T'skya and her heart began to hammer in her chest. Without it she would have no way to relocate her ship and the Mothership would be unable to trace her upon its return. She frantically searched the pockets of her flight suit but found nothing. Her eyes scanned the room but there was nothing technological to be seen. Perhaps if she could prove it was harmless and if she co-operated they might return it to her; assuming the beacon had not been dismantled out of curiosity or destroyed.

Her pack was missing too. Within it was her medikit, a couple of flashlights, fire lighters, some basic tools, spare clothing, a ground sheet, re-hydrating pills and nutrients and her water canister. Nothing of great importance but all she now possessed in the world. But it was too late for regrets; her priority was to survive.

To distract herself she decided to explore the room more thoroughly. Commander Talmana had, after all, expected her to become acquainted with all aspects of the land's cultures and resources, but there was little to see: just a small tree stump chair, a makeshift bed and some shelves upon which various clay bowls and pots were standing. Curious to see what they contained, T'skya nervously sniffed, felt or cautiously tasted what was held within and then replaced them exactly as they had been; disappointed her homing beacon was not stowed away in them. She bitterly regretted the loss of her analysing equipment and data discs; she could have spent days studying the contents. She simply could not have carried it with her from the ship; but then she had never intended to crash.

Picking up a narrow-necked pot, T'skya uncorked it and took a cautious sniff. Minute orange spores flew up her nose and made her sneeze. With tears streaming down her face, she hastily replaced the offending object. 'What the hell is that stuff?' she muttered, wiping her eyes with the back of her hand.

'*Koulumbia*,' came a voice from behind her.

T'skya whirled around. She had not heard anyone come in and it startled her.

There in the doorway, his slim body leaning against the doorpost stood a young man dressed in forest greens and browns. His hair was long and fine, the colour of the early morning sun streaked by the summer rays, and it fell about his shoulders. His skin was pale and unblemished as if he seldom saw the sun, and it contrasted greatly with his dark, almond-shaped eyes. His face looked noble but bore signs of weariness, although he was trying hard to conceal his fatigue. So stood her captor revealed at last.

'It is inadvisable to snoop,' he warned.

'I wasn't snooping!' she replied quickly, feeling uncomfortable under his fixed gaze. 'Well...not exactly.'

He merely raised a sculptured eyebrow.

'Well, okay, I was,' she admitted, 'but you can't blame me for being curious.'

The man continued to stare but said nothing. T'skya felt naked in the silence and shuffled, nervously pulling at the side of her gown. 'Uh...thank you for the, uh, clothes,' she stuttered, wishing he would speak.

He nodded his acceptance of this gratitude. 'Come, you have been here for many hours and you may have needs.' He gestured for her to follow him.

T'skya let out a sigh and nodded, but she could not prevent her heart from clamouring at the thought of leaving the security of the room. Keeping a wary distance she ducked under the blanket and stepped out into the open. She was surprised to find no guards outside; the man seemed content to ward her on his own.

The hut stood near the centre of the encampment. T'skya

had little time to survey the area properly as her host led her through the trees, but she did manage to observe several similar structures, although some were hard to make out amongst the undergrowth. She also saw a clearing in which several people were gathered, paths leading into the forest, and a few stacks of dried wood and some enclosures. She could take in no more than that since the path she was bidden to follow led away from the main camp.

They had gone but a short distance when the blond man stopped. 'From here you will walk alone. At that tree,' he said gesturing to a magnificent old oak which ten men could not have spanned, 'you will find what you need. Be warned! It is futile to seek escape. Our scouts will surely find you and even were you to evade them you would be unable to find a safe path through the forest.'

The man waited patiently with his back turned, although the tree had more than adequately sheltered her from view. As he heard her returning, he watched over his shoulder until she was almost in reach. 'If you are ready, we shall go to the Clanmeet.'

T'skya was intrigued and wary. 'The Clanmeet?'

'It is the name of the circle of gathering. There is much we have yet to know of you.'

T'skya stopped dead. 'You mean you're going to interrogate me again!' she exclaimed.

'If that is how you wish to put it.'

'Are you going to use that *stuff* again?' she asked uneasily.

'Will it be necessary?' he inquired softly, looking at her from beneath his brow.

'No,' she replied grimly.

There was a minute sign of a satisfied smile about his eyes as he beckoned her to follow him.

As they walked towards the Clanmeet T'skya had more time to study her surroundings. To the right of her was a small shelter constructed from dried reeds, around which some animals were grazing. A child who looked no more than ten years old was tending to them, grooming what looked like a shaggy carpet on legs. As the child groomed the beast she collected the loose hair and stuffed it into one of the sacks beside her. It already looked quite full and T'skya could see the girl combing out the hair with such ease it was a wonder the animal had any left.

When they approached the child raised her head. She shouted a welcome to the man and he saluted her back, but then she caught sight of T'skya. Before she could react a stout woman rushed from the shelter, grabbed the child by the hand and bundled her away from sight, casting a fearful glance over her shoulder. The man walked on as if nothing had happened but T'skya felt hurt and dismayed.

To the left of her were some women and boys washing the collected hair in shallow bowls. They were diligently rubbing it before spreading it on to mats to dry. Despite their work, they too paused to stare at her as she passed by. T'skya could hear them muttering, the word Kházakh cropping up in their conversation repeatedly. She felt uncomfortable being discussed, especially in a language she could not understand.

Beyond the hair collection areas the ground to either side of the well worn path was almost pristine. Ferns, nettles, shrub bushes and small forest flowers, wood avens and forget-me-nots with yellow and blue faces, dotted the ground bringing a fresh and attractive air to the place. Here and there elderberry, sloe, brambles and mulberry bushes sat with a heavy profusion of shiny berries, red ones, blue ones and ones so dark they were almost black. Others were still in blossom, their dainty blooms a busy place for the bees and gaily coloured butterflies. T'skya's spirit lifted a fraction.

But it was a short walk to the Clanmeet. Already she could see a gathering of people in the circle wearing garments matching the colours of the forest. They also ceased what they were doing to watch her approach. Eleven pairs of eyes turned towards her and she abruptly felt horribly self-conscious.

The group opened the way as she was led into the clearing. The blond man gestured to a cushion towards the rear of the circle and there she sat, faced by an arc of strangers whose attention gave no respite.

Directly in front of her sat two elderly women, one of which had repaired her suit. The other was slightly younger and of ample proportions, seeming like a rock cemented to the ground. Her face looked solemn, yet not unfriendly, but T'skya instinctively knew she was a woman who, once resolved, would yield to no persuasion.

To their left and right sat the two male leaders. T'skya's blond host seemed exceptionally elegant and refined next to the lump of a woman. The darker haired man with the roguish smile appeared to be more ill at ease and fidgeted constantly until a sharp look from the seamstress stilled him. T'skya noticed the similarity between them and briefly wondered if they might be related in some way.

To the side of the blond man sat a woman who was watching her with such loathing that T'skya wanted to wither up and die. There was no doubt in T'skya's mind that this fiery creature was the one who had treated her so harshly before. Her face reflected the beauty of a semi-wild animal, domesticated yet ready to explode in a frenzy of savagery; the border being but tenuous. Her eyes were deeply set and as black as jet, her nose thin and slightly hooked and her snowy white skin stark in comparison with her magnificent locks of ruby hair.

T'skya had no time to study the others before the company joined hands and raised their arms before them. It was the Rock who spoke first; her voice deep and resonant;

Er lu'loui myali ouryval,
Lu'loui onkylara ourynal,

Mia lu'loui wylkhyli lahli.
Let our wisdom be perfect,
Our hearts pure,
And our judgment just.'

The men and women parted contact and sat expectantly, awaiting the questions to commence. T'skya turned her attention to the Rock since she had taken charge of the meeting.

'This is the gathering of the Clanmeet, our council, and here you will answer to me. What is your name and from whence do you come?' she was asked.

'My name is T'skya and I come from what we call the Homequest,' she answered, hoping she would not have to reiterate.

'Did you not say before that you were from a distant planet?'

So the blond man had reported what he had already learned from her. Yes, of course he had. T'skya did not hesitate to answer; 'I originate from there, yes, but I've never seen my home planet. I was born on the Homequest.'

'What is the Homequest?'

'An intergalactic spaceship.'

'Explain intergalactic to the Clanmeet. We are not familiar with this word.'

T'skya complied, but kept the details simple. She did not want to reveal too much.

'And where is this spaceship now?'

T'skya sighed down her nose. 'I don't know.'

'How can this be?' the woman inquired, her tone flat and neutral.

'Because the ship has left and I'm not in contact with it.'

'My son tells me that others of your kind have also come from there,' the elderly lady broke in. 'Where are they?'

T'skya flicked a glance across to the darker haired man, her suspicions of his relationship confirmed. 'Your son is correct.

Others did come but as I've already explained to him they went to different lands. I'm here alone.'

'You are alone and yet you stated before that you are to dwell here for twelve lunar months. How is that possible unless you belong to the Kházakha?' the Rock objected.

T'skya felt frustrated. She knew she should not answer all of their questions and yet she was not in a position to lie. She did not even know what Kházakha were, although they obviously associated her with the word. She paused, trying to gather her thoughts, knowing that any lengthy silence would be construed as dishonesty and concealment.

'Uh...the ship can't return before then.'

'Why?'

'Look, I'm not the Commander. I don't know why!' she snapped in exasperation. The blond man frowned at her and she instantly regretted the outburst.

The fat woman was incensed and boomed at her; 'Do you expect us to accept such an answer?'

'I'm sorry,' T'skya replied, sounding less than apologetic, 'but I don't know what you expect from me.'

'We expect the truth; no more and no less. There can be no trust in dishonesty.'

'Then you expect too much!'

Twelve sets of eyebrows were raised in surprise. T'skya could feel herself digging her own grave but continued bravely; 'You expect me to open myself to you and tell you what I know so that you can trust me. Well, why should I trust you? Your soldiers took me captive, bound my hands and dragged me blindfold through the woods so that I'd have no chance of finding my way out. They threatened me and forced that vile drink down my throat and stole my property. I don't know who you are, or what you are, or what I'm supposed to have done wrong, but I'll tell you one thing, I'm not going to answer any more of your questions until you answer some of mine.'

T'skya was almost shouting by the time she had finished.

The memories of everything she had endured had come back and filled her with resentment.

The head women muttered together and took counsel with the two male leaders. T'skya waited; her outward appearance one of fixed determination whilst inwardly she was quivering. She had always been stubborn but this outburst had even caught her by surprise.

At length the large woman spoke; 'There is wisdom in your words and though you would behave as we have done were our places reversed, we have erred in our approach. We will answer your questions; though do not expect us to be any more forthcoming in our answers than you, for our reasons run deeper than the seas. What is it you wish to know?'

Now that she had the opportunity she did not know what to ask. There had been so many questions floating through her mind since she had been captured that finding the right one was far from easy. She sifted through the turmoil and came up with a simple, yet very important question.

'What are your names?'

Presently they were just faces; strangers with no real identities. Names would make them real to her, give them solidity and form. Some showed reluctance, thinking it a trap, but the Rock was unconcerned.

'Our true names we will not reveal, for they are not lightly given and would mean nothing to you. We do, however, go by names in your tongue also, which will serve you well enough.' She gestured to the deformed man on T'skya's left to begin.

'I am Knoll,' he said in a voice as rough as gravel, revealing broken, rotten teeth that looked like a line of rusty nails. He sat hunched over, his back bent and crooked, yet there was strength in his limbs as if he had seen many years hard labour and his tufted beard stuck out proudly from his chin. His skin was the colour of rich soil and T'skya could not help but stare. She had never seen dark skin before and its beauty fascinated her.

'I am Ferret,' said a skinny weasel of a man, his voice confident but his demeanour uneasy.

'Badger is my name,' the muscled man said, courteously bowing his fair head to her.

'Fen,' mumbled a man conspicuous by the ragged scar that ran from his left temple to the edge of his displeased lips. Of all those gathered, he was the only one who did not, or would not, look at her. The second leader, having noticed Fen's reticence, flashed T'skya a brief but winning smile, for which she was grateful.

'My name is Hollam and this beautiful lady is Negram,' he said, gesturing dramatically to the old seamstress beside him. Both she and the Rock frowned deeply at his presumption but T'skya could see the twinkle of merriment in the Negram's eyes, suggesting her display of displeasure was more for the satisfaction of the other than deeply-seated disapproval.

'Thank you, son, but I am neither too old nor too senile to introduce myself,' was all she said. Hollam tried his best to look abashed but failed dismally.

With great dignity the Rock introduced herself; 'I am Briar, and as head of the proceedings you will address yourself to me.'

T'skya accepted this and waited for the blond man to speak. For some reason learning his name seemed vital. He had not displayed Hollam's joviality or warmth and yet there was something compelling about him.

'I am known as Cail,' he stated simply. It was not the kind of name she had anticipated, being too short and plain, and yet it somehow suited him.

'Cail,' she repeated, nodding at him.

The red haired woman took exception to the use of his name and flicked her eyes between them suspiciously. 'You will call me Raven,' she snarled.

She had the look of a carrion eater with her sharp beak of a nose and intense black eyes. T'skya became so caught up in this image that she almost missed the last names given of Tarn, and the twins Wolf and Hawk. She found their general use of names taken from nature quite charming, although she briefly wondered what Negram, Hollam and Cail were.

Her ruminations were interrupted by Briar's deep tones. 'T'skya of the Homequest, how came you to our land?'

'I came in a short range A.S.D. One Eleven Landing Craft; uh...a flying machine,' she added.

'Where is this flying machine now?' Briar asked, emphasising the words with a touch of sarcasm. T'skya's arrogant assumption that they would not understand had offended her.

Negram better understood and interrupted. 'Do not fear to speak freely, T'skya of the Homequest. If you are truly from above and newly arrived, we must forgive your ignorance. Simply know this, we are not as ignorant of your ways as you assume.'

'Apologies. My craft is somewhere in the desert.'

'Why did you not land elsewhere?'

'I had navigational problems,' she said trying not to recall those fearful moments during which her life had been so nearly extinguished.

Briar narrowed her eyes. 'Is your craft operational?' she asked slowly.

T'skya's face fell at the thought of her sleek ship lying forlorn in the harsh sands. 'No, it isn't. I crashed and destroyed the nose and flight controls.'

Briar studied her intently and asked with great purpose; 'Then how crossed you the desert?'

T'skya sighed at having to repeat herself. 'I walked and then I fell, or was pulled, down a hole and woke up in the forest.'

She thought she would be commanded to elaborate but to her surprise Briar just accepted the answer with a slow nod of the head. 'And what do you know of the Kházakha's city?' she said at length.

'Nothing more than it's quite technologically advanced

for this world,' T'skya answered truthfully, remembering the information the Mothership's sensors had picked up. No-one had been able to fathom why a large spread of population was almost devoid of industry whilst a sprawling city existed which possessed some technology almost on par with that of the Mothership. T'skya pushed these thoughts aside and added; 'I've never been there.'

This answer raised expressions of disbelief from some and puzzlement from others. Hollam, Negram, Briar and Cail showed nothing. The men had heard parts of her story before and the women were too wise and experienced to show their thoughts that openly.

'It is difficult for us to accept that you know nothing of your own people,' Briar explained.

'I don't understand,' came the slow reply. T'skya did not know what they meant by her 'own people'. She asked for clarification.

'The people of the city are as you are. Nobody in this land has black hair and green eyes except the Khàzakha. Therefore, as logic dictates, you must be one of them.'

'That's impossible!' T'skya objected. 'Ours was the first ship to explore other galaxies. Nobody even had the technology to travel so far before then and I can't conceive anyone reaching here before us. It would've taken thousands of years without the…well, without our new…' she caught herself before she gave the technology of their propulsion drive away, '…knowledge to get beyond our own solar system. And besides, it takes years and enormous funding to build a spaceship capable of intergalactic travel.'

'Nevertheless, our words are true. We have lived under their oppression and tyranny for decades of your years and we know these people well. You claim to know nothing of them and yet you judge us to be wrong.'

'When did they arrive?'

'When I was young.'

'Then I tell you it's impossible. We were the first and even with the decades it took to reach here no other ship from our planet could've made it in that time. We simply didn't have the technology,' she objected.

Briar was not convinced. 'Then from whence did you come?'

'My home planet is called Navenná. It was a beautiful world, but we destroyed it.'

Briar's insistence that others of her kind were in this city seemed sincere yet she could not reconcile this with the knowledge that her ship was the prototype. How could there have been another? Could it have been kept a secret? That was ridiculous! How could something on the scale of a Mothership have been kept a secret? It was too much for her to accept. T'skya needed more evidence.

'How did these people arrive here?'

'They came in small ships, just as you claim to have done,' Briar explained. She went on to describe their size and shape and how they flew and the more she said, the more T'skya believed.

T'skya sat in stunned silence not knowing what to think or say. Everyone, even Fen, was now looking at her. At last she spoke. 'Given that what you say is true, what have these people done to you?'

'What have they *not* done?' someone muttered through clenched teeth.

'Peace,' Briar commanded softly. 'You ask a heavy question, T'skya of the Homequest, for the tale is long and burdensome for the teller and all who listen; but it shall be told, though we should firstly break our fast to strengthen our endurance.'

T'skya found Briar's words a trifle dramatic. How bad could things have really been?

The Clanmeet was adjourned. T'skya was led to a smaller clearing in which cushions had been arranged in two rows and where plates and bowls of clay had been laid out. T'skya lingered behind unsure if the invitation had been extended to her?

'Sit where you will,' Negram told her, gesturing to the cushions. T'skya looked around nervously hoping to sit next to Cail, but he had been waylaid by Raven and did not look as if he would be able to free himself quickly. She sat instead at the far end of the row facing Negram and Hollam. Seats were left for Cail and Raven in the centre. Fen sat hunched over his bowl at the farthest end of the row. *As far from me as possible*, thought T'skya.

Bowls of steaming soup were brought and placed before them by the young girl who had been tending the animals. T'skya soon noticed how the child lingered close by staring in fascination whenever she thought she was not being observed. Nothing escaped Briar's notice and she shooed her away with a wave of her hand.

The soup smelled delicious and was made from a variety of vegetables, flavoured with an interesting assortment of spices. It was served with bread fresh from the ovens. T'skya was curious and braved an inquiry to the man she thought most approachable. 'Where do you get the flour to make bread? I've seen no cornfields here,' she asked Hollam, who was already helping himself to another bowl of soup.

'Not made from corn, from ground nuts, from the Harvesters,' he said his mouth still full of bread.

Negram frowned at her son's table manners and, catching sight of her, he hastily swallowed the unchewed pieces before continuing. 'It is a far trek from here, but twice in every one of your years, though dangerous now, we journey and trade our forest fruits for their flour. We also make flour here from forest nuts though it takes much time to grind and there are fewer nuts.'

'Why do you always say 'your years'? Don't you have your own?' she inquired.

'We do not measure time as you do. It has no meaning for

us,' he replied, waving his soup spoon about dangerously before consuming its contents. T'skya waited for him to elaborate but he was too absorbed in his food to pay her much heed.

'Forgive my son,' Negram whispered. 'He has the manners of a hog!'

T'skya smiled. Hollam had not missed his mother's derogatory remark but it washed over him as if he had heard it a hundred times.

'In our land,' Negram continued, 'we do not always have seasons as you know them for they are not constant. The weather changes as it sees fit and so we do not count the time. We celebrate our births by the flowers and the trees and the nesting of the birds. Hollam was born with the coming of the swiftwings and Cail with the blossom of the hope trees, but we do not really count the years or celebrate male births until their coming of age, and that dawns differently for all our people. Hollam would be seven cycles and Cail but one, though you would age them differently. The Kházakha tried to force their concepts of time upon us, thus we understand it, but choose to follow the phases of the moons and the cycle of nature as we have always done.'

T'skya found the concept fascinating. It had an air of romance about it, something which her world's set time lacked. She suddenly found herself filled with the desire to learn all that she could about these forest dwellers, their customs and habits, their language and songs, their joys and their sorrows. She only hoped that her likeness to the Kházakha would not stand in her way.

She was about to ask what swiftwings and hope trees were when she saw Cail and Raven taking their seats. Soup was placed before them but neither showed much of an appetite. Cail played with his wooden spoon and Raven sat glowering, casting bitter glances in her direction. It put T'skya off her food and dampened her mood. She ate the rest of the meal in silence.

As Cail climbed to his feet to head towards the eating area, Raven waylaid him. 'We must go,' he said gesturing towards the others, who were sorting out the seating arrangements.

'This is important,' she said. 'It cannot wait.'

'Very well. Speak, but be quick.'

'Do you trust me, Cail?' she asked earnestly.

Cail laughed. 'Of course I do. What question is that?'

'Then why do you judge against me in this matter?' Raven demanded.

'What matter?'

'This creature,' came her caustic reply. 'She is one of them and yet she eats with us and sleeps with us and learns more about us every moment that she is here. Where is the sanity and wisdom in that? It goes against all that we have learnt and suffered to learn. It is madness, especially for you.'

'You have heard her speak. Did you not hear her say she has no knowledge of them?'

'And you believed her? How can you be so foolish, you, who are known to be wise in judgment? Have her false tears softened you so?'

'My heart is as it always was, Raven. It does not condemn those who have not been proven false. It is open to all truth and to all those who are in need.' He paused and looked her in the eyes regretfully. 'It is you who have changed, Raven. You have become too hard of heart.'

'If I am, it is the hardship of life that has made me so. I am a warrior because of need, not of choice. There can be no room for softness; softness kills.'

'No,' he said, shaking his head. 'It is bitterness and hatred that kills. It makes us become like those who enslave us and kills what we are.'

'Is what we had then also dead?'

Cail stared at the ground, hesitant to answer. He did not

know how best to proceed. 'You have become so involved in our cause that there is no room left in your heart for anything else…nor for anyone.'

'Is our freedom so unimportant to you?'

'It is the most important thing,' he replied quickly. 'But not if we must pay for it with our hearts. What freedom will we have if we become like those we seek it from?'

'And what freedom will we have if we open ourselves to their trickery? Are you blind? Already you have fallen under her spell and believe her deceits. I will never trust her!'

'Then we are at a stalemate and there is no more to discuss.'

'You are wrong, Cail,' she responded softly.

'Then let it be so!' With that he turned and went to take his place next to Knoll, and Raven sat silently beside him.

❧

Following the soup and when the fruits, nettle tea and clear fresh water had been consumed the company returned to the Clanmeet to resume their discussions. Everybody felt morose; T'skya because of the ill-feeling radiating from Raven, Cail because he felt trapped between his relationship with Raven and his beliefs, Briar because of the gravity of the situation and Negram because she had been chosen to relate the tale. The others sensed the mood and absorbed it.

Negram sighed and rubbed at her eyes. T'skya waited patiently for her to begin realising that many of the questions she had left unasked may now be answered. Negram began: 'I will start my tale before the coming of the Kházakha so that you may know what a land this was.

'Roumanhi, the name of our land, was a place of beauty and of peace. It was, and still is, a land of many peoples and creatures, some of whom are strange to behold or little known. We who dwell in the forests are but one people. Knoll is of the mountains to the west and Breeze, whom you have not yet met, hails from the distant shores of Kalkassa, the Great Divide.

'The land was once bountiful; the forests stretching to the farthest shores and the plains rich and fertile. The desert at that time was insignificant and crossed without adversity, and the passage of people and beasts was unencumbered. It was a time of plenty for all and we lived under the rule of a King, or Castan in our tongue, who was a good and honourable man. Mithdrill was descended from a dignified line of Castans and wielded his authority with justice and love; never abusing his power or those who served under him. Forever by his side was the Castana, his Queen, a woman of unparalleled beauty and grace.

'Under the Castan's rule we lived in great prosperity, though not by your definition of the word, for we do not use money to buy our goods but trade with our produce. There was no war, no hunger or slavery. Everyone worked for the good of the land and that which it contained.

'But then the Kházakha came from the sky in great ships which we thought were falling stars and at first we were afraid for we did not know of other worlds. But as is our want, we welcomed them as something wondrous for they brought great knowledge of marvels we could not have conceived. We tried to teach them our language but they had no mind for it so, being a people of many tongues, we learnt theirs, though we have chosen to maintain the style of our own speech.'

As she spoke Negram's eyes were unfocussed, her memories lost in time and her voice nostalgic. But as Negram continued a shadow fell upon her. Her eyes became hard with recrimination and bitterness showed in her tone.

'It was not long before they began to abuse our laws. They pleaded ignorance of our ways when confronted with their crimes and in our compassion we forgave them and trusted their promises to reform.

'The Castan allowed them to build small, unobtrusive

structures since they seemed unable to live as we do, but they began to ravage the land in order to build huge monstrosities and the Castan was forced to rule against them.

'The Kházakha then used his ruling against him. They corrupted those whose hearts and minds were weak and consorted to discredit him. They claimed his ruling was to keep the people poor and under his domain when they could offer comfort, convenience and riches beyond our wildest dreams. We would no longer have to farm the land by hand nor carry water to our homes. We would no longer need to live the lives which had suited our forefathers for generations beyond count.

'They plotted and plundered and built terrible machines against which we had no defence. They had weapons with beams of light that paralysed or destroyed those they touched, and men of silver with eyes of fire against whom no spear or arrow had effect.

'It was some little time before the Kházakha overthrew the Castan that the Queen fell pregnant. For so long they had tried without success to have a child. Even our greatest healers and those from the Great Divide could do nothing. We had feared that the Castan's line would end, for the King, though strong, was aging. And so, despite our fears, the land became a place of rejoicing. Alas that she should bear a child at such a time!

'The Kházakha feared the birth would unite the people. They should not have feared. We were not fighters and had not the means to assault them. We were helpless against them when they turned on the Castan and took him from us.

'Ah, my Castan, may they be cursed forever!'

In her distress, Negram struck at her breast with such ferocity that Hollam was compelled to restrain her. Briar held Cail back. Seeing their consternation Negram quieted. When she spoke again her voice was bitter but calm.

'The Kházakha came to his court with their machines of destruction. The Castan had foreseen his end and pleaded with his Queen to flee and take the new-born Prince with her, but in vain. Nothing could persuade her to leave her bondmate's side.

'And that is how they died; slaughtered in cold blood where they sat, the Prince cradled in their arms and the Castan shielding his Queen's precious body from the cruel blade. The land where they died is now bare, for nothing will grow where their blood was shed. It is as if the very earth has rebelled against the deed and left its own memorial.'

Negram fell silent again. T'skya sat frowning, chewing her lip. The old lady's story sounded far-fetched, like she had narrated a poorly written fairy-tale, and yet T'skya believed all that she had heard. It was palpable how much their ruler had been loved and respected but T'skya sensed something much deeper; something that only time would reveal.

Briar broke the silence. 'What you have just heard is but the surface of our troubles. Nobody who has not lived it can fully comprehend the depths of our despair, but perhaps now you can understand our mistrust of you.'

T'skya did not know what to think, let alone say. Her own kind was allegedly responsible for these atrocities and now she had landed in the middle of it. If the Kházakha were truly from Navenná, then to whom did she owe her allegiance? Should she seek out her compatriots and plead for their help? If they had already established a home base and secured minerals and fuel, both of which the Homequest was desperately in need of, and if they had managed to adapt themselves to the planet's living conditions, would it not be more sensible to go to them? If she did so, she could fulfil her purpose, to find a home for her people and rescue them from their destruction. She would pass her initiation and be accepted into Navennán society as a fully-fledged adult worthy of full title but, more than that, she would be a heroine, praised and honoured above all else. It seemed to be the most logical step, although she neither knew how to reach the city nor where it was.

On the other hand, the people Negram had described did not sound hospitable or, indeed, the type to offer help freely. Moreover, there were still too many mysteries for T'skya to feel comfortable with the prospect of beseeching them. But the most powerful feeling of doubt came from her instinctive respect for the Clanmeet. Negram's words had moved and shocked her and she felt the desire to make amends for her compatriots' behaviour. T'skya was in a quandary.

Briar disturbed her thoughts. 'T'skya of the Homequest, we have told you much of what you desired to know. Will you now open yourself to us?'

T'skya nodded half-heartedly.

'Then let us open the discussion.' Briar spread her arms wide, gesturing to the people in the Clanmeet. 'You may now voice your questions.' Those who wished to speak placed stones before their feet and waited for Briar's permission to begin.

Ferret was the first to ask. Opening a sack which lay beside him, he brought out T'skya's pack and rummaged through the contents, demanding explanations of their use and the materials from which they were made. T'skya was greatly relieved to see her belongings and readily complied. He then extracted the homing beacon from the pack and examined it cautiously. T'skya hastily warned him off, fearing he would reset the device.

The twelve were highly interested in her explanation of its functions. 'Your ship can actually be relocated with this small contraption?'

'It can,' she replied. 'Without that, I'd have little chance of ever finding it and there's stuff aboard her which is useful to me.'

'Such as?' Briar inquired.

'Equipment for analysing and synthesising materials mainly.'

'Why not bring this equipment with you?'

'It was too heavy for me to carry so far and after crash

landing my first priority was to survive the desert.'

Briar paused for a moment and consulted with those beside her. They talked together in whispers and there was much nodding and shaking of heads, interspersed with glances in T'skya's direction. When some form of agreement was reached, they turned to her again.

'T'skya of the Homequest,' Briar said solemnly, 'you have heard much of our tale and we but little of yours, and there is much yet to discuss. But the time has come, before we progress, to ask you your intentions. Will you aid us?'

Fen and Raven were openly dismayed by the question and the possibility of working side by side with an enemy. Hollam scratched his head, whilst Negram and Briar sat quietly. Cail just stared at her intently, his fingers steepled before his lips.

It was undoubtedly an unprecedented state of affairs for the forest dwellers to appeal to a Kházakh for assistance and T'skya was astounded. The discussion was far from over and she only had tales to go by.

She rubbed her brow wearily, reviewing all that she had learnt. Too much depended on her choice. She was about to ask for more time when a cry was heard and three figures came crashing through the undergrowth into the Clanmeet.

THREE

Slythe

The company scrambled to their feet in alarm as the scouts relayed their messages in a flurry of words and gestures. Orders were barked and people began fearfully scurrying about.

Cail grabbed T'skya's arm and dragged her roughly behind him. 'Follow me! The Kházakha are upon us!' he cried and opening a concealed trap-door in the forest floor thrust her into the hole.

It was only a short drop and T'skya landed safely in a narrow tunnel. It opened into a fairly large cavern that had several other tunnels leading from it. A variety of provisions stood to one side and the cavern was dimly lit with candles which gave out the faint but pleasant smell of honey and shone like stars in the darkness.

Other forest dwellers had already entered from the adjoining tunnels and they stood silently, their faces full of fear; not least because of their proximity to T'skya. They blew out the candles as they passed and it became difficult to see. Cail dropped lightly into the tunnel and helped down Negram, Knoll and Ferret, who was carrying T'skya's belongings. The trap-door was quickly shut and dull scuffing indicated it was being concealed above. The only light now was that trespassing through the narrow ventilation shafts.

'We will have to trust Hollam and Tarn now,' Negram said pointing an accusing finger at T'skya. 'This does not bode well for you!'

T'skya was taken aback. 'I've done nothing!'

The old lady eyed her with grim mouth. 'That remains to be seen.'

'Mother, enough!' Cail admonished, stepping in to defend T'skya. 'Now is not the time.'

Negram fell quiet in deference to her son's wishes. T'skya was surprised; he looked and behaved so differently from Hollam that she had taken the reference to them as brothers as being no more than a term of affection. She assumed he must take after his father, wherever he was.

Cail tensed and motioned for silence. T'skya could hear nothing sinister from above, but already knew the forest dwellers possessed better hearing than she did. Cail put his eye to one of the spy-holes near the roof of the cavern. T'skya doubted he could see much but when she also looked was amazed to find that she could see most of the Clanmeet. The natives were more ingenious than she thought.

Hollam and Tarn were standing talking to one another with the apparent ease of contented and untroubled friends. One or two others were going about their daily business as if nothing was happening and Raven scurried off through the trees. Everything appeared normal; just as it was intended to.

Everyone in the cavern waited anxiously. T'skya could hear nothing but the rattle of Knoll's breath beside her and the faint rustle of leaves beneath the feet of those above. Before long, however, she caught the sound of heavy footfalls as the Kházakha trampled into the Clanmeet. T'skya could just make out a dozen or so figures, each dressed in white and cloaked in dirty green, and even from her concealed space she could clearly see that each had black hair and green eyes. They did indeed appear to be of her own race, even down to the traditional pierced ear for adult males.

'Who is in charge here?' the Kházakha section leader demanded. He was a skinny mean looking man who walked with the swagger of one who relishes his authority and delivers indiscriminate orders just to see them being obeyed. He believed it was a foolish mistake on High Lord Procurator Santovin's part to allow the Roumanhis so much freedom. They were unruly and disobedient, and would better serve as slaves. He was determined to whip them into shape. There would be no disobedience in his sector, no excuses for inadequate supplies, no leaving the enclave. His sector would be the most efficient and productive of all, and then perhaps his majestic leader would finally recognise his worth and promote him to a position in the city.

The section leader did not trust these people and nor did he know how best to handle them. He was not renowned for intelligence himself and relied on brute force to cover his inadequacies; but even that could prove tiresome and profitless. He could not very well kill everyone who displeased him or there would soon be too few left to gather the supplies needed by the city. No, he needed his work-force alive but submissive.

'I am,' said Hollam, stepping forward.

The Kházakh looked him up and down disdainfully, memorizing his face. 'Name?'

'I am Hollam and this is Tarn,' he said, gesturing to his friend. 'How can we be of service?' His voice sounded sincere and his demeanour was one of servility. The Kházakh narrowed his eyes suspiciously.

'We captured these creatures outside your borders. What do you have to say about this?'

Two young scouts, their hands tied behind them and looking the worst for wear, were pushed roughly forward and fell to their knees. Hollam swallowed deeply, the muscles in his cheeks twitching as he fought to contain himself. 'I know nothing.'

'You know the punishment for leaving your enclave?' the man said threateningly.

'We do but they are young,' Hollam reasoned. 'They may have wandered too far in search of food. You tax us a heavy burden.'

'Is that a complaint?'

'It is merely an observation,' Hollam replied calmly.

'Then I suggest you observe this,' the Kházakh sneered. 'Lash them!'

Two Kházakha grabbed the scouts and pulled them to their feet. They were marched to a tree and tied. Taking hold of their shirts, the men tore them open, revealing the boys' smooth backs. Hollam and Tarn were horrified; they knew the cruelty of the lashes.

Hollam leapt forward and grabbed the leader's arm, but immediately backed off, his hands raised submissively as the guards swung their weapons towards him. 'I am responsible for my people. Take me instead and let them bear witness for their crimes,' he begged in desperation.

Hollam stood anxiously, waiting for the Kházakh's answer. The man stepped closer, trying to intimidate him, but as Hollam was some inches taller, the ploy did not work. An evil gleam came into the Kházakh's eyes. 'Yes, you are indeed responsible. Take him!' he ordered, signalling to another guard. 'Lash them all.'

'You cannot!' Tarn objected, trying to intervene. He was quickly silenced by a sharp blow to the head that left blood gushing down the side of his face. He staggered under the impact but remained on his feet, holding the wound to stem the flow as he looked on helplessly.

Hollam was manhandled to the tree and likewise bound. His shirt was violently torn from his back. A powerfully built man came forward and took a whip from his belt. It was made from three thin twisted-leather thongs topped off with jagged stones.

The soldier stood back and raised his arm, waiting for the signal to begin.

'Proceed,' the leader commanded, smirking at their helplessness and excited by the prospect of torture.

Leaning his body into every stroke, the man lashed each prisoner in turn. The teenagers cried out as the thongs tore into their skin five times, leaving angry red welts and jagged cuts to mark their impact. Their agonised cries echoed through the enclave bringing dwellers scurrying from all directions. The mothers of the boys were inconsolable.

Children were so precious to the Roumanhis. Few had been born since the arrival of the Kházakha and those who had found the courage to raise young lived in abject fear that they would be taken to the city. The Kházakh leader seemed to take delight in their distress.

Hollam was not so vocal. He was determined not to give them the pleasure of hearing his pain. As the whip cracked against him he clenched his teeth and grimaced but only the occasional hiss of air escaped. His silence enraged the leader who stormed to and fro, commanding Hollam be struck again and again. Tarn closed his eyes to shut out the sight, silently wishing his friend would cry out just to have the punishment cease. Hollam was enduring too much and his back was being cut to ribbons.

❧❧❧

Inside the cavern, Negram was beside herself. Tears of pity were streaming down her face and her shoulders were shaking with rage at her son's predicament. Cail could not bear to watch and was standing with his arms wrapped around his mother, but his eyes were glued on T'skya. She stood horrified and transfixed, staring through the spy-hole.

At last the lashing stopped. Hollam, his strength spent, sagged against the tree, barely conscious. Tarn stood trembling with anger, one hand still firmly pressed against his head and the other clenched tightly by his side.

The Kházakh leader finally had Hollam released and brought before him. He was forced to his knees, his arms twisted cruelly behind him. The leader leered with satisfaction at the Roumanhi's humbled position, little knowing how courageous Hollam appeared to the forest dwellers as he used what strength he had left to meet the Kházakh's eyes.

'Perhaps now you will follow our rules,' the Kházakh said. 'Let this be a warning to you all. You are in *my* territory now and you belong to me. I, Slythe, am your master and you *will* obey me!'

He walked up to Hollam and gripping his chin yanked his head up even higher. 'Now, you'll co-operate and tell me what I need to know. Three days ago we had reports of a strange light in the sky over the desert that seemed to fall to the earth. What do you know of this?'

'I know nothing of this,' Hollam replied hoarsely, defiantly pulling his head from Slythe's grip.

'Obstinate still? I admire your courage but despise your foolishness.'

'It is not courage, it is the truth,' Hollam rasped. 'The desert is many leagues distant and the trees here are tall. Since we may not leave our enclave, how could we have seen this light you speak of?'

He stared down at Hollam for some moments before signalling the soldiers to release him. Hollam took a deep breath and lurched to his feet. Slythe chose to ignore him and brought one of his men forward. 'Snell, scan the area.'

'What shall I scan for, Sir?'

The question rattled Slythe. 'Anything unusual, you fool!'

'Yes, Sir,' Snell responded with a shake of the head. He did not like his new section leader. He did not mix with his men and was severe with them to the point of absurdity; there was great discontent amongst the ranks. He also had enough compassion to sympathise with Hollam and the scouts, who were not much younger than him. But orders were orders, and if he did not carry them out he would also suffer the consequences.

He unclipped a rectangular box from his belt, drew out the antenna and began walking away from the Clanmeet, sweeping the machine from side to side, adjusting the controls as he went.

❧

T'skya was alarmed. Slythe could only have been referring to her craft as it entered the atmosphere and dropped heavily into the sands. It would only be a matter of time before they found it and learned of her presence.

And now they were scanning the area...

'The beacon,' she gasped. 'Give me the beacon.'

Ferret hesitated. He did not know whether to trust her and turned to Cail who nodded briefly. Ferret unwillingly brought the beacon out of his pocket and held it gingerly towards her. T'skya immediately snatched it from him, threw it on the ground and crushed it underfoot. It was an impetuous action and one that she instantly regretted. In pieces on the floor lay her only hope of salvation.

Cail, sensing her loss, touched her arm hesitantly. He realised the implications of her action and was grateful for it.

T'skya felt no better.

❧

As Snell carried out his duties, Slythe revised the list of taxes due and added another third to his demands. There were gasps and cries of dismay that were silenced by threatening movements from the guards.

Hollam courageously or perhaps foolishly spoke up; 'Sir, as I have said, you tax us a heavy burden. The crops do not grow as they used to and since you limited our borders we cannot forage for supplies.'

'I know your difficulties. Just work twice as hard and eat less.'

'Food grows at its own pace. We cannot change that,' he countered.

Slythe snarled and stepped threateningly towards Hollam. 'Your insolence is intolerable!' he said raising his arm to strike.

Just then Raven appeared. She was devoid of her usual habiliments, dressed in a simple revealing gown. She had untied the ribbons about her neck and chest and the opening of the gown hung wide, exposing her white skin and the curves of her breasts. Slythe paused in mid-stroke. He had a voracious appetite for sensual pleasures and took full advantage of women, whether they were willing or not.

'My Lord Slythe,' she cooed, 'why do you waste your energies on these foolish men? Let them be and entertain me for a while. I have waited long for a man such as you.'

Hollam and Tarn could not believe their eyes. Raven, who hated the Kházakha more than anyone, actually appeared to be seducing one of them. It was unprecedented and foolhardy.

'Had I known such beauties existed here, I'd have added you to my list of taxes,' Slythe slimed.

'My Lord, you tease me,' Raven replied coyly, lowering her eyes in feigned embarrassment but feeling sick inside.

Slythe stepped closer and ran a finger down her bare arm and she shivered at his touch. 'Do I excite you?'

'Is that not obvious?'

'I excite you because you fear me, isn't that so?' he whispered arrogantly into her ear. His breath was warm and caustic on her face, but then he suddenly snapped. 'Do you think I'll succumb to your whims so easily? No, slut, I won't satisfy you when you desire it; but don't worry, I *will* have you, when *I* decide. Until then let this satisfy you.' He pulled her to him, kissed her hard on the mouth and threw her to the ground.

'Women!' he added scornfully and, gathering his troops about him, strode off, collecting Snell on the way. 'We'll return at full moon for the taxes. Don't disappoint me.'

Tarn grabbed one of his scouts and gave him hurried instructions: 'Follow them at a distance and inform us when they are outside our borders. Do not let yourself be seen, and set a double guard tonight.'

The scout scuttled off and the dwellers ran to Hollam, Tarn and the boys to give them assistance. Hollam shrugged them off and stumbled towards Raven. She turned away from him and tried to escape but he grasped her arm. 'I want to thank you for what you did.'

She turned her head and looked him straight in the eye; her expression was cold enough to cause frostbite. 'I did not do it for you.'

❧

Raven half-scrambled, half-ran to one of the bathing ponds. She felt sick and stood retching beside a silver birch. The sight of Slythe had disgusted her and his touch had made her want to shrivel and die. And the kiss! Would she ever be able to wipe away the stain of his lips upon her? She had almost sacrificed her virtue, and for what? True, it had aided Hollam, but she had not acted for him, she had done it for Cail. Would he now believe that all was not lost? Could he now not see that she would do anything to have him love her, anything at all?

Standing on the beach by the water's edge, she stripped off her gown, kicked it aside in disgust and dived into the water.

The pond was spring-fed and pure, surrounded by rushes and reeds, water-plantains and bog asphodel. Raven stayed under the water until she thought her lungs would burst before breaking the surface in a rush of spray. Moving to the shallows, she scrubbed her skin with handfuls of sand, scrubbing until her body felt sore, but she could not scrub away the memory of Slythe's poisonous touch. Regret and revulsion overcame her and she beat her fists into the pond, sending up waves of water.

Cail slowly approached from the trees holding a bundle. Averting his eyes he sat staring into the forest. 'I thought you might need some clothes and a cloth to dry yourself.'

'Thank you,' she said, walking unashamedly out of the water to stand beside him. He turned further away provoking her. 'Are you ashamed of me, Cail?'

'Ashamed, no. Surprised, yes.'

'Do you not understand?'

'I understand that you put yourself at risk and are at risk still. He will return for you,' Cail replied solemnly.

'You are angry.'

'Not angry, concerned. What did you expect to accomplish? How can you hope to win against Slythe and men armed with blasters, you, a lone woman?'

'Not even Slythe is so paranoid to have guards in his bed chamber.'

Cail shook his head incredulously. 'Is that what you intend? To lure him to bed; and do what? Kill him? You would not survive long enough to enjoy it.'

'Have you so little faith in me?'

'You are a brave and skilful warrior, Raven, but even you are no match for their weapons.'

'What would you have had me do?' she demanded. 'Leave your brother to his fate?'

'This is not about my brother.'

'You did not answer my question.'

'And you are evading the issue,' he snapped.

'I did what I had to do. Your precious T'skya did nothing but cower below ground.'

'As did I,' Cail reminded her.

'You had reason.'

'As did she.'

His reply infuriated her. He had understood nothing of her actions and continued to favour the Kházakh. She fought hard to contain her jealousy, fearing it would drive him further from her, and fell silent.

Cail, too, found he had nothing further to say. Raven had a forceful personality and fought for what she wanted, but he found her suffocating in her possessiveness and harsh in her judgments. Now, since T'skya's arrival, albeit but a day, she had become almost insanely jealous, even though Cail felt he had done nothing to warrant such animosity.

It was over between them. It only remained for Raven to accept it. He had not bonded with her and so was free to decide; or as free as she would allow him to be. At length he spoke; 'We should return. They will be missing us and I wish to check on Hollam.'

Raven collected her belongings and stalked off into the trees without saying a word. She had not taken the conversation kindly and it was his sincere hope that no-one would provoke her further.

❦

People were soon gathered in groups discussing the events and there was much heated debate, not least about the lack of warning arrows and Raven's apparent mental breakdown. The atmosphere was fraught with fear and fury. T'skya, forgetting that she was still officially a prisoner, strode off towards the house of healing, but pulled up short at Negram's request. She, too, was hurrying to her son's side, but could not match the young woman's pace. 'You forgot your pack,' Negram informed her, thrusting it into her hands. 'Perhaps your medicines will aid him.'

T'skya smiled with relief at her inclusion. 'Yes, they will.'

The room was surrounded by citizens eager to give their assistance. Although a little taken aback by T'skya's presence, they opened a space for her and Negram to pass. Hollam was awake and the two scouts had already been attended to at his insistence. An elegant slender woman who had the most startling sea-grey eyes and a highly decorated and intricate hairstyle was finishing applying a bandage to Tarn's head. She was clearly not Roumanhi. Hollam was lying face downwards on the bed, his wounded back still open and sticky with blood.

'Breeze! Why has nothing been done for him?' Negram demanded crossly.

'He would not allow it,' placated the adorned woman. 'He said that no-one was to touch him but you.'

'Pach!' she chided. 'No matter how old they get, they always want their mother when there is trouble, even when there is a superior healer amongst us.' She turned to Hollam. 'And you! Do you not think I have enough to do without coddling you as you waste the services of the Great Divide?'

Hollam raised a smile. 'You see how my mother loves me?'

Negram bathed his back with hot water to remove the dirt and blood and T'skya applied a protective gel from her medikit to the lacerations and he was lightly bandaged. Breeze observed their efforts and cast a tender glance at the prostrate man but did nothing to assist, even though it was frustrating and demoralizing to ignore her superior skills.

When their surgery was complete Hollam slowly got to his feet. His determination to be seen drew protests from his mother and the other healers, who advised him to rest. 'My walking out there will raise morale more than words,' he proclaimed, against which they had no counter argument. He grunted his way to the door, hissed as he stooped under the blanket but smiled for the concerned faces that beheld him.

'I am hungry,' he announced to everyone's amusement and relief. If Hollam could still think of food, then his injuries could not be that serious.

'Sit here,' Breeze said, helping him onto a high stump so that he would not have to bend. 'We will bring the food to you.'

Hollam was not accustomed to having so much fuss made over him but revelled in it, taking full advantage of their charity. T'skya was amused and even helped feed him when he complained the effort of moving his hands to his mouth caused him pain. She was just spooning him some broth when Cail arrived to check on his condition.

'I see that you are being well cared for, brother,' he said.

'It could be worse,' Hollam replied.

At that moment a small bundle of energy in the form of a child came whooping through the trees and enveloped Hollam in an all embracing hug.

'Steady there, Catkin, or you will do more damage than they did.' he said, gently prising her from him.

'I was so worried about you,' she replied, her eyes full of concern.

'Well, thanks to my friends I am recovering.' He turned the child to face T'skya. 'Catkin, meet T'skya. T'skya, this is my young friend, Catkin.' The girl had been so intent on Hollam that she had failed to notice T'skya.

'I'm pleased to meet you,' T'skya said, offering her hand.

Catkin looked at it suspiciously and shrank closer to Hollam. He gently pushed her forwards, encouraging her to accept the offer of friendship. The girl was nervous but if he accepted the Kházakh, then so would she. She stretched out her tiny fingers and placed them against T'skya's. T'skya took a gentle but firm hold and shook her hand. 'Why is she doing that?' the girl asked in surprise.

'I believe that shaking hands is their custom,' Cail informed her.

'How strange,' Catkin giggled, and proceeded to show T'skya how their people greeted one another. 'You see, *we* take hands and place them to our brows. It symbolises the union of our minds and bodies,' she explained proudly.

'It's a very good greeting,' T'skya put in. 'Better than ours.'

Catkin beamed and then looked thoughtful. 'Why are you being so nice?' she asked. 'You are a Kházakh and hate us.'

'Catkin, that was not polite,' Cail admonished.

'It's all right,' T'skya said quickly. 'She has the right to ask. I look like the Kházakha and I believe I may be one of them by blood line, but I'm not the same. I'm your friend and I want to help.'

Hollam grinned and Cail looked relieved. 'Have you then made your decision?' he asked.

'Yes,' T'skya replied distantly. 'Yes, I suppose I have.'

⁂

Things soon returned to normal in the camp, and T'skya was given a burrow to make her own, together with clothes, linen and one or two objects of convenience. It was not safe for her to sleep above ground in the huts and so like many of the dwellers she was confined to the burrows at night. There she had time to rue the destruction of her beacon and all that it signified, and when the camp fell silent she would think of the Mothership and question the decision she had made.

During the first few days, to keep busy, T'skya spent her time getting to know the other inhabitants of the enclave and learning as much about their ways as she could. She was curious how she had been found when the Roumanhis were meant to be confined to their enclaves.

Cail explained that all excursions were carefully planned and that scouting parties were always present in the forest, foraging for supplies and keeping watch on the enemy. The forest dwellers could travel quickly and silently and had exceptional camouflage capabilities that rendered them practically invisible to the Kházakha, who, fortunately, had not developed their skills and could easily be tracked. The two young scouts had been captured because they were careless. They had ventured out without permission or an experienced guide, and had walked straight into a group of Kházakha who were resting by a brook.

'What if the Kházakha visit the camp while Hollam and Tarn are absent? Won't that raise suspicion?' she asked.

'The Kházakha visit rarely, but should it happen we would simply say they are out foraging; besides, they seldom venture together,' he said, making a complex and highly dangerous venture sound so simple and safe.

In the daytime T'skya also explored the burrows, an intricate network of tunnels and caverns that spread a considerable distance and had escape routes deep into the forest. She was amazed by Roumanhi ingenuity. The original burrows were centuries old but since the arrival of the Kházakha, extensions and renovations had been laboriously carried out; a job which the aptly named Badger now supervised.

The burrows remained secret places of refuge and allowed the Roumanhis to hide essential items that would have been confiscated or led to severe punishment. There were grain and wool stores, stores of wood, water, mead and wine, dried and fresh fruit and vegetables, and stores of primitive weapons: bows and arrows, spears, boluses, knives and swords, but nothing that could constitute a threat to the Kházakha. It made T'skya shiver to think of these simple peaceful people reduced to this. They were, however, fighting a war; a war they were destined to lose if this was all they had to rely on.

Another query raised was why Cail had taken refuge in the burrow, leaving Hollam and Tarn to face Slythe alone. Knoll she could understand; he was from a different race and would have been punished for being in the land. Negram was too old and the children too young. But why Cail?

He was hesitant to answer and what he did impart was evasive. It took T'skya some time and a lot of different approaches to understand anything.

Cail was wanted by the Kházakha. If he were found, he would be taken from the camp and executed. He would not say what had done to deserve their interest but his tone implied there was more to the situation than he dared reveal aloud. The secret roused T'skya's curiosity and made Cail romantically mysterious. Negram's refusal to elaborate only furthered her interest and caused wild flights of imagination to surface. To T'skya, Cail was every type of hero rolled into one and yet he was no hero at all.

'You know, telling someone you have a secret and then not telling what it is must be the worst kind of cruelty,' she chided.

'You do yourself an injustice,' Cail replied, raising his blond eyebrows at her.

'Hmmm,' was all he heard in reply and thankfully she let the subject drop.

✦

T'skya spent a great deal of time with Hollam and Cail. Hollam's back was healing and it did not look as if he would be badly scarred. He had a strong constitution and was walking about within a few days, scouting and foraging, spontaneously bursting into song and playing tricks on everyone to keep the camp's morale high. The injured parties never remained angry for long; they were used to his exploits. The only one who remained unscathed was Raven. Hollam understood that she would find no humour in his escapades and would undoubtedly repay him ten-fold for his actions.

A week after the Kházakha's visit, Briar came raging into T'skya's burrow, where Cail and she were engaged in deep conversation.

'Where is Hollam?' she demanded.

'What has he done now?' asked Cail warily.

'This!' she thundered, holding up her favourite gown.

On the fine creamy-white surface of the dress, just where her large breasts hung, two large crossed-eyes had been painted, and around her rotund stomach a toothy, smiling mouth had been scrawled to encircle half her bulk.

T'skya coughed as she tried to contain the laughter and Cail desperately attempted to bite back his mirth but only succeeded in letting a loud snort escape from his nose. As she crossly disappeared from sight, the pair exploded into laughter.

Cail shook his head. 'Briar will not contain her wrath if she catches him.'

'It will come out, won't it?'

'Oh, I should think so. Hollam may be a clown but he is not cruel. He has not done any permanent damage, yet.'

'You are so different, yet I see Negram in both of you. He has her kindness and merriness and you her integrity and wisdom. But what was your father like?'

'I do not know,' Cail replied sadly. 'He died shortly before I was born, during the conquest of the land. Mother does not speak of him openly; I fear the memory is too painful.'

'I'm sorry.' T'skya placed her hand on his arm. 'Your people have suffered greatly. I wish I could do something to help make amends.'

'Perhaps you can,' he replied quietly, and with that he left the burrow.

❧

Nearly two weeks had passed by T'skya's reckoning since she had been found and still nobody had suggested any plan of action against the Kházakha. She was growing more and more frustrated. The longer they waited, the more chance of the Kházakha finding her ship. She hoped Briar would hold a council soon but the time was nearly upon them for Slythe to return for the taxes and everyone was so busy preparing the supplies that perhaps they had no time to take the matter into consideration.

T'skya had been allowed out foraging and was impressed by their laws of selection. As Negram explained, the fruits of the forest were not picked randomly. They had defined sectors which were harvested in rotation and only a percentage of the fruits were taken, ensuring the plants' continued reproduction. Since the varieties of plants bore fruit at different times of the year there was always food available, but the Kházakha were demanding and severely affected what the dwellers had managed to achieve. Indeed, oftentimes they found a sector plundered by the aliens, the bushes hacked down and burnt or else trampled underfoot. It was a continual struggle to propagate and pick, despite their expertise.

Although T'skya had worked in the environmental section of the Mothership she had never set foot in a real forest and was astonished by the variety and abundance of plant life that grew wild there. She spent hours learning how to find and differentiate between edible and inedible species, increasing her chances of survival alone.

Cail had also taken it upon himself to show her some of the animals that inhabited their land. He led T'skya down a path which led to the southern edge of Wilderwood, ever alert for Kházakha patrols. As he neared a small glade he put his finger to his lips and slowly dropped to his knees. T'skya was alarmed, half expecting to see the white uniforms of her people honing in on them, but Cail had a smile on his face. Cautiously he pointed away to their right.

'*Kamaara*,' he whispered.

T'skya caught her breath as a herd of deer came into view. The does were a dappled golden red and had the softest brown eyes and the daintiest velvet noses. Their nimble hooves made no sound as they picked their way through the undergrowth, nibbling at the fresh buds on the bushes. A large stag with a magnificent set of antlers was proudly patrolling with them. He stopped and sniffed the air, but Cail had kept them downwind and out of his senses. T'skya stifled a giggle as a couple of fawns made their appearance, staying close to their mothers for safety. And then they were gone, startled by a large fowl that exploded from the undergrowth where her nest lay.

Cail remained still and scanned the canopy. He flicked his eyes towards an unusually tall moss covered buckthorn. T'skya followed his gaze and finally saw the bird he was observing.

'That is a male *marra marra*. The nearest translation is 'vanity'. In our tongue it is humorous for someone who thinks only of their own beauty but does not possess the looks to warrant it.'

T'skya was curious. 'Why is it called that?'

'Ah, you see his plumage is plain compared to many of the birds you see here. He has not the vibrant colours nor the sweet call, but he struts and poses and ruffles out his feathers as if he were the prince of all. See, he tries to attract a mate.'

The *marra marra* began his ritual and the brighter plumaged female watched the puffing and strutting and preening and the peculiar beak tapping and squawks as the proud male did his very best to entice her. And then she flew away. T'skya burst out laughing as the poor deflated male watched her leave. But T'skya's education did not stop with zoology and botany lessons.

Catkin and her mother, Bramble, showed her how to make bread from forest nuts and various types of soup; wild potatoes stuffed with herbs and cheese, and honey cakes. T'skya had never cooked anything apart from dehydrated survival packs and she found the whole process fascinating, although she doubted whether it would be so appealing if forced upon her every day.

It was during one such occasion, as they sat down to eat, that she learnt another difference between the Kházakha and the dwellers.

'This soup is wonderful,' she said, saluting Bramble. 'What kind of meat is it?'

Food fell from hands, cups were slammed onto the mats, conversations ceased and expressions of revulsion spread from face to face. T'skya looked around in bewilderment. 'What did I say?'

'*We* do not murder animals for their flesh,' someone said pointedly.

T'skya ate the rest of the meal in silence.

Cail came to her afterwards. 'I hope you do not think us impolite, but the idea of eating our fellow creatures is offensive. It is the same as if you suggested eating our children.'

T'skya shook her head. 'That's a heavy simile.'

'To you, perhaps, but to us all life is sacred.'

'Even the Kházakha's?'

Cail hesitated. His expression suggested conflict and furrows deepened on his brow. 'All death is regrettable, but sometimes necessity dictates; we do what we must to survive.'

T'skya read many things into this and, although she knew she did not have the right, asked; 'Have you killed?'

Cail's reaction was instantaneous and made her regret the question. He did not need to speak; the answer was obvious, he had taken a life and had not yet come to terms with it.

T'skya touched his fingers. 'I'm sorry, Cail. Forget I asked.'

'Do not apologise, Green-Eyes. You have the right to ask such things.'

T'skya shook her head. 'I have so many things to learn I forget myself.' She studied him carefully before adding; 'You know, sometimes it helps to talk about things. I'm here if you need me.'

'I thank you, T'skya of the Homequest,' he replied, bowing to her. 'It is a difficult subject for me, but I believe the tale will answer many questions you have not yet raised. Come, let us go to a more private spot; I do not wish to be disturbed.'

Taking her arm, he led her along a winding path through low-lying, uncurling ferns, stopping at a secluded embankment beside one of the fresh-water ponds.

He sat upon the moss, as was his custom, with his legs in front of him bent at the knees and with his elbows resting upon them. T'skya sat cross-legged and stared out across the pond watching the mayfly courting.

'It's so peaceful here,' she whispered. 'It's hard to imagine you are fighting a war.'

Cail studied his fingernails. 'Have you ever fought for anything, T'skya?'

'Not in so many words, at least not in this type of war, but my people are fighting for survival in their own way.'

'Due to others or themselves?'

'Because of our own greed and stupidity,' she answered bitterly. 'We destroyed our home world in the name of progress and technology. Our attempts to improve our lives succeeded only in destroying them, so here we are, searching hopelessly for a solution to our own mismanagement.'

'It is neither hopeless nor in vain if your people have learnt the error of their ways.'

T'skya picked at the vegetation and tossed it aside in disillusionment. 'We have learnt but I think it's too late.'

'Just as we learnt too late,' Cail agreed. 'We saw the dangers but did nothing until we were overpowered. But I did not bring you here to talk of this. I have brought you here to relate an event that occurred nearly four of your…nearly four years ago. I hope you are comfortable, it is a long tale.'

T'skya nodded that she was ready and sat in anticipation, studying his body language and feasting on his handsomeness.

Cail's eyes drifted across the pond becoming unfocused as he cast his mind back. 'At the time I refer to, the Kházakh in charge of this section was a man named Tresk. He was not like Slythe, but a gentle man who caused us little trouble. The laws then concerning our movements were lax and we were not confined to our enclaves as we are now.

'A group of five of us set out to gather flour from the Harvesters, myself, Willow, Hawk, Spider and Elm. We were a young, inexperienced group but somehow it fell upon me to be the leader.

'We were into our third day of journeying, travelling through a region that borders the fertile plains known as *Voulhama*, or Poppydown in your tongue, where the forest narrows so that it takes but a day to walk from one side to the other. Before long we recognised a change in the forest's mood. We then smelt smoke and our hearts began to race. There is little rain here sometimes and the forest, downs and plains become parched dry. This was such a year. We were filled with dread and hurried towards the fire.

'We had travelled only a short distance when we came upon the cause of our fears. In a clearing, a short walk from the plains, we saw a small dwelling barely alight by that time, smouldering and charred. The soil and the grass beside it were scorched and a group of Kházakha was standing around, stamping on the embers. We believed they had happened upon the fire and had thought to extinguish it before it could spread to the trees, but a curdling scream snapped our attention to the truth of the matter.

'To the right of the fire, and a little way back, there was a man on his knees, bloodied and blackened with soot. In front of him stood a Kházakh dressed in grey and hooded. I could not see his face and yet I could sense a sinister, formidable power burning inside him. He seemed to tower over the man and all the Kházakha shrank away when he glanced in their direction.

'We were too far away to hear what he said, but I do not fear to be corrected if I say his voice was one of unremitting evil. He

bent towards the man and took his hand, twisting the grimy
fingers with sadistic intent, demanding answers to questions
we could not hear. The man screamed, his face contorting with
pain. Again the Kházakh demanded and again a finger was
twisted...and snapped.

'Three times we witnessed this cruelty, and three times we
remained hidden in the bushes, horrified and sickened yet too
fearful to move. It was my decision to make; I was their leader,
but I panicked and froze. Elm, the youngest, could bear it no
more and exploded through the bushes. Before we had formed
any strategy we found ourselves following, screaming war cries
and waving our staffs as threateningly as we knew how.

'Our sudden rush gave us a moment's advantage and we set
upon the Kházakha fiercely, though they outnumbered us. We
fought hard trying to make our way to the tortured man, but
we were not skilled fighters. Valiant though our efforts were,
we were overpowered. The hooded man did not even move;
he simply watched our endeavours with disdain. He was never
in danger and knew it. I even heard him laugh; an unnatural,
harsh sound that I still shiver to think of.

'We were restrained, our staffs taken and our hoods were
thrown back so that he could view the faces of those who had
been foolish enough to confront him. I stared him full in the
face but I could see nothing other than his chin below his
hood. It was pitted and wrinkled, a deathly white and his jaw
was set with distaste. He was clearly an aged man.

'He approached us slowly and surveyed each one of us in
turn. I could almost taste his acrid breath as he hissed through
his teeth. Not one word did he speak but turned away and
went to stand next to his victim, pointedly snapping the one
remaining healthy finger.

'As the unfortunate man cried out, my guard's attention
was momentarily distracted and I took the only opportunity
I knew I would have. I snatched the weapon from the guard's
hand and fired before anyone could react. I had witnessed their

use before and knew of their force, but little did I realise what the consequences would be.'

Cail paused, unwilling or else unsure of how to go on. He bent his head in sadness and stared down at his hand. He curled his fingers as if clasping the blaster's butt and his forefinger made one swift movement, the impulsive squeezing of the trigger.

'I fired and the Kházakha fell. Two of the remaining soldiers leapt to defend their leader, but he raised a hand and forbade them to approach us or shoot. I thought he feared I would kill or perhaps he was simply studying us. It was then I noticed that Elm was not free. His guard was holding a weapon to his head and had twisted the boy's arm behind his back.

'I was at a loss. Should I surrender and hope they freed Elm, or sacrifice him for the sake of the others' lives? I had little faith in the Kházakha's mercy, having witnessed the severity of their punishments.

'The guard was nervous. I turned the weapon towards his master, who had given him no clue as to what action to take, believing this threat would weigh heavily upon him and give Elm a better chance of freedom. I looked towards the leader and, out of the corner of my eye, I caught a movement. I swung the weapon around and fired, but being unused to the design I held the trigger too long and the beam struck Elm. He collapsed as if his legs had been severed.

'I was too stunned to move, but the others, heedless of the danger, dashed to his side. Elm was dead. I had not checked...I had not...'

Cail broke off, his voice cracking with emotion. T'skya put out a consoling hand but he pushed it away. That very act of sympathy, something he felt he had no right to, strengthened his resolve. He took a deep breath, wiped his sleeve across his eyes and looked to the sky.

'I had not checked the setting. I assumed they were always set on stun. Not only had I taken the lives of four Kházakha, but I had murdered my friend. I fell into a fog, unseeing and unhearing, wrapped within the shell of my own misery and self-disgust. The remainder of the tale is as I heard it from Willow; I can recall nothing of it but my own self-pity.

'While we were concerning ourselves with our companion, the Kházakha made their escape into the forest. I will never understand why they did not fire on us; we were vulnerable then to their attack. Perhaps they were just uncertain of us since it was not our custom to take lives and they did not wish to risk losing another.

'My companions gathered the bodies of the Kházakha and gave them burial but wrapped Elm in cloaks so that he could be transported home. The injured man was tended to as best we could and invited back with us. We only sought the sanctuary of home.

'The journey back was slow and solemn. Elm was placed upon a crude stretcher and the injured man was in need of assistance, he was weak and in shock. I could offer neither comfort nor aid for I was shut within myself. I was an unforgivable burden on my company.

'When we returned I was too frightened and shamed to enter the camp. I feared the reactions and the recriminations, though I believed I deserved no better. It was the man I had rescued who gave me the strength to face the consequences of my actions.'

T'skya took the opportunity to speak as Cail paused. 'The man you rescued was Fen, wasn't it?' she said quietly.

'Yes,' he replied. 'And it was Fen who came to me as we sat a short distance from the enclave. Fen is a reticent man, even more so since your coming, I fear, but that day he opened himself to me. There are some who shun the Clans and choose to live solitary lives within the forest. We call them Wanderers. Fen was one of those. He had lived for many years wandering the land, settling here and there, and harming no-one. He had eventually come to live near Poppydown to make a home for his bondmate Holly and child. They lived happily and trouble-free until the day the Kházakha came.

'They had tried to violate Holly - they think nothing of taking a woman for their own use. Fen had tried to defend her and they beat him fiercely, slashing at his face with a knife. Blinded by the blood and delirious from the pain, he could do nothing to prevent their deeds. In the ecstasy of their passions, the Kházakha torched the dwelling, trapping Holly and her son inside. Again and again Fen had tried to rescue them, but the Kházakha held him back. He was forced to watch as his family burned; forced to hear their screams as clothes and hair and skin smouldered and charred, and the Kházakha looked on smiling. The horror of it is unimaginable.

'Then they questioned him, stupid questions he could not answer. As a punishment for silence his fingers were broken. Such was the damage that even Negram could not save them all and one had to be removed to prevent further infection.

'What were my troubles compared to his? None of us could have foreseen the events and no-one, not even Elm's mother, held a grudge against me. It was only I who judged myself. As a consequence, the entire group has had to hide from the Kházakha, though we have not all been successful. There is a bountiful reward for my capture. I am, perhaps, the most wanted criminal in the land.'

'And you still see yourself as a criminal?' T'skya asked bluntly.

'Yes,' he heaved himself to his feet, 'and no. I have learnt to accept what happened to the Kházakha since they were killed with a weapon of their own design, a weapon designed to persecute us. But I shall never be at peace over Elm.'

'It was an accident, Cail. You can't spend the rest of your life brooding over a mistake. There are always casualties in war. Elm's life saved another's.'

'Are we then at war?' he asked, almost to himself. 'Yes, I suppose that is true, but we do not wish to take lives; it is against our custom.'

'Then you will have to change your customs. You can't expect the Kházakha to change.' She added more forcefully; 'Do you think you can reason with them and make them relent with words? If they won't change, then you must or you'll surely lose.'

The corners of Cail's mouth curved into a thoughtful smile. 'You sound like Raven.'

'Then her advice must be sound.'

'Sound but unwelcome.' He offered his hand and helped her to her feet. 'Come, it is late and you must be hungry.'

'Cail, thank you for telling me. I'm glad you trust me enough, though I don't know why you should.'

'I like you,' he said simply, and led her back to the camp.

FOUR

In trust there is hope

The day of taxes was upon them. It was still early morning and the camp was a hive of activity. People were ferrying supplies from the burrows to the collection point, meticulously covering all traces of disturbance from the areas above and around the trap-doors. Fen, as the supply-master, was overseeing the operation and everyone obeyed his commands without question. He counted sacks of nut flour, berries, fungi, barrels of mead, balls of yarn and lengths of finely woven cloth.

T'skya resisted the temptation to offer help, fearing rejection. She understood his reticence and the discomfort her proximity afforded him, yet she desired his recognition. It would be a sign that she was trusted; something she badly needed.

There was still over an hour or so until the Kházakha were due to collect the taxes but the atmosphere in the camp was already tense. Those who must not be seen would shortly take to the burrows to spend several miserable hours anxiously waiting for the day's events to unfold. Hollam and Tarn would again be left to face Slythe, and what of Raven?

T'skya had little contact with the woman and was content to keep it that way. Fen simply avoided her, but T'skya could feel the animosity pouring from Raven like the cascades of a waterfall. This was a woman she had no hopes of ever reaching. If it were not for the fact that she would bring ruin on the whole camp, she was sure that Raven would not hesitate to betray her. And yet T'skya felt no animosity towards her. Rather, she pitied her, an emotion Raven would have despised had she known.

T'skya was well aware of the warrior's passion for Cail. She saw it in the way Raven watched him as he went about his business, in the way she moved and held herself when he was near, and in her coldness towards any woman who dared speak to him when she was close by. Yet she only seemed to alienate herself further from him. Each conversation they shared left him sighing and in low-spirits, each moment together was heavy with misunderstanding and hurt, every look was filled with doubts and questions. T'skya found it hard to imagine they had ever been happy together, although she knew it must have been so, long ago.

At a loss and bored by inactivity, T'skya sought out Hollam. He was always good company and he welcomed her cheerfully.

'I feel like a rotten potato,' she declared miserably.

Hollam looked puzzled. 'You wish to eat rotten food?'

T'skya was unsure whether to explain her meaning or to laugh. 'You are joking, aren't you?'

He touched his chest as if the suggestion were ridiculous. 'Me?'

Her face relaxed into a smile and she playfully punched his arm. Hollam feigned intense pain. 'Aren't you ever serious?'

'When necessary,' he replied, shrugging nonchalantly.

T'skya was intrigued. He gave the appearance of one who took everything in his stride and quailed at nothing. T'skya wished she possessed just an iota of his fortitude. 'Aren't you afraid of Slythe?'

Hollam took a deep breath before answering. 'Only a braver man than I or else a fool would not fear the Kházakha, and

I consider myself neither a coward nor a fool, though some might say I was the latter.' Then he added; 'What do you require, my little potato?'

T'skya laughed. 'Give me something to do. I feel completely useless.'

Hollam considered the options. He knew Fen would not appreciate her presence if she assisted with the taxes and he respected the man's feelings too much to force the issue. 'You could start sending people to the burrows. It is early yet, but the Kházakha are not renowned for punctuality.'

'Don't the Kházakha wonder why there are so few people in the enclave?'

Hollam grinned. 'They have never known our true numbers. A census was conducted many seasons back but we hid away then and now they only do head counts. As long as their figures match they ask no questions.'

She squeezed his hand softly ready to leave. 'Be careful.'

T'skya went about the task somewhat nervously. She still found it difficult to approach some of the forest dwellers, ever aware that her people were the cause of their troubles. In less than half an hour, however, a third of the camp had taken to the burrows and it was time for her to go into hiding. When she reached her designated cavern she found Negram, Knoll and Ferret already housed.

Negram appeared agitated and was tapping her foot impatiently. She regarded T'skya expectantly. 'Where is Cail?'

'Isn't he with you?' T'skya replied, despite his obvious absence from the cavern.

'We thought he was with you,' Knoll accused.

'I am not his keeper Knoll,' she rejoined, somewhat upset by his tone but more so by the empty space her friend should have been occupying. 'I was with Hollam. I haven't seen Cail for some time. Do you think he's coming through the tunnels?'

'I rather fear he is seeking Raven,' Negram sighed.

T'skya turned to leave. 'I'll go and find him.'

'No, T'skya of the Homequest. It is not safe for you to venture out at this time. Cail will come when he can.'

T'skya was unhappy but knew that Negram was right. She would be more of a hindrance than a help to Cail should the Kházakha come before they had taken shelter. Instead she glued her eye to a spy-hole hoping to spot him and chewed her nails impatiently.

✦

Cail had indeed gone to seek Raven. She had refused every plea to hide and remain safe from the clutches of Slythe, but he felt he had to try once more, before it was too late.

'The decision is made,' she snapped. 'What do you care what becomes of me now that you have that black-haired plaything?'

Cail was both frustrated and angered by the accusation. 'What has T'skya to do with this?'

'You know very well,' Raven replied darkly, loathing and scorn inflecting her voice.

Cail decided to avoid the subject of his Navennán friend and concentrated on the matter in hand. 'Slythe will violate you if he finds you, and he *will* find you if you do not seek sanctuary with us.'

'And do you not think it will appear strange that I am gone? Do you not think he will require an answer?'

'We will say that you have gone foraging.'

'That will not suffice. Our enclave is not so great that they could fail to find me. It is you who are not logical. I must appear or Slythe will grow suspicious. Would you have Hollam suffer again for disappointing him?'

'No, of course not, but...'

'There are no buts, only choices, and here there is but one choice,' she declared firmly.

Cail could see that he would never be able to change her mind and he was tired of reasoning with her. 'Yes,' he said in a surprisingly calm voice, 'there is but one choice.'

Raven's jaw hardened. 'We all have to live with the consequences of our actions.'

Cail blanched. He knew what she was referring to and her accusation stung him. He turned away to master himself. Raven knew that she had wounded him and no sooner had the words left her lips than she regretted them. 'Cail, I am sorry.'

'So am I,' he replied, swinging a well-aimed punch that struck her jaw squarely and sent her tumbling into an unconscious heap. 'Damn stupid, obstinate woman!' he muttered to himself as he picked up her limp body. 'I have never hit woman before. Why did it have to be you? There is going to be heavy penance for this when you wake up, Loukhala Ravenwood.'

He quickly made his way to the Clanmeet, hoping to stow his passenger below ground before the Kházakha arrived. His appearance and the sight of Raven hanging prostrate over his shoulder drew gasps of astonishment from all he passed and Cail just had time to hear Hollam's jovial proclamation about his magnificent way with women before the warning signal for the approach of the Kházakha was given. As the red-tipped arrow struck the ground, Cail snatched it up and carefully climbed into the cavern closing the trap-door behind him. Hollam kicked leaves over the surface to conceal the entrance.

No-one in the burrow had time to register their surprise before the trampling of feet overhead compelled them to silence. Cail said nothing as he grimly unloaded his burden. He propped Raven up in the corner and made her as comfortable as possible, ignoring the quizzical glances that flicked from face to face. He turned to his mother, who was sitting eyebrows raised but her expression otherwise calm, and whispered darkly; 'Do not ask!'

Slythe came into the Clanmeet as arrogantly as if he owned the place. He was surrounded by his usual squad, some of whom were leading beasts of burden. The men were grievously few to patrol such a large designated area, but what they lacked in manpower they made up for in brutality and technical advancement. One man armed with Kházakha weaponry was worth twenty armed with sticks and stones. Slythe felt no threat to his safety. He need only raise his hand and all who stood before him would be slain.

Hollam stepped gingerly forward to meet him. 'I hope that everything meets with your satisfaction.'

'As do I,' said Slythe, stressing each word dangerously.

The dwellers waited impatiently as he perused the goods, stopping to open this sack and that, tasting the mead and touching the cloth. 'Everything is as it should be. We'll require the same amount in two full moons; I trust you have no objection?'

Hollam had many objections but knew better than to air them, even though Slythe had generously cut the usual collection time by a third. The reduction of time and the extra demands would strain the inhabitants severely and he doubted whether they could meet Slythe's requirements without enormous struggle and further deprivation. 'We will do our best,' he said stoically.

'Yes, I'm sure you will.' Slythe steepled his fingers before his face and wagged them at Hollam thoughtfully. 'There is just one more thing...'

Hollam swallowed and waited for the bad news.

'I've unfinished business here. Where is that woman?'

'We have many women here. Which one do you require?' the anxious man said, trying to buy some time.

'Do not try my patience, fool!'

Hollam had to think quickly. He had seen Cail carry Raven

below ground and understood his brother's reasoning, but it had now put him in a tenuous position. It was impossible to produce her and yet not to could infuriate the Kházakh. 'She is not here,' he said lamely, slipping into a lopsided placatory smile.

'You speak the obvious,' Slythe replied impatiently. '*Where* is she?'

'I do not know,' Hollam admitted, intonating shame and fear to make his words carry more weight. 'Such was your effect upon her that she feared to show herself. She is hiding and we know not where.'

Slythe erupted. 'Are you so incompetent that you can't find the creature within the confines of your own enclave? Don't tell me you've let another leave your borders.'

'No, Sir, she is not foolish enough to leave the enclave. She fears to face you and she would surely fear your punishment more. But she is a skilled woman and if she wishes to remain hidden, then none will find her.'

'And what is the creature's name?'

'Ra - Radish,' he blurted in blind panic. His nearly revealing her name, a matter he considered unwise if they were to protect her, and the ridiculous name he had conjured up filled him with anguish.

'Radish!' Slythe thundered incredulously.

'It is her childhood name, Sir,' Hollam said hastily, desperately trying to salvage the situation, 'for her skin is white and her cheeks pink when roused, hence the name, Radish.'

'Her real name!' the Kházakh demanded, growing more and more infuriated by Hollam's prattling.

'Er...her real name is...er...Blackbird,' he stammered, 'because she...er...sings a lot, though to hear her one would think she was more suited to the name Crow. Though I hate to say this of a beautiful woman, her voice leaves much to be desired. Never, Sir, never I say, ask her to sing to you. It is enough to turn milk to cheese. I think...'

'Enough!' Slythe raged, 'I have heard enough! Let's go before my sanity is destroyed by this babbling fool.' He strode up to Tarn. 'You,' he snarled, poking him sharply in the chest, '… next time I will deal with you.'

As Slythe turned, his men did their best to wipe the smirks off their faces and stifle their sniggering. It was obvious that Hollam was bantering with the man, but Slythe was too ignorant to realise it. His anger blinded him to the truth and he left the enclave so hurriedly that his troops had to scramble to catch up with him.

Hollam let out a sigh of relief and sagged at the knees. Tarn slapped him on the shoulder, amused. 'Very controlled. Very believable!'

Hollam said nothing. He was still shocked that his raving had not condemned him to another beating.

When the all-clear was given, those in hiding streamed out of the burrows. Raven was one of the first to emerge. The side of her jaw ached where Cail's fist had connected and it was beginning to blacken and she had not failed to hear Hollam's insanity. Now she stood in front of him, her eyes ablaze. Hollam smiled nervously and tried to explain but no more than a few words had escaped his mouth when she struck him a sharp blow across the cheek that brought water to his eyes and made his face burn. Unrepentant, she turned on her heels and stalked off through the trees.

Cail faced his squirming brother. 'Radish? Sings like a crow?' Shaking his head and laughing raucously, he left Hollam standing alone.

❦

Collection time had passed without calamity bar two sore faces and two dented egos. Hollam feared it would take a long time before the commotion caused by his unorthodox behaviour died down and it seemed that, for once, he was the butt end of the jokes. He smiled, a fixed resigned smile, and accepted what was due to him.

Raven, on the other hand, was seething. She felt humiliated; Cail and Hollam had made her a laughing stock. That they had done it for her own good was irrelevant; she felt betrayed and conspired against. It would be a long time before she could forgive them.

Cail, resignedly, went to find her. He located her some way from the Clanmeet, sitting on a shaded tussock. Her slim trousered legs were parted and she was holding a delicate flower by the stalk between them, pulling off its petals one by one. He watched from the shelter of the trees, undecided whether to approach, but knew that the longer he waited, the more difficult it would become.

'I am sorry,' he said quietly.

She refused to look at him but her reply was surprisingly soft. 'You made a fool out of me.'

'That was not my intent.'

'And what of Hollam?'

'He panicked.'

'And you?'

'I suppose I panicked, too.'

She glanced across at him, letting her anger subside just a little. 'Hollam is a fool but I expected more from you.'

'You left me with no choice,' he sighed. 'What else could I have done?'

'The decision was mine alone to make.'

'Did you expect me to stand by and let you be violated? I could not bear to be the cause.' Then he added quietly, 'Whatever you may think, I care about you deeply.'

'Do you?' Raven asked as if his words were a lie.

'You know I do, but our paths do not lie together, Raven. You must see that. We are too different, you and I.'

'With whom *does* your path lie?' She sounded bitter now.

'I cannot foresee the future; I do not know.'

Raven fell silent, submerged in her churning emotions. He was rejecting her, finally telling her the words she had dreaded to hear.

'We spend all our time fighting and I am tired of it,' Cail explained crouching down. 'It is *they* we should be fighting, not each other. I do not want to hurt you; I have *never* meant to hurt you, but if we continue down this path that is all we will do. I am sorry.'

Raven spoke, her voice cracking with emotion. 'Please, leave me.' She could not bear sympathy, it stuck in her throat.

Cail nodded and rose to his feet. She looked so sad, so young and fragile as she stared at the ground. 'I *am* sorry,' he whispered.

He walked into the tree line, feeling at once both troubled and relieved. He was worried about Raven; her passions ran so deeply that he did not know how she would react. He felt guilty for being the cause of her pain yet at the same time it was as if a heavy burden had been lifted from his shoulders. He had finally told her the truth and put an end to her futile hopes. Now he could start afresh, free from the shackles of their relationship.

In his contemplation he failed to catch the penetrating glare which followed his movements from beneath Raven's brows. A gleam of pure malice had entered her eyes, her heart cold with rejection and jealousy. As he disappeared from view, she muttered dangerously; 'It is not over, Cail. You will be mine. Oh yes, you *will* be mine.'

❧

T'skya found herself devoid of company for the first time since her arrival and resigned herself to an evening of solitude. She threw herself down on her ferny bed and sighed as memories of the Mothership and the friends she had left came flooding back.

There was Danon and P'tala, R'tangi and Valish, sitting together in the recreation hall, sipping fruit concentrate and flicking cream substitute at each other, for which they were duly chastised for wasting precious food. She remembered her first real kiss. It was her eighteenth birthday and her friends had thrown a surprise party. During the celebration everyone paired off and she found herself with Danon, a youth of twenty and a particular favourite with the girls. She had been surprised by this and secretly pleased. She had assumed that he would be with P'tala; they were usually together, but she had paired off with Chalmis, probably the most talented pilot the ship had ever had. Then she remembered the terrible ache of loss and the disaster of Voltan Four.

It had appeared a favourable planet from the scans and there was excitement on the ship as the scouting parties were sent out. T'skya was disappointed not to have been selected, still considered too young at the turn. The initial surveys were positive and a decision was made to send a team of five scouting parties to the most promising sector to prepare a base camp. They remained for a week before returning to the Mothership. The planet's atmosphere was breathable, the water drinkable and there was an abundance of vegetation, much of which was edible, but there were very few animal species. Those that had been found were primitive organisms with the most basic nervous systems, and no trace of anything remotely resembling a mammal could be found.

Although puzzling, Voltan Four seemed ideal. Animals from the Mothership could be introduced and controlled and, since no-one was there to object to aliens inhabiting the world, preparations were made to disembark from the ship and settle on the planet.

Shortly after the first supplies had been ferried down, members of the original team began to feel weak and disorientated. They were kept in isolation and further transports were halted until a diagnosis could be made. Despite stringent decontamination, the scouting parties had succumbed to a bacteria never encountered before; a bacteria that had somehow failed to be detected by any of the diagnostic tests run on the planet's surface. Within days all those who had been in contact with Voltan Four had fallen ill.

Twenty-six of the crew eventually died, Danon, Chalmis and P'tala included, and all plans to inhabit the new world were abandoned. Thereafter, individuals were sent to each sector of a promising world and thus T'skya found herself on Roumanhi with a year in which to survive or perish; a necessary sacrifice for the good of all.

She wiped away the tears which had fallen with the memories. Had she betrayed her friends by siding with the natives? She did not know and had no wish to dwell on it, but she did know that her inactivity was helping no-one. It was only a matter of time before her small ship was discovered, if it had not been already, and then she would no longer have the safety of secrecy on her side.

The forest dwellers appeared unconcerned. They had done nothing to rectify the situation nor appeared likely to do anything in the near future. She convinced herself there and then she had but one choice.

⚜

Day dawned neither bright nor enthusiastically. It had rained heavily during the night and a thick fog lingered over the camp. The birds were silent, too concerned with keeping warm to sing and the enclave had an air of melancholy.

T'skya awoke suddenly. Her sleep had been fitful and remnants of dreams still troubled her as she sought the outside world. One or two early risers were out, wrapped in waterproof cloaks to ward off the cold and damp. She saw Bramble stomping through the mud towards the ovens and wanting to rid herself of her demons walked across to see if she could help.

'On days like this a hearty meal does wonders,' Bramble said, glancing at T'skya's dismal expression.

T'skya tucked a strand of damp hair behind her ear and stuffed her hands deeply into her pockets. 'If only food could cure all our ills,' she said miserably.

'Something troubles you,' Bramble observed, but seeing T'skya's reticence decided to probe no further. She bustled about and before long a good fire was blazing. 'It requires a little more work in this weather,' she said, 'but with the right kindling and a little know how...'

T'skya puffed out her cheeks impressed by the ease in which the fire had been lit despite the unruly elements. 'You make it look so simple.'

'It merely requires practice. Now you light the other one.'

T'skya set to work, building the kindling pile as Bramble had done but the fire remained unlit. Bramble looked on saying nothing but her eyes were merry.

T'skya began muttering under her breath in frustration. 'I can rewire environmental components, I can genetically engineer plants, I can fly a space-ship. I will *not* be defeated by the most basic discovery of man. I *will* light this stupid, damned, ignorant...I've done it...NO, don't you dare go out!' She sat back on her heels smiling triumphantly as the flames burnt through the kindling pyramid.

'At last,' Bramble said, deflating her somewhat. 'Now fetch me some water.'

Bramble was right. The breakfast they supplied brought a good deal of cheer to the camp, especially when the fog began to lift, although dark clouds still threatened rain. T'skya, however, still felt morose. Her expression was not missed by those who knew her, but their inquiries into her well-being were dismissed with feeble excuses.

Hollam and Cail set about preparing to lead the scouting parties, but T'skya declined invitations to accompany them.

She was thankful they would be absent when she followed through with her decision; their presence would only have hindered her and weakened her resolve. She retreated to her burrow and spent an hour arranging the room before going to find Negram.

She found the old lady in the house of healing, occupying the same stool on which T'skya had first seen her. Negram rose to greet her, but on seeing T'skya's Navennán apparel and the look upon her face sat down again.

'You are leaving us,' she stated calmly. T'skya gave an almost imperceptible nod. 'And where will you go all on your own?'

'To my spaceship before the Kházakha find it.'

'Through the forest and across the plains and the desert without your beacon and with no-one to guide you? You must indeed be accomplished.' The old lady's tone was plain, but her words were laden with sarcasm.

She chewed her lips and frowned, drawing the courage from deep within herself to argue her case. 'I must at least try,' she insisted. 'I can't wait here doing nothing whilst they're out searching. I've been here for several weeks now and nobody has even suggested a course of action. What other choice do I have?'

'So you think we have been idle?' Negram said dourly. 'You think we failed to catch the significance of Slythe's words?'

'Truthfully?'

Negram held her eyes although T'skya thought she detected unease behind them as she stated; 'The truth is always best.'

T'skya held her ground. 'Then yes, I do. You asked for my help and I agreed, but you've requested nothing of me since. You haven't questioned me further or given any indication as to what you want me to do. The longer I wait the more of a hindrance I'll be.'

Negram stared at her coldly. 'I had not considered you a coward.'

'What?'

'A coward departs with no farewells and a coward seeks blessing for foolish ventures. Or was it that you hoped I would prevent you from following this path? I will neither bless you nor prevent you, for the choice is yours, but I say this, alone you have no hope of success, alone you will endanger us all. Should you be caught they will extract the knowledge you have gained here and the consequences for all will be dire.'

T'skya was dumbstruck. In the back of her mind the coward within her had longed to be forbidden. Now the choice had been given to her and she did not know what to do. Abruptly her forced determination withered and crumbled and her shoulders sagged in defeat. She opened her mouth but found she had nothing to say.

'A journey such as you desire is not to be undertaken lightly,' Negram continued more kindly. 'The forest and the plains are patrolled by the Kházakha and the desert is formidable. We have not been inactive all this time, as you suggested; we have been formulating a strategy. You must learn patience. Scouting parties have been gathering information, travelling deep into the forest and following the movements of the Kházakha. The enemy has not yet found your craft so time is on our side.'

T'skya waved her arms in exasperation. She had sweated and deliberated, worried and schemed and none of it had been necessary. 'Why didn't anyone tell me?'

'Of what? Would it have eased your frustration or increased it? No journey has been possible until this time.'

T'skya jumped on her words, eager for an answer. 'Is it possible now?'

'A meeting shall be held to decide it.' Negram sat still and cocked an eyebrow at her. 'My sons would not have forgiven me had I let you go. Already they are fond of you.'

T'skya smiled and felt the tension begin to slide out of her body. 'And I of them,' she answered warmly.

'These are indeed strange times. Now leave me. There is much to be done.'

❧✦❧

T'skya made herself as useful as she could, but impatience made her irritable and clumsy and she was more of a hindrance than a help. Eventually she went to help Bramble prepare lunch and, as if on cue, the weary scouting parties trudged into the camp. Hollam and Cail disappeared to be debriefed by Briar and Negram whilst the others went to change and wash before eating. As they hurriedly reappeared, anxious not to keep Bramble waiting, T'skya helped Catkin set their places and began to serve the food. Although now officially on rations, the meal was adequate, a tribute to Bramble's culinary skills, and even Hollam's cavernous stomach was satisfied.

T'skya had changed back into her Roumanhi clothing of dark green trousers and baggy cream shirt, over which she wore a long russet jerkin. From Hollam and Cail's speculative glances, however, she knew that Negram had told them about scheme. She did her best to avoid their eyes and did not tarry by them.

At the end of the meal she rose to leave but Cail caught her hand. 'Trying to steal away again?' he whispered.

'Trying to avoid your criticism!'

'Well said,' he smiled. 'Do not go far. We are holding a meeting shortly and you are to attend.'

T'skya was grateful for his discretion. She squeezed his hand in gratitude and turned to leave but his hold lingered for a moment before he released her. T'skya's stomach whirled.

The twelve council members soon assembled in the Clanmeet but T'skya, instead of being the focus of their attention, was this time invited to sit in the arc next to Knoll.

Briar called the meeting to order with the usual ceremony and then spoke in a sonorous tone. 'For many days our scouts have been gathering information concerning the movements of the Kházakha. Let us hear their accounts to better judge the choices we have to make. The floor is open to Cail.'

As was customary, Cail nodded to Briar to acknowledge the opportunity of addressing the Clanmeet. 'We all know what would happen to us if the Kházakha discover we are sheltering T'skya and until recently we were not too concerned about Slythe's words. But nor have the Kházakha been idle. They have interrogated many dwellers from the Clans bordering the plains and the desert and have now, we believe, gathered enough information to make the matter urgent.

'Yesterday, we learnt they are planning an expedition into the desert. Fortunately the desert area prohibits the use of their scanning equipment and their vehicles are unsuitable for desert terrain. Instead, they have chosen to train the troumaloks to bear their burden.

'Unfortunately T'skya destroyed the homing beacon and now our hopes of finding the craft before the Kházakha are negligible. I now ask permission to open the floor to Tarn.'

Briar consented and Tarn began:

'From the descriptions gathered we estimate that the craft fell at *El Greezma*, The Treacherous. Few who have dared to cross its sands have returned. It is a wonder to me how a woman as unfamiliar with the terrain as T'skya could have made it out alive, but I digress.

'Even if we set out now, the Kházakha would far exceed us in speed for the troumaloks can travel swiftly and have great endurance. However, troumaloks are susceptible to a precious herb which can render them unconscious. We have gathered enough, we hope, for our purposes and can delay the Kházakha's departure, but it will involve great risk to those who undertake the duty.'

Tarn fell silent and Briar waited patiently until their attention was directed to her. 'Perhaps it is time to hear from the cause of our concern. I open the floor to T'skya of the Homequest.'

T'skya was taken completely by surprise. She was still trying to make sense Tarn's words. She began hesitantly whilst hoping to make a strong case for herself.

'My spacecraft contains equipment that could endanger you if the Kházakha find it, but it will also aid you against them. I have devices that can analyse and multiply some of your produce which may ease your burden a little. I also have weapons that match the power of the Kházakha's and equipment to scan for your enemy. More importantly, if we don't find the ship before they do, they won't rest until they've found me and in their searching they will terrorise, torture and destroy. We need to find my ship for all our sakes.'

Briar spoke again: 'Is there anyone who wishes to elaborate on what we have learnt before I open the floor to questions?'

No-one spoke and Briar was about to commence when Raven placed a stone in front of her. 'There is one other possibility we have not yet discussed,' she said cautiously. 'We could scramble her memories and just hand her over.'

Loud cries of dissent erupted from the group, but Raven continued; 'Consider. Even if this mission is successful, we still imperil ourselves with her presence. The Kházakha are the enemy and whether she belongs with them or not, we should not endanger all our lives to aid one of them.'

'You go too far, Raven,' Briar warned. 'That is not an option here, so clear it from your mind.'

'My apologies,' Raven replied insincerely. 'I merely wanted all options to be clear.'

'It is *not* an option.'

'Then I withdraw it,' the warrior said, slowly collecting her stone.

Briar scanned the group before continuing. 'If you accept this mission, do not concern yourselves with the passage through the desert for I believe I can help; though I cannot reveal my knowledge since I am bound by an oath too old for words.'

In saying so little, Briar had managed to say a lot. She had not only presented them with an intriguing riddle but had implied the situation was not as hopeless as it seemed. If Briar was in favour of the quest then there must be a reasonable chance of success; she was not a woman prone to rashness or foolish venture. She then allowed the debate to begin. The first to raise an objection was Badger.

'Supposing all goes to plan and we succeed in finding this ship before the Kházakha, what then? Has any thought been given to how it will be hidden or removed?'

T'skya had an answer, but one she was unwilling to contemplate. 'I can destroy the ship. It has a self-destruct mechanism, but I don't know how to disguise the size of the explosion.'

'Why not use this device when you first arrived?' Wolf asked.

'I had no knowledge of your land and its troubles. I'd hoped to go to the city to find help in repairing it. Without the ship, how will I return to the Homequest? They won't be able to come to me without the beacon or co-ordinates and now I can't look to the Kházakha for aid. If someone can come up with a better solution, I'd be grateful. I really don't want to lose my ship!'

There were few other questions and even Raven remained unusually quiet.

'Does anyone need for more time in which to contemplate the quest?' Briar asked.

No-one requested it and the vote was cast. There were no abstentions. Thirteen stones lay on the ground, insignificant in themselves but crucial to T'skya and the Roumanhis. All that remained was to decide who would undertake the mission, when and how.

T'skya felt a sense of relief when she saw the favourable vote, but underlying it was a whirl of tension and doubt. She wanted to go, she needed to go, but at the same time she was fearful, not only for herself, but for those who would also be putting themselves at risk.

Briar adjourned the meeting and suggested reconvening in her burrow. It was cold outside and this did nothing to inspire debate. The company made their way to the trap-door, leaving the Clanmeet forlorn and empty as they filed along the narrow underground passageway to Briar's abode. It was larger than most, but then so was Briar and as head of the Clanmeet her position warranted some small concessions. The room itself was sparsely furnished with a chair, shelves neatly stacked with clothes and ornaments, and a large ferny bed covered with cushions. Curled in the corner, and wrapped in a blanket so that only her small head was visible, Catkin was sleeping soundly.

Briar gently shook Catkin's shoulder and the girl sat up with a start. 'I did not do it!' she squeaked fearfully. Then she caught sight of the others. Their grave, grim expressions seemed aimed at her and she began to tremble. 'It was not my fault, Root made me!'

Briar stared at her from under white brows and the child shrank away from the fearsome gaze. 'We will discuss this later. Leave us now.' Briar clapped her hands and the child fled.

The meeting began again but it progressed slowly. There was much debating and questioning, and tempers ran high as it dragged on. All knew the mission was necessary, but few could agree who should take part.

Throughout, Briar, Negram and T'skya sat in silence.

Eventually, it was decided that time was of the essence and the parties would venture forth that day. The weather, whilst unpleasant, would not hinder them as much as it would the Kházakha; the poorer visibility and the sodden ground making the passage of the troumaloks more difficult. Next was to decide who was to go and to formulate their plans. On this Briar would have the final say.

'Since you can do no more than squabble like children, the decision shall be made for you. It is a sorry state of affairs when we cannot even agree amongst ourselves. With me shall go T'skya, for she alone has knowledge of this ship; Cail, for without him the path across the desert cannot be attempted;

and Wolf, for we shall need a second scout to guard our way.'

Cail was surprised but honoured to be chosen, although how he was vital for the desert crossing was beyond him. He had never ventured there and knew little more than old tales. Still, he could not doubt Briar's words, even though they were tied in riddles.

'Hollam and Badger shall be responsible for the troumaloks. We know where the Kházakha imprison the beasts and the tunnels should aid their part. Tarn, you must remain here, lest the enemy comes upon the enclave during our absence. The rest count themselves lucky to remain, for this undertaking is not without hazard. Ferret, Fen, prepare the provisions. Raven, furnish the weapons. Hawk, Tarn, instruct the scouts to double their watch. Knoll, have you obtained all that I required of you?'

Knoll nodded and showed his rickety teeth. 'I have indeed. I think you will be pleased.'

'T'skya of the Homequest, do you consent?' Briar asked her.

'I still wish I knew what you intended after we reach the boundary,' she replied. 'But I'll trust you in this since everyone else does.'

'I thank you,' Briar answered. 'Without trust there is no hope, and without hope there is despair. The time to despair is not yet upon us and I pray that it never shall be. I will summon Bramble and Catkin to prepare a hasty meal. We must leave before supper is called.' It was clear that she did not relish the thought of the coming journey. She was not built for exertion and whatever secret plan she intended weighed heavily upon her. 'We shall join you shortly. But first I have a matter to discuss with Negram.'

'Is there no other way?' Negram asked despondently when everyone had departed.

'If there were, I would be glad of it,' Briar responded, leaning against the shelves. She rubbed a dumpy hand across her cheek and looked at Negram intently, as if trying to penetrate the elder woman's mind. Negram met her gaze and held it. It was not a battle of wills; it was the sharing of two troubled souls.

At length Negram reached into her pocket and brought out a carefully wrapped bundle. 'Guard this well. Without it, we are lost.'

'In trust there is hope.'

'I fear it is too soon,' Negram whispered, her voice cracking with the strain of her emotions.

Briar placed an understanding hand upon her friend's shoulder, trying to give what comfort she could, although she knew nothing could touch the inner depths of Negram's fears. 'It is his destiny and we are not yet wise enough to rule above it.'

'No, we are not yet wise enough; that is my concern.'

FIVE

Parting of the ways

The rain was now coming down in sheets and the dwellers had chosen to eat underground rather than in the shelters which dotted the enclave. T'skya found herself in a narrow, low-ceilinged hall that had been carved out of the stratum. She had never seen the room before and would have considered it claustrophobic and oppressive were it not for the rows of candles that sweetened the air with the scent of spring blossom and honey, and the decorations disguising the grey walls.

Down the centre of the cavern ran a long stone table carved from the living rock. Etched designs decorated its edges which followed no pattern and yet were in harmony with the contours of the stone, breaking the monotony. Down either side ran two low stone benches worn smooth through decades of use, upon which those present sat munching a cold buffet.

Whilst the others sat eating, T'skya scrutinised the brightly coloured arras that concealed much of the walls. Near the doorway, was an image of the land; the first depiction of Roumanhi she had seen. It was clearly of a time long past. The desert was conspicuous by its absence and a large river wound its way like a lazy serpent through a swathe of vibrant grass. The next depicted a handsome but untamed young man with a quiver slung across his chest and a sheathed sword about his waist. He stood upon a rugged hill top, looking to the snow-capped peaks of the northern mountains. The tapestries went on to reveal his life: his true love, his children, the fierce battles he waged against fell creatures from the north and his sad demise at the hands of a monstrous beast.

But it was the final arras which really captured her attention. There hung a solitary black sheet, unbroken in its emptiness. T'skya searched to find an image but failed to see anything. She turned to Hollam, who was sitting with his back to her engrossed in his meal. 'Hollam, can you tell me the story behind these?'

Hollam continued chewing but turned to face her. 'It is a story I would not dare to shame by being brief. Ask me again when time is less pressing.'

'But what of this one?' she said, pointing to the black one.

'For that you must ask someone more learned than I, Negram perhaps, or Briar. Now come and eat. Today we must look to the future, not the past.'

T'skya sighed but sat down beside him and tucked into the buffet with relish. Negram and Briar entered the room and Bramble brought some packages, small in size but filled to capacity.

'I have supplied you with the best I could find. Within is enough to last a week with care, though I dare say some would find it insufficient,' she added winking at Hollam, who flashed back a roguish smile. 'I have included some *coulhi* sticks to aid you if delayed.'

T'skya was curious. 'What are *coulhi* sticks?'

'Potent roots which can sustain you for many days. They are scarce and difficult to find, but we keep a small supply in store,' Bramble explained.

'Won't we find food on the way?'

'There is plenty in the forest, but we must cross the downs and plains and there will be no time for foraging,' Briar answered.

'We will also be open to view for even our cloaks fail us when we move and move we must.'

'Talking of cloaks, why don't the Kházakha use them and why do they let you keep them? Wouldn't it be more sensible to confiscate them all?'

T'skya was surprised when her question drew laughter. 'They deprived us of many and attempted their use, but they lack our knowledge and the cloaks failed them,' Cail said, smiling at his memories. 'They take time and skill to retain their potency and without *meckhalin* the colours fade and they become as any other cloak.'

'*Meckhalin*?'

'Caelcáladrim preserve us!' Cail groaned, shaking his head in a mixture of disbelief and mirth. 'You are as inquisitive as Catkin! If your feet work as quickly as your tongue, we will soon arrive at our destination.'

'Well, now you've added another question to my list; who or what is Caelcáladrim?'

'Which answer do you require first?'

T'skya leaned across the table towards him. 'Either.'

'*Meckhalin* is a gum from a tree which mainly grows in the area of forest known as the Blackwood, *Roumázisraoun* in our tongue. From the gum we make a powder which, when mixed with the fibres of the cloaks, produces the camouflage effect. The powder wears off in time, and so the Kházakha found the cloaks became useless. As for your other question, *that* is Caelcáladrim,' he said, pointing to the tapestry hanging on the wall behind.

'So he is a hero of the land,' she said.

'*The* hero. But enough, we must make ready to depart.'

Briar rose to her feet. 'Collect what you require from your burrows and meet again here. Be swift!'

T'skya trotted off as ordered and rummaged around her room indecisively. She finally donned her warrior garb but put her own boots upon her feet, taking comfort from their fit and familiarity. They were not as light as the dwellers' footwear and caused more noise than she liked, but they had gone through a lot with her and she considered them lucky, her amulets of fortune. She tied her hair back and filled her pockets with hydrating pills, her small flashlight and the larger one for Badger, and one or two odds and ends. The main provisions were already waiting for them in the hall.

When she returned, she found the others waiting for her. Everyone had hoisted their packs on their backs and slung their canteens around their waists. T'skya picked up her pack and was surprised by its weight but accepted the burden with no further query. She was supplied with a duly treated cloak and copying the others wore it over her pack. The bulging packs made them appear deformed, as if they were hunchbacks, but Hollam and Badger, who were not travelling so far, carried less.

Raven had put a supply of weapons in the hall. T'skya took a staff, simply made but ideal for someone of her stature. She also chose a stone knife with an engraved and gilded handle and she passed it from hand to hand testing its weight and feel. She frowned thoughtfully as she slipped it into her belt. She had some knowledge of self-defence but was no warrior and she hoped the weapon would remain dormant at her side.

When everyone was ready they met together in a circle. The joking stopped and solemnity enveloped them. Bowing their heads and joining hands the seriousness began to penetrate T'skya as Briar offered up a prayer of protection and good fortune for their quest. They held each other's hands for several moments more, each caught in their own private thoughts, and then, as if by telepathic command, made their way silently to the surface.

Despite the downpour which still lashed the earth, the inhabitants of the enclave had gathered in the Clanmeet to wish them well and say their goodbyes. Catkin rushed to Hollam launching into his arms for a monstrous hug and then threw her arms around Briar's vastness, burying her face in the woman's stomach. Briar kissed the child on the brow and smiled kindly.

'Fear not that I am departing, little one. Fear rather my return, for I am curious to learn what it was that Root made you do.'

Breeze approached and wished them well but held Hollam long in her sea grey eyes; they had spent much time together of late. Negram stood silently by, her head bowed in despondency, evidently still ill at ease with their chosen path. Her sons tenderly kissed her brow and whispered words of encouragement. With effort she managed a weak smile.

The farewells ended and the fellowship left their friends and families and began trudging through the mud, heading eastward. They walked in silence, picking their way through the rain drenched trees. Before long the path petered out and they had to cross rougher ground covered with snaking roots and soaked bracken that slapped against their legs and shook its drops upon the earth. They were soon forced to walk in single file with Briar leading the way. T'skya was surprised at her speed. Briar fairly bustled along, although her progress was hampered by the treacherous ground. It was boggy and slippery, covered with twigs and brambles that snatched at their feet and conspired to trip them as they walked. But the dwellers were a surefooted people and had little trouble picking their way through the encumbering undergrowth, whereas T'skya found the going difficult and tiring. Soon she was forced to use her staff for support and was grateful to have it; the forest no longer seemed such a welcoming place.

A short distance further they came to a rounded boulder standing isolated amongst the vegetation. Each dweller touched their brows with their fingertips and caressed the stone, seeming lost in their own thoughts. It was one of the boundary stones marking the borders of their enclave. Courtesy of the Kházakha, the surrounding trees had been daubed with a red smudge of paint that dribbled down the bark like blood; a less than sanguine reminder of the perils they would face if caught. As such, Hollam and Wolf bounded into the forest on either side of the line to keep watch and were soon obscured by the greenery and the blinding rain. Cail lingered at the rear whilst Briar stomped in the vanguard leaving T'skya and Badger isolated in the middle. She concentrated on Briar's distant form, concerned that she would lose sight of the woman's determined back which lured her onwards, despite fear and growing weariness.

A few hours of such marching and T'skya was exhausted. Her legs ached and her back was stiff and sore from repeated jarring as she slipped in the mud. She was relieved when they came to more solid ground on which their passage was easier.

The rain continued unabated and whilst their hoods and cloaks kept them dry, their skin was damp from the sweat of their exertions. T'skya found that water was beginning to seep into her boots making her socks wet and uncomfortable and she was thankful when Briar called a halt. They sipped water from their canteens and took a mouthful of food, but no one was in the mood for feasting or conversation.

'This is an ill rain!' Briar muttered to herself.

The feeling of despondency grew and they ventured on, each step taking them further from home and closer to danger.

༺═⚜═༻

T'skya walked on oblivious, her mind wandering over maybes and ifs, strategies and plans. Her legs worked independently of her will, propelled by a need for urgency and Badger's strong form behind her. A sharp whistle snapped her back into reality and she turned to locate the reason for the warning.

Badger pulled T'skya down roughly, forcing her prostrate. They lay still, hardly daring to breathe in case the sound carried into the trees. The forest floor was uncomfortably uneven and some roots and stones were digging into her flesh. Her face, only partially protected by the hood, squelched against the water-logged earth. Badger's eyes warned her not to move. They heard nothing bar the torrential drumming of the rain and the slap of leaves in the strengthening wind.

It felt like an eternity; waiting fearfully for detection, straining to hear signs of movement above the din, but at last the all-clear was given and they could breathe freely. Badger helped T'skya to her feet; they were covered in mud, growing up from the soil like stunted trees. But they had no time to reflect. Briar had headed off and was already disappearing from view and Cail was urgently waving them onwards.

T'skya's inactivity was beginning to tell on her. She had hardly done any strenuous exercise since her arrival and now, lacking fitness, her breath began to come in desperate sobs. She gripped her side, trying to ease the stabs of pain her exertions brought, but it had little effect. Badger was concerned and helped her when she slipped; an increasing necessity the further they travelled.

'We will rest soon,' he encouraged.

'You said that an hour ago,' she rasped between breaths.

'This time I mean it.'

They then reached the glade in which she had first endured the test of truth. It did not look so becoming now; the flowers lay battered on the ground and the trees danced wildly in the frigid wind. No birds greeted the weary travellers and the mossy mounds were puddled and slick.

Briar beckoned them to take what shelter they could find. Hollam and Wolf soon appeared and Cail joined them. The group huddled together beside a grand old oak and took a bite from their rations. The men were scarcely breathing anymore deeply than usual, but Briar was panting and T'skya felt as if her legs had been weighted with concrete and her lungs scoured. She trembled with exhaustion and needed her staff to stand. The food provided energy, but they took no pleasure from the taste. Even Hollam, who usually ate with enthusiasm, chewed with lackadaisical spirit.

They had reached the parting of their ways.

It was a solemn occasion and nobody could find the will to move. Hollam shuffled nervously from foot to foot and Cail toyed with his spear, neither having the courage to speak.

Briar broke the awkward silence. 'It is time,' she said, shouting above the wind.

The brothers clasped hands and held them long. They could find no words to express their love and their fear. T'skya felt her throat clogging. She embraced Badger's solidity and kissed his muddy cheek. She then caught Hollam in her arms and held him tightly, afraid to let go. He flashed her one endearingly embarrassed smile before saluting Briar and Wolf and hastening into the trees with Badger. Those remaining watched until they were no longer visible.

'We cannot remain here,' Briar boomed. 'The rain is too fierce and we have no proper shelter. Come, we shall march a while longer. Darkness will be upon us soon and we will have no moons to guide us this night.'

T'skya groaned. She did not feel that she could move another inch but Briar was right. This was no place to make camp. 'Where are we going?' she bellowed to make herself heard.

'There is a haven not more than a league from here. There we can rest.'

Their progress was slow. The day was darkening into night and T'skya had difficulty seeing the terrain. She did not possess the dwellers' keen night vision and dared not risk her flashlight. She concentrated upon Briar's back, compelling her onwards until at last, they came to the haven the woman was seeking.

T'skya would have walked past it had she been alone, thinking it no more than another hoary tree. She could see nothing through the foliage; the leaves closed over the branches as if hiding some dark secret but Briar clearly intended them to find shelter above. T'skya looked up but could conceive no way of reaching the boughs. The trunk had no hand holds and was too wide to grip, and she was far too short to reach the branches.

'Up there?' she asked. 'How?'

'Watch and learn,' Wolf said. He walked around the tree three times, running one finger along the bark. He stopped, uttered an incantation, tapped the trunk three times with his spear, and stood back expectantly.

The tree seemed to tremble for an instant, and then, to T'skya's astonishment, began to lower its boughs towards them. T'skya had seen touch responsive plants before but never one so huge. There was no sound, save the howling of the elements, as the tree appeared to wilt like a dying flower. As the tips of the boughs reached the ground the three Roumanhis lightly bounded up them and disappeared from view. T'skya followed hesitantly, fearing that she would slip on the slick bark and was amazed to find that her footfalls were secure. As she reached the top of the bough, the branches sighed softly and began to rise. The dying flower had found sustenance and was returning to life.

She found herself standing on a flattened circular platform no more then six feet in diameter. The others could not be seen and for a moment she panicked, fearing some evil had befallen them or that they had abandoned her. She was relieved when a hand reached down from the second tier of branches above her and Wolf's face appeared amongst the leaves.

'Give me your hand.'

T'skya reached up and clasped his wrist. He hauled her up with ease and she passed through the second tier, now some twenty feet from the ground. At first she could barely see, but soon either her eyes became accustomed to the darkness or it grew lighter within and she saw she was standing in a large room, walled and roofed by a thick canopy of silver backed leaves. The edges of the branch on which she was standing spread outwards, forming a solid floor and curved upwards at the outer edge like a parapet.

Briar was already seated on the wooden floor taking supplies from her pack. Cail had removed his cloak and was preparing their beds using ferns that had been stored under a mat at one end of a different platform. Wolf joined Briar and soon they had prepared a light meal, but they lit no fire.

'How? I mean, what? This tree, is it alive like us?' T'skya asked.

'It eats. It drinks. It grows and so it lives. But if you mean does it think and feel then I have no answer,' Cail replied, 'though we would like to believe that it does.'

'But how did you make it do that?' she probed Wolf.

'That is a difficult question to answer,' he replied. 'There are many tales concerning the *Silhvran* trees. But if you will permit me, I will briefly tell you the legend of Caelárian and then you can decide for yourself.'

T'skya nodded eagerly. With no written language and no written law, the Roumanhis relied on their historical narratives to keep the past alive and their customs and traditions pure. Tales were a joy to them and were a way of dispelling their sorrows.

The company eagerly settled down. Wolf's ochre eyes burned brightly as he began.

'Caelárian, the daughter of Caelcáladrim and Kilcáerian, saviours of our land, lived long ago in the northern plains. As she grew up a restlessness entered her blood and she would stand for hours staring to the west seeking out the hazy glimmer of the forest beyond. But her father was a stern man, bound by duty and protective, and he forbade her to approach them, expecting his word to hold. He distrusted the forest for his travels there had been fraught with danger and he had scarcely escaped with his life.

'There lived close by a young man, Yvan, who won her affections and for a time she appeared to settle. Her parents then spent more time away, rallying the land to their cause against enemy invaders from the north and her brother, Gilgarad, was sent to the east, leaving Caelárian under the watchful eye of her beloved.

'With her family gone she began her wanderings again, compelled onwards by the lure of the trees until she reached the edge of the great forest. She stood breathlessly before it wishing to enter, but the memories of her father's warnings and the fear of the unknown stayed her feet.

'As she pondered the dilemma, the sound of faint, enticing music caught her ears. She was entranced and braved the trees and made her way into the forest's mottled greenery. She was awed by the beauty of the blossoms and the patterns the sunlight made through the leaves, soon becoming lost; yet no fear was upon her as the strange song impelled her onwards.

'At last she came upon the source of her gladness; a mighty *Silhvran* tree magisterial in its girth and its leaves dancing silver and green. Spellbound, she remained sustained by the forest, charmed and mystified by the ever present song, and gradually she began to understand the *Silhvran's* message; its loneliness as it stood bereft of companionship, tales of ages past, and the love the tree bore for her. But she did not learn of the peril she faced, for the tree grew on the borders of *Roumázisraoun*, the Blackwood, where fell creatures lurked and where all men feared to tread.

'One night, a band of fell beasts came upon her, their eyes pale like death and their fangs dripping with the lust for blood. Caelárian circled the tree slowly, caressing the bark in terror for her life. Three times she circled and the pack followed, waiting for the time to strike. She called to the *Silhvran* in desperation and the tree let out a shudder and lowered its branches to the ground. Embracing her, the *Silhvran* set her securely amongst its boughs and in retribution pounded the beasts into the ground so they would trouble her no more.

'In gratitude, she swore fealty to the trees, promising to spend her days in their service, but the tree refused to set her down until she met its terms: The *Silhvran* would sing to its kin and order them to provide a haven for her and for all who came in her name, and in return she must forsake all other loves and return ten years hence, to be its companion until the end of her days.

'Caelárian could not refuse. In keeping to her oath, she spurned Yvan's love and returned, when the time was nigh, never to be seen again. But her passing from the land was known, for the trees ceased to sing and one of the glories of Roumanhi was lost. Yet, the *Silhvran* kept its word and its kin offer sanctuary to all who are pure of heart and call upon them in her name.'

Wolf fell silent for a respectful time and then asked, 'It is a moving tale, is it not?'

T'skya nodded silently. 'Do you believe the tale?'

'Believe?' Cail asked in some surprise. 'We know no other. It may be that there is some scientific reason, but we have no desire to know it.'

His distaste was evident. Science was of no importance; it was enough to know the trees aided them without knowing why or how.

'I believe,' she whispered, easing herself on to the bed and falling into a deep untroubled sleep.

⟡

The company woke early. The sun had not yet broached the horizon but the sky had taken on the first glimmers of light. The four packed their belongings and made ready to depart. Cail lowered T'skya to the ground and then, with Wolf's help, assisted Briar down. The rain had stopped but the sky remained overcast and whilst the ground was sodden and boggy their march would be easier without the lashing rain.

A night of rest had done wonders for T'skya. She felt refreshed and eager to get started. Briar set off at a rapid pace, concerned to reach the plains quickly. The Kházakha would begin their journey the following day if Hollam and Badger failed in their quest.

They walked in the same formation as before, although T'skya now paid closer attention to their path. Last time she had been blindfolded and they had gone at a more sedate pace. At the group's present speed, they should reach the place of her discovery before long.

Dotted here and there, she noticed wild primroses, their yellow petals like spots of sunshine amongst the dark foliage of the forest. Birds greeted the dawn with their song and for a short while T'skya forgot her troubles and took pleasure from the fresh scents which rose from the flora.

Briar soon quickened the pace and in the heavy going T'skya became tired again and had to focus her attention on remaining upright and pumping one leg before the other leaving no energy to enjoy the surroundings. Briar's sense of urgency increased with each passing moment and penetrated them all. The only solace T'skya could find was that they would soon reach the plains.

Indeed, half a league more and Cail signalled they had reached their destination. Briar drew to an abrupt halt and forbade them to go further. She confirmed with Cail the exact tree by which T'skya had been found and approached the spot. The men did not ask Briar's intentions, but curiosity was evident in their eyes.

Briar stooped low as she walked, taking each step slowly. Her eyes scanned every inch of ground as she surveyed each leaf, stone and blade of grass, muttering to herself constantly until she reached the tree.

T'skya watched in bewilderment. 'What is she doing?' she whispered.

Cail shrugged dispassionately and continued to watch, his eyes flicking into the forest, alert for danger. Wolf had gone scouting to ward them whilst they waited. Eventually, Briar came towards them looking grim and anxious, and Wolf came trotting back to see what the outcome was.

'It is as I feared,' Briar said wearily. 'I had hoped to find a sign allowing us to avoid the plains, but the forest has been washed clean by the rains. We must venture into the open. Hold hope that your brother will succeed,' she said to Cail.

'If there is a way, he will succeed,' Cail replied. 'He knows the perils as well as we.'

'We must hurry. Be warned, T'skya of the Homequest. In movement, our cloaks will not aid us. We will be open for all to see, so be alert and do not let your mind wander as it has done until now.'

T'skya had expected to see a broad flat plain and was surprised to find a rolling landscape of green-clad hills, dotted here and there with meadow flowers and the occasional bush. The hills swept away into the distance and, although there was no cover, there would be some protection from prying eyes once they had climbed over the first crest. 'How long will it take to cross?' she asked Cail.

'That depends on our speed, but about a day should suffice.' He touched her elbow, encouraging her into motion.

There was little conversation as they climbed the first slopes. Wolf remained at the back to keep watch and Briar bustled ahead, anxious to put distance between them and the sheltering trees from which they could be espied. As they crested the first hill and the forest disappeared, the company drew a sigh of relief and Briar slackened the pace to be comfortable, although not leisurely.

Briar cast anxious glances at the sky as it blackened ominously and a chill wind began to pick up, making them wrap their cloaks more tightly about them. T'skya groaned inwardly at the prospect of more rain. If a storm broke, the going would be arduous, if not impossible. The thoughts had scarcely entered her mind when the first dots of rain began bombarding them as they struggled on their journey.

They scrambled onwards, ascending the steep incline of another hill. By the time they had reached the top, T'skya was gasping for air and Briar was leaning heavily on her staff, her breath rasping in her chest. Even the men were inhaling deeply. From the summit, the plains stretched before them and despite the rain T'skya could see that the hills would shortly peter out and they would have to face a broad, flat expanse without any cover. As she stood on the hill, leaning into the wind, the land was lit by a blinding flash of forked lightning which split the sky and made her shiver with fear. Darkness followed and the air was rent with a deafening crack of thunder that made her cry out in alarm and cower on the ground.

Cail called out in concern, but his words were being torn away by the wind. 'What ails you? We cannot remain here. We are not yet in the heart of the storm.'

Between them, Cail and Wolf managed to manoeuvre T'skya downwards but the going was difficult. The grass was slippery underfoot and with the burden of their packs and weapons they had only one hand free with which to assist her.

'What is this? What's happening?'

'It is nothing but a storm. Why do you fear it?' Cail bellowed above the wind.

'The light and the noise...I thought I was going to die!'

'Have you never seen a storm before?'

'No.'

'Thunder cannot hurt you, it is but noise. Lightning is another matter, but it would be misfortune indeed to suffer at its hands. Can you continue?' he asked, peering intently at her sorrowful face.

She nodded, determined not to let fear waylay them any longer. But the wind soon became impossible to fight against. It howled around them tearing at their clothes and their sanity. They were forced to huddle in a group, protecting each other from its brunt, whipped by the rain.

Then, as quickly as it had come, the storm passed, leaving

them soaked, despondent and weary. The company lingered for an hour, trying to regain their strength. T'skya's head hurt and she felt chilled. She rubbed at her temples hoping to ease the throbbing pressure. Cail and Wolf, although tired from their exertions, looked no worse for wear, but Briar was shivering and her face was flushed.

T'skya was anxious. If Briar ailed badly there was little they could do. They were too far from the enclave to summon help and there was no shelter, no medication and no decent wood for much of a fire.

'Briar's sick,' she muttered to Cail. 'I think she has a fever.'

He went to kneel by the old lady, put his hand to her brow and shook his head grimly as he touched her burning skin. 'We need fire,' he said anxiously.

'Fire could be seen!' Briar croaked.

'No-one in their right mind would be out in such weather!' T'skya countered.

'It is a risk we must take,' Cail added firmly.

Briar reluctantly gave her consent and Cail set to work. He unclasped his cloak, removed his pack and took out a scant bundle of twigs. T'skya was relieved to see he had thought ahead and that a fire was possible. She rummaged for her fire-lighter and handed it to him, glad to be of use.

'This will not last long,' he said ruefully, 'but at least we can heat some water and make broth.'

Cail gave Briar a *couhli* stick to chew and one to T'skya, who was both pleased with its flavour and surprised at the rapidity of its work. She felt energy returning to her muscles and the pain in her head eased.

They gathered their strength until mid-afternoon before beginning the next stage of the march. Briar's colour had improved but she found the going tough and their pace was slow, despite the improvement in the terrain and the weather.

'We now cannot hope to reach the desert before tomorrow,' Cail told T'skya. 'I hope this delay will not bode ill for us.'

That night they made camp out in the open. There were no trees to shelter under or in, no bushes or rocks; nothing to provide a sanctuary. The ground was still wet; the water held remorselessly by the long grass, and the air was cold. But at least it was not raining and the earth was soft beneath their bones.

Briar slumped down where she was standing, too weary even to remove her pack. Wolf and Cail helped her and, despite protest, sacrificed their own cloaks in an effort to keep her warm. She had begun to shiver again. Her condition was growing progressively worse and it cast a shadow over the company.

They took turns watching Briar throughout the night, unwilling to leave her unattended. T'skya gamely volunteered to go first. She doubted if she would be able to remain awake during the middle of the night and as the men settled into sleep she counted the minutes, keeping one eye on Briar and the other on the darkening landscape for signs of danger.

It was tiresome work and she caught herself drifting off at times, but she managed to survive her watch and woke Cail. Then, despite the less than salubrious surroundings, she quickly fell into sleep.

Wolf roused her early. Briar was much the same and Cail looked weary, having been unable to relax after his watch. They all chewed *couhli* sticks, heedless of the fact their supply was limited. The sky was clear and the sun rising over the horizon as they set off.

They crawled forward, Briar unable to manage more than a shuffle. She leaned more and more upon her staff and had to take frequent rests. Her face was drawn with strain and she frowned constantly at her own inability to travel faster. Cail and Wolf took it in turns to aid her, lending their strength to support her bulk. T'skya had taken some of the burden by relieving Briar of the contents of her pack and storing most of it in hers. She was determined to help, even though her own strength was limited.

The sun had set when Briar finally called a halt. They had come to the edge of the desert and it stretched before them like a pale blanket. The sky was devoid of clouds and the two waning moons cast an eerie light upon the sand. The grass upon which they were standing was coarse and dry, untouched by the storm that had soaked the verdant growth further westwards. The ever encroaching desert was like a starving leech absorbing any water that did fall, depriving the plants of life. Those that did manage to survive close to such inhospitable terrain were the hardiest, but even they struggled and were withered and twisted, seeming to claw their way towards the sky.

T'skya stared out across the seemingly endless expanse of sand. The desert did not make sense to her. She knew it was very real, so real it had left her burned, but it simply should not have existed. Squeezed between the mountains to the east and the forests to the west and in a climate too temperate, the desert was an anomaly; another unexplainable phenomenon in a land of puzzles, and somewhere out there was her ship.

Briar told them to make camp several hundred feet from the desert boundary where some low dunes had been formed by the winds that swept the region. Tufts of long pampas grass grew there, as sharp as knife blades, and the company was careful not to brush against them.

Cail and Wolf sat silently, letting the rough sand run through their fingers. Neither of them had seen the desert before and both were deep in thought about the next stage of their quest.

Briar chose to sit some distance from them, wrapped in her own thoughts. Her fever had not yet broken and, despite the sweat on her brow, her colour was like bleached bones. T'skya stared at the woman through the dimness, studying her face and trying to discern her intentions. Briar had given no indication what their next step would be but her plans clearly lay heavily upon her.

For an hour or more, Briar sat motionless. Time dragged on and the company's inactivity gnawed at their nerves, but they did nothing to disturb her. At long last she stirred. Her intake of breath was so sharp that it caused Cail to snatch for his knife.

'I must depart to secure your path to the ship. If I do not return by dawn then I have failed and I am lost. You will then have to decide amongst yourselves if you wish to walk the sands.' Abruptly she walked into the darkness, heading for the perilous desert.

Eventually T'skya spoke, although she could raise no more than a whisper. 'What did she mean, lost?'

Cail paused before answering. 'That she would not return - or could not.'

'You mean dead?'

T'skya was horrified. Briar was putting her life at terrible risk because of her. If she had not crashed her ship; if she had not been found by the forest dwellers, then Briar would be safe, not hazarding her life so far from home. T'skya groaned aloud and buried her head in her hands. Cail, seeing her torment, placed a comforting hand on her shoulder.

'If there lies a way, she will succeed. Briar would not have dared the venture if it were futile. Hold faith. The rising of the sun will decide it.'

※※※

It was a long wait. None of them could sleep. Their aching eyes scanned the east, searching for signs of their companion. Illusionary images played tricks upon them. Every so often, one of them would become stiff and alert, as if they had seen something, and then sink back into despondency as they realised their mistake. The stars began to fade as the first light of the approaching sun brightened the sky. The temperature rose slowly yet resolutely, even though the first dazzling glimpse of the star had not yet broached the horizon. An overwhelming sense of urgency filled the company and they rose as one, peering into the landscape.

Wolf gave a cry and pointed to the desert. His eyes were the keenest, but by following his outstretched hand they saw a stumbling form making its way erratically towards them. The men flew to her aid, running like stags across the coarse tufts of grass and onto the energy sapping sand. As they reached her, Briar collapsed in their arms. T'skya came panting up behind them and was shocked by what she saw.

Briar looked as if she had aged twenty years. Her face was grey and lined, her eyes sunken and yellowed. Her cheeks were hollowed and her mouth hung loosely; a thin trail of saliva running down her chin.

Cail groped for his canteen, tore a piece from his shirt, moistened it and sponged the dirt from Briar's face. He gave her a sip of the tepid water to refresh her mouth. Then, wrapping her arms about their shoulders, Cail and Wolf half-carried, half-dragged her out of the sand and back to their camp. Unable to help them, T'skya ran ahead, wanting to prepare food and a comfortable place for the old lady to rest.

After they had lowered her to the ground, the men paced about unable to relax in their concern, whilst T'skya fed Briar small pieces of *couhli* stick. The old woman's breath rattled in her chest. She coughed violently and T'skya noticed that the ground was spotted with blood. She was no medic, but understood that without help Briar could die. Even the potent *couhli* stick seemed to be having little effect. When T'skya mentioned the blood to Cail he paled.

'What shall we do?' she asked, hoping he would have a magic solution.

'I do not know! She is in no condition to travel and help

is too far away. I could send Wolf back to the enclave, but at best it would take five days before anyone reached us here. We shall have to tend to her ourselves and hope that she recovers enough to travel.'

Wolf called to him. 'She asks for you, my friend.'

Cail hurried to the old woman's side and knelt down. 'I have secured your passage,' she rasped. 'You must walk two-hundred paces directly eastward into the desert. Whatever happens, do not be alarmed, and show good courtesy. Now go. *Klúlat lu'vari quylas, lu'ari Cail!*'

'I cannot leave you like this!' he protested.

'*Liállat!*' she commanded as strongly as she could. '*Liállat!*'

He looked to T'skya and Wolf for support. They just stared helplessly waiting for his decision.

'*Reh var furtra, ce aertru mora,*' he said softly. 'As you wish it, so shall it be.' He turned to Wolf. 'I do not know how long we shall be. Guard this woman with your life. You need not wait for us if you think it unwise.'

Wolf nodded but said nothing. He was young to have such responsibility placed upon him, but Briar had chosen him for the mission and he was determined not to let her down.

'Fetch your things,' Cail told T'skya, his concern showing in the abruptness of his speech.

T'skya quickly did as she was told. She, too, felt like swearing and shouting at the futility of it all but instead she hoisted the pack on to her shoulders, fastened her cloak over it and stood waiting for his next command. She was in his hands now; she had no clue what they would do.

Cail hesitated, studying the ground as he kicked at it with his toe. It was time to leave. Together, Cail and T'skya turned to depart but were stopped by Wolf's sudden cry of fear.

'Aieee! The troumaloks! The troumaloks are upon us!'

SIX

Strange revelations

'How far is it to this tunnel?' Hollam asked glumly, his heart heavy with worry.

'Not much nearer than the last time you asked!'

'Sorry.'

They had been walking for almost two hours when they came upon the trap-door they sought. It had lain unused for many years and without Badger's vast knowledge of the forest network they might have missed it. The entrance was overgrown with weeds and bramble and a wych elm had toppled over, partially covering the door. It took some while to clear the incumbent growths enough to lever it open.

'Once we are inside there is no hope of properly concealing the entrance again,' Badger informed his friend.

'I know, but the Kházakha are unlikely to come this way; there are no people here to persecute,' Hollam replied bitterly.

'Come, then. I will enter first.'

Badger squeezed through the opening. Hollam followed and attempted to drag some branches across the door as he closed it. The drop was longer than expected and he fell to his knees in a puddle of muddy water.

'Thank you for the warning, friend!' he growled sarcastically.

'You are, as ever, welcome,' came Badger's jovial reply.

'Did I ever tell you how annoying you can be?'

'Watch your ...' Badger warned, but too late.

'Head?' Hollam finished as he smacked the top of his skull against the mud-encrusted roof of the tunnel. 'This is going to be fun!' he muttered, rubbing at his mop of soiled hair. 'What say you to a little light in here?'

He heard some rummaging and soon the narrow beam from one of T'skya's flashlights cast its illuminations. 'I do not know how long this will last,' Badger said, 'but we should make use of this light while we can before we hazard fire.'

They set off at a rapid speed with Badger leading. The tunnel was a little too low for Hollam with his long legs. He hurried along with his head bowed, trying to avoid scalping himself or getting his hair entangled in the dangling tree roots.

They were negotiating a passage created centuries before as one of the two major highways through the forest and beneath the detritus the floor was smooth from attrition of use. Even before the arrival of the Kházakha, however, it had sadly fallen into disuse. One length of it, near the Blackwood, had been destroyed in a great earthquake during the reign of the Castan Laecus, and since the downfall of the King's line few had desired or dared to venture outside their enclaves to traverse its length.

The other highway lay far to the west, where the towering cliffs that separated the lower land from the upper stood in awe-inspiring grandeur. Millennia before the land had split, creating a chasm stretching from the northern mountains to the Great Divide. This second highway followed the path of the chasm, but whether it was still passable Badger did not know.

'How long before we reach the exit?' Hollam inquired.

'Less than four leagues.'

'And if that door is blocked? What then shall we do?'

'It will not be.'

Hollam was surprised. 'How can you be sure?'

'I am not. I am merely attempting to be optimistic; something we normally expect from you.'

'And so I would be were my brother's life not at stake!'

Badger stopped and stared his friend in the face. 'We shall find a way, whatever assails us.'

'I hope so,' Hollam muttered darkly. 'I hope so.'

They continued for another league; the passage becoming progressively more difficult. The carved rock gave way to earth and soon they were splashing through deepening puddles. In places, where the walls had crumbled or the roof given way, they were forced to clamber over mounds of debris and slash their way through thick tangles of roots.

'I do not like the look of this,' panted Hollam as he wiped beads of sweat from his brow with the back of his hand.

'The rain is weakening the walls.'

'Perhaps it would have been wiser to chance the forest.'

Badger scratched his head. 'I am inclined to agree with you, now,' he said, hacking at a thick root with all his strength. 'Perhaps it would be best to rest here. We have another day until the Kházakha are due to depart. It would be wise to conserve our strength.'

After an uncomfortable and restless night they made ready in the early morning and continued their difficult path. Suddenly there was a rumble and a slosh of wet soil. Hollam only just had time to shelter his head as the roof collapsed, knocking Badger to the ground and obliterating the light. Hollam yelled and groped his way forward, trying to locate his companion in the darkness. His hand came upon the heel of Badger's boot. Locating Badger's other leg sticking from the mud he began to pull with all his might.

The bulky man would not move!

Hollam began to dig the earth away with his hands,

heaving large stones aside as if they were weightless. Calling on Caelcáladrim for strength he attempted to extricate his friend. Badger had been buried for what felt like an eternity. With one final desperate exertion Hollam pulled his prostrate companion from entombment. Hollam rolled Badger over onto his back searching for a sign of life. He was not breathing! Despite working blind, Hollam's movements were precise. He opened Badger's mouth, removed the muddy blockages and urgently began to breathe life back into him.

At first there was no response but then Badger let out a splutter and coughed, his body convulsing violently. Hollam sat back on his heels and laughed. He was overjoyed to hear his friend's discomfort; it meant he was alive.

'You kissed me!' Badger wheezed through his explosive coughs.

Hollam chuckled wickedly; 'Aye, I thought you were Breeze.'

But now they faced another dilemma. Badger had lost everything including his flint and with no wood they could not make fire, the way before them was blocked and the nearest exit lay over eight leagues behind them. Even if they were able to run all the way back to the exit, they would still be unable to cover the return distance through the forest in time to carry out their plans. Their only way was forward, and that lay hidden behind a tonne of earth and rock. They dared not think of misfortune if the blockage extended far.

'I fear we are in for a long morning,' Hollam said wearily. 'Are you well enough to move?'

'I have never felt better!' the large man replied stoically. 'Come, let us begin.'

They began to dig laboriously away at the mountain. Using his knife, Hollam cut away chunks of the heavy clay earth whilst the well named Badger used his enormous spade-like hands. With their combined efforts they managed to dig a channel big enough for one man to crawl through, but it was slow work.

Badger let out a cry of satisfaction. 'I can feel air.'

They redoubled their efforts and soon both men were slithering through the narrow gap into the tunnel beyond. Although they still had over a league to go and had lost a great deal of time, they dared not hurry in the blackness. One false step and injury would only delay them further.

It took a frustrating hour to cover the distance to the trap-door. Morning was growing old. Ahead of them, they could see dim shafts of light illuminating the tunnel where the exit lay. They hurried to the opening and stood looking up. Now they dared speak in no more than a whisper; the camp of the Kházakha lay only a short distance beyond.

Badger extended his arm and tentatively pushed at the door; it opened almost half-way before hitting an obstruction. Badger hoisted Hollam up until he could push his head through and look around. No-one was in sight. Being the slimmest he wiggled through the gap and removed the branch blocking Badger's escape.

Both men welcomed the fresh air and the sight of the forest around them. They were coated in a thick layer of mud; only the whites of their eyes and gleaming teeth betrayed the fact they were people and not creatures of the soil. But there was no time to contemplate their appearance, it was almost noon and a drizzle had begun to fall. Stealthily, they made their way towards the Kházakha's camp, their ears alert for any sound and their eyes focused on the area around them.

It was quiet. Too quiet!

Within minutes they reached the camp and were careful to approach downwind so the troumaloks would not pick up the scent, if any could escape their mud encrusted bodies. To their consternation the camp was empty. The only signs of habitation were the camp fire ashes, the rubbish and the trampled ground.

Hollam rushed into the clearing and went to the fires to see what he could glean, but they were cold and the ground was trampled and awash with puddles.

'I need a clear print,' he said, searching for a clue.

Badger began to explore the perimeter and gave a low whistle that brought Hollam scampering over to inspect a large cloven hoof-print left by a departing troumalok.

'Judging from the rain and this track, I believe they are not so far ahead of us,' he said, scratching at the itchy covering on his face.

'What chance have we of catching them now?'

Hollam rubbed his eyes as he tried to make his tired brain think of a solution. Mud crumbled from his brow as it furrowed. Then he began to pace, muttering to himself. Badger stood gravely by and awaited the verdict. Suddenly Hollam froze. His visage brightened and he garbled out his thoughts with semi-forced optimism.

'The Kházakha are heading northwards, but their path lies to the south-east. What tells you this?'

'They have no sense of direction,' came Badger's dry reply.

'No!' Hollam cried. 'They go northwards to reach the ford at Iselbach. The rain will have made the stream swell. The troumaloks will not pass fast-running water. They have to use the ford. That is why they have departed early, to make up for the time they will lose with this diversion. We still have a chance.'

'You intend to get ahead of them,' Badger said slowly as Hollam's plan became clearer to him.

'Yes. They will have no other choice but to head for the pass in order to reach the plains. It will mean flying like the wind to get there before them, but it is possible.'

'We have slept little and are already weary,' Badger replied, casting doubt on Hollam's scheme. But seeing the younger man's avid expression, added; 'But we shall not fail through lack of trying.'

Hollam slapped his friend on the back and set off as fast as his legs would carry him and the terrain allow. Badger matched his speed, although he was too muscle-bound to be much of a long distance runner. He knew the pass Hollam referred to and counted the leagues in his head. The Kházakha would need to travel six leagues northwards to reach the ford and a further seven to the pass. Hollam's route would save them almost half as much, but the enemy had a head start and could travel at a pace far exceeding their own if they spurred the great beasts on.

It was now a race; a race dependant on Roumanhi courage and endurance.

❧

Hollam kept his speed constant, trying to conserve what energy he could. His sense of urgency demanded an increase in pace, but logic dictated the distance forbade it and Badger would be unable to match him. Indeed, they had scarcely covered two leagues before Badger was forced to stop. The big man clutched at his chest and gasped for breath.

'I cannot...I cannot keep this...pace,' he rasped. 'Go on, my friend. Your long legs are better...suited to this race. I will follow...as I can.'

Hollam was dismayed but Badger was in no condition to run any further. He buried his head in his hands and inhaled deeply as he accepted the unwelcome news. He rummaged in his pocket and produced a *couhli* stick, snapping it in half.

'Take this. It will aid you. Here also is my spear. I do not think I will need use of it and I like not to leave you unprotected.'

Badger accepted the gifts and managed a smile. Hollam, for once, could not match it. He scraped roughly at his face and pointed a warning finger at his friend. 'Do not take too long. I think I will have need of you,' and without waiting to hear the reply dashed off through the trees.

It was not long before the grasslands opened in front of

Hollam and he started to ascend the hills. They were steep and climbing made his legs burn. Only sheer grit, determination, and the fear of what failure might bring kept his legs pumping up the slopes. By the time he had reached the third crest, however, he was practically crawling.

From the top he strained his eyes westwards, searching for a sign of Badger. Perhaps it was only his imagination but he thought he caught a glimpse of his friend, a tiny spot atop the first hill. Although glad to see him moving, he had fallen so far behind Hollam knew Badger would never reach the pass in time to be of use.

The pass was still over a league away. Hollam could just make it out between two long ridges that had sides too sheer for the troumaloks. To the south he could see the remains of dark storm clouds. His thoughts turned to his brother; had he been caught in the storm?

Hollam pulled his thoughts back and lurched forward, ignoring the pain in his legs and chest. His goal was in sight; and so were the Kházakha! From his vantage point, he could just discern their dark shapes as they moved southwards across the plains. They were making good speed, but were still at least two leagues from the pass.

Hollam had no time to lose.

As he bounded down the hill he made swift calculations in his head. In his present condition it would take him at least half-an-hour to reach the pass and the Kházakha, if he had gauged their speed correctly, would arrive shortly after him.

As yet he had no idea what he would do when he finally reached the pass. Once there, he was sure that something would come to mind; or at least he hoped so. Cail was the real planner, having studied strategies with grave seriousness since the tragedy with Elm. Hollam was more spontaneous, relying on instinct, which, although not always proven the wisest choice, often wound up successful.

His descent was rapid, aided more by the steepness of the

hill than his own abilities. He stumbled onwards, forcing one leg in front of the other. Only his resolve kept him going; he had come too far and suffered too much to let exhaustion defeat him.

At last he reached his destination. The pass was in front of him and the Kházakha had not yet arrived. But there was no time to rest. Now Hollam had to conjure a scheme out of the air. He crawled up the sharp incline of the ridge to find a vantage point.

The ridge was decked with abstract boulders and he wedged himself between them, allowing a view across the plains. The Kházakha were less than half a league away and would arrive in minutes. Their forms were clearer now; a dark mass of strength trotting its way remorselessly forward. He could discern eight huge beasts, each carrying two riders; far more than expected and he groaned aloud.

The scouts had told the company of four troumaloks, meaning a squad of eight men. Now Hollam was facing twice as many! Others must have joined them at the ford. He looked about, his eyes examining the terrain, and his mind working feverishly, rejecting possibility after possibility. He toyed with the idea of causing an avalanche of stones and boulders to bar the path but the pass, although narrow, was too wide to be blocked from one side alone.

He could attack the Kházakha as they passed. They could not ride more than two abreast and perhaps an assault from above would disable some of the riders and dismay the rest. But they were sixteen and he was one. They were heavily armed and he carried only a knife.

The troumaloks were now almost upon him. He could see the faces of the riders; their expressions tired and grim. The great beasts swung their heads from side to side as if uneasy approaching the narrow gap, or perhaps they sensed danger. They champed at their fierce bits and stamped their feet. The riders reprimanded them with a crack of the whip.

Hollam had just made up his mind to risk his life and attack, when, to his amazement, the enemy stopped. Halting no more than two hundred feet from the pass, the riders dismounted and set about making camp. The beasts were unharnessed and tethered together; their feet in irons to prevent them from wandering. The riders erected shoddy two-man tents and started preparing their evening meal.

Hollam breathed a sigh of relief. Unable to smother a smile, he found a comfortable position and settled back against the rocks, observing the enemy.

Before long, the smell of cooking wafted across on the breeze. Hollam stuck a fist into his stomach as it rumbled in loud anticipation. If things had gone to plan, he would have been half-way home, or at least satisfying his cravings with berries and mushrooms or something. But here he was, starving to death with only half a *couhli* stick, far from his burrow and being teased by the aroma of stewed herbs and potatoes!

He watched as they ate and sat around talking, so arrogantly unaware of their own mortality. Had the Roumanhis gathered an army there, the Kházakha would have been overcome, despite their weapons. And yet they were so sure of their invincibility that no guard was set and no-one even scouted the area. Hollam shook his head at their stupidity. If all the Kházakha were as lax then perhaps his people would be able to fight them.

'You have grown careless!' Badger chastised without warning.

'And you have grown stealthy! What kept you?' Hollam moaned, stifling his joy and waiting for his heart to stop jumping.

Badger did not deign to answer, but asked instead; 'What plan have you?'

'I thought I would wait and see what you suggested.'

Badger gaped at him. 'You have no plan?'

Hollam shrugged his shoulders looking vaguely apologetic

as Badger settled down beside him. 'We have time.'

᯽

It was a long wait for night to fall. The pair took it in turns to sleep, but got little. They were stiff, cold and tired, and as yet did not know what to do. They shuffled ideas but came up with nothing feasible until Hollam grew excited and grabbed at Badger's arm. 'I have it,' he said as quietly as his enthusiasm would allow. 'What will panic the troumaloks and make them uncontrollable?'

Badger thought for a moment; 'A vixil cat, I suppose.'

'Remember as a boy I found a wounded one and raised it? It has been many years, but I believe I can still do a fair imitation.'

'The beasts are tethered and shackled. We would have to release them if they are to be scattered. Would it not be simpler to drug them as we intended?'

'We only have enough herbs for four, though if we spread it thinly between them they may stay calm long enough to free them without disturbance.'

Badger pulled at his chin thoughtfully. 'It is open here, but you know the beasts' ways. Perhaps they would not betray you.'

Hollam nodded. 'Perhaps.'

He checked his pouch of herbs and silently descended the ridge. He made his way through the narrow gap, straining to hear any signs of movement from the Kházakha, but they were all asleep in the tents. Hollam crept onwards towards the dozing beasts and could hear deep breaths rumbling down their long snouts. One or two troumaloks shuffled, causing their chains to rattle. Hollam froze until he was sure no one had been roused.

Slowly he made his way to the imprisoned animals, clicking and purring to calm their fears. Cautiously he extended a hand

119

and caressed the muzzle of the nearest troumalok. The beast snorted with pleasure as he reached up to scratch it behind the ear. It rubbed its head against Hollam and almost knocked him from his feet, but he braced his legs and allowed it to rub to its heart's content, careful to avoid the sharp horns above its nose.

Hollam took a small handful from the pouch and offered it to his new friend. The troumalok sniffed at it suspiciously and extended its long sticky tongue. Hollam screwed up his face and tried to shake the gluey saliva from his fingers. He proceeded along the line and by the end was covered in stinking slime. Hollam was soon thankful he had not eaten.

He waited as patiently as he could for the herb to take effect. Before long, all eight beasts had shut their eyes and stood dozing. Hollam scurried round them and quietly unlocked their shackles and loosened their tethers before making his way back to Badger, who was anxiously waiting for him.

Badger knew of his approach, he smelt him some distance away. 'I am gladdened by your return, my friend,' the big man whispered, 'but please sit away from me. You stink worse than your socks!'

'Funny!' Hollam growled sarcastically, trying to rub his hands clean on what little grass there was. Then he added; 'You need not fear. I will go to the other ridge. Should they try to pass this way, we will loosen the boulders upon them.'

He hurried across the pass to the opposite ridge and found himself a nook from where to watch the camp. He did not intend to mimic the vixil cat until the last possible second. Besides, there was no point in doing anything until the troumaloks awakened.

As morning dawned, and as Cail and company set off with the feverish Briar, Hollam became alert. Noises came from the tents and the Kházakha came blinking into the light. As no Roumanhi would do, they seemed intent on seeing to their own needs before tending to the beasts. The troumaloks had awakened and seemed none the worse for wear.

Hollam waited until the Kházakha were tucking into their breakfast and then took some deep, deep breaths. The roar of the vixil cat was no easy task and required extensive lung power, together with a throat of iron. He cupped his hands to his mouth and let out a strangled high-pitched wail that echoed off the hills and made the Kházakha bolt to their feet.

The troumaloks reacted instantly. They wheeled around to where the noise was coming from, snapping their loosened tethers, and began to plunge, desperately attempting to remove their shackles. Hollam had done his job well and the iron restraints fell from their legs as they reared and bucked in panic. The Kházakha ran to them, trying to snatch at the ropes that dangled from the halters; but they were fearful of the animals' leg spurs and horns and of the madness that was upon them. The men grabbed their whips and tried to beat them into submission, but the troumaloks were uncontrollable. Three broke away and galloped off towards the north whilst another two charged through the pass. The three remaining were attempting to break free of ropes the Kházakha had thrown around them. One man went down beneath hooves and another was thrown through the air and lay still, pierced by the animal's sharp horns.

The Kházakha fought fiercely to control the beasts but fearing for their lives reached for their weapons and fired. It took several blasts to stun them but eventually the troumaloks fell.

The Kházakha's camp was in uproar. Two were dead and another five injured. The wounded were tended to and the dead unceremoniously buried. Three able men were sent to retrieve the troumaloks which had headed northwards. They were unlikely to have gone far; their herd instincts were strong. The other men stood arguing about who should take charge; their Commander was one of the dead.

Hollam and Badger looked on in grim satisfaction.

After a couple of hours everything which could be done had been done and the uninjured Kházakha prepared to mount their now conscious troumaloks and head through the pass. Instructions were left for the three who had gone in search of their mounts to follow as best they could. The six then climbed aboard, two on each animal, and with a farewell wave headed towards the gap where Hollam and Badger were concealed.

Through a series of hand gestures and urgent pointing the two men had agreed on a rough plan of action. As the troumaloks approached, Badger clasped a large stone in his strong hand and made ready to launch it at the leading rider. Hollam wedged his feet against the rocks and braced his back against a boulder, preparing to create a wall of falling debris to disrupt their path.

As the leading troumalok came parallel to the lurking figures, Badger propelled the rock at the rider's head with such force that it knocked him senseless to the ground. The troumalok spun around in fright and the second Kházakh was unseated and fell awkwardly onto the grass, lucky not to be trampled underfoot as his mount galloped off. The remaining troumaloks, seeing their companion disappearing, started to plunge and their riders fought hard to hold them back. The pillions drew their weapons and started firing at Badger, who was forced to make a hasty retreat as stones shattered and splintered around him. Hollam strained against the rocks and with a mighty heave sent an avalanche of boulders down upon the enemy. The nearest troumalok stumbled under the weight of the stones and fell to its knees, nearly unseating the rider. Hollam leapt from the hillside with startling speed and, before the Kházakha could react, he was upon them. He charged like a bull and rammed his arms into the pillion's stomach before he could fire. The man was thrown from the beast's back, his weapon dropping from his hand as he tumbled from the saddle. The rider, unable to both control the beast and defend himself was also dispatched with one swift jab of an elbow.

Meanwhile, Badger had started a furious assault upon the other Kházakha. Volleys of missiles rained down from the outcrop and although they tried to protect themselves, Badger's targeting was too accurate. The rider hauled at the reins so his companion could take steady aim, but it was futile. The troumalok danced nervously on its cloven hooves, trying to escape the hail of missiles; the gunman cursed as each beam missed its target. The attack then began from both sides. Hollam, having dispatched the other riders, swiftly went to his friend's aid. He picked up the fallen weapon, checked its setting, and fired on the men.

The wounded Kházakha left in the camp were approaching as fast as their injuries allowed. Deadly beams from their weapons disintegrated rocks all around Hollam as he dashed for the troumalok. As the riders fell from its back, he grabbed the reins and deftly leapt on board. Badger raced from his place of concealment and with a mighty bound settled himself behind the younger man.

Hollam spurred the great beast forward with a yell and a jab from his heels and the troumalok sprang away, eager to follow its companions. The Kházakha fired after them and a beam hit the animal's hind quarter causing it to lurch, but it was not enough to prevent their escape. In a matter of moments they were out of range and safe.

As they rode away from the pass, Badger summoned the courage to shout into Hollam's ear; 'Know you how to ride this beast?'

'No,' Hollam yelled back.

'What?'

'I said no.'

'I know you said no.'

'Then why did you ask?'

'Because we are sitting atop and it is moving very quickly!'

'It cannot be difficult,' Hollam consoled. 'I suppose you pull the left rope to go left and the right one to go right.'

'I care more about stop!'

'Both, I think.'

'Then try. I like not this speed,' came Badger's supplication.

Hollam leant back on the reins hopefully, but the animal had taken the bit between its teeth and refused to slow. 'We could jump,' Hollam suggested.

'Are you serious?'

'If we chose somewhere soft?'

'I am not jumping.'

'It could work.'

Badger's reply was a resolute no.

Hollam thought for a moment. 'Then we must wait until it stops.'

'My friend, your logic astounds me!' said Badger, wrapping his huge arms even more tightly around Hollam's waist.

It was not long before they caught sight of the beasts their steed was pursuing. To the men's consternation their ride quickened its pace before coming to an abrupt stop before its herd.

'Now what?' Badger inquired.

'We are far from home and could be pursued if the Kházakha have regained their mounts. What say you we remain aboard a while longer?'

'I have heard more pleasant suggestions, but the decision is wise, if you can control it.'

'Now that he has his herd, perhaps he will co-operate.'

Hollam tentatively pulled at the reins and the troumalok obeyed instantly. He scratched its neck gratefully and relaxed his hold. He turned his steed and the strange company set off at a more sedate pace.

❦

T'skya's first instinct was to run, but there was nowhere to hide.

Cail took her hand and stood still, patiently awaiting his fate. Wolf peered into the distance shielding his eyes with a slim hand. 'There are five beasts, but I can see only two riders.'

'Only two?' Cail said in surprise.

Wolf suddenly laughed. 'Either my eyes deceive me or these riders are well known to us. It is Hollam and Badger - look!'

'He rides?' Cail cried, relieved there would be no battle and overjoyed his brother was alive. He ran forward eagerly pulling T'skya with him.

Before long, the grinning form of Hollam and his not so happy companion were clearly visible. T'skya, however, found herself less interested in the riders than their mounts. The troumaloks were a strange concoction of beasts all rolled into one. Their heads had two lethal-looking horns projecting from above their flaring nostrils, and their pale eyes rolled incessantly like a whirligig, ever alert for danger. The animals looked mighty as they approached with muscular chests and loins, and sturdy legs that ended in massive cloven hooves; legs that propelled them with apparent ease. Fighting cock spurs curved dangerously above their elbows ready to rend and tear and T'skya determined to keep her distance. The troumaloks' bodies were covered with plates like an armadillo protecting all but their soft, hairless bellies. Coarse sandy-coloured hair sprouted in tufts around their short thick necks, similar to a lion's mane, and was also present on the end of their whip-like tails. They were strange beasts indeed.

Hollam reined his troumalok to a halt and jumped down into his brother's arms. Despite his exuberance, Cail found the reek from the troumaloks' spit too potent for his refined nostrils. 'I see you have a tale for the telling,' he said laughing, backing away with his hands raised in mock defence.

Hollam cast an acerbic look. 'Indeed we do, but first tell me how you fare.' He caught sight of his Clan leader, who had not reacted to his arrival and asked sharply; 'What ails Briar?'

'This journey has taxed her a heavy burden. She will not last long without aid!' his brother replied, his voice now devoid of joy.

'Then it is good that we came when we did. With these beasts we can return her to the forest, if she can manage such a journey. Have you accomplished your mission?'

'No. We were about to attempt the desert when Wolf saw you.'

'Then do not delay. The Kházakha were on our trail and I do not know how long it will take them to pick up our path. Badger and Wolf can escort Briar and I will lay false trails to keep the enemy at bay. If it is possible, I will return for you - now go.'

Cail closed his eyes thankfully. As Badger went to Briar's aid, Hollam stood and watched his younger brother walk out on to the sand. Then, resignedly pulling his attention away, he set about helping his friends mount the beasts.

❧

T'skya and Cail briefly turned to watch their companions depart. They were relieved Briar would soon get care, provided she met with no mishaps on the way, but now they only had each other to depend upon.

As they approached the desert boundary, Cail stopped and looked across at T'skya questioningly. 'T'skya, I do not know what will happen. Briar has only hinted at such things. If you wish to change your mind about this, I will not forbid it, though I must go on with or without you.'

T'skya crossed her arms, staring at him for some moments before answering. 'I'd like nothing more than to leave this place and sit safely in my burrow. I'm not a warrior and this scares me almost witless but as long as you are with me, I'll deal with whatever's out there.'

Cail smiled and took her hand. T'skya lowered her eyes, embarrassed by the awkward silence that followed. Cail laughed nervously and taking comfort from each other's touch, they walked, as commanded, two hundred paces into the desert sands.

At the end of their count they halted, unsure what to do or expect. T'skya tightened her grip on Cail's hand and looked about her anxiously. He gazed across the sands as if he were expecting something to approach them, but nothing moved in the glimmering heat.

'Now what?' T'skya whispered.

'We wait.'

'For what?'

Cail shrugged and tucked a strand of hair behind his ear. T'skya studied his patient profile as he stood erect against the glow of the yellow expanse. He reminded her so much of the figures on the arras, although he was slimmer and less wild-looking. He sensed her eyes upon him and turned his head to meet them. This time she did not look away, but held his gaze. He was about to speak when the ground beneath them abruptly gave way and they were plunged into darkness.

T'skya only just had time to register the eerie feeling of déjà-vu and let out a squeal of fright before she found herself alive and well in an open space below ground. It was as black as pitch. She could not even see her hand in front of her face and she felt disorientated and frightened.

'T'skya?' came a soft voice from somewhere to her right.

'I'm all right. Where are you?

He reached for her, grasped her hand firmly and carefully edged towards her until they were sitting shoulder to shoulder. He put a protective arm around her waist and they sat in silence, waiting. T'skya quietly suggested using the flashlight from her pocket, but Cail forbid it. Briar had taken no means for light and she had returned, albeit in poor health.

Before long, they heard a strange scrabbling sound approaching. It was almost like stones scraping over each other; a rough inorganic sound which was unnerving in the darkness.

T'skya shrank closer to Cail. He cocked his head sideways attempting to pinpoint and identify the noise.

'Whatever happens, remain calm,' he whispered.

The scraping sound stopped a few feet from them. T'skya strained her ears but could only hear the pounding of her heart as it pulsated in her chest as if trying to escape and flee; a desire she related to.

A rough grating noise broke the silence and then stopped abruptly. T'skya squeaked in fear; biting her lip to gain courage. Cail again said nothing. The noise was repeated but Cail remained obstinately silent. The sound of water receding over a pebbly beach followed in what could have been a sigh.

'*Grznkhssh kzik*. Speak,' the noise commanded.

Cail searched for suitable words, tentatively asking in both Navennán and Roumanhi; 'Know you our tongue?'

'*Shka*. Tongue knows us yes, yes. Her knows us. You not!' the creature replied in Roumanhi.

'You know T'skya?' he stuttered in surprise.

'Says that not us? Who you?'

'My name is Cail of the enclave Wilderwood. Will you not tell us of yourselves?'

There was much rumbling and grating and it became obvious they were surrounded. The voice spoke again. 'Words of welcome speak. All will know you us. No words, no life! Words - you us helps.'

'How can I speak your language when I do not know who or what you are?'

'Knows us you not, you not she claimed you are!' the creature muttered, appearing angry.

'What the hell was all that about?' T'skya hissed. She had understood almost nothing of the conversation. Her knowledge of Cail's language was too basic to follow the exchange.

'I believe we will die unless I say the correct words of welcome,' he replied bluntly.

'So say them,' she urged.

'I do not know them!'

'What? I thought you were a people of many tongues!'

'We are, but I cannot speak to them in their language if I do not know who they are. They seem to know you though.'

'Me?'

'I think we have just met your mysterious helpers.'

'Why would they help me if they won't help you?' she responded in confusion.

'I was hoping you could tell me.'

'I told you, I don't remember anything.'

They sat in silence pondering their fate until she added hopefully; 'Briar knew this would happen. She wouldn't have sent you here if you didn't know what to do. What did she say to you?'

'She told me to remember my youth,' he replied, frowning thoughtfully.

'What did she mean?'

'I wish I knew.' Then he began to mutter to himself. 'What about my youth? Come on Cail, think!' Suddenly he laughed and pulled her to him, planting a kiss upon her cheek. It felt wet and warm and she touched where his lips had been in happy bewilderment.

'What? What is it?'

'This is a moment I will treasure for all eternity.'

T'skya shook her head in total confusion and found she could think of no reply. Cail raised himself to his feet and, clearing his throat, spoke in a loud, solemn voice the words that they were waiting to hear.

'*Shnakhash Grish-Grish-Gûri, tsozgleck psitch,*' he said, his throat screaming with the effort. He gracefully lowered himself onto one knee and bowed his head. 'This day I am humbled before you.'

Cail slowly stood up, removed his pack and pulled out the strange rocks Knoll had supplied. With ritual precision he placed them at the creatures' feet and poked T'skya to indicate she should do the same. From the noise she understood his actions and promptly complied, although she could not fathom the symbolism.

There was a chittering and grating of pleasure from their audience and a dim light was produced. It cast shadows over the walls of the cavern revealing them at last.

T'skya could hardly contain her amazement. She had thought the troumaloks strange, but these creatures were something altogether different. There were hundreds gathered and they were staring at the couple intently, or at least she felt they were; there was nothing to indicate eyes of any shape or description.

Each animal was shaped like a dull fat worm with smooth, interlocking plates running down the length of the body like millipedes. Their heads were oversized, mainly comprised of massive, stone-crushing jaws. They had no teeth to speak of, but rough grinding ridges that ran along the inside of their mouths in rows. Their noses were broad flat slits covered with a delicate fringe of rubbery feelers and looked very much as if someone had glued surgical gloves to their faces. Their ears were no more than vertical slits covered with movable flaps for protection.

Despite their worm-like appearance, the creatures had six legs; the front pair like twisted iron ending in four sucker-tipped fingers and one sharp hook in the middle. The central legs had three sucker-tipped toes, and the powerful back legs ended in shovels. Their tails were long and solid, weighted like a hammer at the end.

These peculiar creatures, the Grish-Grish-Gûri, rustled with pleasure for their gifts. The ones closest picked up the rocks with their strange hands and held them aloft. Delight shone in their faces as the lilac pink stones caught the light and the crystals within glittered and sparkled like the bright night stars.

'What are those for?' she whispered in Cail's ear.

'Lunch,' he grinned.

'They eat those?' returned her shocked reply.

Then as one, and much to Cail's surprise, the Grish-Grish-Gûri bowed to him, their heads to the ground. T'skya was looking at him questioningly. He just shrugged fractionally in answer. The creature who had first spoken to him moved forwards and sat perched on its back legs, supported by its tail.

'One more test asks us,' it said so that T'skya could also understand.

Cail frowned but was courteous in his reply. 'If it lies in our power, we will comply.'

'Not both. You only. Pass she already,' it said.

It was Cail's turn to look questioning, but T'skya was as ignorant as he. 'Very well,' he consented.

'On knees,' the creature commanded, and Cail slowly complied. Tentatively, the creature raised one arm and placed a suckered finger against the centre of Cail's brow. His only reaction was a slight widening of his eyes and then his face relaxed and became expressionless. An eerie chanting came from the onlookers as the first creature concentrated on Cail. T'skya edged closer to her companion looking at the creatures askance. The ritual was unknown to her and with Cail the focus of their attention, she did not like it.

When it had finished, the creature released Cail from its touch. He slumped forward, drained of energy. T'skya leapt to his side, her eyes ablaze with anger. 'What have you done to him?' she demanded. A rustle of disapproval circulated the room, but she held her ground.

'T'skya, I am unharmed,' Cail said shakily. She relaxed a little but her mouth remained grim.

The creature sat back on its haunches, looking satisfied. 'Spoke she truth. It is he.'

A cacophony broke out as the entire company began banging their tails on the ground. The din was tremendous in such a confined space; Cail and T'skya were forced to cover their ears.

The creature signalled for peace and again turned to Cail. 'Lord, speaks not good I. Here Trik-nak is. You will he helps if wishes you that.'

At that, a granite coloured creature came slithering forward on its belly and presented itself to Cail. 'Trik-nak am I. How may I serve you, Lord?'

Cail was a little taken aback at the title but shrugged it off. 'We have come seeking a strange craft that fell into the desert many suns ago. Have you knowledge of this?'

'Of it we know,' Trik-nak replied cautiously.

'Can you take us to it?'

'As you command, Lord,' Trik-nak said, bowing.

Without any discernible gesture of command, four other creatures came forward to escort them to the ship. 'This way. This way,' they cried, rushing ahead and waving their hooks.

'They are young,' Trik-nak explained.

T'skya raised an eyebrow wondering how it was possible to tell. 'How old are they?' she asked hesitantly, unsure of protocol.

'They have not yet reached their second century,' he replied simply.

Cail drew down his brows and fell quiet, but continued to follow the Grish-Grish-Gûri through the winding tunnels. In places they had to stoop low; the passage had not been designed for people and was cramped. For a time they travelled downwards, the incline leading them further from the planet's surface. The temperature was cool, almost cold, and a breeze ventilated the passageways although no shafts or inlets could be seen, but it was still hard work and made them sweat. Trik-nak led them through turn after turn until T'skya had completely lost all sense of direction. Trik-nak, however, was sure of his path and never hesitated in his choice, finally stopping by a blank wall for them to catch their breath.

'I will not enter, but what you seek lies behind this wall,' he said with a wave of his peculiar hand.

'That's not possible!' T'skya objected. 'My craft landed much deeper in the desert. We haven't been walking long enough.'

Trik-nak cocked his head at her but said nothing.

'T'skya!' Cail warned through clenched teeth.

'No, wait a minute,' she whispered. 'How do you know this isn't a trap? They might have won your trust, but they haven't won mine! First of all, what did that creature do to you and why did he say that I'd already passed the test? I didn't speak any words of welcome and don't remember anyone touching me. They speak in riddles and don't explain anything yet you are so ready to trust them.'

She had tried to speak quietly, but she had forgotten Trik-nak's sensitive ears. Trik-nak pulled back his lips and hammered his tail on the ground in anger. T'skya flinched. 'You doubt *us?*' he grated, trying to contain his wrath.

Cail intervened using his best diplomacy. 'My companion is naturally suspicious. She is ignorant of your kind and all they have done for the land. She also serves to protect me and so should not be wrongly judged. She has undergone much hardship on this journey. If someone must be punished for discourtesy, then it should be I, for I have failed to ease her fears.'

Trik-nak ceased his drumming and his face relaxed. 'I will forgive her mistrust if you command it, Lord. But you,' he said thrusting his face at T'skya and bristling his nose, 'should place more trust in your master.'

'Well, then I ask my master's forgiveness,' she said in a tone not entirely devoid of satire.

Cail smirked.

'Do you now wish to enter?' Trik-nak inquired.

Cail nodded and Trik-nak pressed his palm against the stone and slowly the outline of a concealed door became visible. He grated some words and the door swung open to reveal a darkened room. He handed them some smooth glowing rocks that reacted to warmth. Cail and T'skya evidently produced more heat than the Grish-Grish-Gûri, for the stones were now burning brightly.

'We will return when you wish it,' Trik-nak said, shielding his face from the light. The Grish-Grish-Gûri scuttled down the passageway, leaving the couple alone.

'Are you ready?' asked Cail, kindly not criticising her for the outburst.

'What are we waiting for?' she replied, and thrust herself through the doorway.

The room they entered was spacious and high-ceilinged. Their stones were not powerful enough to illuminate the space in its entirety, but they could see enough to realise that the ship was not there or, at least, not there in one piece. 'My shi...my ship!' she stammered. 'What have they done to my ship?'

She had good reason to be alarmed. Her ship lay about the cavern in pieces. There were parts scattered everywhere. Most of it was hardly recognisable, having been twisted and chewed, hammered and crushed. T'skya walked slowly around the cavern touching this and examining that, mumbling miserably to herself. Then she just flumped to the floor, her head buried between her knees, and burst into tears.

Cail knew what this meant to her; she had lost her way home and was trapped on the planet, on a world she did not belong to or understand. 'I share your pain but remember what our mission was, T'skya. There was the chance you would have been forced to destroy the ship. Now, at least, we do not have to fear discovery by our enemy. And we will find a way to get you home, if that is what you really desire.' He took her head between his hands and forced her to look at him. 'If that is what you really desire, I *will* find a way.' Wishing to give her something to focus on, he added; 'Can anything be salvaged?'

'I doubt it!' she replied bitterly, but gamely climbed to her feet to examine the dismantled parts more thoroughly. As she went about her business, Cail held or carried whatever he was asked to and made a pile of equipment near the door.

'This is the machine I was telling you about,' she said, turning a largish tubular object about in her hands. 'It has parts missing, but if I can find them, I might be able to fix it.'

Cail rummaged about and held up various objects for her inspection, but she shook her head at each and every one. 'Is this it?' he asked, preparing to give up.

'Yes!' came her enthusiastic reply. She dashed over to him and snatched the part out of his hands. 'Keep looking,' she urged whilst she set about trying to reconnect the wires and sort out the circuitry. Before long, Cail let out a triumphant yell and pulled the other device from under a mass of battered metal sheets.

'Will it work?' he inquired.

'I don't know yet; it may take some time.' She avidly set to work and paid Cail little or no attention. To keep himself busy he continued to search to room, every so often daring to break her concentration to show off his finds.

At last T'skya let out a sigh and gestured for Cail to join her. 'If this doesn't work, there's nothing else I can do.' She closed her eyes and keyed in the codes. The machine sprang to life and its screen became bright, awaiting data. 'Well, I can't get home, but at least I can analyse and synthesise to my heart's content,' she said sardonically.

'I found the weapons you spoke of,' Cail replied. He held up some twisted guns for her to see. 'They have been destroyed!'

'Great for shooting around corners!' she said tossing them on to the pile. 'Come on. There's nothing more we can do here and seeing all this junk is breaking my heart. Besides,' she said waving her arm at the ship, 'I'd really like an explanation for all this.'

'As would I,' he agreed, filling their packs. 'But ask nicely.

You do not comprehend who you are dealing with.'

No sooner had they reached the door to leave than Trik-nak appeared and gestured to his companions to assist them with their salvage. They followed Trik-nak back through the labyrinth.

The first, Yyishgur, was waiting for them, but the former assembly was absent. Cail bowed to him elegantly and T'skya bent a little. Yyishgur touched his head to the ground in welcome. 'Lord, pleased yes?' he said.

T'skya opened her mouth but Cail quickly intervened, fearing an outburst. 'We are most gratified by your hospitality and aid, but we are puzzled by how the ship came to be here.'

'Disturbs sleep, yes. Makes noise and shakes ground. We hears, we sees, we inv- investigates, yes. Not likes what we finds. Dangerous for us if they comes. Bites it, tastes bad, not nice rocks. We finds it, we takes it, pieces by pieces so they not finds it.'

'That is well,' Cail replied. 'I have one further question. Did you rescue T'skya from the desert?'

'Rescues us, yes. Finds her and tests her. We finds no guilt in her and so sends her to trees.'

'How did you test her, Yyishgur?'

'We reads her thoughts,' the creature replied simply, as if it were a natural skill that all possessed.

'And Briar? What test did you give her?' T'skya asked in a grating voice, feeling violated.

Yyishgur's nose quivered. 'That knowledge not for you, yet.' And then, as if dismissing T'skya from his thoughts, he turned his back on her to face Cail. 'We takes you to the forest, Lord. Plains not safe. The *Psitznkkhss* there,' he continued in what sounded rather like a violent sneeze.

'We thank you but my brother Hollam may be awaiting us at the desert boundary.'

'Waits not. We knows. Will meets you in trees.'

Cail looked at T'skya to learn her thoughts on the matter.

She raised her eyebrows, raised her arms, shrugged and left the decision to him. Cail gave his consent and was surprised to see small sleds brought into the room. They were made of polished stone and shone like mirrors. They glided almost noiselessly over the ground and were pulled by two solid-looking creatures.

'Sit. Sit,' they insisted. Cail and T'skya sat down with their packs behind them. The Grish-Grish-Gûri took the harnesses between their jaws and prepared to leave. Yyishgur held up a forbearing hand. Trik-nak shuffled forwards and announced solemnly; 'Lord, when the time comes and you have need of us, we will answer. Our debt will then have been paid and we will serve no more, so choose wisely. Fare you well.'

With that the Grish-Grish-Gûri disappeared into the darkness giving Cail no time to contemplate Trik-nak's words. The sled leapt forward with such a spurt that T'skya and Cail were nearly unseated. They sped through tunnel after tunnel, never pausing for breath.

❧

T'skya and Cail were awakened with a poke and found that they had come to a stop. Neither had been aware of falling asleep and both felt slightly disorientated and groggy. T'skya blinked against the sunlight and was surprised to see sky, trees and Hollam's smiling face above her.

'I am pleased to see you both alive and well, though grieved to find you sleeping when I have been galloping about the countryside with no rest.'

'How did you know where to find us?' his brother asked, looking about in confusion.

'I did not, but my friend Stinker would follow no other path and brought me here with great speed. But tell me, how did you arrive before me? You must have sprouted wings to have outpaced a troumalok.'

'Well, we came...we...I do not know,' Cail replied, puzzled by his inadequacy. He frowned deeply. 'T'skya?'

She just stared blankly and shook her head. Cail looked at the bulging packs beside them and, springing upon them, tore them open. Inside, the salvaged parts from the ship gleamed dully in the sunlight.

'I do not understand it. I remember walking into the desert and feeling like I was falling and then - then nothing! Yet we have parts of the ship, so we must have been there. I do not understand it,' he repeated, scratching his head.

'Perhaps you are not supposed to,' Hollam said calmly. 'Now there will be no tale to brighten my day and you will have to be content with mine. But come, we must delay no longer. The Kházakha have increased their patrols and our way will be hazardous. The troumaloks I will release. They have served long enough and would be of no aid amongst the forest growth.'

He went over to the giant beasts and unharnessed them, concealing the saddles and bridles amongst the undergrowth and then gave each animal a hug and a pat on the neck.

'I thank you for bearing me so far. Now be free as you should be and roam safe from harm. Beware the Kházakha, but know me as your friend.'

The troumaloks shuffled their feet and rolled their eyes, unwilling to leave. Stinker blew down his nose and gave Hollam a sloppy lick across the cheek. The man screwed up his face as the stench hit his nose but did not shrink from the contact.

'Go on, you are free,' he said, waving his arms half-heartedly. Stinker snorted and stamped his foot, turned and then, followed by the others, disappeared from view.

Hollam opened his canteen and used what little water he had left to wash his face.

Cail knew him too well to be deceived. 'You are too soft, my brother,' he said, slapping him lovingly on the back.

'What are you talking about? I had something in my eye, 'tis all,' Hollam replied gruffly as he hoisted T'skya's pack onto his back to save her the trouble of carrying it. 'Come on,' he said setting off into the depths of the forest.

SEVEN

Analysis

The travellers arrived back at the enclave in the late evening. They had made good time, despite encountering the enemy on route. Hollam's activities had not gone unreported and, although sure they could not identify him, the Kházakha's movements so close to home caused him concern.

T'skya, Hollam and Cail entered the enclave to a warm welcome. Badger and Wolf embraced them enthusiastically relieved to see them safely back. To Hollam's delight Breeze was there and he wrapped a strong arm about her slender waist and held her tight.

'I will prepare hot water for bathing. You have need of it, methinks,' Breeze said, her eyes shining.

Hollam looked bashful but said he would be glad of it. Raven was also present and she greeted the men warmly, even sparing a word for T'skya. Bramble hurried away to prepare some hot food.

'How is Briar?' Cail asked Tarn, who was standing nearest.

'She is poor but stable. Your mother attends her and awaits your presence eagerly.'

'We will go to her.'

'She does not request that Hollam attend,' Tarn said

awkwardly.

Hollam looked momentarily wounded but covered it well. 'Perhaps she has heard tell of my odour!' he said softly, and putting T'skya's pack down stalked off after Breeze.

Cail's eyes followed his brother and T'skya frowned. 'You'd better go' she said, retrieving her heavy pack and nodding towards Negram's hut.

Cail made his way to the house of healing. He found Briar asleep and his mother seated, as always, upon her favourite chair. She did not rise to meet him but sat staring, looking him over from head to foot.

'How is she?' he asked, gesturing to Briar with a tilt of his head.

'She will recover given time, but will never be as she was,' Negram said sadly. 'What of you?'

'I am well in body, but my mind is troubled,' he replied, kneeling at her feet. 'My tale is short in telling; I recall so little. I remember nothing of the desert and nor does T'skya, though I feel something wondrous occurred there. I cannot explain it.'

Negram smiled and placed a hand upon his hair. 'My son, do not tax yourself trying to remember that which is meant to be hidden. There is reason in all things. You have returned to me, but not as you were. You have grown and will continue to grow until this mystery is resolved.'

'And when will that be?' he asked.

'Soon, my child, soon.'

Cail looked into her eyes. 'You know the answers,' he whispered.

Negram said nothing. Cail had taken his first steps towards his destiny and she could no longer interfere. She only hoped it had not come upon him prematurely; hoped he would not fold under the challenge.

❦

The Kházakha soon gave up their search and reduced patrols back to normal, and the scouting parties returned to their daily routines. Briar's strength grew day by day until she was able to rise from her bed and sit in the sunshine. T'skya spent most of her time with her equipment, attempting repairs. She could not remember how she had come by the parts and was puzzled by strange scour marks on the casing.

Without knowing why, T'skya also found herself drawn to the underground cavern where the arras hung. Surrounded by candlelight, she wrestled with the wiring and connections finally managing to construct one operable weapon and restore most functions to the analyser unit. But her thoughts were ever drawn to the tapestry by the door which suggested much but revealed nothing. It reminded her of something, something that remained elusively at the back of her mind. Cail also found himself drawn to the hall, less so by the arras than by T'skya's presence.

'You promised to tell me the tale of Caelcáladrim when there was time,' she said one day.

'Actually, it was Hollam that promised,' Cail replied.

'Well, he isn't here and you are.'

'Yes, his spare time is much taken up by a certain young woman,' he smiled.

'But he still won't admit that he's in love with her.'

'Nor she with him, even though it is obvious to us all.'

'I'd never have thought him shy,' T'skya said.

'Nor I,' Cail agreed, 'but I fear there is more to it than we can see.'

'Because she is Kalkassian?'

'Amongst other things.'

T'skya pondered for a moment. 'How come Breeze came here with the Kházakha about? Isn't she in danger?'

'You would have thought so, yet the Kalkassian Premier

still allows their presence here. The Kházakha never harm people from the Great Divide. I do not think they dare provoke war.'

T'skya drummed her fingers on the table and leant on her elbows. 'The tale?' she prodded.

Cail seemed reluctant and T'skya almost gave in but knew deeply inside it was something she needed to hear. 'Please,' she pleaded, touching his arm. He hung his head as he came to a decision and rubbed his eyes. He stood resignedly and drew her to the first tapestry.

'This was the land, or at least the nearest image we have, at the time of Caelcáladrim's birth. The people then did not live in Clans and nor did they serve the land as we do; over time areas were deforested and the grasslands grew to about the size you see today; though the desert has encroached upon large stretches since the arrival of the Kházakha.

'Caelcáladrim was born here,' he said, pointing to an area below the northern mountains. 'Though he came from a simple farming family, his parents raised their son to respect the land, for they knew that only by nurturing and protecting it could they provide a sure future for their young.

'This way of thinking is the foundation of our lives today, but at that time they suffered much scorn for it. The people of the north had enough problems with the constant threat from the Blackwood to concern themselves with such ideas, and so the family moved eastward across the plains to an area that was then rich and fertile, and for a time they prospered.

'As Caelcáladrim grew to manhood, he was troubled by reports of barbarous raiders from beyond the mountains and organised his siblings to fight. When a savage band of Saxskotnaks invaded their land Caelcáladrim was ready. Despite being outnumbered, his family drove the enemy away with few losses.

'When the other people learnt of this, they begged Caelcáladrim for his aid. He agreed and poured his energies into training and teaching the isolated farmers to work together. This was the first step towards a united race.

'At one of these farms Kilcáerian came to his notice. She became his bondmate and bore two children, Gilgarad and Caelárian. Together they patrolled the northern reaches, aiding those who requested it and mastering those who did not.

'The incursions continued for many years but few were successful. The raiders then ceased to come and the land grew peaceful. The farmers, no longer threatened from the north, soon forgot their debt to Caelcáladrim, and resented his interference. Caelcáladrim was furious but vowed he would never cease to serve them. Believing the raiders would return, he journeyed through the treacherous mountains.

'He saw the Saxskotnaks gathering their forces, employing strange and mighty beasts. He then had to convince the farmers of the danger and persuade them to fight for their lives. Few paid him any heed, though a small group joined his cause and settled on his farm.

'The Saxskotnaks began to make small forays across the mountains, testing their strength. Caelcáladrim was alarmed and sent Gilgarad eastwards to implore the Harouks, a warrior people from beyond Roumanhi, to come to their aid. The Kházakha city lies in what was once their land. He sent his mate southwards and he went to the west, whilst his brothers and sisters rallied the people of the north. It was during this time that, according to legend, Caelárian ventured into the forest and swore her oath to the *Silhvran* tree.

'During Caelcáladrim's absence the Saxskotnaks struck their first blow. An army larger than any the land then possessed passed over the mountains and slaughtered all who stood in their path. Having encountered so little resistance, they withdrew and prepared to launch the throbbing mass of their power upon Roumanhi.

'The raid stirred great alarm and people rallied to the cause in droves, bringing all the weapons they possessed. The

Harouks readily joined Gilgarad and so it was that troumaloks first entered the land. Led by Gilgarad, a mounted brigade of some five hundred beasts was sent in the vanguard whilst foot soldiers marched in their wake. But when the Saxskotnak army came swarming over the mountains, the Harouks were still well distant and Kilcáerian's southern army was still three days away.

'The north and western farmers put up fierce resistance, but were pushed remorselessly southwards suffering heavy losses. Caelcáladrim and his siblings sent their armies into full retreat to close the distance with Kilcáerian. The enemy was on their heels and those that fell were mercilessly slayed. Caelcáladrim and a small group of men then flew eastward to intercept Gilgarad, hoping to trap the enemy between the allied forces.

'The farmers from the north and west fled in desperation and were soon in sight of Kilcáerian. Her army, though large, was pitifully weary, and many quailed at the sight of the approaching deadly horde, fleeing in terror for their lives. Battle raged and although Kilcáerian's army was outnumbered almost five to one they held the day.

'As the second dawn rose, Gilgarad's Harouk army came upon the bloodied battlefield and were dismayed by what they saw. Kilcáerian had lost over half her forces and those remaining were half dead through tiredness. The Saxskotnaks, however, were thrown into confusion by the Harouks' sudden and fierce assault.

'A cry went up as the Saxskotnaks broke and dashed for the great river, which at that time split the land in two. The Harouks set off in pursuit, knowing the troumaloks would not follow should the enemy cross the water and the invaders were driven back towards the east.

'But Caelcáladrim was not amongst them. He had made his way to the mountains bordering the Saxskotnak and Harouk lands, impelled by an ancient Harouk legend. It told of a race that lived beneath the mountains who were wise in law, mighty in strength and whom the Harouks worshipped as gods. With the impossible hope of securing their aid he travelled as fast as the troumalok beneath him could manage. Leaving the beast, he climbed the rugged slopes until he reached a plateau and there stood supplicating the unknown race in every tongue he knew, but to no avail. He sank to the ground and wept bitter tears.

'Then, in the darkness, he saw images of the fight he had left behind and knew the raiders' strategy. The dash towards the river was a ruse luring the smaller weaker army towards the jaws of an advancing Saxskotnak reserve.

'Caelcáladrim wailed aloud and damned his own stupidity. He should have seen the trap! Now he was days away and could never hope to warn his compatriots. But through the darkness came a voice with no solidity for him to grasp. It penetrated his mind; he saw and felt the words clearly, though he did not understand from whence they came.

'As thus spoke the voice; "*We have read your soul and find you pure. Thus we will aid you for we have suffered greatly at their hands. Bring the enemy to us and we will crush its heart utterly, as we have already crushed those who have tainted our homeland. Do this for us and we will serve you thrice more. But beware! None may seek us save three. The King, his heir, and one who shall communicate between us.*"

'The annihilation of the reserve army heartened Caelcáladrim, but he was also at a loss. "I cannot meet your needs for we have no King," he replied.

'But the voice was adamant. "*You are a King amongst men. When victory is yours, the people will humble themselves before you and your kin.*"

'Caelcáladrim was doubtful. "I am but one man. How can I do so much?"

'And the voice answered; "*The King is all the land. Hold faith and you will not fail.*" And so it was that Caelcáladrim vowed to do as they bid.

'Strangely, his mount seemed as fresh as the day and together they raced like the wind across the golden plains. His armies were leagues away, yet by nightfall he came upon the Harouk foot soldiers and left orders to march no further. He raced onwards and by morning the enemy was in sight. The Saxskotnaks stretched across the plain like a dark stain upon its back, whilst his army was in a pitiful condition, few in number and marching no more.

'Gilgarad, troubled by the Saxskotnaks' retreat, had commanded his army to halt and encamp upon the plain. A roar of gladness erupted at the sight of Caelcáladrim returning to his faithful troops and he cried openly with pride as he revealed his vision. He implored them to redouble their efforts, for in three days victory would be theirs and peace would return to the land. He asked the impossible, yet something in his tone and the fire in his eyes allowed of no refusal. And so the long march began.

'At length they came upon the Harouk foot soldiers who had let the enemy pass through. They then joined their compatriots in pushing the Saxskotnaks towards the looming mountains.

'On the morning of the third day the enemy stopped at the base of the mountains in dismay, for they had expected to be greeted by their reserve army; but not one man nor fell creature could be seen and the army became disarrayed. As the Commanders desperately tried to regroup their troops, Caelcáladrim gave the order to attack. With a cry of fury, the Roumanhis and the Harouks launched a fierce assault upon their foes forcing the Saxskotnaks backwards up the mountainside. Those who set foot upon its purple hues were never seen again, for the enemy disappeared as if consumed by the mountain itself.

'Caelcáladrim closed his ranks and the enemy was forced back, their numbers becoming fewer and fewer with each passing moment.

'But the Saxskotnaks rallied one last time. From their midst came a monster so hideous to behold that it cast fear upon man and beast. Caelcáladrim alone stood to face it. Gilgarad fought savagely but was engaged in battle too far away and could not reach him.

'Great was the battle between man and beast that day. Caelcáladrim fought as no man could, but the beast was mighty and cunning and overcame the man. But even as the monster's jaws closed upon him did Caelcáladrim find the strength to raise his sword and hew its neck asunder. As he lay there, his blood mingling with his foe's and the light in his eyes fading as the light in the sky was fading, Gilgarad reached his side and was commanded thus; "My son and heir, this night you shall have victory. Climb upon this mountain to the plateau above and find the wisdom our people need. You shall be their saviour now!"

'And with those words he passed from this life and the people praised him. With the slaying of the monster the Saxskotnaks were defeated and few, if any, survived that night and peace reigned upon the land.

'Gilgarad did as he had been bidden and for three days and nights remained upon the plateau, seeking knowledge from the Harouk gods. A strange peacefulness was upon his soul when he returned. The people declared him King and using the wisdom he had gained, Gilgarad set about creating the foundation of the lives we live today.

'The Harouks returned to their homeland but what became of their people we do not know. Each party sent to find them never returned and so all contact was lost with those brave people. All that remained were the troumaloks, which had been given to Gilgarad in honour of his victory. Those beasts he freed, for under his rule no man was to be mastered, no creature enslaved; and we live that way today.

'This arras,' Cail concluded, pointing to the one which interested T'skya, 'symbolises the Harouks' gods and the darkness in which we lived before we were freed by them.'

'Who were these gods?' T'skya asked quietly.

'No-one knows. Only the King, his heir and the one known as the Communicator possessed knowledge of them. And now that knowledge is lost,' he replied sadly. 'So, you have heard the tale, though I feel I have disgraced it. I wished not to tell it and have not told it as I should. My words did not do it justice.'

T'skya stared at the arras. 'I needed to know, don't ask me why, but I thank you for it.'

❧

Time passed and another collection day arrived. The dwellers had laboured to meet Slythe's demands, but the required provisions were gathered and laid out for inspection as usual. The flurry of activity ceased with the hope Slythe would be satisfied with their efforts. If he believed the taxes were supplied too easily he might increase them. If he deemed their efforts too poor they would be punished. Heedless of the taxes, his venom was ignited by Raven's continued absence.

With Hollam banned from Slythe's presence Tarn bore the brunt. In a petulant outburst Slythe swung his weapon at the unarmed man and struck Tarn heavily in the face. The blow left a deep cut under Tarn's left eye which bled profusely and required some of Negram's delicate needlework to staunch the flow. Tarn held the cynical belief the Kházakha disliked his face; this was the second time they had assaulted it in a matter of months.

Apart from that, little of interest broke the mundane routine of the dwellers. Briar regained most of her strength but refused to take over any former responsibilities and spent most of her time in her burrow. The scouts, foragers and weavers went about their business as usual and T'skya set about analysing the enclave's flora.

She found the abundance and variety of plant life fascinating.

That anything was remotely familiar still perplexed her. Statistically the evolutionary path should have created something utterly different, but she was not going to complain. The more she studied the more she came to understand the bio-diversity and the ecological balance the dwellers fought so hard to maintain.

T'skya soon took a particular interest in the fungi which seemed to grow in every accessible nook and cranny the forest provided. There were beautiful spotted fungi, red and shiny, standing proud like soldiers at the bases of trees. Brown, sweet smelling fungi fanned from trunks, their serrated bellies in black and tan, and delicate, white, bell-shaped fungi clustered on the forest floor in crowds. Then there were the golden puff balls hidden in the ferns waiting to set free their spores and the stinking trumpets lurking in the damp rotting wood of trees long dead. T'skya analysed them all.

One afternoon she came across a small nondescript toadstool that really caught her interest. As she broke the plant into its component parts it revealed some fascinating qualities. When she asked Negram about it the old lady laughed.

'What interests you so in that common thing? We seldom have use for it except to aid with sleep.'

T'skya furrowed her brow. 'Can it knock you out?'

'If you consumed enough of it, I dare say, but not even Hollam has the capacity to manage such a feat.'

T'skya gave the old lady a soft smile and departed, looking extremely thoughtful. Negram shook her head at the youngster's curiosity and settled back to work. The first bite of winter had come upon the land and it was time to prepare for a Knoll's birthday.

When the first frost flowers opened, the celebrations began. Bramble prepared a sumptuous feast of Knoll's favourite food and there was dancing and singing throughout the day. With flowers woven in her hair Breeze enchanted them with Kalkassian storm dance, Hollam and Tarn had them in fits with their clowning and Cail performed a skilful weapons display. Many tales were told and Knoll took delight in recounting stories from his people's history.

Knoll also burst into laughter and tears when he beheld T'skya's gift; a clay sculpture in his likeness. 'You have been kind,' he said, 'for surely this is more beautiful than I have ever been.'

For the whole day the Clan put their cares and fears aside, but T'skya found she could not clear her mind. Wild schemes fluttered inside her head as she tried to find a way to put her knowledge to use. Feigning tiredness, she left the celebrations early and sought the solitude of her burrow.

By morning T'skya had formed a sketchy plan but needed more detailed information from the knowledgeable dwellers. It was with great impatience that she waited for the people to rise from their beds; the revelling had gone on until the early hours and few felt inclined to rise with the sun.

Eventually one or two weary faces appeared in the daylight and set about trying to find the energy to follow the day's routine. T'skya thought it best to wait until they had eaten and regained their strength before burdening them with her questions.

Hollam rose as lunch was being served and looked much the worst for wear. His hair was more tousled than usual and dark rings circled his bleary eyes. He sat hunched over his bowl with one hand clasped to his head and the other clasped to his stomach.

'Too much mead, brother?' Cail asked loudly, chuckling at his sibling's fragility.

Hollam eyed him unhappily and flinched. Breeze stared down at him with her hands on her hips and a wry expression on her face. Feigning disapproval she poured a thick, dark substance from a flagon and slammed it down in front of him. Hollam groaned and reluctantly accepted the unpleasant concoction.

'I think you are trying to poison me,' he said gloomily.

Breeze tutted in disdain. 'I think you have already done that to yourself.'

'Very funny!' Hollam muttered. Then forcing his voice and face to look bright and cheerful, he turned to the approaching Negram. 'Good afternoon, mother.'

'Good afternoon, my son. Well, since you have evidently recovered, Hawk has twisted his ankle, so methinks you shall take his place and lead the next scouting party. Be quick. They are awaiting you.'

T'skya could hardly contain her laughter as Hollam's smile faded into horror. 'Is there no end to my suffering?' he moaned, rising to his feet and eyeing his friends for support. He received none with Negram standing near.

'Thank you all!' he said sarcastically, before shuffling off to put on his gear.

'That boy needs to learn self-control,' his mother said as she seated herself beside T'skya.

'Oh, I don't know,' the young woman replied. 'I think we all need to let go once in a while.'

'Perhaps. But is drinking yourself into a stupor the way to do it?'

T'skya laughed as she remembered her own less than sober experiences on the Mothership. 'Haven't you ever been just a little drunk?' she inquired.

Negram's expression became almost wicked. 'On several occasions,' she admitted, 'but do not tell that to my son!'

<hr />

After lunch, T'skya went to see Tarn. Cail, like his brother, had gone scouting, and Tarn, who had only just had the stitches removed from beneath his eye, had been ordered to have another day's rest before resuming heavy duties. She found him sitting in the sunshine near a hazel thicket, laboriously chipping away at a rough stone which would ultimately become another spear tip. It was skilful work and when done by a craftsman there would be little waste. Many of the chips that fell were sizable and sharp enough to be used as arrowheads. Tarn already had a collection by his feet.

'Would you like to try?' he asked, holding some tools out to her.

'I'll have a go, but I don't think I'll be good at it,' T'skya answered sitting down next to him.

It saddened her that his people had to resort to such measures. She had seen some of the intricate metal work they were capable of in the rare belt buckle or ancient knife handle. But the Kházakha had outlawed Roumanhi use of metals and the punishment was death.

As she chipped away at the stone, careful to avoid the flying splinters which resulted from her less than skilful attempts, she began to dig away at Tarn. 'You know, the Kházakha are my own people and yet I really don't know anything about their lives here.'

'What is there to know?' replied Tarn, evidently uncomfortable with the subject.

'Well, for instance, their city. Who lives there and how is it governed?'

'The majority of the Kházakha live there. Most of the troops you see here have families there and so they rotate after two or three collections. The Section Leaders tend to be unattached so they can remain here longer; they get to know the Clans, and thus control us more easily.

'The city is a stain upon the land, built of stone torn from the earth by slaves. Many Roumanhis live there, either in enforced service to the richer families or in the slave quarter, a perilous place to live. From there our people are taken to the mines and forced to dig for minerals. Their life span is notoriously short.'

'But who is responsible?'

'The Kházakha are ruled by High Lord Procurator Santovin. All the orders come from him. Below him is Commander Travis. He coordinates the military. The Chief of Operations responsible for the mining and tax collections is Slavik.'

'Have you ever been to the city?'

'T'skya, none who have gone to the city have ever returned, at least that I know of, save one.'

T'skya's interest grew. 'Who?'

'A man named Gilgarad.'

'Gilgarad?'

'Not *the* Gilgarad, yet a man of equal might who resides in the forest to the north of us at Vinewood. He is unusual for our race.'

'In what way?' she asked, pleased that Tarn was being so forthcoming.

Tarn paused and swallowed heavily. Looking grim he answered; 'He does not fear to kill. He seems to have developed a taste for it.'

'Do you know him?'

Tarn stopped what he was doing and laid his tools on the ground. Then he faced her squarely, his brown eyes glittering with emotion. 'Yes, I know him. He is my cousin.'

'Your cousin! Then why isn't he here?'

'We are not close. He is a difficult man to get along with. I dislike his savagery and he despises my compassion. But in a fight there is no other man I would rather have by my side.'

T'skya pressed on, hoping the pull as much information from him as she could before he tired of the subject. She could sense she was entering sensitive areas but his answers were fascinating. 'What about the rest of your family? Why haven't you ever got married?'

Tarn's posture and expression sagged and his eyes became dull. It was as if all his energy and joy was draining from him. 'Many of the people you see here have been, or still are married; though we use not that word. We call it bonding. When a man comes of age and joins with a woman, there is also a spiritual bond that remains for all time.'

'I don't understand,' T'skya interrupted.

Tarn sighed and picked at the ground, looking even more uncomfortable. 'We are not like you. Our males reach a certain age and change within. They become capable of bonding. Cail and Raven are not bonded because they lay together before the change came upon him. It is our misfortune that until we meet the one we wish to unite with, we must lie alone once we have reached the age of maturity. Hollam's time came early; he has waited many years for someone like Breeze. It is difficult for him as the call to bond is strong and not easily overcome. Cail has waited little more than a year by your terms; it is different for each of us. But once we have chosen and lain together, we become as one, sensing each other's emotions and needs when near, and ever aware of the other's life-force.'

'What if you choose badly? Can the bond be broken?'

'The breaking of this bond can only be granted by the Clanmeet and then only broken by the few skilful enough to master the melding. It is something I have never witnessed nor heard required in my lifetime despite the hardships we face, and it is said to be a dangerous ritual.

'The Kházakha have split up most of the families, taking the men and women and sometimes even the children to work in their houses or mines. My bond-mate, Lily, was taken nine of your years ago. I have not seen her since. Word of her has only come from the city twice since then. I sense she lives yet, and believe she works in the household of Commander Travis - she is luckier than most. I have chosen to remain bonded, for I yet have the hope we will be reunited one day.' Tarn's voice was flat when he spoke. Behind his eyes T'skya could see the pain he was suffering as he thought of his beloved wife so distant and yet so close in his heart.

'Oh Tarn, I'm so sorry. Forgive me for asking.' She knew her words were not enough.

'It is not for you to apologise,' he said softly. 'You are not responsible. You look the same, but they are not your people. You have never raised a hand against us or mocked our simple ways. You are welcome amongst us, T'skya of the Homequest.'

'Not everyone feels that way,' she replied sadly.

'Raven cannot see beyond your face. To her you are a threat, not least because of Cail.'

'But why?' she protested. 'We haven't done anything. We're just good friends.'

'Perhaps,' Tarn replied, 'but is that not also what Hollam says of Breeze?'

T'skya considered Tarn's words and asked hesitantly; 'So this bonding, does it work on other races? Can a match be made?'

Tarn glanced at her face sure the inquiry was not entirely focussed on Hollam. 'It is only the men of Roumanhi who possess the gland for bonding. Our women are free to lie with whom they choose. It is their freedom and their curse for it leaves them vulnerable to the Kházakha who are known to take them by force. The males of this land are forbidden on pain of death to lie with the Kházakha women.'

T'skya frowned. 'Is that your law or theirs?' she asked softly.

'Theirs. They are afraid we will weaken their bloodlines and their hold over us. The bonds are too strong for them to break. Mixed birth children would also be an effrontery. It is doubtful that such a bonding would ever occur with or without the law. Would you wish to lie with your enemy? So the answer to your question is yes, we can bond with other races. Breeze could follow her heart's desire and bond with Hollam though no Kalkassian has ever done so before to my knowledge, and you could bond with a Roumanhi male if you chose to flout the law.'

Tarn smiled to himself, picked up his tools and newly-wrought weapon heads and strode off through the trees without another word, leaving T'skya sitting stunned beside a pile of misshapen chips of stone.

❧

T'skya spent the much of the afternoon wandering around the camp feeling half dazed by the realisation that Tarn was right. Her feelings for Cail ran deeper than mere friendship and she sensed he also felt the same, yet whichever way she looked at it she was an alien of enemy race and a bond was surely impossible. Besides, the future was uncertain and they might not survive the coming turmoil if she could make her sketchy plans reality; and there was still the possibility the Mothership might return for her and then...

To momentarily take her mind off these fantasies, T'skya went about extracting information from those who were not too busy to talk. She learnt more about the silver men with eyes of fire which could only have been androids of some kind. Their existence was not a surprise to her; there were plenty on the Mothership programmed for menial chores. What worried her was the suggestion the city androids were programmed for more hostile tasks.

She also learnt about the city's water supply and how the great river, which had meandered like a thick winding ribbon across the plains, had been dammed by the Kházakha, the valley flooded and a dark lake formed behind the mountains to the north-west of the city. This had caused the central plains to grow dry and allowed the desert, which was, as Negram had said, formerly of no consequence, to encroach upon the grasslands with excessive speed. Water was channelled from the lake and kept in huge storage tanks in the foothills north of the city. The excess water produced by the rains and thawing snow in these mountains had been diverted to an artificial lake on the city's south-western side.

It was the storage tanks and the knowledge that all the water consumed by the city's inhabitants came from there which most captured her attention and she retreated to her burrow, spending the remainder of the day and night avidly huddled over her equipment.

❧❦❧

At last, T'skya sat back with satisfaction as she beheld a vial of clear, inconsequential-looking liquid. According to her analyser, it had no particular flavour and was, she hoped, as potent as the machine indicated.

The plan was clear in her mind, but first she needed to ensure it would work. She carried the precious fluid across the enclave to where Negram was instructing Catkin on the fine art of needlework.

T'skya was hesitant to try the experiment in front of the old lady. It was an exceptionally arrogant thing to do and was, without a doubt, unethical. However, she was confident there would be no ill effects on the child.

She greeted the two females and held the cup out to the girl. 'Catkin, I'd like you to try this drink I've made for you. Tell me what you think.'

'What is it? It looks just like water.'

'Just try it. You'll see,' T'skya replied as casually as she could.

Catkin shrugged and downed the lot. A puzzled expression crossed her face. 'It tastes just like water,' she said, and then fell off her chair.

Negram jumped to her feet in alarm.

'She's only asleep,' T'skya said hurriedly. 'I made a solution from that fungus - a sleeping drug. She'll be out for a few hours but there's nothing to worry about; really.'

Negram was about to give T'skya an angry lecture on ethical behaviour when the connotations of what she was doing began to sink in. 'I presume it is a tremendously concentrated potion,' she said.

'One drop in a flagon is more than enough to knock several large men out for a good twelve hours,' T'skya replied eagerly.

'You have a use for this in mind, I suppose.'

'I think you could say that. If the Clanmeet were assembled...'

'It will be done. But T'skya,' the old lady warned, 'no more surprises. I am too old for such shocks.'

T'skya nodded, but could not help smiling brightly. She scooped Catkin into her arms and, cradling her like a baby, took her to the house of healing and laid her on the bed. Breeze was there and looked anguished until T'skya explained what she had done.

As T'skya turned to go, the grey-eyed woman waylaid her. Her face was as pale as her eyes and a deep furrow lay upon her brow like a scar. T'skya had never seen Breeze look so troubled, not even when Hollam was cruelly beaten by Slythe.

'What is it? What's wrong? Is it Hollam?'

'No...yes...T'skya, I do not know what to do. I have grown to love him and would gladly accept him as my bond-mate, but it cannot be. I have chosen another path and I know he will not follow.'

T'skya was surprised and disconcerted. 'What other path?'

'I am returning to my people,' Breeze said sadly.

T'skya was shocked. She liked the woman and knew what her departure would mean to Hollam. 'Why?'

'My time is over here. I came as an apprentice to learn the forest art of medicine and healing to enhance my own skills. He has always known the time would come and thus we fought our feelings but to no avail. But it has come sooner than I expected and I must soon return to share my knowledge with my people.'

T'skya thought for a moment. 'Does Hollam know?'

Breeze lowered her head and studied the ground. 'No, I have not yet found the courage to tell him.'

Not only did T'skya feel desperately sad for them, but she also knew that the timing was bad. She would need Hollam complete and ready, not nursing a broken heart with his mind elsewhere. She sighed a troubled sigh.

Breeze gazed at her with moist eyes. 'You, too, will face this dilemma.'

'Me?'

'I am no more blind than you are. You are in love with Cail.'

T'skya blushed and gave a nervous laugh. 'I wouldn't put it that way exactly.'

'But your feelings do run deep?'

T'skya nodded and quickly changed the subject. 'You must tell Hollam before he hears it elsewhere. That would be too cruel.'

This time it was Breeze's turn to nod. 'I will tell him when he returns from his duties.'

'He has returned. I saw him and Cail before I came here.'

The news did nothing to comfort Breeze. But just as she was about to leave, the signal for the Clanmeet was given. Negram had done her work quickly and arranged for the council without delay. Breeze seemed relieved to have the moment postponed, but T'skya felt a stab of fear run through her. Now it was the opportunity to sell her idea. She had better not fail!

❧

Everyone in the council was gathered in the Clanmeet. Briar took her usual position at the head, which pleased them all immensely, and T'skya took her place beside Knoll. Despite the importance of the meeting, she could not help staring at Hollam as he sat cracking jokes, oblivious of his imminent pain.

The bantering stopped and everyone fell quiet as Briar brought the meeting to order. 'This council has been called by T'skya of the Homequest,' she began, the revelation causing a few eyebrows to be raised. 'I believe she has something of great importance to tell us, but before we commence, I too, have something to say. I have made a decision which many of you will not accept easily. Throughout my life I have had but one goal, one mission to accomplish for the good of the land. I have now fulfilled my obligations and in doing so my purpose here is at an end. I therefore practise the right which is mine alone to resign my position and cede the leadership to one now more worthy than myself.'

Without allowing her to explain, the Clanmeet exploded in uproar. Cail and Hollam caught each other's eyes. They both knew Negram had no desire to take Briar's place. It was several minutes before Briar could continue. 'My good friends, it is inevitable that the old must one day make way for the young. I therefore cede my place to Cail.'

Nobody was more surprised than he. He sat with open mouth, not knowing what to say. Raven sat triumphantly and several others looked pleased although slightly shocked, but Hollam sat glowering. He was the older son and by rights should have been chosen above Cail, and at first the slight stung him badly. But after some reflection he appeared to accept that Briar was right; he had never considered himself a leader of men. Hollam graciously tilted his head in acknowledgement and gave his little brother a brief congratulatory smile. T'skya showed no reaction. She felt that things were leading down dangerous paths.

Briar broke her train of thought with an unsatisfactory explanation for her untraditional choice. 'I have chosen Cail for reasons which will become clear to you, though now is not the time to reveal them. Now that my work is done I shall be leaving you soon. I have been offered a haven by the people of Kalkassa, the Great Divide, and shall leave to take my place with them seven moon rises from today.'

Her news was met with silence until somebody asked, 'Surely you do not mean to venture on such a journey by yourself? The way is long and fraught with danger.'

Briar raised a placatory hand. 'I shall not travel alone.' T'skya longed to interrupt. Her heart sank to her boots when she realised where the conversation was leading; but the words came out of Briar's mouth too soon. 'Breeze has offered to escort me and I have accepted.'

T'skya bit her lip in dismay. Hollam's head snapped up as if he had been shot. 'NO!' he cried, lurching to his feet like a drunk. Hands quickly took hold of him and pulled him to the ground before he could cause harm. 'No!' he mumbled in utter distress. 'Why did she not tell me?'

'Hollam,' Briar said forcefully. 'I am sorry. I assumed you already knew. We all have our paths to follow and sometimes they are hard. Accept what must be.'

'I must go to her!' he insisted. 'I must stop her.'

'No, you must not. You cannot change anything. You must stay and do your duty to the land. You will have time to say all that you intend, but now is not that time. You are too emotional to see things rationally and I would not have you say anything that you might regret.'

Hollam was forced to obey and sat like a dead one staring morosely at the ground. He did not move for the remainder of the meeting or give much indication that he heard a word spoken.

Briar shook her head sadly and motioned to Cail to take her place. She bowed to the company and left them to their discussion. Her absence weighed heavily and Cail felt awkward in her place. He ached for his brother and longed to comfort him, but his duties forbade it.

He called the meeting to order again and opened the floor to T'skya. She hardly had the heart to begin but knew she might not get a second chance if she failed to impress them now.

'When I first sat here, it was as your prisoner and not as your friend. I was asked my intentions and I chose to side with you. I was asked for my aid and I agreed. Now, having lived amongst you for these past months, I'm finally in a position to give you the help you wanted.

'Over the last few days I've made a discovery using the equipment we recovered from my ship which should allow us to overcome the Kházakha with the minimum of force and without engaging in a prolonged war. What I'm about to tell you is the basis of my scheme. I'm not a strategist so I want you to look at my idea logically and without any personal prejudices and tell me whether it will work or if there's a better solution.'

She had begun forcibly and her opening remarks had captured their attention. She believed the plan was not only plausible but ingenious, but as she related her ideas as simply as she could and noted the dwellers' reactions, she began to lose confidence. Some stared at her in dumb amazement, others shook their heads, and one or two winced. Cail looked surprised but Hollam showed no reaction. Only Tarn, who knew Gilgarad's character, and Negram, who had seen evidence of the drug's potency, showed any favourable signs.

T'skya's scheme basically fell into three stages:

Firstly, to rally the forest dwellers into an army under Gilgarad's leadership, just as Caelcáladrim had done in ancient times, to fight the Kházakha troops stationed in the countryside who would be unaffected by her plan for the city.

Secondly, to infiltrate the city's slave quarter; spread the word and be ready to launch an assault against those unaffected by the third stage of her plan, which was to subdue the Kházakha in the city by adding the potent sleeping drug to the water storage tanks. In this way she hoped enough Kházakha could be vanquished without needing to fight and risk the shedding of blood. Any soldiers unaffected could be overcome quickly with the help of the forewarned slaves.

With the Kházakha out of the picture, the Roumanhis would have access to the arms supply and would undoubtedly find weapons capable of destroying the dangerous city androids if they needed to.

When T'skya finished her speech it was met by protracted silence. Much their surprise, Hollam was the first to speak up. *So he has been listening after all*, she thought.

'If you are looking for volunteers, you may consider me the first,' he said grimly.

'We are not sending anyone on a suicide mission!' Cail snapped, his anguish for his brother making his tone harsh.

'And I was not suggesting it!' Hollam growled, as close to anger with Cail as T'skya had ever seen him. 'Her plan has merit, though you are too much in love with yourselves to see it. Ask yourselves this; what do I love more, the land or my life? In all my years I have never heard one of you suggest a solution which even had the slightest chance of success. Now we have been presented with one and you balk at it. You are afraid to kill or be killed. Well, I am no longer afraid. If anyone goes, I will go.'

'We have not decided one way or the other, brother,' said Cail softly; disturbed by Hollam's tirade. 'There is much to consider. It would be folly to accept the scheme merely because it is the only one we have, just as it would be folly to dismiss it because it presents difficulties.'

Tarn then appealed to speak. 'Even if we accept, it is of little consequence without cooperation. I should not assume my cousin's reaction, but it is not in his nature to refuse a challenge and if any man can raise an army, it is he. Most Clans have skilled fighters amongst them, just as we do, and with the right leadership and the right weapons, what T'skya suggests might be possible. I would be willing to approach Gilgarad if the council so decides.'

Raven was the next to speak and T'skya was astonished by her words. 'It is no secret that I have not always seen eye to eye with T'skya, but I am a warrior and my sword arm itches for conquest. I do not balk at death. I, for one, will fight.'

Cail intervened. 'We are running ahead of ourselves. Do not forget who we must conquer. It is all very well to agree to something we are not yet facing. The key is: how will we set about doing it?'

'As I see it,' Tarn said, 'forming an army is possible if it is only the troops in the forest that we must subdue. My main concern is how to infiltrate the city without being captured or slain.'

'Perhaps we ourselves need not go. We need only get a message there. The people themselves will spread it,' Wolf added.

'Many know people who have been enslaved,' Hawk continued, 'and each three full moons another slave transport is taken to the city. We would only need to put a person on the slave ship or pass a message to one who will be taken.'

'But we never know who will be chosen,' objected Ferret. 'How could we guarantee that a message would get through?'

'Nothing can ever be guaranteed,' said Badger, 'but it sounds plausible to me.'

'When is the next transport due to leave?' T'skya asked.

'In less than two full moons,' Fen replied. 'The transports of slaves will coincide with the transport of taxes.'

T'skya was surprised, not only by the answer but by the fact that Fen had deigned to speak. It was the first time they had really conversed since her arrival. Was it a sign he was accepting her at last?

'Is there any way we can ensure someone will be chosen?' she continued.

Nobody spoke for some moments. T'skya got the impression that if there were a way, it was not a pleasant one.

'I think I could arrange it,' Raven said at last. 'I have people in the city that would care for me. I could get a message through.'

'How?' T'skya asked.

'That need not concern you. You have asked us to trust you. Perhaps you should do likewise.'

There was something in Raven's eyes which made the hair stand up on the back of T'skya's neck. She could not put a finger on what was bothering her, however, and let the matter drop when Knoll began to speak.

'The city is a long trek from here. How do you intend to reach it and how will you drug the water? The storage area will not be unguarded.'

'We'll get there on a transport ship, unless anyone knows a better way. As for the water, I won't know until I get there,' T'skya admitted.

'Remember also,' Badger said, 'the last Clan which tried to poison the Kházakha failed. They laced their taxes and made several Kházakha sick. The dwellers were executed one by one. What makes you think we will succeed where they failed?'

'The drug is efficient,' Negram said. 'I have seen it work.'

'Yes,' T'skya added, 'and remember, everyone uses water. Everybody drinks in the morning. This drug has no smell, no taste and no colour, and it acts almost instantly. There won't be anyone left awake to retaliate; not if the rest goes according to plan.'

'And if it does not?' Badger asked.

'Then we will face the bloodiest battle in our history!' replied Cail grimly. He waited for his words to sink in before continuing. 'There is much we have to consider. Even if we agree to attempt this scheme, there is nothing we can do without the cooperation of others. Still, it is a weighty decision and I will not rush into it. This meeting is adjourned until sunrise tomorrow. Consider it well.'

When the meeting was adjourned the people formed into small groups avidly discussing the plans. Cail refused to be dragged into further conversation and T'skya left him alone. Hollam slipped away.

He was, as T'skya guessed, going to confront Breeze. It would not be an easy time for either of them. Beneath his rugged, happy-go-lucky exterior, Hollam was the most emotional man T'skya had ever met. The news had devastated him. Cail was different although no less attractive. He was cooler, calculated, honourable to a fault and yet still retained an inner warmth and compassion that was especially evident where his family was concerned. Now he stood watching his brother disappear and his posture betrayed his sympathy.

It was going to be a long night.

EIGHT

Gilgarad

Day dawned overcast and cold. The council gathered in the Clanmeet and everyone looked tired and listless. Nobody had slept well, and some had not slept at all. Hollam, in particular, looked dishevelled. His hair had not been brushed, he had not changed his clothes and dark rings circled his bleary eyes. Whatever he and Breeze were discussing had clearly not been resolved.

Cail soon called the meeting to order. 'We all know why we are gathered here so I will delay no longer. Let us cast the vote.'

In the centre lay only six smooth stones. Some of those who had seemed to favour the idea the previous day had evidently changed their minds during the night. The vote tied, the final decision now lay with Cail.

He stared at the pile grimly; his mind foggy and the burden of responsibility lying heavily upon him. He was about to make one of the most important decisions of his young life. Thoughts ran wild and he struggled to bring semblance of order to his over-taxed brain.

When Cail eventually spoke his voice was solemn and he hid the sickness in his stomach like a professional. 'As head of the

Clanmeet, I now use the right to weigh the balance. I do not say this lightly but I think we should liberate our people.'

Now that he had cast his vote there was no going back on it and those who had voted against the scheme had no choice but to accept it. T'skya sat back with a relieved sigh. Raven was showing her teeth; she could already see the blood dripping from her sword, and Hollam bowed his head in sad resignation.

'Tarn,' Cail said abruptly, 'I do not like the idea of sending you from here when you are our spokesman, but since you stand the best chance of procuring Gilgarad's aid, I elect you for the task. The more time he has to organise the people of the land, the better. I advise you to leave as soon as possible. You may take another with you if you deem it wise, but do not delay in Vinewood; we have need of you here.

'T'skya, I leave the drug and its preparation in your hands.

'Raven, I will not risk your going to the city alone, whether you will find shelter there or not. There are almost two moons until the transport leaves. In that time you must come to me with a workable strategy. I will not allow you to chance your life on a fool's errand.' Raven's eyes flashed like burning coals. She was about to protest when Cail cut her off. 'That is my final word.'

Raven closed her mouth grudgingly. She blamed T'skya for his distrust.

Cail continued; 'The rest of you will have much work to do once we have heard from Gilgarad. However, I wish our decision to go no further than this Clanmeet until his aid has been confirmed. I suggest we resume normal routine accordingly.'

He called the meeting to a close and the council members headed off for breakfast. Hollam shuffled along as if the smell of the freshly baked bread had hypnotised him and taken control of his legs. T'skya followed behind him with Cail.

'I'm worried about him,' she said quietly. 'I've never seen

him so despondent.'

'As am I. I too have never seen him like this.'

'Have you talked to him?'

'I have tried and so has Tarn. He would not discuss it.'

'I'll talk to Breeze after breakfast,' she suggested.

❦

With breakfast over, everyone except Raven and Tarn went about their normal duties. Tarn had chosen the warrior to accompany him that afternoon on the three day trek to Vinewood, rejecting the tunnels in favour of the forest. Their path, however, would take them close to a Kházakha's camp, unless they chose to make a wide diversion. They were still arguing about the merits of each choice when T'skya went to find Breeze.

She found her in the house of healing. The Kalkassian was weeping. T'skya rushed to her side to console her. 'Don't cry. Everything will be all right,' she whispered tenderly.

'He will not listen to reason,' Breeze sobbed, 'and I am so afraid!'

T'skya felt her stomach tighten. 'Of what?'

'He has told me of your plan. He is going to get himself killed.'

'What makes you say that?' T'skya asked, becoming afraid for the kind hearted rogue.

'He told me that I am his life and without me he has no reason to live.'

'Oh Breeze, he loves you so much he'd say anything to stop you from leaving. He wouldn't throw away the chance of seeing you again by doing anything foolish. You're only going to be away for a while, aren't you?'

Breeze hung her head and said nothing.

'You are coming back?' T'skya asked sharply.

Breeze shook her head. 'I was born of the sea. It is where I belong. I did not come here looking for love; it is not our way to mix our blood and yet when I beheld him my heart was sorely tried for I knew he could capture it completely. T'skya, I have wronged him. I should have sought my home when I saw his passion and thus would he be free. There are many reasons why I cannot return here; too many to mention.'

'Breeze, love doesn't come in a package. It can't be opened when you choose or shut away when it gets difficult. Hollam shines when he is with you, and you positively glow. If it is meant to be then he will go to you.'

Breeze smiled a sad resigned smile. She understood the divide between their people and knew it was not so simple. 'T'skya, he was born of the forest. It would destroy him to leave the trees. Our people are not like yours. We cannot change our ways so readily.'

'You're wrong, Breeze, so wrong,' T'skya said forcefully. 'Love is much stronger than that. You're doing yourself an injustice by believing this. If you truly love each other, you will find a way.'

'If we were bonded I might agree with you, but he has refused me. Hollam knows the offer was not lightly made; it goes against tradition and the wishes of my father. He said he could not cause dishonour or bear to bond when we will soon be parted. I told him that if we bonded we would always be together, no matter what distance lay between us. It was then he scared me, for he said he would not leave me halved! I cannot fully sense what he intends, but I fear for him.'

T'skya thought for a moment. 'Tarn's his best friend and knows about such things. Perhaps if I spoke to him?'

'Tarn will have left before Hollam returns.'

'Then I'll speak to Hollam.'

'Thank you, but I do not believe you will reach him. What lies between us cannot be resolved. I just wish him safe,' Breeze answered in distress.

T'skya forced strength into her voice. 'I still have to try.'

❦

T'skya would have to wait several hours before Hollam returned from foraging. Cail had not trusted his alertness to risk sending him further afield on a scouting mission. It was a tense time for T'skya as she contemplated his return.

She was due to join a scouting team in the late afternoon, but Cail had also changed this. He wanted her to concentrate on the fungi, even though he could not guarantee it would get used for its intended purpose. And so, since the sun had decided to show its face and brighten the day, and since she could do nothing to help Breeze until Hollam's return, she chose to gather her equipment from her burrow and head for the outside world.

She saw Cail approaching and wondered if he had come to object to her working in the open, but he was simply interested in learning everything he could. He also seemed in need of conversation. He was not finding it easy to adapt to his sudden promotion. 'How fared you with Breeze?' he asked.

'Not well, I'm afraid.' She did not wish to burden him further and refrained from mentioning the details of their conversation. 'I'm going to try talking to Hollam when he returns.'

'I wish you luck. He was not willing to open himself to me.'

T'skya placed a consoling hand upon his arm. 'I'll do my best. When are Tarn and Raven leaving?'

'Shortly, if they can agree on a route. I hope I will not be forced to choose between them, for I favour Tarn's. Raven is already, shall we say, displeased with me. I would not wish to further her blame.'

'This Gilgarad, do you think he'll agree to it?'

'I hardly know the man, but he is an exceptional warrior. I do not think he will refuse the chance to put his knowledge and instincts to use.'

They were then distracted as Catkin bounded towards them. She seemed none the worse for wear after her enforced sleep and was unconcerned by the fact that she had been unconscious for nearly six hours. Seeing T'skya's equipment for the first time, she was filled with curiosity and could not resist inspecting everything. The conversation between T'skya and Cail was brought to an abrupt end by the stream of questions that flowed from her small mouth and T'skya answered as best she could, wary of revealing too much.

Cail seated himself on the ground and watched her carefully from under his brows. His intense gaze made T'skya nervous but she managed to satisfy the sharp-minded child.

'You are so clever, T'skya. Cail thinks you are clever and wonderful too,' she said dancing around him.

T'skya smiled coyly and turned her face away, embarrassed.

Cail gallantly tried to rescue T'skya from her squirming. 'Catkin, is it polite to talk to a lady so? You have caused her embarrassment and should apologise.'

Catkin stood stock still when his words reached her ears. All signs of celebration ceased and a worried, almost horrified look came upon her face. 'I did not mean to make you upset. You will not tell Briar, will you?'

T'skya cast a reproachful look in Cail's direction, silently chastising him for frightening the child. 'It's all right. I'm not angry with you, though I am going to speak to Briar and tell her how friendly and helpful you've been and that you can talk to me whenever you want.'

The change in Catkin's disposition was immediate and she bounded off into the forest singing to herself.

'Now you are asking for trouble,' Cail chuckled. 'Giving Catkin free permission to talk is akin to asking Hollam to taste your supper!'

T'skya laughed and slumped down next to him. 'If you hadn't upset her I wouldn't have needed to cheer her up.'

'You are too kind-hearted, Green-Eyes. It will cause you naught but trouble, though I would not have you change. There is now too little kindness in this world.'

'Do you think it will work, our plan I mean?' she asked suddenly.

'If it does not, then we are lost.'

Their train of thought was interrupted by the news that Tarn and Raven were about to depart. T'skya and Cail took deep breaths and climbed to their feet. Lost in their own thoughts they walked towards the Clanmeet, where everyone had gathered for the farewells.

It was commonly believed Tarn and Raven were going to visit some of the neighbouring enclaves to gather news of the Kházakha and keep relations strong between the Clans. Some dwellers were surprised by Raven's inclusion; she was hardly their greatest diplomat, but they supposed it was to keep her safe from Slythe and that her survival skills would be an asset on the march.

Uncharacteristically, Raven had accepted Tarn's route, sparing Cail the task of over-ruling her. He embraced them both and kissed them on their brows but said little as they prepared to depart. Tarn whispered a few words in his ear and Cail nodded in reply. 'I will tell him.'

❧

In the early evening, T'skya sought out Hollam. She waited until after he had washed and rested a little before locating him by one of the bathing ponds on the outer reaches of the enclave. It was a place he was accustomed to visit when he needed time to think.

He did not appear to notice her approach despite her heavy footfalls, and jumped at her touch. Such inattention at the edge of the enclave could reap terrible results. Disturbed by his behaviour, T'skya found herself unexpectedly angered and all thoughts of a gentle approach vanished.

'Why are you doing this?' she snapped.

Hollam seemed genuinely puzzled. 'What am I doing?'

'You know what I'm talking about. Why are you hurting us?'

'I am not hurting anyone,' he replied glumly, keeping his eyes averted from her harsh stare.

'No? Well, I'm hurting, and Cail, so is Tarn and your mother, not to mention what it's doing to Breeze. You won't talk to us or let us help you. Don't tell me you don't need help,' she blurted, pointing an accusing finger at him.

Hollam hung his head and ran his hands through his dark shaggy hair. 'Have you spoken to Breeze?'

'Yes. She's frightened for you Hollam. She thinks you've given up on life.' She peered at him intently; 'Have you?'

'I said many empty words. She need not fear,' he replied flatly.

'She also said you refused her because you would not leave her halved. Were they just empty words or don't you really love her?'

For a moment, T'skya thought she had gone too far. Hollam stood abruptly as if to leave, his face clouded with anger, but then let out a heavy sigh and sat back down. 'I suppose it does deserve some explanation,' he said wearily. 'Please understand, our personal lives are meant to be just that, personal, and to talk of them is not easy and is not something I do readily. I refused Breeze not because I do not love her, but because I love her too much. She is a *Jaidus*.'

T'skya was confused. It was not a word she recognised.

'A *Jaidus* is a rarity amongst the Kalkassians. They are empaths and feel emotions more deeply than we can fathom, though I understand they have learnt to shield themselves to some degree. If I were to bond with her, she would always feel what I feel tenfold to a normal bonding: my fears, my joys, my pain, my death. I would not be able to shield her from it. I will not put her through such torment when I cannot foretell the future. This plan of yours has too many risks. I will not have her be one with me only to lose me.'

T'skya was stunned. She had no idea that Breeze had such abilities or that her plan would be the cause of so much tribulation. She felt as if she were responsible for all their woes. 'If she weren't a *Jaidus*, would you accept her offer, even though it would mean leaving Roumanhi?' she asked.

'It would grieve me deeply to forsake the forest and my Clan, but for her...' He paused unsure of his thoughts. A passion entered his face, intense and powerful. 'My desire for her fills my blood. I can hardly contain my hunger; it is a growing fever in my mind. The change came upon me long ago and consumes me.'

T'skya had not expected him to be so forthcoming but she could almost feel the hormones raging in him, desperate to be assuaged. She found she was flattered by his openness rather than embarrassed by it. 'Have you told her this?'

'I have not.'

'Why not?'

'I was too angry and proud, and also too fearful. I have always known that she would return to the Great Divide and yet I hoped she would stay. I cannot blame her; she is of great importance to her people. I was too stubborn to admit it though, or even to think about leaving my homeland to be with her. But I cannot expect her to do what I am not prepared to do myself, yet I cannot contemplate my life without her.'

T'skya could see a change coming upon him as he pondered his dilemma. It was as if years were lifting off his face. 'So you would go to her when all this is over? You would leave the forests?' she probed.

'T'skya, I would leave my body if I could be with her.'

'Then what are you waiting for?' she asked, urging him to go.

'Nothing,' he cried with a giant grin and bounded off

through the trees, calling out Breeze's name even before she was in earshot.

T'skya did not really comprehend what she had done or said to cause such a reversal but she could not help feeling very pleased with herself. Later, when supper was called, she was happy to see Hollam and Breeze looking more relaxed in each other's company. The sadness of the forthcoming departure still cast a shadow upon them but there was also a new strength, a new resolve in their faces. Hollam's change of heart had given them a chance.

When Breeze saw T'skya she rushed to her and squeezed her hand. The light in her eyes and smile on her face conveyed more gratitude than words could ever have done.

Cail also seemed in a buoyant mood now that his brother had recovered somewhat and spent the meal chatting contentedly. He was also more outgoing with T'skya and planted a grateful kiss upon her cheek in view of the Clan. T'skya was startled by his impulsive action, and more than a little pleased.

The meal over, Cail announced his new schedule for weapons practice. Nobody objected to their inclusion, but many were surprised. Cail had to offer some sort of explanation for this change; combat-training was usually only performed by the scouts. Now he was asking some of the foragers and weavers, the animal tenders and teachers to participate. He did not relish deceiving his people despite his wish for secrecy. Briar was watching him carefully, adding to the pressure, but he rose to the occasion well.

'You may be wondering why I have taken this decision. Rumours have come of plans afoot in the north and we may be called upon to fight. Although unlikely at this time, I would not have us unprepared. You all received basic training in your youth, but many of you have not touched a weapon since. It is time to reacquaint yourselves.'

Clever, T'skya thought to herself. He did not lie and yet did not tell the truth. He was proving himself a worthy politician.

❧

The following morning, T'skya found herself in a group wielding swords and spears and firing arrows at targets made of matted reeds. Although she had done basic training in hand to hand combat and the use of fire-arms on board the Mothership, she had never used weapons requiring such skill to master.

She had been given a light, blunt sword for ease and to prevent injury through unskilled use. Cail demonstrated some simple thrusts and parries and counted time while they copied his moves. The sword felt awkward to begin with and rubbed the skin from her hands, but once T'skya began to get the hang of it she started to enjoy herself. When they had mastered a few basic strokes, he allowed them to fence with one another. Cail, of course, chose T'skya as his partner and in one stroke had disarmed her and put his blade to her throat.

'That was not nice,' she grumbled, retrieving her sword.

'Combat never is. Try again.'

This time she was more prepared and managed to counter his first attack, but within seconds he had his blade only inches from her abdomen.

'You are not chivalrous,' she complained.

'Would you have me let you win before my students?' he asked smiling.

'Would you have me lose?'

'I *am* the instructor,' he said by way of apology.

'Yes, and this student feels tired.'

Cail lowered his sword but he did not allow them rest. Next came work with the spears; how best to hold them, defend with them and throw them, and lastly came the archery.

Cail set up the targets facing away from the Clan and at no great distance from the students. He took a bow and arrow and scored an instant bull. T'skya was the first to try. She followed the procedures with some difficulty and let go. The arrow sailed over the target and landed in the bush behind. She let out a squeak of pain as the bow-string sprang back and caught her arm.

'You must not straighten your arm. Keep it locked at a slight angle and you will suffer no harm. Your release must be smoother; you are snagging it,' Cail instructed. 'Try again.'

She did, and although again missed the target she was closer and her arm remained unhurt. By the time the session had ended, she had managed to hit the target three times, pierce a tree, lose four arrows and break two. Her arms ached, her fingers were sore and Cail was happy with her progress.

'Why do you look displeased? You have done well,' he told her.

'I was worse than all the others put together,' she replied, beating the ground with an arrow.

'Remember, this is not the first time they have done such things. You cannot expect to be perfect.'

'I know,' she said throwing the arrow aside to rub her sore fingers.

'They will harden in time and pain you no more.' He gently took her hands and lightly kissed them.

T'skya felt excited by his touch but withdrew her hands, mumbled a garbled excuse and hastily escaped to her burrow. Cail watched her retreat with a mixture of confusion and amusement. He had not failed to notice the trembling of her body, nor the red flush which had crept across her cheeks, and it pleased him. And Negram, who had been approaching to see how things were faring, had not failed to notice their brief exchange.

Stopping where she was, she waited to see Cail's reaction. He looked startled, but then his face smoothed and he approached her as if nothing had happened. 'Mother,' he said by way of greeting.

'Son,' Negram replied, nodding her head at him. She expected him to stop and speak about what she had witnessed but he continued on his way. Negram decided not to pursue it - for the time being.

❦

A week had passed since Raven and Tarn departed and, as yet, no word had come from them. It was now time for Briar and Breeze to take their leave and start the journey to the Great Divide. It was not a happy time for the dwellers of Wilderwood.

Catkin had been wailing for the past hour and showed no inclination to stop. Bramble kept tight hold of her and promised a million and one things to brighten her mood, but the girl's misery would not relent. Perhaps Hollam would have had more success but he was standing far distant, talking to no-one. He could not face this moment in front of everyone and had already said his goodbyes.

Breeze enveloped T'skya in her arms and pressed a small object into her hand. 'Perhaps you will come and visit my homeland one day,' she whispered hopefully.

'When all this is over, I will come.' T'skya opened her hand and looked at the object, an iridescent blue shell, a symbol of farewell to the people of the sea.

'Take care of Hollam for me. I cannot bear to see his pain.' T'skya cried.

Briar tore herself away from Cail, to whom she had been giving some last minute advice, and nodded that she was ready. It was not easy turning their backs on so many friends and Briar was glad that Negram, like Hollam, had already said goodbye. Soon Briar and Breeze were gone.

The dwellers lingered in the Clanmeet for a short while feeling awkward and upset and resumed their duties with little enthusiasm. Hollam simply stood rooted to the spot, his eyes never leaving the trees. Cail took his arm and quietly guided him away.

❦

News finally came of Raven and Tarn's approach. By early evening, the two weary travellers were within sight of the camp. T'skya did her best to hide her anxiety and stood beside Cail, awaiting a sign. Tarn caught Cail's eye and gave a solemn nod.

Another meeting was abruptly called. Cail chose to hold it in the underground meeting hall since dusk was deepening and there was still the need for privacy. Hollam was doing his best to look cheerful and interested, but his mind was clearly elsewhere. Cail appeared unduly tense; his eyes fixed upon his mother. She looked tired and worn. Briar's departure was already taking its toll and whatever secret they had shared now solely lay upon Negram's shoulders. Briar had been the strong one, lending Negram the strength to withstand the pressures of her knowledge. Now that strength was gone. A constant frown dwelled upon her face and she sat more bowed than usual.

T'skya was too eager to hear the tale to pay much attention to anyone except Raven and Tarn, and she was oblivious to the heightened tension in the room. The arras on the walls gave Tarn and Raven the perfect venue to recount their story.

❦

Raven and Tarn set a rapid pace. The sooner they could reach Gilgarad, the more time they would have to convince him to fight. Their first day's travel, however, was met with some difficulty. The Kházakha were patrolling the forest between Wilderwood and Rowanwood, and it was only due to the Roumanhis' expertise that they managed to pass unseen.

The second day passed without incident except a brief visit

to the blighted enclave Rowanwood where the taxes had been tripled twice in four collections. Raven and Tarn promised to send whatever aid they could.

On the morning of the third day as they approached a wide track known as the Clearway, trouble struck again. Tarn raised his foot and was about to take a step when something cannoned into him, knocking him to the ground. He bit back an alarmed cry when he realised it was Raven. She said nothing, but answered his consternation by jabbing a long flat stick into the ground where he had planned to tread. The leaves exploded as the jaws of an evil animal trap snapped shut, cracking and splintering the wood.

'*Tjakhash!*' he growled angrily, using the closest equivalent to a swear word that the Roumanhis' possessed. '*Tjakhash!*'

The trap would have sliced through his flesh like butter and crushed the bone. An animal would be lucky to die through loss of blood or shock; spared the torture of slow dehydration or having to gnaw its own foot off. Tarn shivered at the thought. 'How did you know?' he asked when he had caught his breath.

'The leaves. They looked unnaturally placed,' Raven answered casually, and then with a snarl added: 'Where there is one, there will be others. They must be destroyed.'

'Raven, we cannot. We have no time and to destroy them could bring dire results on those blamed. Rowanwood has suffered enough.'

'Would you have me leave them and let man or beast be caught?'

'I like it no more than you. These traps are an abomination. They violate all that we believe in but we must beware and consider the consequences.'

'To see and not act makes us as guilty as those who perpetrate the crime. Would you have this on your conscience?'

'I do not wish it,' Tarn replied sadly.

'Then let us at least spring them all. The Kházakha do not

check them regularly. Perhaps we can prevent some innocents from falling prey this day.'

Tarn nodded and found a stick. Together they sprang seven more traps and when they were satisfied the area was clear, went on their way probing the ground ahead. There were sure to be more on the opposite side of the track and indeed they found another five, one of which had already been sprung; its victim lying dead, imprisoned by the steel jaws. It was a young lazat and had been trapped for some time. Its eyes were glazed and dried blood splattered the ground. Flies were busy on the wound, but there was no smell. The cat had not been dead long.

Raven let out a sob and knelt beside the beast, stroking its back. She bowed her head as if in prayer and when she rose her mouth was hard as steel, her eyes like ice. No signs of warmth remained behind their blackness and Tarn flinched at the sight. Only a solitary tear winding its way down her face betrayed her humanity.

'This must stop!' she said in a deathly voice that made Tarn shiver inside. He could sense something menacing in her which if released could be catastrophic. Raven was dangerous, but they had a mission to accomplish and in that he was sure she would triumph.

Gilgarad had no sympathy with weakness. Any sign of it and they would be dismissed from his presence and his mind. He only understood forcefulness, determination and courage, and in those Raven was strong.

They left the lazat where it lay. The Roumanhis did not kill beasts, but neither did they interfere with nature's cycle and saw no wrong in using discarded bones or horns, as Negram's needles had shown. The lazat was dead. They could do nothing for it now, although the thought of its fur being draped over the shoulders of some rich autocrat caused them nothing but revulsion.

By late afternoon they had reached the borders of Gilgarad's domain, Vinewood. It was appropriately named, for here the trees were ancient in years and of majestic girth, laden with creeping vines which gave the place an ominous appearance. Thick coils wound their way around the trunks like pythons, and rooty offshoots dangled from the branches akin to unkempt hair.

Raven's single raised eyebrow conveyed what they were both feeling and they cautiously made their way in to the gloomy interior. The thick foliage and abundance of vines reduced the light penetration significantly and what plants grew beneath were small and scanty, whilst the canopy above provided an ideal hiding place from which to spring a trap. As they moved, their eyes scanned the branches above them.

Despite their caution, they failed to observe green-clad figures lurking in the treetops observing them vigilantly. Without warning, the watchers dropped from their concealment and surrounded the two intruders.

Raven unsheathed her sword with startling speed and adopted a defensive stance, but Tarn put out a forbearing hand and forced her arm to lower.

One of the watchers spoke. 'What brings strangers to these parts? Speak truthfully or be slain.'

Tarn stepped forward with his hands held open and a placatory smile upon his lips. 'Has it been so long, Malvern, that you no longer recognise a friend? And has it become thus that all courtesy has been lost?'

Malvern drew back his hood in surprise. Malvern was about Tarn's age and almost as rugged, but his complexion was even paler, as if he seldom saw the sun. Roumanhis had their own inborn protection from the sun and their naturally light golden skin scarcely darkened with exposure, but Malvern's visage was almost ghostly. He stepped closer, viewing the man from Wilderwood with curiosity and delight. 'Tarn, is that really you?'

'I am none other,' Tarn said with a grin, and the two men

embraced. Raven re-sheathed her sword, although her hand never strayed far from its hilt. She was wary and slow to trust but Tarn's relaxed manner pacified her.

Tarn introduced her to the company. She nodded formally but her expression was not kind. She was still cursing herself for failing to detect the scouts. Her negligence could have cost their lives and Malvern understood her fury. 'Raven, there is no blame. Even our own people cannot see us amongst these trees unless forewarned of our presence.'

She pouted, deliberating his statement.

'It is not wise for us to remain here,' Malvern continued. 'I take it this is not a social call and so will provide guidance to the Clanmeet. I cannot escort you, but Dell and Birch will see you safely there. I shall expect a full account of you, my friend, when we meet again.' They clasped each other's hands to their brows and bade farewell.

Dell and Birch led the Wilderwood pair away and the scouts scaled the trees and disappeared from view. Birch flashed Raven a brief smile. She was heartened to be in the company of another female warrior; there were too few in the land. Raven felt nothing at the sight. Gender was irrelevant provided you could fight. Her coldness did not escape Birch, but the woman from Vinewood was not offended. She knew only too well the effects their present way of living could have and did not judge her badly.

Raven and Tarn were led on a winding path towards the camp and their journey was slow. Security was tight and they were forced to go through many check-points. Although no mention was made of his blood-bond to Gilgarad, Tarn's friendship with Malvern ensured their safe passage.

Messages were relayed ahead and, when they finally arrived, a group of people had gathered to meet them. Tarn looked about anxiously for Gilgarad but he was not in sight. A wizened old man shuffled towards them. He was older than Negram and needed the support of a stick to walk yet, despite his bent spine, he still surpassed Tarn in size. His eyes were bright amidst the folds of skin. 'Tarn, be welcome. Your coming is a joy to me,' he croaked.

'Greetings uncle Galdim,' Tarn said bowing deeply. 'It has been a long time.'

'Too long,' the old man replied, shaking his head. 'I began to believe you had forgotten me.'

'Forget you? Never! But times are hard and my duties are many.'

'This young woman and you have not come to please an old man, I see. It is Gilgarad you no doubt require.' Galdim shakily raised his stick in the direction of a large sapling house, grander than any in Wilderwood. 'He is within.'

Tarn bowed and taking Raven by the arm propelled her towards the house. She needed no encouragement; she was eager to meet the man of valour and gently released herself from Tarn's grip.

Tarn did not wait for permission to enter the house. He swung the portiere aside with vigour and strode in. Raven also ducked boldly under the blanket and came face to face with the man they had journeyed to meet.

Gilgarad was more impressive than she had imagined and the force of his presence made her take a step backwards. He did not deign to stand but she could tell that he was nearly a head taller than Hollam, who was the tallest member of Wilderwood. His girth made even Badger seem puny and his bare, muscular arms were covered by a network of scars; permanent reminders of battles fought.

But it was his face that consumed her gaze. It held the image of great struggle and undauntable will. His greying hair was tied into a tight pony-tail and his brow was deeply furrowed. His nose had obviously suffered serious assault and was twisted and flattened, partially covered by an eye-patch. Deep scars lined his cheeks and a ragged one ran vertically down the length of his face. His good eye looked at them with relative disinterest and, despite not having seen Tarn for several years, he dispensed with all greetings and got straight down to business.

'Who is she?' he demanded in a voice that betrayed the refinement of his upbringing.

Without allowing her companion the time to answer, Raven haughtily introduced herself. 'I would that you spoke with the respect my position demands, for I am Loukhala Ravenwood, council member and warrior of the enclave Wilderwood, and I am neither daunted by your bulk nor your reputation.'

Her fearless disregard caused Gilgarad's mouth to curve into a lop-sided smile. 'I see you are keeping better company these days, Tarn.'

'And I see that your hospitality is, as ever, none existent. We have travelled far. Will you not have us sit?' Tarn snapped in reply to his cousin's snide remark.

Gilgarad shrugged and gestured to the bench opposite him. Tarn and Raven sat and stared across the broad table separating them, glancing at the piles of paper littering the top. Gilgarad did not miss the direction their eyes had taken but did not attempt to hide what was there. He knew they could not read.

'Literacy has its advantages,' he said, waving a massive hand at the table.

Tarn shrugged dismissively and did not reply.

'You do not approve,' Gilgarad said, but Raven had a different point of view.

'Anything giving advantage over the Kházakha is desirable,' she said.

Gilgarad leant his arms on the table and brought his giant face close to hers. 'On that we agree. Now, I am a busy man. Speak your mind or leave me to my work.'

Raven did not even glance at Tarn for approval before speaking. In a steady voice she told him of their plans, neglecting only the existence of T'skya and her Navennán apparatus.

Gilgarad listened carefully with no hint of an expression. When she finished, he sat back and sucked a lungful of air between his teeth.

'That was well spoken, but not complete. Do not hold back if you expect my help. A warrior I may be, but that does not mean I will blindly take up any fight that comes my way. You must either trust me with all or with none.'

Raven was perplexed. She was not prepared to reveal T'skya without Tarn's permission. If things went amiss the residents of Wilderwood would be sure to hold her responsible and accuse deliberate betrayal.

'Is this house secure?' Tarn asked at length.

Gilgarad raised an eyebrow. 'Naturally.'

Tarn was taking a great deal of responsibility on to himself, but seeing Gilgarad's impatience, told of T'skya's arrival and her part in the scheme. His cousin's eye widened at the news and he almost seemed impressed. And then he smiled. It was the only similarity he had with Tarn. But it did not last long and was soon replaced by his usual stern exterior.

'I think I would like to meet this T'skya,' he said slowly, adding; 'I also have someone I think you should meet.'

Tarn and Raven exchanged glances. Gilgarad stood and revealed his full stature. He was a veritable Goliath and suddenly the room seemed unusually crowded. He squeezed under the blanket and strode across the camp. His pace was unhurried but Tarn and Raven had to scramble to match his long stride.

He led them to a trap-door and they all dropped below ground. Being tall clearly had its disadvantages and Raven was interested to see that an extra channel had been carved into the roof of the tunnel. He led them through a series of passageways, coming to a halt in front of a door covered by a brown drape. He moved aside to let his visitors enter.

Tarn allowed Raven to precede him and she stepped into the room beyond. Before Tarn was even halfway through the door he saw Raven draw her sword with a cry of alarm and advance on a very startled looking man who was hastily backing towards the rear of the room.

It was a Kházakh!

Tarn reached for his weapon but Gilgarad's roar of laughter waylaid him. 'Put away your weapon, my pretty warrior. You are frightening my guest,' he told Raven, who was now holding her blade against the terrified man's throat. Raven eased the pressure fractionally, but did not re-sheath her sword.

'Satisfy my curiosity and I might obey,' she hissed.

'The man you wish to slay is a deserter and our ally. He has lived amongst us for six full moons and has served us well. Now, release him before I lose patience.'

This time Raven did as she was told. The man touched his neck and wiped away the thin trail of blood from where the tip of her blade had pierced his skin. 'Perhaps next time you should warn newcomers, Gilgarad. I do not enjoy your little games,' he said in awkwardly pronounced Roumanhi.

'What, and spoil my fun, Prell? Never,' the giant grinned.

Prell shook his head and stepped warily past the flame-haired woman. He sat on a low stool and looked at his friend sourly, switching to his own tongue. 'I'm not on exhibition, Gilgarad.'

'Where is your sense of humour, Prell?'

'Seeping away with my blood!' he answered bitterly. 'I presume you have a reason for bringing these people here, other than to see me suffer?'

'Oh, indeed I do. I think you will find their news of the utmost interest.'

Prell looked curiously at the pair as they seated themselves opposite him. Gilgarad remained standing with his arms folded across his mountainous chest. Tarn hesitated, doubtful. However, since Gilgarad trusted the man he relayed the information clearly and simply. Raven regarded Prell coldly. With their black hair and green eyes they all looked the same to her, but this man was vaguely familiar. He reminded her of Snell.

She pushed these thoughts aside as Prell suddenly lurched to his feet. 'That's ludicrous, impossible! It goes against everything we've ever been taught!'

He was not taking the news of T'skya's existence well.

'It is true, nonetheless,' said Tarn, puzzled by the man's reaction. 'Just what were you taught?'

'That *we* are the native people of the land and that *you* are the invaders. Nobody's ever openly refuted this and no literature or records exist that I know of to prove differently. *Your* people tried to drive us from the land, you slaughtered our young. That's why our leaders retaliated. That's why we rule with such resolute ferocity. Admittedly, it's a notion many of us find difficult to accept; there's too much conflicting evidence, but our laws are strict and anyone caught doubting Santovin's word is swiftly dealt with.

'So please understand my scepticism, it stems from a life-time's indoctrination and, despite the evidence, it's not an easy thing to accept your whole life's been a lie. Won't you tell me more about T'skya and my world,' he appealed.

Tarn had purposely told him little of Navenná and its fate. If Prell knew the whole truth, he might not be so willing to help. Raven also had this worry.

To give her credit, Raven had managed to listen to Prell's speech without sneering, but she could not refrain from showing contempt when she spoke. 'You ask a lot from us and I, for one, am not prepared to answer until I know exactly what it was that made you desert your *master* race.'

Prell knew better than to take offence and answered promptly. 'I couldn't stand watching families being torn apart any longer, seeing the suffering. I was forced to work on a slave ship - those screams have never left my memory. I rebelled, despite Commander Travis's warnings, and took my complaints to Santovin. What a mistake! I was reduced in rank and sent to the mines. There I witnessed the horrors my duties had contributed to. So when the opportunity came I escaped and, knowing me, Gilgarad gave me shelter.'

'It was Prell who brought word of Lily,' Gilgarad added.

'And it was men like Prell who took her!' Tarn reproached.

'Tarn,' Prell said quietly, 'there are many among our people who feel as I do but don't have the will to resist. Our ruler is as harsh with us for failure and weakness as he is with you. Don't judge everyone who commits crimes badly; they just fear for their own lives. My brother Snell is one.'

Raven seemed satisfied with Prell's explanation and, since Gilgarad had accepted him, they decided to give him the benefit of the doubt. The man's face withered with sadness when he learnt of Navenná's plight.

'You bring news of my world and then tell me it's destroyed. You gave me hope and now it's gone. I'll help you all I can; this is now the only home I'll ever have, but it's not as I'd like it to be. I don't want to remain in hiding for the rest of my life. I want to live in peace.'

Raven and Tarn were heartened by the news. Prell was a well of invaluable knowledge and with his help their goals could be accomplished with less guesswork and less risk. Gilgarad, however, had not yet given them a definite decision and was, for the moment, content to listen and absorb information. Savage and brutal as he seemed, he was not devoid of sense and protected his followers with unremitting passion. He also had more patience than his brusque manner of speech implied. These qualities, together with his might and tactical excellence, made him a formidable opponent.

He settled comfortably on the floor, his massive legs stretched out and his back against the hard surface of the wall, and remained a silent observer as the others discussed possibilities like eager children.

Prell sat up attentively. 'Did you say Slythe?'

'Yes,' Raven answered. 'Do you know him?'

'Oh yes, I know Slythe. He was in charge of the mine I helped supervise. His family is influential in the city; that's the only reason he was promoted to troop leader. He's as brainless as he is cruel. You should have no trouble manipulating him. It's the men under him that may cause problems. They won't be as easy to fool.'

'I think we may have fortune on our side there also,' Tarn said. 'Snell is under his command.'

'Snell? That's great. I hadn't thought to see or hear of him again. How is he?'

'He is well, and seems to share your compassion, though Slythe keeps a tight hold on all his men. Snell appears to resent his leader and, of all the Kházakha, he would be the one most easily turned,' Tarn replied.

'He is your brother,' Raven continued. 'Would he do it?'

Prell considered the question deeply before answering. 'We've been apart for a long time and my treachery's brought shame on our family name. But as you say he's my brother and we were close. If you carried a message to him from me, I'm sure he would help you as much as he dared. He lacks courage, but his heart is good.'

'Is there a way you could ensure my safe passage on the transport?' Raven asked.

'How long has Snell been on patrol?'

'Three full moons. The next will be his fourth.'

'Excellent. Then he's due for rotation. That makes things easier. He'd be able to escort you.'

'And Slythe? He has his own personal interest in me,' she said, full of disgust.

Prell raised his eyebrows considering the dilemma. 'Slythe's a lecherous dog but wouldn't dare disobey a direct command from his superiors.'

'That is all well and good, but just how do you intend to get these orders?' Tarn inquired disparagingly.

'Forgery,' Gilgarad said, unexpectedly breaking his silence. 'I told you literacy has its values. Prell, here, is an excellent forger. He will make the papers you need if you intend to proceed with this scheme.'

'Our proceeding depends on you. I would not like to think we are wasting our time here. Will you not tell us your decision?' Raven urged.

'I have not yet made one,' Gilgarad said calmly. 'We have waited a long time; a few more days will hurt us none.'

'I cannot delay here, cousin. I am the spokesman of our Clan,' Tarn replied.

'Indeed? You have risen through the ranks, at last.' His tone was mocking but his face held signs of respect. Tarn did not rise to the bait. Gilgarad then informed them his duties required him elsewhere and departed.

Raven, Tarn and Prell stayed in the burrow for the remainder of the day, discussing some of the difficulties their plan presented and exchanging information. Tarn was surprised by Raven's open attitude but assumed the hope for freedom outweighed her loathing of Prell's people. It pained him to realise that his own people were now almost as prejudiced as those they accused.

Late that evening, Gilgarad remembered that he had guests and sent Birch with refreshments and instructions to guide them to a place where they could sleep.

❦

Raven and Tarn arose early and disturbing Prell from his sleep resumed their discussions. By lunchtime they were satisfied with their plans and Prell began working on the documents they would require for the city. Raven and Tarn unwillingly sat down and as a contingency methodically began to learn the seemingly meaningless squiggles which represented the Navennán alphabet. It was frustrating work and the quills felt awkward in their hands but after several hours of practice they had mastered the letters and began to form the names of their Clansmen and women. Prell helped them with the spelling and before long they were scribbling names with fluid hand.

Two hours later, Prell viewed his handiwork. Raven and Tarn looked over the documents with interest, although scarcely understanding what was written upon them. 'This one,' he said, holding up the most elaborate sheet, 'should guarantee your safe passage. It is signed by Commander Travis himself.'

'I thought Slavik was in charge of the transports,' Raven said with a hint of suspicion.

'Of the taxes, yes, but Travis controls the movement of slaves. Since troops are involved, it falls under military jurisdiction.'

Raven nodded and studied the paper more carefully. She held it almost tenderly and stuttered her way through some of the words before handing it back. 'And the others? Where must we fill in the names?'

Prell indicated the small space he had left on each paper. 'It doesn't matter if your script differs from mine. The names are often filled in by clerks.'

'How are the names arrived at?' Tarn asked tightly.

'The troops are given a thorough debriefing when they return to the city. They provide the names of those they think suitable for our purposes.'

'Ah,' he replied quietly, wondering just who it was that had so kindly suggested Lily was taken into servitude.

A little later they were granted another audience with Gilgarad. They stood before him expectantly as he perused Prell's forgeries. From his great height, Gilgarad looked down upon their eager faces as if they were children demanding cake. He fixed them with his good eye and did not move for what seemed an eternity. Then he tore his gaze away and seated himself on a large chair.

'Well?' Tarn insisted.

Gilgarad closed his eye and sat considering, and a hushed

silence fell upon the room. When his lid opened there was a gleam in his eye and a twisted smile upon his face.

'It shall be done.'

NINE

Confrontations

Two weeks passed since the trip to Vinewood and the dwellers of Wilderwood had been busy. As promised what supplies could be spared were carefully smuggled to Rowanwood. Gilgarad also sent provisions from Vinewood. Tarn knew tactics not altruism lay behind the seemingly compassionate gesture. Feed your armies and they will be fit and strong; starve them and you have nothing.

The citizens of Wilderwood were also paid unexpected visits by the Kházakha. They were only random checks and passed without incident but Cail was forced to set a double guard and as much weapons training as possible was moved underground.

Raven kept a careful watch on Snell, but Slythe kept his men in tight formation and Prell's brother was never far enough from his unit to dare the approach. If something did not happen soon, she would have no choice but to seek him far outside the enclave.

As the close of the third week approached, reports from the other Clans began to trickle in. Gilgarad had sent his people far afield and most Clans were only too willing to fight for their freedom.

At the beginning of the fourth week, Gilgarad himself boldly strode into the camp. He was led to the burrows where he could talk freely with the Wilderwood council. Only Negram was absent, now too ill to attend. Gilgarad immediately got down to business, telling them in plain words about his progress. He was vaguely satisfied by his accomplishments but concerned about the time limitations.

'Drugging the water will have to take place after the city has been infiltrated,' Cail replied. 'We must be sure the slaves are ready. You will have several days from Raven's arrival in which to finalise your strategy.'

'And how do you intend to signal your success? I will not have my army blindly attack. Your success is not guaranteed,' said Gilgarad bluntly.

This was something T'skya had already considered. It was imperative the forest enclaves did not start fighting while troops remained active in the city. 'With these,' she announced, holding out some innocuous looking boxes made from equipment cannibalised from her ship. 'I'll transmit a signal from this machine to these receivers on our success. Unfortunately I only had enough parts to make a couple.'

'Their range?'

'Enough, if the land's geology doesn't interfere. I've tried them in the enclave without a hitch, but I can't guarantee anywhere else. I don't know enough about your land for that.'

Gilgarad was incredulous. 'The make-up of our land varies considerably, and there are mountains to consider. You cannot expect me to rely on these alone!'

'Well, don't look at me,' T'skya replied huffily. She knew the receivers did not suffice, yet they were the best she had to offer. 'You think of something. I'm out of ideas.'

'The horns of Camaldriss,' Hollam interrupted softly. 'We could use the horns.'

T'skya looked at him blankly. 'The horns?'

'They were gifts to the enclaves from the people of the Great

Divide when they first entered the land. They are no more than sea shells really, but they carry sound incredible distances upon the wind. There are Kalkassians in the land still. They would hear the call.'

Gilgarad nodded. 'That is a worthy notion. I, too, possess one, though it has lain unused for much time. We can use a horn if someone will be there who has mastered its use.'

'I will be there,' Hollam said flatly. 'I have mastered its use.'

Cail and T'skya looked at him with concern. No decision had been made as to who would accompany T'skya, or even if she herself would go. Cail frowned at his brother but Hollam met his gaze with stubborn determination. Uncharacteristically, it was Cail who backed down first.

When Gilgarad was satisfied with their plans he demanded to see the progress Cail's warriors were making. The combat took place in the tunnels and the rooms within and he watched silently as the people of Wilderwood wielded their swords and spears and sent arrows flying down the brightly-lit passageways.

When Gilgarad was content that his additional techniques had been understood and sufficiently practised, Cail led the tired warriors to the great hall, where Gilgarad painstakingly explained a variety of battle plans. By the time he had finished it was late evening and Bramble brought them food, watching with horror as Gilgarad swallowed several days' supply. Even Hollam's voracious appetite was like a mouse compared to the giant's. When he had dampened his hunger, Gilgarad requested time alone with T'skya. She was happy to oblige but remained wary of the brusque and fearless man. He seemed to notice the unease behind her eyes.

'Are you afraid of me?' he asked.

T'skya did her best to sound strong and calm. 'Should I be?'

'Only if there is betrayal in your heart.'

T'skya leapt to her feet looking offended. 'To hell with you! I didn't stay here to be insulted. If that's all you intend to do, I shall leave!'

'And lose the opportunity of learning more of me, and Prell?'

She gave him a hard look and resumed her seat. 'Likewise,' she pointed out. 'You didn't ask me to stay for my own benefit.'

Gilgarad did not react but his questions indicated the verity of her words. He extracted all he could about her home planet, the Mothership and her reasons for siding with his people. He dug deep and she found it hard to answer without violating all of Commander Talmana's orders. She hated to think of the trouble she would be in if Talmana ever returned for her.

She also found it difficult to retain her composure under Gilgarad's watchful eye. He saw her glancing at his eye patch and leaning his face close to hers suddenly flipped it upwards. The socket was empty; a gaping dark hole.

'Pretty, eh?' he said. 'You wish to know how I came by this.' It was not a question, but T'skya nodded dumbly. Flipping the patch back in place he asked; 'Have you heard of the Arena?'

She shook her head.

'It is a large circular pit with tiered seats and a sand-covered stage near the city centre, where the citizens go to watch the games. It is a place of strength and skill and courage. It is a place of terror and death.

'Many years ago, I was taken to work in the mines. I did not remain there long. Santovin learnt of me and chose me as his gladiator and so I was taken to the Arena for the Grand Festival. The senior officers would partake, each with his own fighters chosen from amongst our people to fight to the death. It is their way of providing entertainment and eliminating worthy men who might otherwise cause trouble. I was well-fed and trained, and was put into the ring to test my skills. It galled me to slay my own people but to have refused would have brought slaughter to my Clan. Acceptance reduced the cost.

'I was victorious but suffered many wounds. Santovin was delighted and retained me in his service for the annual Grand Festival. I remained victorious for three years. In all, I had killed over thirty men.

'It then came time for the fourth Festival but it was also time for me to make a stand. The prize for victory was meant to be freedom but Santovin had denied me three times. I would not be denied a fourth! And thus when I had defeated all but one I made my declaration. I had struck my opponent such a blow he was unable to stand and victory was within my grasp, but instead I laid down my sword, and retained only my knife. I faced Santovin on his throne of gold.

'I cried aloud so all could hear. "Santovin, you have denied me freedom for three long years. I will be denied no more. Grant freedom before all your citizens or I will seek liberation through death!"

'Santovin quivered with rage; he had no choice but to agree. He had laid enormous bets upon my victory and stood to lose too much. But so overcome was I by the chance of freedom that I almost lost my life. My opponent had resumed his feet and the thirst for his own liberation was upon him. Before I could retrieve my sword, he struck me a fierce blow across the face which sliced through my eye and left me blinded. I staggered backwards and fell, my face on fire and gushing blood, and I all but lost consciousness. My opponent knelt by my side and raised his sword to the sky, preparing for the final stroke. I could hear the crowd screaming for my death. My opponent, in his moment of glory left himself open to attack, and with my last remaining strength I plunged my knife into his chest as he brought his sword down upon me. The knife went in deep and victory was mine.

'When I awoke, I found myself in Commander Travis's quarters. I was no longer of interest to Santovin and he had left me to die; but my bravery had won the Commander's favour and he refused to leave me to such a fate. I owe that man my life; it was he who had me carried from the Arena and ensured my survival. He also saw me safely from the city and spared me the fate that Santovin had in mind.'

Gilgarad sat back thoughtfully as he considered Travis's actions. T'skya was silent, shocked by the tale and by the Commander's unexpected compassion. Travis was responsible for many of the atrocities against the people of Roumanhi: it was he who sent troops out on the transport ships, he who made the rules concerning the people's movements, and he who set the punishments and T'skya could not reconcile these facts with Gilgarad's revelations.

'Was it Travis who sent word of Lily?' she asked.

Gilgarad nodded. 'Via Prell, yes. He took a risk in doing so.'

'If he's so concerned, why doesn't he just set her free?' she replied suspiciously.

'He cannot. All documents of movement or liberation within the city must be signed by Santovin. What reason could Travis give? He dare not jeopardise his position or his family.'

'I see,' she said thoughtfully and fell back into silence. Gilgarad also seemed reluctant to speak further and so they brought the meeting to a close.

T'skya retreated to her burrow and fell into sleep, exhausted by the day's activities. When she awoke the next morning, she found that Gilgarad had taken his leave during the night, eager to reach the southern enclaves.

❧

T'skya was sitting on the edge of a clearing when Catkin approached. Since Briar's departure, the child had spent a great deal of time with the young woman from Navenná and approached so quietly that T'skya did not hear her. The hand that touched her shoulder jerked the woman violently from her repose. She swung around with a cry of alarm, snatching up her knife ready for battle.

Catkin leapt backwards, looking both apologetic and scared. T'skya let out a sigh and lowered the weapon. 'Oh Catkin! You frightened me. Please, don't ever creep up on me like that again. I could've hurt you.'

'I am sorry, T'skya. I will be very noisy from now on, I promise. T'skya...can I ask you something?'

T'skya nodded, wondering what the question would be this time.

'Well, I wanted to ask you...well, the thing is...it is like this... why do you like Cail more than Hollam?'

T'skya raised an eyebrow. The child continued without noticing. 'I like Hollam much more. Cail is always telling me off and he is so serious. Hollam always cheers me up and is much more fun. I asked Bramble and she told me to mind my own business, so I asked Tarn and Badger and they said I would understand when I was older and had boyfriends of my own.' At this, Catkin blushed but pressed on: 'And when I asked Hollam he just smiled and said there was no accounting for taste. Nobody will tell me anything!'

She paused and frowned as she contemplated how to phrase her next words. 'Oh, and T'skya, I think I made a big mistake. When I asked Raven she looked like a thunder was upon her brow. She spat and cursed at me, and...and then she took up her sword and hewed a branch off a tree!'

T'skya was perturbed by this revelation. For one of these peaceful, nature-worshipping people to purposely wound a tree was unthinkable. She knew Raven disliked her and begrudged the influence she had on Cail, but this was unexpected. Nor was she happy about her business being relayed to all and sundry by Catkin's overworked tongue. The girl certainly knew how to stir up trouble that was for sure! T'skya knew, however, that Catkin had not meant any harm and could not bring herself to reprimand her.

'Don't worry about Raven. Sometimes people get angry and

do things without thinking. Raven likes Cail too and felt bad when you asked about me. She's also worried about the Kházakha. You don't want to go making her feel any worse, do you? So say nothing further to anyone. Now as for your question; I like both Hollam and Cail a lot, but in different ways. Hollam is strong and funny and makes me laugh, but he's also a bit of a rogue. Cail *is* more serious, but he's also sensitive and gentle and I feel relaxed in his company. And, well, I think that's enough explanation for now.'

'I will not say anything, I promise,' came the solemn reply. Catkin touched her heart and brow and spread her arms outward in the familiar gesture of the oathtake.

'Go on now, child. I have much to do and I can't sit here chatting with you all day,' T'skya grinned, waving her hands in dismissal. Catkin instantly obeyed. Instead of her usual springing, dancing steps, she walked tall and straight, trying to give T'skya no doubts that she would keep her word.

T'skya sat for some moments and then rose to her feet. She pulled herself up straight, her shoulders back and her head held high, trying to give herself the courage and determination to carry out her intentions.

⚜

Raven was drenched in sweat brandishing her sword with the utmost ferocity, her hair clinging to her face in curling streaks of fire. T'skya watched in admiration as Raven whirled and leapt with graceful precision and deathly intention, and abruptly came to the conclusion that it was, perhaps, not the best time to interrupt her.

As she was about to slip quietly away, Raven turned to face her with a malicious gleam in her eye. She stood with her legs braced and the sword planted in the ground between them. T'skya felt obliged to approach and moved forwards with some trepidation, but she met the woman's stare head on. 'I want to talk to you,' she said as forcefully as she could.

'I have no time for idle words,' Raven snarled. 'If you wish to talk, you must also fight. The choice is yours.' She picked up another sword lying close by and threw it to the startled Navennán.

T'skya caught it by luck and held it tentatively. It was heavier than she was used to and she knew that Raven far excelled her in skill. If she backed down now, however, she would lose whatever chance of respect she had with the Roumanhi warrior. It was not a pleasant choice. Finding her courage, T'skya stepped into the clearing. She held her sword defensively, expecting Raven to commence the attack immediately.

She was not disappointed.

Raven swung a heavy blow that T'skya managed to parry, although it left her arms tingling. Raven tried another to T'skya's left and was again blocked. The warrior was smiling wickedly and T'skya knew her opponent would not remain generous for long.

'What right do you have to frighten Catkin?' she demanded.

Raven raised an eyebrow and laughed. 'Is that what you have come here to challenge me about, Kházakh, a child? Or do you have some deeper motive for your foolishness?'

'There's nothing foolish in defending the innocent,' T'skya replied defiantly as she blocked another attack.

'You dare to moralise to me, you, a Kházakh?' raged Raven. 'I should slay you where you stand!'

'Do you really hate me so much?' T'skya panted in angry amazement.

'You will never know the depth of my loathing!' Raven hissed, launching a savage attack. T'skya staggered backwards, trying to defend herself. Raven was no longer pulling her strokes and T'skya's arms felt like lead.

'You don't hate me for my race. You hate me because of Cail. Raven, you lost him yourself. I didn't steal him from you.'

On mention of Cail, Raven's face contorted into a look of insane fury. With a curdled scream she launched herself at T'skya and beat the terrified woman to the ground. T'skya could barely raise her sword to block the attacks.

Raven slid under the defence with ease and held her sword against T'skya's throat. She was panting heavily and her body was trembling. The sword swayed precariously above T'skya's bare neck. T'skya swallowed deeply, her face drained of colour. She forced herself to look into Raven's eyes and could see the battle raging within her. T'skya dared not speak, but then she heard a voice.

'Raven!' Cail thundered. The clashing of their swords had drawn his attention and he stood some feet distant, holding a sword and pointing an accusing finger at his compatriot. 'If you intend to kill her, you will also have to kill me!'

Raven lowered her sword, realising what she had done. She had come so close to murder, to breaking all the laws of her society and permanently alienating her beloved. But she was a fighter and stubborn of will. She would not lower herself and admit the mistake, especially in front of the enemy. 'You worry needlessly,' she spat. 'If I had wished her dead, she would not have survived my first stroke. I was merely testing her abilities. She needs more work!' She glared at T'skya, daring the Kházakh to contradict her words, and stalked off through the trees.

T'skya was too shocked to move as Cail raced to her side. 'Are you hurt?' he asked, checking her over. T'skya shook her head and began to sob. Cail gently lifted her to her feet and held her tenderly. 'Did Raven speak the truth?'

T'skya had no wish to lie to him, but neither did she wish to further antagonise the woman. Cail chewed his lip in deliberation. The truth was clear and need not be voiced.

Raven made herself scarce for the next few days and let the tension in the camp dissipate. Despite Cail and T'skya's secrecy, word of the women's clash had spread. T'skya had an inconspicuous guard put on her and was touched by their concern, although she felt it was unnecessary. She had provoked Raven's volatile character and did not believe the warrior would take any cold-bloodied action against her; at least, not while there was still a chance of defeating the Kházakha.

Raven had not yet found the opportunity to reach Snell and was growing anxious. She was also brooding about Cail. She had alienated him but refused to give up. She would find a way to win him back, she promised herself that. She would get to the city and carry out her part and then - then time would tell.

༄༅

A week later, as a group of Kházakha was returning from Springbrook, a minor enclave to the west of Wilderwood, Raven finally found the chance she had been waiting for. The alien men had decided to take a rest on the mossy banks of a stream that carved its way lazily through the forest and Snell had wandered off to pick berries. Raven stealthily made her way towards him keeping herself hidden in the undergrowth.

She crouched to his left, invisible beneath the folds of her cloak, took a deep breath battling down her fears and hissed for his attention. Snell started and reached for his weapon.

'Who's there?' he whispered sharply. 'Come out or I'll shoot!'

'It is Blackbird,' she said, recalling the name Hollam had used.

'Blackbird?' Snell repeated. Then it dawned on him and he moved cautiously towards her hiding place. 'What do you want?' he asked in surprise.

'Keep picking,' the bush commanded, and Snell complied, trying to look as natural as possible, but feeling confused by his own compliance.

'You are outside your enclave. I should report this.'

'Prell sent me,' she replied quickly.

On mention of his brother, Snell choked. One of the Kházakha called across to him but Snell smiled and waved and the Kházakh returned to his conversation. 'What do you know of my brother?'

'He is my...friend,' she answered. 'I have a message from him.' Snell gaped in amazement as a hand bearing a small piece of folded paper thrust itself through the bush. He looked around before grabbing the note and stowing it inside his jacket. 'If you agree, get word to me within two days. Betray me and you will also betray him. Think on it well.'

Snell stood in a state of shock and Raven made a hasty, but silent, retreat. She watched him from a safe distance, her heart racing, but Snell showed no sign of betrayal as he followed his team through the forest towards their base camp. Now she would have to wait until she received a reply.

❧

Two days later, as demanded, Raven got her reply. How Snell managed to get away from the rest of the Kházakha she never found out, but in the very early morning, before the sun had broken over the horizon, there he stood in the middle of the Clanmeet.

Tarn and a very weary-looking Hollam stood on either side of him and one or two others crouched around the edge of the Clanmeet. Snell shuffled uneasily; it was the first time he had been faced by so many dwellers without the security of his comrades. Raven approached and stood within arms reach. She was just as tall and met his nervous gaze head on. 'I don't know why you want to do this and I won't ask,' he said solemnly, 'but I will do it. Give me the papers.'

Raven took the forged documents from her pocket and thrust them into his open hand. 'There will be three of us.'

Snell looked at the papers and nodded at his brother's

handiwork. Then catching the names, he frowned. 'Raven, Ash and Ferret. Where is your name?'

'I am Raven,' she proclaimed proudly.

Snell turned and looked accusingly at Hollam. The latter gave a cheeky smile and shrugged his shoulders. Turning back to Raven, Snell warned; 'Slythe will not be pleased to learn that he's been lied to. Why use this name?'

'I am known as Raven to those I seek in the city. I have no wish for misunderstandings upon my arrival.'

Although Snell did not appear ready to accept her explanation, he nodded and tucked the papers away. He brought out a note he had written and held it out to Raven. 'For Prell,' was all he said before taking his leave.

Raven fingered the paper and then handed it to Tarn. 'Have T'skya read it,' she said blandly.

Tarn raised his brows at Hollam, who just shrugged again and walked aimlessly off. With Snell gone, the others lost interest and went about their business, although many were curious why the Kházakh had come amongst them. They were informed that evening.

Cail called a general meeting after supper and relayed the plans to the adult population of Wilderwood and his words were met with silence. Everyone had realised something was afoot with the military exercises, the extra secrecy and the comings and goings of strangers, but none had guessed the true intentions of their leaders. Objections were raised but in the end they accepted their fate with good grace. T'skya had expected an outcry; their calmness in the face of adversity awed her and she could not help feeling proud of the people she now considered friends.

So far, everything was going according to plan. Gilgarad was raising an army, Raven had secured Snell's help and passage on the VST - Vehicle for Slave Transport - and T'skya had produced as much of the sleeping drug as she felt necessary. Furthermore, Prell had solved the problem of reaching the water tanks.

He had told Tarn and Raven of an extra hold on board the transport ship large enough for three people. The hold was seldom used since it was awkwardly placed to load. It was there that T'skya, Hollam and Cail would hide. Some of the Clan, especially Negram, were averse to risking such valuable members but Hollam's mastery of the horn compelled his inclusion and Cail felt duty-bound to accompany him. It was definitely risky and would be extremely uncomfortable, but since T'skya and Cail could not travel openly like Raven and it would take weeks to arrive on foot, there seemed little choice but to follow Prell's suggestion.

It would mean leaving the camp early and sneaking past the guards, breaking into the hold and remaining there silently until they reached the city, sneaking out again, travelling unseen through a city filled with their enemies and drugging the guarded water tanks.

Simple.

❧

Time passed quickly. T'skya's group were to leave early the following day and it was also expected the Kházakha would arrive to collect the taxes and nominate the slaves. The enemy was not prepared to risk their chosen workforce escaping if given prior warning of selection. Those unfortunate enough to be picked would be given little time to prepare themselves; they were allowed one bag of possessions and a few moments to say goodbye, no more. The slaves would then be shackled and marched to the transport ship.

Raven was unmoved by the prospect of her enslavement. Ash, a young scout whose entire family had been taken to the city over the years, was avidly awaiting the chance to be reunited with those still living, and Ferret, being Ferret, was as nervous as any natural coward. He did not consider himself cut out for such adventures and had been horrified by his inclusion. On reflection, he could see his scavenging qualities would be more useful in the city than the enclave. He was, after all, a poor fighter and would be of little use in the forthcoming events, but the prospect still filled him with dread.

Hollam showed little reaction one way or the other to his approaching challenge. He was morose without Breeze and it was as if the danger held no meaning. Cail was filled with quiet determination and hope. He saw their mission as the chance of a lifetime; a chance for freedom and peace. He refused to be intimidated by the difficulties and the million possibilities for failure. T'skya, on the other hand, was becoming overwhelmed. As the day approached, she grew more and more fearful and could hardly sleep. Her dreams were troubled with images of betrayal and discovery and she wore a permanent frown.

Later that day, she found herself alone with Cail by the main bathing pond. It was a cool evening and the water was being fanned by a gentle breeze. She sat down by an old twisted tree and played with the end of her braid in absent-minded distraction. Cail stood looking over the dark water. The wind caught his golden hair and ruffled it. He quickly tied it back in a loose pony-tail as if it was annoying him and glanced over his shoulder at T'skya.

She caught his look and tried to hide the solemn expression on her face. Cail was not fooled. 'Tell me,' he said softly and resumed watching the pond.

T'skya bowed her head. She was feeling so weak and agitated it was difficult to think clearly. After some moments struggling with herself she spoke; 'Do you fear death, Cail?' She stared intently at the profile of his face as if her eyes were trying to eke their way inside his mind. She so desperately wanted to understand him, to assimilate his strength in order to bolster her quailing spirit, to make his steadfast intent fill the void of her own incapacity.

He paused, surprised by her question, took in a lungful of

air and then sighed deeply. He turned towards her and, in a steady voice, answered; 'I do not.' Then he posed the question she feared. 'Do you?'

'Yes,' she quavered. 'Yes, I do. I fear death as any sane person would.'

'Do you then believe I am not sane?' he asked reproachfully.

T'skya pressed herself deeper against the rough horny bark of the tree, despite the discomfort it caused her. It was almost pleasurable to feel the reality of its existence; it made her aware of her own. Fearing to look at his face, she stared at the mossy undergrowth. 'It's insane to fight a power so much mightier than you with sticks and risk the lives of those you love, so I guess you're not sane,' she rasped. 'I guess *we* are not.'

'You have nothing but your life to lose. I am risking my life, my Clan and all the people of the land; perhaps the land itself and yet I do not shrink from it. T'skya, death awaits us all. It is pointless to try and defy the laws of life.'

'We aren't defying them. We're doing our best to succour them!'

'We are following your plan, remember?'

'Well, maybe I was wrong,' she considered flatly. 'Why don't you just leave here? Take everyone with you and find a place where you can live in peace. You could easily go south to the Great Divide. What's so special about this place anyway?'

At that, Cail began to stride away as if he could not abide being in her presence any longer. Then, as abruptly, he swung around to face her. 'Are you blind?' he snapped. 'Have you understood nothing? This land, which you dismiss so readily, is our *home.*'

Home. The word seemed to rebound off every tree. The birds, too, seemed to scorn her. Their songs turned to a cacophony of cries as if they could not believe her treachery. She felt ashamed of her arrogance and cowardice, and ashamed of the reaction she had caused. 'I'm afraid.' she stated simply.

'We are all afraid, T'skya,' Cail said more gently.

'But you said...'

'I said I was not afraid of death and that is true. Dying is easy and is not a matter we can avoid forever. It is survival that is difficult; our life brings pain and suffering, not the peace you hold so dear. Nevertheless, were I to do as you suggest and find the safety of another land, I would never find peace; my heart would be grieved and guilt is not a source of merriment.

'Do not misunderstand me. I have no wish to die, but if by this action I could save my world, I would ask you to strike me where I stand. This land and these people *are* my life and I will not abandon them. If death is what you fear, you should not stay within our borders nor accompany us on our quest, for the way is perilous and few will return unscathed.'

His clemency made her cheeks burn and she could feel her eyes prickling as tears began to well. She swallowed hard and fought to keep the water from rolling down her cheeks. 'You shame me,' she murmured, using every ounce of self-control she still possessed to keep her voice steady. 'I'm not as brave as you, and never will be. I had the idea, but now it's actually happening...I don't know; I'm just so afraid. Anyway, you're wrong. I do have more than just my life to lose; I have you.'

⁓⊱❧⊰⁓

It was cold when T'skya woke and a beneficial mist was covering the enclave. Cail had already roused his brother and Bramble had packed enough supplies to see them through the night. Each pack also contained a dozen vials of the potent sleeping drug and a space for their cloaks. T'skya carried the transmitter and Hollam had his horn.

Raven and Tarn stood waiting and soon Negram appeared looking drained and pallid. She now seldom rose from her bed and the brothers were obviously concerned. She was too old and fragile to have such worries placed upon her, and since

Briar's departure her health had deteriorated further.

Hollam embraced his mother gently and whispered words of encouragement. She clasped his hand and smiled sadly. Cail then held her but had to bear Negram's weight as her knees gave way. Gravely concerned he helped her to a seat but resignedly left T'skya to say her farewells.

T'skya kissed the ailing woman lightly on the brow and smiled a comforting smile. 'Don't worry. We will succeed. I'll see they don't get into any trouble.'

'Ah, T'skya,' Negram sighed. 'There is more to this than you could possibly imagine.'

There was something deeper lying behind Negram's eyes than simple concern for the safety of her sons. Once again T'skya wondered if it had something to do with Briar's secret. There was no time to think about it, however, and the adventurers took their leave.

They had come too far to turn back now.

It would take the trio less than half a day to reach their destination. The Kházakha had cleared large areas throughout the forest to allow the transport ships to land fairly close to the multiple enclaves. The VST they were planning to catch was usually parked in an area to the west of Wilderwood and Rowanwood so that it could serve several enclaves in one go. Slythe did not wish to travel further than need be with heavy sacks and unruly slaves.

Unfortunately, towards mid-morning the concealing mist began to lift. Hollam, Cail and T'skya travelled swiftly and in silence. The men looked grim and T'skya was preoccupied with trying to keep her footfalls light.

Oftentimes Cail would motion them to a standstill. T'skya scarcely dared to breathe and strained her ears and eyes for signs of the enemy. She trusted Cail implicitly, knowing his senses were superior. When she had first arrived, he had warned her that she would not get far on her own and he had been right. She possessed neither the Roumanhis' instincts nor their heightened senses and would have walked into trouble. She also knew they would be even more at risk that day. There would be great enemy activity in the forest and she half-expected to see a patrol of Kházakha bearing down on them. She had not noticed Cail had chosen a path which veered off to the left in order to avoid this; she had been too busy watching the ground.

It was not long before Cail halted them again and it was several minutes before T'skya could perceive the noise that had alerted him to the danger. To the distant right, she made out the sounds of heavy feet crunching through the forest as Slythe led his troops towards Wilderwood. His voice was clearly audible as he snapped instructions to his men, criticising them for their slowness and ordering the beasts of burden to be whipped onwards. The sounds faded and the companions' thoughts turned to Raven, Ferret and Ash, who would soon be facing Slythe's tyranny. They were all concerned about Hollam's absence; his lie would become evident once Raven declared her true name, leaving Tarn at Slythe's mercy.

The trio continued on their way, trying to push these thoughts from their minds. They had their own problems to contend with and the coming hours would require all their concentration. But they had travelled no more than a league when disaster struck.

They had reached a steep incline where the land dropped away some thirty feet into a grassy dell. The valley was long and narrow, and thickly forested along its rim. Cail indicated they needed to descend and warned that the ground was treacherous. The mist had soaked the tufty grasses and many areas were devoid of growth. It was extremely slippery and there was little to hold on to. It was also an open space where they could be seen.

T'skya peered down as Cail carefully descended, determined to find the best route for her to follow, and Hollam kept watch, eyeing the opposite bank suspiciously. Something was gnawing at him. Then, with a gasp he flung himself flat, pulling T'skya down along with him. Cail froze a few feet down the bank.

'What?' he whispered sharply to Hollam.

'The birds. No song,' Hollam replied in a low voice.

T'skya cocked a look at him and listened. He was right. The forest was quiet; too quiet.

Hollam peered over the edge of the bank into the forest beyond. It seemed safely empty but then he caught sight of a distant shadow flitting between the trees.

'Movement!' he hissed in warning to his brother, who was desperately trying to maintain his position.

Cail was precariously placed and could feel his grip slipping. The tussock he had his foot wedged upon was beginning to give and his fingers were starting to cramp. He gritted his teeth in effort and attempted to dig his fingertips into the heavy soil. 'I cannot hold on!'

'You must!' Hollam insisted.

'I am slipping!'

'Wait. I am coming. Try to reach my hand.' Hollam edged over the side and T'skya held his legs. He reached towards Cail, who was anxiously looking up at him. If Cail let go, he would surely fall and draw the attention of whoever was lurking opposite.

'Lower,' Cail gasped.

Hollam wriggled another few inches forwards and T'skya clung to his ankles. She could see the other side of the valley and was frightened to see several figures making their way towards them.

'Hurry!'

Suddenly, a cry went up and the figures began to run.

'Cail!' Hollam demanded, stretching as far as humanly possible. Cail pushed upwards from the tussock with all his strength and grabbed for Hollam's outstretched arm. He was within an instant of locking his fingers around his brother's strong hand when he lurched and his aim went wild. With a cry he tumbled down the slope. He clutched at his thigh in agony as the effects of the Kházakh's weapon took hold.

As Hollam looked on aghast and T'skya strained to haul him up from his perilous position, Cail struggled to remove his pack. As the Kházakha poured down the opposite bank, firing wildly at Hollam's retreating form, Cail staggered to his feet and hurled the pack towards his brother. Hollam managed to clutch one strap and pull it up after him.

The pack and its valuable contents were safe. His brother was not.

❧❦❧

Slythe arrived with his men before lunch. Fen had already ensured the taxes were ready for inspection and had hidden himself away. Tarn stood waiting in the Clanmeet as though it were just another collection day. He did not show additional anxiety as he formally greeted the Kházakha and watched the hard-earned produce being loaded onto the beasts. Nor did he show it when the warrants for his people's enslavement were extracted.

Snell waited impatiently for his leader's attention and handed the documents across. Slythe scanned them briefly and gave Snell the honour of announcing the names. Snell shuffled his feet. Even though the Roumanhis knew who would be taken, he was nervous about the deceit. He cleared his throat and declared in a loud voice; 'Our gracious leader, the High Lord Procurator Santovin, requires the following people to accompany us to our city: Ferret, Ash and Raven. Step forward and be accounted for.'

Ferret and Ash did as they were bidden, miming shock and horror. Ferret licked his lips and wrung his hands and the younger blond man hung his head and trembled. Slythe surveyed them with some disdain and awaited the arrival of the third. When Raven stepped out from behind the crowd, a hushed silence fell upon the enclave. Slythe's jaw dropped open in bewilderment. He glanced at Snell and Tarn, clenching his teeth in annoyance.

'What is this trickery? Your name was not called,' he snapped at the woman.

'You are mistaken, Sir,' Raven replied calmly.

'And which of those called do you claim to be?' he sneered.

'I am Raven.'

'Raven, is it now? Someone must pay for this deceit. Where's that fool I had flogged?'

'There was no deceit,' she said quickly. 'Blackbird is my Clan name. I, however, choose to answer to Raven. It is more fitting.'

Knowing that Slythe was an impatient man, Tarn added; 'Hollam is foraging. It may take some time, but I will have him brought to you if you wish it.'

'I do not wish it. I have more pressing matters to attend to than waste time on him,' Slythe replied, much to Tarn's relief. Then he turned back to Raven. 'And you, my dear, have sorely disappointed me! But no matter. You'll have ample opportunity to make it up to me on our little journey, won't you? I have plans for you.'

He moved closer and cast his hands along her body. Raven shivered but this time made no effort to hide her disgust. Easing his hand behind her head, he began to pull her mouth closer to his.

With a snarl, Raven spat in his eye and pulled sharply away. Slythe's face contorted and with a cry of rage he struck her across the face, knocking her down and leaving blood on her lip. Never taking her accusing eyes off him, she started to rise. Slythe stepped in, ready to kick. Before he could reach her, Snell jumped between them. 'Sir, you must not!' he pleaded.

'Get out of my way or I'll shoot you where you stand!' his leader threatened.

'This warrant comes from Santovin himself - for his *personal* service; undamaged it says,' he added hastily, shoving the paper under Slythe's nose.

Slythe snatched the document away and stared at it wrathfully. 'Undamaged, you say. Pity!' he hissed, trying to regain his composure. 'Santovin's getting more than he bargained for with this one. Snell, Daravin, guard her well. She has five minutes to pack and say her farewells. It should be more than enough time.'

Snell stayed close to Raven and flashed her a sympathetic smile, whilst Daravin tarried a short way distant watching his partner. Snell had been acting strangely for the last few days. He seemed strangely protective towards the forest dwellers and although Daravin was not a cruel man, he found such charity unbecoming in a soldier of the state. He was growing more and more suspicious of where Snell's loyalties lay. But luckily the man also considered him a friend and would not willingly expose him to Slythe's retribution. Besides, Snell had come to the end of his tour and was returning to a post in the city; all his uncharacteristic behaviour would probably stop once he escaped from the uncivilised confines of the forest. If not, if Snell had really turned renegade, then Daravin would have to do his duty and report him. It was not a prospect he relished.

Raven, who was the most observant, sharp-minded creature, had seen Daravin's speculative glances. She resorted to insulting Snell as he stood over her, dragging her feet when he led her and made his passage difficult until he lost patience and began to bully her back. Daravin's face showed nothing.

When the five minutes was nearly up, Ferret, Ash and Raven were allowed to bid their Clan farewell. The three were leaving, perhaps never to return. Tarn chose his words carefully when he addressed them. 'Our hearts go with you as you carry our wishes to the city.'

Raven flashed a wicked grin. She would enjoy her revenge no matter what she would have to face to accomplish it. Ferret and Ash, however, showed no such relish and stared sullenly at their captors as shackles were fastened to their wrists and necks, linked by a chain that bound them one behind the other. In this degrading fashion the prisoners were led from the enclave towards their temporary place of incarceration aboard the VST.

❦

They travelled at a decent rate; a long line of people and beasts. The three slaves were placed in front of the laden animals, with armed escorts on each side. There was no chance of escape, not that it even crossed their minds. They were content to follow Slythe, but acted their roles as unwilling captives with realism trying to give Hollam, Cail and T'skya more time to stow themselves away. The fewer Kházakha in the vicinity of the ship, the better.

Snell and another walked on either side of Raven. Daravin walked behind Ash and Ferret, and guards paced to the front and rear of the group. The other Kházakha clustered around the provisions whilst Slythe, fearful of attack, stalked onwards behind his pointman.

He was still smarting about Santovin's acquisition of Raven. If only he had taken her that first time then his glorious leader would not have demanded her. Santovin had little interest in used products. Now Santovin was denying him the triumph of mastering such an exciting woman and it made him choke with regret.

After some time trudging they came to the wooden bridge that spanned the dell, not far from where Cail had tried to descend. The bridge was wide enough for two people to walk abreast but was not railed on either side. The valley was narrow here and some forty feet deep there but the bridge was strong and there was little risk of falling.

Raven walked grimly, wishing she could sweep some of her enemy into the gorge. Ill-feeling radiated from every pore.

Snell glanced at her nervously and dropped back next to Ash until they had crossed. He might be aiding her, but that hardly qualified him as a friend. The beasts were hesitant to cross. They did not like the sound of their hooves upon the wood, but feared the cruelty of the Kházakha even more. Man and beast therefore reached the other bank without incident.

They marched onwards, stopping only once before they reached the VST. The vehicle was large and looked ungainly but the Roumanhis knew that it was heavily fortified, well armed, capable of travelling on land as fast as a troumalok, and able to fly at low altitudes. It was within that dull grey hulk that they would live until they reached the city.

There was a hive of activity around the VST. Troops were unloading supplies for the forest soldiers and ferrying sacks and barrels from the other enclaves into the holds at the back. Several slaves, most of whom the dwellers from Wilderwood recognised, were unwillingly assisting the Kházakha. Ash was incensed to see one of them pole-axed for cracking a barrel when it slipped through his shackled hands. The young man plunged against his chains, drawing protest from Raven and Ferret as they were choked by their collars. To still him a guard jabbed him in the stomach with the butt of a blaster. Doubled up in pain, Ash protested no more. Snell looked on sadly but with Daravin scrutinising him closely he made no effort to intervene.

The captain of the VST pulled Slythe aside and talked urgently to him for some moments. Ferret drew Raven's attention to their activities. She just shrugged but her stomach tightened. Neither of them could make out what was being said, although it was evident from their gestures that something important was being discussed.

When the captain had finished explaining, Slythe's scowl changed into a smile. He hurried to the side door of the transport ship, pulled it open and leapt aboard. The door swung closed, muffling the sounds within. All the same, from the banging and shouting, it was not unwarranted to assume that some poor wretch was suffering in there.

Raven flicked her eyes across to the small hatch beneath the ship. If Cail and company were not aboard now, then there was little likelihood of them succeeding; there were too many Kházakha to sneak past. The hatch looked secure and none of the Kházakha was paying it any attention. Knowing that Cail had left early, Raven began to relax.

Her thoughts were disturbed by Slythe's reappearance. He was rubbing his knuckles looking furious. His brutality did not seem to have produced the desired results. Raven smirked, knowing he dared not touch her. Slythe just gave her a deadly glance and then, seeing that the supplies had been loaded, ordered the slaves aboard.

Raven's group was the last to go. The chain was removed from their necks but the collars remained and one by one they were led to the door and seated on cramped benches. Their hands were chained to a bar in front of them and their legs fastened to the floor, preventing movement.

With the slaves securely tied, the Kházakha left to exchange keys with their replacements. Snell and Daravin would accompany the captives to the city and see that they arrived at their designated destinations before their debriefing sessions and reassignments; but for now the hold was enemy free.

Out of curiosity, Raven tested the strength of her bonds and sighed. The light was dim and she could barely make out the faces of those sitting near her. Nobody spoke. In the stillness all she could hear was the occasional rattling of chains, the odd sob of misery and some hoarse breathing. She sensed that she was being watched and peered through the gloom, trying to locate the interested party.

There in the corner, his hair dishevelled and his clothes filthy, sat a man staring at her through one eye. The other was too bruised and swollen to open and blood was trickling from his nose and mouth, courtesy of Slythe no doubt. Raven paled and choked back a cry of horror.

TEN

Tragedy and transformation

Cail desperately tried to clamber up the slick side of the dell but his right leg would not support him and he was giddy from the pain. Even unwounded, he knew he could not have made it to the top before the Kházakha were upon him. With a final burst of energy he took a swipe at the nearest man and yelled at Hollam to flee before being obliterated by the beams of the Kházakha's blasters.

T'skya screamed as Hollam hauled her from the valley sides. Shots flew over their heads, making their ears ring and their skin prickle. From the curses of the Kházakha, Hollam gathered that they were having difficulty scrambling up the steep banks, but they would make it eventually and if he and T'skya remained they would suffer the same fate as Cail.

T'skya resisted Hollam fiercely, determined to go to the man's aid.

'Do as he says!' Hollam cried, cursing at the enemy and at her recklessness. 'We cannot help him if we are captured.'

He was furious and nearly pulled her arm from its socket as he dragged her through the forest. Gradually his urgency penetrated her and she began to run under her own steam. When they had retreated far enough to be temporarily safe, they flung themselves down in despair.

'We can't just leave him,' T'skya objected, her face drawn and wan. She was terrified for Cail. She knew his life was in grave danger. She did not care about their plans; she did not care about herself. She cared only that Cail should be safe. She felt responsible for his downfall. Her wild ideas had caused this and she had done nothing to help him. Now she was powerless, frustrated, riddled with guilt and empty; bereft of the man she had grown to love. Her wrath was directed at Hollam; it had nowhere else to go.

Hollam struck his fist on the ground and leapt to his feet in agitation. He paced about, scraping roughly at his face; his own fear expressing itself in fury. 'Do you think I wished to leave him there? Do you think I wanted that?'

'Of course not!' she snapped. 'But he needs us. We could still get to the ship. Why don't we go to the ship? They'll take him there. They'll take him to the city. We could still go to the city,' she ranted.

Hollam, despite his grief was thinking more clearly. 'They saw us. They know we are out here. We would not get within fifty feet of the ship without being caught. It is impossible.'

'Did they see *me*?'

'Your shape only, I think. Not your appearance.'

'Hollam, will they kill him?' she suddenly asked in a trembling voice.

Hollam stopped pacing; his ire calming in response to her pain. 'I do not think so. At least, not yet. That would be too easy. Santovin will question him first,' he replied grimly. 'We still have some time on our side.'

'You'd better be right,' she muttered darkly. 'I can't lose him. Do you understand me? I can't lose him. I love him!'

'As do I,' he whispered. 'Come, let us return to Wilderwood and find another way.'

'Negram!' T'skya gasped. 'What will we tell Negram?'

'The truth,' he replied bitterly. 'Caelcáladrim preserve us!

The truth.'

✌︎❀✌︎

Although filled with urgency, Hollam took T'skya the long way. He could not risk running into Slythe. Despite this, they still managed to arrive back at the enclave in the afternoon. The scouts spotted them easily as they dashed through the trees and fired arrows to warn of their arrival. One landed by Tarn's feet, making him jump back in alarm.

'There is trouble!' he roared, but seeing the yellow flight feathers knew those approaching were not the enemy. He dashed across the camp, leaping obstacles in his path as Hollam and T'skya tore through the trees. Hollam pulled up sharply to avoid running into his friend.

Tarn stared at the two of them with large troubled eyes. 'Cail?' he asked.

'Captured!'

Tarn paled. 'The drug?'

'Safe, for all the good it will do us!' Hollam snarled, roughly pushing Cail's pack into Tarn's hands.

'What now?' Tarn asked.

'Good question. Where is my mother?'

Tarn hesitated, fearful to add to Hollam's pain. 'She is resting in the house of healing. She felt...unwell after you left.'

Hollam sighed heavily and raised his eyes to the sky. Tarn caught his arm as he moved off. 'Hollam, she need not know.'

'Would you have me lie?'

'I would have you say nothing and spare her. She is too frail to hear it.'

T'skya gasped in warning, making the men swing round. They followed the path of her eyes and saw Negram standing a short way behind them.

'Where is Cail?' she asked shakily, but her face showed

224

comprehension. Hollam found no words to say. 'We are lost! Lost!' Negram cried.

Hollam only just managed to catch her before she fell to the ground, mumbling incoherently about the Castan. Tarn rushed to his aid and together they carried the frail old woman back to the house of healing. The healers set to work at once, chaffing her hands and feet and oiling her with aromatic herbs. Hollam and Tarn were dismissed, but lingered for a time outside the portiere.

'If only Breeze were here,' Tarn muttered before realising his tactless mistake. 'Sorry! Look, I will call a meeting of the council. Together we will find a solution. We will rescue Cail, defeat the Kházakha and give Negram something to smile about.'

Hollam's mouth twitched. 'Call me when you are ready. I need to change.'

He hurried off, leaving Tarn and T'skya alone. The rugged man looked kindly upon her and wiped away her tears with his sleeve. 'T'skya, you must be strong now. Everything is in jeopardy and we need your wits. Do not succumb to your despair whilst a chance still remains.'

T'skya nodded. 'I promised Negram I'd keep Cail out of trouble. I've failed in that. I will not fail again.'

❧

It did not take the people long to gather underground. The council seemed oddly inadequate; the absence of Briar, Negram, Ferret, Raven and Cail weighed heavily upon them. Hawk was the last to arrive, having awaited his replacement amongst the boughs. He took his place next to his brother.

Hollam took Cail's place at the head of the table, with T'skya beside him. With great strength of character, he relayed the day's events. 'We need a quick solution. Raven's group will arrive in the city before long and it is probable that Cail is with them. We cannot rely on them to rescue him; it would jeopardise their mission in the city. Our main hope is to poison the water tanks before the Kházakha decide to execute him.'

'Then you mean to continue with the plan?' Badger said.

'He would wish nothing else,' Hollam replied. 'We cannot afford to lose this opportunity by affecting his rescue.'

T'skya was aghast. 'You mean you'd be willing to sacrifice your brother just to win your war?'

'Is that not what he would wish?' he said darkly, barely able to hold his voice steady. The decision was crippling him inside although he dared not show it. If he faltered then they would all falter. He could not afford to follow his heart now; he had to follow his head.

T'skya grimaced, thinking back to her conversation with Cail. *"If by this action I could save my world, I would have you strike me where I stand,"* he had said. 'Yes, that is what he would wish,' she agreed sadly, her voice cracking under the strain.

'Catching the VST now is out of the question. What do you suggest?' Knoll rasped.

Hollam chewed his lips and blew out his cheeks. 'We cannot walk to the city or use the troumaloks. There is another transport due to leave in two days but we cannot hope to gain passage on it. It is for Kházakha troops only.'

The room fell silent as they tried to find a solution. T'skya scowled, wishing there were some way of boarding the other ship. Every moment was one nearer to Cail's demise. 'Are there any female soldiers in the forest?' she asked slowly.

'There are some Kházakha women, but they do not fight. They are used for cooking, cleaning and as nurses mainly.'

'Are they rotated?'

'Yes,' Hollam replied. 'Why?'

'Could they get transport on that ship?'

'Possibly.' He saw her hopeful expression and understood her intention. 'No! I will not allow it,' he said decisively.

'Why not? I'm a Kházakh. Who else would stand a better

chance? Hollam, what other choice do we have?'

'Cail would never accept it.'

'Cail is not here!' she cried.

'I cannot let you go alone,' he objected. 'The risk is too great. We cannot afford to lose you too.'

'I won't have to go alone. I have an idea.'

❦

T'skya battled hard and Hollam finally agreed to her insane plan. He could scarcely believe he had consented, but now stood with Tarn outside the trap-door, clutching a sheet of writing that T'skya had told him to learn. She had gone to her burrow, leaving orders not to be disturbed.

Fen was busy with the seamstresses, explaining exactly what was required and rummaging through the stores to find the needed goods. Hawk was standing in the centre of the Clanmeet blowing on a small whistle that emitted a signal too high for human ears to hear. Wolf was nearby with a peculiar-looking harness in his hand.

Despite her demand for peace, Badger went to fetch T'skya, believing she would be interested in the imminent events. The sun was sinking quickly but there was still some daylight left and, apart from one or two clouds, the sky was clear. As she waited, a long shadow passed overhead and T'skya gasped as an eagle came to rest on Hawk's outstretched arm. He had wrapped a thick cloth around his wrist and now she knew why. The talons of the bird were sharp and powerful and could pierce a man's flesh as easily as a blade.

'This is Braithwheir, Lord of the Eagles,' Hawk said proudly. 'You said an urgent message must be sent to Prell. Here is your messenger.'

T'skya's face broke into a grin. With their fastest runners it would have taken at least three days to receive a message, too late for the troop ship. Now she could have a reply from Prell that evening.

Wolf fastened the harness around Braithwheir's body and secured T'skya's note inside the small pocket that lay against the eagle's chest. 'Take this to Gilgarad, my friend, with as much speed as your mighty wings allow. We have need of a reply this night,' Hawk said softly.

Braithwheir blinked his intelligent yellow eyes and, with a shriek of farewell, lifted into the air. His wings spanned the length of a man and caused whirls of leaves to scatter across the earth. In a matter of moments he was gone, heading with all speed towards Vinewood.

'That's incredible,' T'skya muttered. 'He seemed to understand you.'

'Of course he understood me. He is Braithwheir,' Hawk chuckled, amused by her ignorance.

'Ah, that explains it,' she replied, not understanding anything. 'So why don't you use him for all your communications?'

'Because he is Braithwheir, of course,' Wolf answered as if it were all self explanatory.

'Ah,' T'skya repeated.

Badger laughed and explained more fully as he accompanied her back to the burrow. 'Braithwheir sees much and knows much and chooses when to answer our call. We do not use him. He elects to aid us when the need is great, as it was tonight.'

T'skya was astonished. 'You mean he thinks like we do?'

'You cannot put our thoughts into a creature's mind, T'skya. He thinks as an eagle thinks, but he is wise and knows the perils the land faces. Before the Kházakha, he ruled the skies and had no enemies. Now the eagles are few. He seeks his freedom, just as we do.'

'It's funny,' she mused. 'I've never really thought about the other creatures and their needs. To me an animal was an animal; something to be treasured or used; but ruled by instinct without logical thought. I see I was mistaken.'

'Yes, sorely mistaken,' Badger agreed, and left her to her work.

Braithwheir returned later that night, but his presence was scarcely noticed and, sensing that all was not well within the enclave, he departed swiftly. Prell had done his job hastily but effectively, and without disturbing her already fitful sleep, Hawk placed the papers in T'skya's burrow.

❧❀❧

Shortly after the eagle had left for Vinewood, T'skya was again roused from her work by a message from Negram. She hurried to the house of healing without a second thought and was shocked to find that the old woman's condition had deteriorated. She was shrunken, her skin seemed almost transparent as if she were fading from the world, and her breath was shallow. The healers commanded T'skya not to remain for long.

T'skya seated herself on the tree stump by the bed and took the old lady's hand. Negram lay with her eyes closed and T'skya began to think she was asleep. She studied her friend's face and suddenly found herself looking into a pair of golden eyes.

'Who would have thought it possible that I would ever trust such a one as you,' the old lady said weakly, staring at T'skya. 'For many decades your people have been our enemies and yet in you I put all our hopes for the future. My time is short; I am old and weary, but to you I will tell a thing of great import.'

'Don't say such words, Negram. You have many years of life yet.'

'I will not survive this night,' Negram replied calmly.

T'skya felt a stab of fear in her guts; fear of loss and fear for Negram's sons. 'Then I must fetch Hollam at once.'

'No, not yet. These words are for your ears alone, child.' She paused; 'You have heard the story of the Castan's murder and the slaying of his child as I told it?'

'I have,' T'skya agreed.

Negram's eyes clouded with tears as she remembered the terrible flight from the Castan's palace. She took a moment to gather her thoughts and bring her emotions under control. When she continued, her voice was steady, but the movement of her hands as they twisted the blanket betrayed her emotions. T'skya listened attentively, her curiosity turning to shock and from shock to astonished understanding.

In those few months before the Castan fell, the King and Queen had foreseen their impending doom. They had realised the Kházakha intended to overthrow their rule and to end the Castan line. Their son's life was in jeopardy; he was the heir to the throne and would surely be killed. In conference with their loyal servants, the Castanaries, they had devised a scheme to save the Castan line. In place of their son, a sacrificial baby of similar age was laid. Negram had left her own infant son to die in order to save the Prince. She had been given the honourable task of raising the heir. She had taken the baby, together with Hollam, and left the Palace not more than a day before the Kházakha came.

Negram had travelled far, with as much haste as she could muster until she came to Wilderwood. It had not been easy with two wailing children in tow and the small amount of luggage she had taken with her. The forest dwellers under Briar's recent leadership accepted her willingly and did not question where she had come from.

It was difficult for T'skya to accept what she heard and yet there could be no doubting it. Now everything made sense: Briar's wisdom and secrecy, Negram's protectiveness towards Cail and overwhelming concern for his future, and...the Grish-Grish-Gûri!

Suddenly T'skya could recall them clearly: their faces, their names, their voices and their smell. They had blocked all knowledge of their existence to protect the King, but now it all came flooding back. Now T'skya knew of them; she could remember every detail.

'That was what Briar meant by accomplishing her sole purpose!' T'skya muttered.

Briar had been the Castan's Communicator; the one chosen by the mysterious Harouk gods to be the Castan's mouthpiece, but she had left the land. Now T'skya was the new Communicator; Briar's replacement. Why else would they have made it so easy to recall them? Why else would languages and information she had never learnt about be floating around in her head? They had planted it there. T'skya blanched, stupefied by their deeds, but Negram paid her no attention and continued to tell the tale whilst her strength lasted.

'I had thought to tell the heir King of his heritage myself, but he has been cruelly taken from me,' she croaked. 'I leave that now to you. T'skya, the heir King must be saved or all will have been for naught!'

So the man she loved was who she had imagined him to be. Cail was the heir to the throne; the last of the Castan line. T'skya's head was reeling from the implications of the old woman's words. The Roumanhis had made such great sacrifices and people had died to ensure Cail's safety. Now he was endangered by a people who did not even know how important he was. But while he lived there was still hope. A thought occurred to her. 'Does Hollam know?'

'No, child, he does not. I would that I could have told him, but every ear that hears endangers Cail's life. Now my time is near and Cail is gone. The knowledge must not die with me and so I have chosen you.'

'But why me and not Hollam?'

'How would it aid Hollam to know his blood brother was sacrificed? How could he endure it unbonded as he is? From where would he draw strength? You are the Communicator and Hollam will have enough to bear with my parting. I would not add to his sorrow. It is for you to decide when the time is right to impart your knowledge.' The old lady was clearly dying now. The words rattled in her throat and her breath came in harsh gasps. The effort of telling the story had weakened her considerably and she appeared to shrink in the ebbing candle light. 'Save my Castan,' she rasped.

'I will. I swear it on my life,' T'skya said with as much conviction and determination as she could, and, with tears threatening to fall, she touched her heart and forehead and spread out her arms in the gesture of the oathtake. 'I will fetch your son,' she added softly, kissing Negram lightly on the brow before leaving through the curtained door.

She made her way through the Clanmeet and down the well-trodden path that ran beside a small brook. She followed it until the lights of the fire-bugs and the chattering of voices had faded. All that could be heard was the twittering of the night birds, the rustling of leaves in the breeze and the water splashing over stones as it made its way southwards.

At the grey boulder marking the boundary of the Wilderwood enclave and which looked curiously out of place amongst the trees, she turned left. Now there was no path, but the undergrowth was thin enough for her to walk without difficulty and she knew her route. Before long she came to a clearing that bordered a large pond surrounded by reeds and rocks, silver birches and willows and there she found Hollam sitting cross-legged on top of a grassy embankment. His head was bowed and he was perfectly still. A sheet of paper lay crumpled at his side.

Not wishing to startle him, T'skya took pains to shuffle her feet as she approached.

Hollam spoke without turning his head. 'There is no need to stamp your feet,' he chuckled softly. 'I heard your footsteps some while ago.'

'Sorry,' she replied, moving closer to him.

He raised his head and gazed across the inky water. 'Have you also come for a moment of peace?' he asked. 'I often come here to watch the setting of the sun or to view the stars. I find it calms my soul. Even such a one as I has need of comfort in this harsh world. Does that surprise you?' he said, looking at her shadowy form.

T'skya could see his eyes as they caught the reflection of the golden sky. They looked sad and mournful, so unlike his usual visage. Could he already know the news she had brought?

'Everyone needs comfort, Hollam. Even ruffians like you,' she replied.

He tossed back his head and laughed, his shaggy hair catching the wind. The laugh was like a rainbow after a storm, but short lived. He had seen the pain behind her eyes even as she had tried to lift his mood. 'You tease me, Green-Eyes, but that was not the reason for your coming.'

As gently as she could, she told him of Negram's condition. 'Her time is short, my friend. She bade me bring you to her.' She paused, unable to find suitable words of consolation. A tear trickled its way down her cheek and she pawed at it roughly, as if it were offensive to her.

Hollam said nothing but she could see the tension in his whole demeanour. His jaw was clenched so tightly she thought his teeth would shatter, and his hands had formed fists of stone. He squeezed his eyes shut for a second and exhaled steadily to calm himself. 'I will go to her.'

T'skya watched him walk away into the night. She should have gone with him; she had no light by which to make her way back to the enclave, but she felt her presence would have been an intrusion. Cail was gone, Negram was dying and Hollam had the woes of the world on his shoulders. The sadness was more than she could bear. Grief and isolation overwhelmed her and she collapsed to the grass, sobbing pitifully.

❧

T'skya woke with a start. Through the black of the night she saw the flickering of a light bobbing as it came towards her. She had the inclination to hide, but quickly dismissed the idea. The light was coming from the direction of the camp and was approaching confidently.

It was Tarn. He stopped an arms length away and surveyed her with great concern. 'Are you well?'

Caelcáladrim preserve her! With all that was going on, they still had the compassion to inquire about her health.

'How long have I been here, Tarn?' Her voice was unsteady. She was reluctant to hear the answer although relieved to learn not long had passed since Hollam had left. 'Negram, is she...?' She hesitated, unable to find the courage to finish.

'Negram lives yet, but I fear her passing is nigh.'

T'skya nodded and asked how he had known she was there.

'Hollam sent me,' he replied. 'He knew you had no light and do not possess a night vision as efficient as ours. Come, I will guide you back.'

She took his arm as he led her from the pond. They walked in silence, too concerned with their own thoughts to pass the time with idle chatter. When they reached the Clanmeet they were likewise greeted by silence. Everyone had gathered in the clearing. They were sitting closely together, taking solace from each other's company.

T'skya sat at the edge of the clearing beside a gnarled old oak tree, trying to find comfort in its maturity and wisdom. That tree had witnessed the changing of seasons, the birth of generations and the passing of countless lives. It had seen all the changes and yet was unchanged itself, continuing to grow and live just as these good people would.

She felt a hand slip into hers and glancing to her side saw Catkin's tiny form huddling against her. Her face was wet with tears and she sniffed continuously. T'skya drew the child closer and put a supportive comforting arm around her. She wondered where Bramble was but did not air her thoughts.

They sat unmoving, unaware of the passing time, awaiting the inevitable. The fire died low. The sombre light now barely illuminated the glade but no-one had the heart to stoke it or collect more wood.

A movement caught their attention. The curtain to Negram's den pulled back and the grief-stricken figure of Hollam stepped out. His face was contorted with pain and he was shaking. The dim embers caught his skin and made it appear awash with blood.

He walked, transfixed, towards the fire and stood before it. His misty eyes passed over all their faces, reading their silent words of condolence, and then he began to sing, quietly and softly. She had heard him sing before, but never with so much feeling or in such an enchanting way. It was mesmerising.

He sang the long requiem and as the last notes died away into the night he took the hot stoking iron from the fire and gripped the end in his palm. T'skya leapt to her feet as his howl of pain shattered the peace but Catkin gripped her arm fiercely and hissed at her. 'No! Leave him. You must not interfere.'

Hollam turned his eyes upon her. The intensity of his supplication overcame her and she withheld.

After what seemed an interminable time, but was only moments, he withdrew his hand. It was badly scorched, but he stood numbly whilst some liniment and bandages were placed upon it. When the healers' work was done, the dwellers approached him, kissed his hand, and made their way back to their burrows, until only he and T'skya were left in the glade.

He seemed relieved by their departure and some of the tension left his body. T'skya quietly went to him and gently taking his wounded hand, placed it to her lips.

Her action stirred him and he gazed at her apologetically. 'I am sorry. I should have explained the ceremony to you. I had no thought to shock you. Come, let us depart from here and I will answer your queries, for there is also a question I have in mind to ask you.'

He gathered a torch from the fire and led her away to where the children learnt their songs. As they sat, building another small fire to ward off the chill of the night, he explained about Negram's passing and the ceremony T'skya had witnessed.

The ceremony of branding was an act of grieving. It symbolised the pain of parting and the slow healing that would follow. It was an act of compassion, for it showed him willing to take upon him the burden of the world and the sorrows of his people. The scars would remain to remind everyone of Negram's life and as a witness to the love her son had for her.

T'skya's eyes widened. She had often wondered about the fine white scars upon Negram's palms but had been hesitant to ask. Now, knowing what she did, the answer was obvious. After the slaying of the King and her own son, she had performed the symbolic ritual, burning reminders into both her hands. Now that she thought of it, T'skya had seen scars on most of the older dwellers' hands, but very few on the younger ones.

Hollam explained the ritual was seldom performed any more. Other ways had been found to seek solace and few saw the need to inflict further pain. Indeed, some even tended to view it as barbaric, but T'skya had seen only respect on the faces of those who had witnessed Hollam's ceremonial burning.

Hollam's face changed. He had talked impassively about the ritual but something was troubling him. He studied the ground for a moment and then cautiously took her hand. 'T'skya,' he said, 'we talked much, my mother and I before she died. She told me to put my trust in you and I will do so. But there is something she said that I do not comprehend. Perhaps you can shed some light on it.'

'I will try,' she replied, hoping he was not going to ask anything awkward.

'These are the words as my mother spoke them: "*Son. Blame not Cail or myself for what must be. Though things are not as they seem, our destinies are clear and may not be altered for the needs of the one."* Can you make sense of it?' he asked hopefully.

T'skya knew what Negram was referring to, but it was neither the time nor the place to add to Hollam's distress. How would he react to find that his mother had lied to him all those years? To learn that Cail was not his brother but the heir to the throne? To discover that his true blood brother had been sacrificed to save the heir? Hollam had suffered enough from Breeze's departure, Cail's capture and Negram's death. Yet he had put his trust in her and deserved the truth.

'I think she means that sometimes we all make choices that have to be made, even if those choices cause great suffering to the people we love. Perhaps she was talking about her death, or about Cail. You knew her better than I did. I can't read her meaning.' T'skya felt ashamed for taking the easy way out. Hollam accepted her words but still looked discontented.

'I am also puzzled by this,' he said, pulling a small amulet from his pocket. 'I have never seen my mother wear it, nor known of its existence, yet she placed great importance upon it when she gave it to me. She told me to keep it safe and present it to the Castan! Methinks she had already crossed the path towards the spirit world and knew not what she was saying, yet her eyes still held light and her voice was strong when she spoke it.'

He shook his head as he puzzled over the meaning of the amulet. Its polished stone caught the light from the fire and glistened as he twisted the woven chain in his fingers. T'skya recognised the stone and knew of its purpose. It was the same as those Cail and she had given to the Grish-Grish-Gûri. But it was the chain which drew most of her attention. Hollam saw her closely observing it.

'It's beautiful,' she said.

'It is woven from my mother's hair,' he said, smiling to himself as he remembered times passed. 'She had such beautiful golden hair that fell to her hips and we would forever annoy her by sitting upon it when she was sewing. But it soon turned white and became like the moon's reflection on the water. She must have carried this amulet for many years.'

He passed the amulet to her and she touched the fine hairs that had been so lovingly woven. They felt like silk and T'skya could almost picture Negram as she cut the tress from her head and set to work.

'Ah, mother,' he said to the night sky, 'you were always a woman of mystery and now you leave me puzzles I am too foolish to solve. I would that my brother were here.'

❦

The following morning, Negram was laid to rest in a simple cemetery on the outskirts of the enclave. The ceremony was brief and each dweller laid a stone and some flowers upon the grave to mark her departure. They bade her farewell and left Hollam to himself. He did not remain long, despite his grief. It was time to resign himself into T'skya's hands and suffer the fate that awaited him.

Hollam had endured much in his life-time, but losing his hair was insufferable. He moaned and fussed like a small child as T'skya cut off lock after lock. But Kházakha soldiers wore their hair short and so his had to go.

'Is that not short enough?' he said mournfully, holding handfuls of his magnificent mane.

'No,' she replied and kept cutting. 'Will you please keep still? I'll have your ears off if you persist in fidgeting. I have to lose most of mine as well, you know.'

'Good,' he muttered and quieted considerably.

When she had finished, she stood back and viewed him with interest.

'Well? How do I look?' he asked, nervously touching what was left of his hair.

'You are still very handsome. It suits you.'

'My neck feels cold,' he complained, unable to keep his

fingers from examining the new style.

'Now for stage two,' she said, picking up a pot of black sludge.

Hollam heaved a sigh and resigned himself to spending the next hour with his head covered in the gunge. 'Does it come off?' he inquired suspiciously.

'It will have to grow out, I'm afraid,' she admitted, although she did not sound particularly sympathetic. Hollam believed she was getting some kind of perverse pleasure from his suffering. In truth she was relieved to have something to occupy her mind.

While he sat waiting for the dye to work, T'skya took hold of her own long hair and began to cut away to her shoulders. She waited for his opinion but he was too surly to answer.

'Now then,' she said, taking a tube out of her pocket. 'I want you to try these. You will need to get used to them so they don't hurt your eyes.' She knelt before Hollam and showed him the sliver-thin green contact lenses she had laboriously prepared.

'What are those?' he spluttered.

It took a great deal of persuasion to convince him they would do him no harm despite the temporary stinging. By now a crowd had gathered to watch the transformation. Tarn was enjoying his friend's discomfort and roared with laughter at his protestations. Catkin was giggling, seeming happier than she had done for a long time. She thought Hollam looked funny.

Putting in the lenses was no mean feat. Hollam kept flinching and T'skya was worried she would poke his eyes out. Eventually, however, he succumbed and sat blinking furiously with tears running down his face.

Just when he thought the last of his suffering was over, T'skya surprised him once more. Taking a needle and a small round earring, she told him she needed to make a tiny hole in his ear. He groaned as he remembered the jewels in Slythe and Snell's ears and knew he had no choice but to comply.

After sterilising the lobe, she jabbed the needle through

the flesh and deftly inserted a hoop. Hollam yelled, more in protest than from pain as his ear began to burn. By then his hair was ready and she set about removing the back residue. She rubbed his head vigorously with a cloth and stood back to admire her handiwork.

There, naked to the waist with his smooth toned chest heaving and with his hair standing on end, was a sullen but remarkably handsome Kházakh. Hearing a round of applause from his audience, Hollam's spirit picked up a little and he bowed deeply. As yet, he had not seen himself, and when he looked into T'skya's compact mirror, he scarcely recognised himself.

'I wonder what Breeze would think of me now?' he muttered.

'She would be very proud of you,' T'skya said softly.

Hollam's mouth twisted. 'Either that or leave me again!'

The seamstresses had prepared uniforms for them and, once dressed, Hollam seemed almost perfect. He had learnt to read basic Navennán and had spent hours trying to master the correct accent. He had managed to remove his own lilting tone, but it was difficult to dispel the formality of his own language and slip into the casual speech of the Kházakha. T'skya decided it was better if he spoke as little as possible.

The plan was simple. Dressed as a nurse, T'skya would present her documents and secure passage on the troop transport ship, accompanying a badly wounded soldier - Hollam - who needed the services of the city's medical centre under the pretence of a weapon malfunction.

Hollam's scorched hand was authentic but T'skya also decided to bandage his head and half of his face to disguise his smooth skin. Roumanhi man did not grow facial hair and lacked the blue tinge of the Kházakha. After all, a wounded soldier was scarcely likely to bother shaving before getting on a transport ship.

To T'skya's amazement and relief the plan went without a hitch. The troops leaving the forest were only too willing to help a comrade in need. They made extra space for Hollam and complained furiously about the design of their weapons. It was not the first time a soldier had been injured and each had a story to tell. T'skya pretended to show a keen interest and kept them talking for some time hoping to avoid any awkward questions.

Hollam acted a wounded man with great aplomb; his proximity to so many Kházakha and extra anxiety as the ship launched turning him pale. Although he had no fear of heights and was often to be found sitting in the tree tops, flying was another matter. He groaned occasionally feeling rather sick. T'skya pretended to doze and soon the compartment fell quiet.

It was not a long trip to the city. The troop transporters were much smaller and lighter than the slave ships and travelled quickly. The ground passed by in a blur but Hollam soon turned away; he did not like the view. The land near the city had been desecrated and he could see no forests to cheer him. The city sprawled in an ungainly fashion across the ruined landscape like a stain across a masterpiece.

The troop transport touched down with a thump in docking bay 5 on the western periphery of the city. The two impostors stood at the hatchway and gained their first real view of the drab concrete bay where metal glinted in the sunlight and slaves, their faces as grey as the pre-fab buildings, served the Kházakha.

T'skya helped Hollam alight and sighed. The ugliness hit her like disease. It was not as she had imagined it. Hollam clenched his jaws battling distaste. The slaves glanced his way but lowered their eyes quickly if he looked at them. He was an enemy, feared and despised. Hollam wanted to flee; his disguise abruptly revolting him, but he held his peace and hid behind his lenses. T'skya wanted to get him out of the bay as quickly as possible. She knew how he must be feeling and did not entirely trust his self constraint.

She marched forwards appearing furious to see no ambulance waiting for them. The ship's Captain offered to radio but she declined; she wanted a vehicle and she wanted it now. Hollam groaned persuasively and leaned on her for support. The Captain barked an order and a clerk scurried across from a shabby office carrying some paperwork. The Captain scrawled his permissions and directed T'skya to the vehicle pool. Inside she was grinning. Hollam was not. He did not like the Kházakha modes of transport; he liked his feet.

Helping the 'injured' man inside, T'skya slipped into the driver's seat and studied the controls. Driving looked simple and after a shaky start, she eased the vehicle towards the gate. Hollam's knuckles whitened on the armrest as they approached the guarded barriers. The guard, however, on seeing Hollam's bandages and T'skya's uniform, waved them through without even checking their papers. T'skya and Hollam were free.

Checking the area she found a deserted place to park and removed the bandages from Hollam's head. It would have looked strange to see a wounded man away from the hospital.

'So far so good,' she said optimistically.

'If you say so,' he replied glumly. The lack of vegetation was upsetting him and the sight of his people enslaved had shaken his spirit.

There was little point in trying to lift his mood; Hollam would bounce back soon. Instead she ran through their plans again and headed towards the edge of the shanty town. Hollam gazed through the windows and grew more solemn. T'skya stared ahead, trying to remember the route, ignoring his grim expression and the grimmer buildings. She pulled in and laid her hand on his.

'Cheer up. In a few days you'll be back in the forest, a free man with Cail bossing you about. And don't forget Breeze is waiting for you.'

A smile tugged at his lips as he stared at the dilapidated shacks. 'I have not forgotten, but we have much to do to gain our freedom. We should go.'

T'skya squeezed his hand. 'I'll join you later at the hospital port as agreed.'

Hollam frowned. 'We should not separate; this place has many dangers. What do you intend?'

T'skya explained and Hollam grudgingly gave his consent. He shouldered his pack and watched her drive away and with a heavy heart walked down the crumbling road towards the filth of the shanty town.

ELEVEN

Family reunion

After a long wait, the roar of engines finally reverberated around the cramped hold of the VST. The craft shook unsteadily before raising itself laboriously into the sky. Raven was smarting inside. She was desperate to check on Cail's condition but the presence or Daravin and Snell forbade it.

Ash was more daring. 'Is that what happens to all your slaves?' he growled, indicating Cail with a nod.

'Only if they disobey,' Daravin answered, eyeing Ash and alert for trouble.

Ash snorted.

'I am not a slave,' Cail said sullenly. He was cursing himself for allowing such an easy capture, especially when he had evaded the Kházakha for so long. He was also grimly contemplating just how excruciating they would make his last few hours of life. He knew the punishment his crimes carried and was in no doubt his death would come slowly, but whatever his fate Cail would not concede to slavery. He was a free man as long as he held that freedom in his heart.

Daravin snorted down his nose at Cail's proclamation but there was no pride in his voice when he answered; 'Well, you are now.'

'He was captured outside his enclave,' Snell added as if it justified the savage beating Cail had received.

'Is flogging not the usual punishment?' a slave asked bravely, scowling through the dim light at the bruises and swellings on Cail's face.

'Not for wanted men. Now keep your mouths shut and we'll get along just fine,' Daravin said, wanting the conversation to cease.

'Wanted for what?' Ash asked, ignoring the warning.

'Murder! Now shut up or you'll get some of the same,' he threatened.

Snell shuffled uncomfortably, upset to be surrounded by angry Roumanhis but Daravin seemed fairly relaxed despite his desire for silence. Snell glanced at his friend. 'Talking passes the time.'

Daravin tilted back his head unconcerned. He squinted at Snell disdainfully through a half opened lid. 'Fine, I'll sleep, you talk. Just watch yourself - they're more cunning than you think.' He closed his eyes and listened attentively to his partner. If Snell was a renegade it may show in his conversation.

'So what will happen to him?' Ash asked.

Snell shook his head and fidgeted in his seat. 'That depends on the High Lord Procurator.'

'And us? What will happen to us?'

'The women will be taken to market and sold. The rest of you will probably end up in the mines,' he replied bluntly and then, deciding he was not enjoying himself, fell into silence and refused to answer anything more.

Daravin fell asleep.

There were no windows in the hold or the Roumanhis might have seen the land slipping by beneath them. Their route followed the same path that Hollam and T'skya would take and took them across the north-west tip of the golden peril, over the brown wastelands, through the pass between the mountains where the Saxskotnaks had met their doom and past the southern edge of the great lake. It was then be a fairly short flight to the landing platforms of dock 9 on the eastern side of the city, where land vehicles would be waiting to be loaded with supplies and where slaves would be crammed aboard wagons, ready for distribution.

The passage through the pass was rough. Winds buffeted the cumbersome craft causing it to lurch. The chained slaves were thrown about unable to brace themselves adequately. Some cried out in alarm frightened the ship would disintegrate or crash in the turbulence. Daravin and Snell remained calm. They were used to the experience and knew that winter winds could be fierce in the north; snow had already fallen on the higher mountain peaks. The VST banked sharply right and headed southwards towards the city and before long the flight became smoother.

Shortly they arrived and the pilot set down on the landing pad with a gentle bump. They were in the city from which no-one, save Gilgarad, had ever returned.

There was a lot of banging and shouting as the holds at the back were opened and emptied. Before long the side door was swung open and light flooded the chamber. The slaves screwed up their faces, blinded by the sudden brightness, and the guards shielded their eyes with their hands. Daravin and Snell exited to file paperwork with the supervisor of Port Control and a Kházakh soldier stood guard, eyeing the slaves suspiciously.

Almost an hour later, Slythe's men returned and began unfastening the shackles. Ash was the first to be taken and met the sight of the Port with fascination and disgust. He had never seen constructions so enormous or ugly before. Around him was a sea of concrete and hulking ships. Kházakha were everywhere, doing their jobs quickly and efficiently, and one or two slaves were assisting them. Ash stared and they stared back unhappy to see more of their people having their liberty stolen. They did not hesitate for long. The Kházakha did not like malingerers and allowed them no rest. Ash tore his eyes away as the rest of his company joined him.

The men and women were deftly segregated. Ash and Ferret found themselves bundled into the back of a truck, whilst Raven was led to one side, separate from the rest of the women. They would be taken to the holding pens, ready for market. But Raven was a special case. She was destined for the Palace.

Daravin stepped beside her, preparing to transport her himself. Snell intervened. 'What are you doing? I can manage her. Your wife and child will be waiting for you. Get out of here!'

Daravin hesitated. He longed to see his family but no longer completely trusted Snell. He was about to dismiss his friend's words when he heard his name being called. He turned joyfully and without a second thought dashed off to greet his wife. Raven sighed and gave Snell a grateful smile. Snell did not smile back. He scowled and pushed her forwards with no uncertain force.

Raven staggered and regaining her balance cast a spiteful look. He directed her towards a small, four-wheeled vehicle and locked her in the front. Raven twisted in her seat trying to get one last look at the VST. She had not seen Cail brought out and was desperate to see him, but Snell slipped in beside her and moodily gunned the engine, making for the security gate.

The guard rifled through the paperwork and eyed Raven with interest. After making a few crude remarks he waved them on and they passed into the suburbs of the city.

The road was wide and all the traffic moved quickly. Raven gripped an arm-rest as Snell manoeuvred through the streets. The barrack houses were squat and square, without any exterior design or decoration to break the monotony. They were either grey or white, with small square windows and brown square doors. It was oppressive and disheartening and Raven felt caged.

Before long the buildings began to grow larger and grander.

The occasional plant decorated a window box and, here and there, a thin strip of grass provided relief to the eye.

They were moving towards the city centre and Raven became uneasy. She was sure they should have turned down the last street. Her destination was the shanty town, which lay to the north. Snell passed another turning and another, and Raven's guts lurched in panic.

'Snell, stop this thing…SNELL!' she commanded.

Snell ignored Raven until her violent attempts to be free from her bonds made the vehicle difficult to control. Bashing his hand on the steering wheel, he pulled to the side of the road and killed the engine.

Raven stopped fighting.

'What the hell was all that?' he barked.

'We had an agreement, remember?' she thundered.

'Yeah, I remember.' He gripped the steering wheel tightly until the skin over his knuckles turned white and his chin fell to his chest. Then he added more gently; 'Raven, I can't do it. I'm sorry.'

'So you are taking me to Santovin,' she stated coldly.

He nodded.

Raven was incensed and desperate to be freed. If Snell took her to Santovin now the plan would be in jeopardy. Cail had already been captured which meant the water tanks relied on Hollam and T'skya, and Ferret and Ash would have difficulty spreading the word to all sectors of the slave zone without her. She used the only card she had. 'And what of your brother? Would you have him suffer for your cowardice?'

'You won't harm him. He's too valuable,' Snell rejoined.

It was a clever reply, but spoken with too little conviction to worry her. 'Perhaps he has outgrown his uses. Are you willing to take that risk? My friends will not take your treachery kindly.'

'Nor will mine!' he said bitterly.

Raven changed her tact. 'Two days Snell. That is all I ask,

two days. After that I will turn myself in to Santovin, I swear it.'

'If Santovin learns of this…'

Raven emptied her tone of threat. 'Why should he? He is not expecting me.'

'Daravin or any of the others could tell him,' Snell replied.

'Is that likely?'

'No, I suppose not,' he had to admit.

'Two days for your brother's life,' she pressed.

Snell sighed and resigned himself to his fate. Directing the vehicle down the street, he swung sharply to the right and headed for the notorious slave zone, dropping her off at its borders.

Raven watched Snell's vehicle disappearing and rubbing her abraded wrists checked her bearings. She was on the outskirts of the shanty town and could see the dilapidated buildings stretching out before her. There was a vague smell of decay and stale sewage that grew stronger as she made her way towards the heart of the ghetto. The buildings became cruder and shabbier, constructed from an odd assortment of materials. There was rubbish everywhere and Raven was shocked by her people's disregard for their environment, and for themselves.

Things were worse than she had imagined.

Raven took out a worn cloak and covered her clothes, hoping to blend in. The streets were relatively empty; most of the inhabitants occupied in the mines during the day or fulfilling their functions in the more civilized part of the city. There were a few young children running about totally unsupervised and wearing little but rags and their slave collars. One or two old women, too weary to watch over the children, stared at her blankly from their doorways as they knitted or sewed clothes for the Kházakha.

Raven moved warily onwards. Twice she was forced to duck into a doorway to avoid the law patrols, and was compelled to defend herself from the unwanted attentions of a drunk. The

Roumanhis here had been de-civilised by the Kházakha; de-humanised by their abject lives and the savage brutality they witnessed hour after hour, day after day. Raven cursed and her purpose grew stronger.

Eventually, she came to the house she was seeking, if it could be called such a thing. She paused for a considerable time outside the doorway, uncertain about her presence there. Taking hold of her courage, she tapped lightly on the flimsy wooden door and stood back expectantly. Receiving no reply she cautiously went inside.

The room was empty and what furniture existed was poorly constructed. In the far corner was a ragged blanket which constituted a bed. Next to it was a wooden crate which served as a table or chair, and opposite were some shelves crudely attached to the wall. On the uppermost shelf, Raven was touched to see a sickly looking flower sticking out of a pot. She scooped a small amount of water out of a tin bucket and gave the plant a well needed drink.

Looking around her, she spotted a disturbance in the floor. Within seconds she had unearthed a wooden box. It had been tightly bound with numerous ties. Opening it, she held back tears as she saw a scanty supply of food: some dried biscuits, a shrivelled apple and a stale piece of bread. There was also a lock of golden-red hair that had been carefully preserved in a delicate cotton handkerchief. Feeling ashamed of her prying, she gingerly replaced the box and sat on the crate, awaiting the return of the owner.

Raven had a long wait. It was almost dark when she heard footsteps approaching the house. The sector began to come alive with the sound of voices and the trampling of feet. Despite their exhaustion, some of the men began shouting and cursing each other and Raven could hear the distant sound of weapon fire as the law enforcers moved in to break up the disturbance.

A shadowy form carrying a stick tottered through the door

and made its way to the shelves. Taking down a candle, it proceeded to light it and check if its hidden treasure was secure. Raven, watching from the shadows, said nothing.

Sensing it was being observed the form swung around and held the candle out with a trembling hand. The light illuminated Raven's pale face and dark eyes.

'What do you want? Get out of my house. There is nothing for you here!' the shrunken creature said, waving the stick threateningly and eyeing the warrior with fear and suspicion.

'Do you not recognize me?' Raven asked softly, rising to her feet.

The form inched closer, moving its head from side to side, trying to comprehend. 'Raven, is that really you?'

'Yes, Rosie. Have I changed so much?'

Rosie laughed and embraced her as enthusiastically as her crippled bones allowed. 'You were such a small girl when I last saw you. You have grown so much. You look so beautiful; the image of your mother,' she crooned.

'Am I? I scarcely remember her,' Raven said. She had spent so many years fighting to master the distress and burning rage of her mother's aimless death that she dared not allow the feelings to surface. To do so would not serve the cold intent of her purpose. She was a warrior and warriors did not succumb to useless emotions. They were impenetrable, as hard as mountain and as cold as glaciers, passionate only for their purpose and that purpose was to fight. Raven's mantra swirled in her consciousness as she pushed the frighteningly vivid images of her mother's last moments to the cemetery of her mind where they belonged.

'Raven,' the old lady said, seating herself on the crate, 'I am blessed by your presence, but in truth I cannot say I am pleased to see you. There is no joy in seeing one so vital and young sentenced to a life-time's hard labour.'

Raven smiled at her concern. 'I am not a slave - at least, not yet. I came here of my own free will.'

Rosie looked amazed. 'Now, do not tease your old nanny, dear. I am not yet too decrepit to box your ears!'

Raven laughed. Following the death of Raven's mother she had been a precocious, unruly child given to wild moods and even greater stubbornness; she had truly given Rosie a difficult time. Rosie had taken on the responsibility of raising the child, but had been taken to the city when Raven was Catkin's age and had lived there ever since. Raven felt the Kházakha had deprived her twice. Evacuated to make way for the Kházakha's deforestation schemes she had moved to Wilderwood and spent her teenage years with Cail. Through a combination of patience, kindness and physical training he helped her combat some of the demons. And so she became the warrior and learned to love Cail with the same intensity of feelings she had learned to bury. Raven had and never would do or feel anything in half measures.

Raven's laugh receded into mute solemnity. She knew it would not be an easy task to convince the woman of her words. And yet Raven needed Rosie's help.

In a hushed voice and as simply as she could, Raven explained what she needed. She had to repeat it many times and still Rosie's mind failed to grasp what she was saying. The crippled old woman shook her head in disbelief.

'That is a nice story, dear. And you say your chosen is here, too? What a pity; the two of you enslaved. I do not think you will see much of him!'

Despite herself Raven was growing impatient. It was clear Rosie had lost her capacity for rational thought. Raven tried a different approach. 'I take it you know everyone here?'

Rosie looked coy and cocked her head in confirmation.

'Do you not want to show me off to whichever Roumanhi is in charge here?'

'Why, yes,' Rosie replied happily. 'I will take you to Kilmar. I have talked to him often about you. Let me get my shawl - the nights have grown so cold - and we shall go. It is not far.'

Raven helped Rosie to her feet and watched as she draped the thread-bare shawl about her shoulders.

Kilmar lived only two blocks distance but with Rosie's inability to walk at more than a shuffle it took them a while to reach it. A dim flickering light illuminated the window and Raven observed movement behind the tatty curtains. Rosie tapped at the door.

Kilmar was a muscular man of about fifty, with greying hair and sloping coffee coloured eyes. His chin was long and his lips too thin to be considered handsome, but he was certainly charismatic. He introduced his squat side-kick Stumpy and gestured for the women to sit.

After a pleasantly aimless chat, Rosie informed them that she was too weary to continue and made to leave. Anxious to speak with Kilmar alone, Raven made excuses to remain; Stumpy escorted the old lady home.

Once sure she could trust him, Raven related the reasons for her visit as efficiently as she was able and noted his reaction with satisfaction. Kilmar listened avidly and could hardly contain his enthusiasm. He had long awaited the chance to take action against the Kházakha and had already organized a strong underground movement which was growing every day. There would be no problem spreading the news in his sector. It was late indeed when Raven left him, and she smiled as she walked the quiet street back to Rosie's.

Raven spent much of the next day and night alone and in hiding. She could not afford to let herself be seen by the Kházakha patrols and a young woman like her would be conspicuous. She sat quietly, considering the circumstances and her drastic intentions, but as time passed the frustration of inactivity overcame her. Disguising herself in some of Rosie's rags she finally ventured into the streets.

She walked slowly, keeping to the shadows as she studied all the houses and street numbers in the sector. Kilmar had warned her of the dangers, forbidding entry to areas where some slaves would not hesitate to betray her. The reward of food and clothing outweighed desire for loyalty in the weak-minded and weak-spirited. Raven dared not walk too far.

Concealed in a doorway, she watched the movements of the law patrols, remaining for some time to calculate the frequency of their attendance and studying their route. Finally, she decided to return to her safe haven. Rosie would be worried if she found her missing. Passing a half-opened doorway a long arm reached out, covered Raven's mouth to prevent an outburst, and hauled her through the door.

Feeling a man's body close behind her, Raven fiercely jabbed an elbow into his sternum and jerked her arm upwards, her balled fist catching him in the face.

With a muffled curse, the man let go, staggered backwards, tripped over a packing case and landed heavily on the dusty floor. The light was poor but Raven could make out the white uniform and black hair of a tall Kházakh as he lay there rubbing his nose.

As she advanced, ready to assault him further, the man reproached her. 'That hurt!'

'Hollam?'

He raised himself to his elbows and grinned. 'The one and only. I just wish you had realised sooner.'

She helped him to his feet and dragged him to where the dying light streaked in through the tiny window. 'You know me, strike first, ask questions later,' she said by way of apology as she turned him round to get a proper look. 'What happened to you? Why do you look like a Kházakh?'

'It is a long tale. What of the others?'

Raven explained what she knew before turning the conversation to Cail. Hollam narrated the events at the dell and told her of Negram's death.

'Oh Hollam. I grieve with thee,' she said, taking his wounded hand in hers and kissing it. 'I should have realised when I saw the bandages. How did you know it was me?' she added after a pause.

'That swing of your hips,' he replied, sucking on his lips.

'I did not know that you had observed my hips so closely.'

'I may be a clown, but I am still a man, you know. And I have not forgotten you from old,' he said with a knowing smile.

'I know,' Raven replied, thinking back to their brief romance. But she thrust the thoughts aside. There were more pressing issues to attend to. 'And would this man please tell me what he is doing here dressed like this, and be quick. I do not wish to be found by the owner of this place.'

After Hollam had finished explaining Raven inquired thoughtfully; 'Where is T'skya?'

'She has gone to find Snell.'

'Snell? But why? He does not know of her.'

'Exactly. He will not know she is connected with you. She is going as a friend of Prell's. There is little cause for concern.'

'I am not so sure. He is nervous and nearly betrayed me,' Raven said grimly.

'You are not a Kházakh,' Hollam pointed out.

Raven looked strangely uncomfortable and abruptly changed the subject. 'I am late. How will I contact you?'

'You cannot. We are leaving tonight for the water tanks. You will have about two moon rises to accomplish your task.'

'Tonight!' she muttered. 'How will you get there?'

'T'skya will pick me up from the hospital port later. We will go to the edge of the city and then separate. If one of us is taken, then at least the other will stand a chance.'

'Your route?' she asked with great interest.

'I will approach the tanks from the north and T'skya from the south. I can cover more ground than her.'

'I must go.'

'Will you not wish me luck?'

'I do not believe in luck,' she replied, leaving him alone.

Raven hurried back to Rosie's house and found the old woman waiting anxiously in the doorway. 'Where have you been?' she asked.

'Nowhere - Look Rosie, I cannot explain but I must leave you now.'

'You are returning to your master?' Rosie inquired.

Catching her meaning, the flame-haired woman nodded. Rosie still believed Raven was a slave. 'Yes, Rosie. I must return.'

'Take care, dear. And come to see me soon if you can. Your master must be a kindly man to let you visit your old nanny.'

Raven smiled at Rosie's ignorance and kissed her on the brow. 'I will. I promise.' With that, she dashed off through the dusky streets, heading for the city centre.

༄༅

The sector where Ferret and Ash were housed was less serene than Rosie's. Within minutes they were set upon by youths hoping to find supplies in the men's packs. Ferret gave his up without a word, but Ash was less obliging. He fought like a wild cat until he observed their skinny bodies and the pathetic rags they called clothes. Backing off Ash handed them his pack and his cloak. His kind intent resulted in a violent struggle between the boys as they fought for the goods but the battle soon ended with the approach of the Kházakha law keepers. The boys scattered leaving Ferret and Ash alone.

They entered their shack and looked about in disgust. It was filthy. They backed out quickly and stared at each other in agreement. The smell outside was none too pleasant but it certainly excelled that within. They chose to remain outside.

With nothing better to do until their duties began that night Ferret and Ash decided to explore the sector. Some people were trying to catch up on a little sleep, exhausted from hard labour. Many others were sitting in their doorways holding conversations, some heated. The only women to be openly seen were old; the younger ones housed in a different sector or in the homes they served. The children were probably stolen from the enclaves, used for work requiring their dainty fingers. They were unlikely to have been a result of a bonding between the city slaves; sexual contact was against the law, although appropriate bribes could sometimes ensure a blind eye was turned.

Ash was eager to track down his family but their inquiries met with no success. The male slaves would not give information freely and Ferret and Ash had little in the way of supplies to bargain with now their packs had been stolen. Soon they were dressed in dirty rags, having traded their shirts and trousers for knowledge. They met with better luck from the old women, who retained some generosity of spirit, but for the most part their information was worthless and Ash began to lose heart.

Nevertheless, a clue reunited Ash with Reed, one of his cousins. The blond boy was in his early teens and had been taken to the city almost a year previously. Being a hardy sort and quick-witted, Reed had managed to achieve a fairly important position in the sector. The Roumanhi section leader used him as a messenger and ensured he was adequately fed and housed and that he lived unmolested. The name Reed gave drew gasps of disbelief from the newcomers.

'Spider! Not *the* Spider from my enclave?' Ash asked in astonishment.

'From Wilderwood? Yes, that is he,' young Reed replied.

'We assumed he had been executed.'

Spider had been involved in Fen's rescue and the killing of several Kházakha. It was astounding to hear that not only had his life been spared, but that he had risen to lord over a section of the shanty town. Suspicious, the two men conferred together quietly. If he had turned traitor, it could ruin everything. If not, if he still retained his loyalty, he could be invaluable.

It was a tough decision.

They chose the risk but would have to wait until the following day. Bidding Reed farewell, they hurried back to their ramshackle dwelling to await the transport which would take them for their first taste of the mines; a taste they would never forget.

By morning Ferret and Ash were almost dead on their feet. They stumbled into their filthy house and dropped to the floor. Their necks and backs ached terribly and their fingers were blistered and cracked. Blood oozed from their gashed knees, visible through the rips in their trousers. They were covered in dust and both looked as if they had come off a battle field.

They had dug and lifted and ferried and dug without respite for most of the night. Ferret had suffered the most. He was not a strong man and had nearly collapsed under the weight of the rocks he was forced to carry. The Kházakha did not take slacking off kindly and their whips stung anyone unable or unwilling to keep pace.

So ended their first shift in the mines.

After sleeping on the uncomfortable floor for several hours, the duo stretched stiffly and went to find Reed. The young boy greeted them cheerfully, a short distance away from their house. He had been sent to fetch them and was glad to see them up and ready.

The route he took was complicated and seemed to double back on itself and criss-cross roads they were sure they had already walked. 'Do you not trust us?' Ash asked, stifling a yawn.

'I do, but perhaps Spider does not. I am only following orders. Besides which, this avoids all the patrols,' Reed answered sincerely.

He spoke the truth. Neither Ferret nor Ash saw a single Kházakha vehicle and they were happy to keep it that way. Before much longer, Reed escorted them down some steps which led to an underground chamber. It was like a home away from home as they stepped into the candle-lit stone room. The boy took his leave and the two men found themselves alone. As they surveyed the chamber, the grandest they had seen in the ghettos, a man bustled into the room and embraced them heartily. It was Spider.

'Well met, my friends. What Ash? Can it be you? You were this high when I last saw you,' he said, indicating his chest in wild exaggeration. 'And Ferret. Still scavenging?'

Ferret shrugged, smiling in spite of himself but retaining suspicions of his so-called friend. 'I had not thought to see you again. How did you escape execution?'

'Ah, Ferret, Ferret, always straight to the point. Surely you do not wish to hear that boring tale? What of you and all my friends at Wilderwood? How fares Cail and Hollam?'

'Hollam was well the last time we saw him. Cail, we believe, is imprisoned at the Palace, and we *do* wish to hear your tale. If you escaped death then perhaps he, too, can manage it. It is of *great* interest to us,' Ferret stressed.

Spider's smile slipped from his face. 'That is grave news indeed. Cail captured?' He shook his head sadly. 'Santovin is less likely to be charitable with him. I was merely present; Cail pulled the trigger. I am afraid you must consider him lost.'

'You are well suited to your position, Spider. You have avoided answering our questions twice,' Ash interjected.

Spider's face darkened and his voice was tight. 'I did not realise I was under interrogation!'

Ferret eyed the sandy-haired man and made to leave. 'We have heard enough,' he said at the foot of the steps.

'It was a deal. I made a deal,' Spider suddenly admitted, giving them a baleful look. Ferret and Ash stared at one another and in silent agreement seated themselves in front of Spider. They waited for him to continue but their accusing faces troubled him and he was unwilling to speak for some time.

The original bargain turned out not to be as bad as they had imagined. Spider's deal was simply to inform the law enforcers about any potential trouble makers from either side. The High Lord Procurator did not tolerate people doubting his word or spreading scandalous gossip about the goings-on at his Palace.

Spider took pleasure from reporting the Kházakha soldiers when he heard them criticising their divine leader. It was the one thing that made his city existence bearable.

His deal had cost him more than he had bargained for, however. Santovin kept changing the rules and embroiling him in treacherous schemes which had clearly taken their toll. Although only twenty-four years old in Navennán terms, Spider looked worn and weary. His cheeks were hollow, despite the extra allowance of food, and his hair was already streaked with grey. He had many enemies and feared for his life everyday. If something were not done soon, he was afraid he would not live to see his twenty-fifth year! He wanted out.

After a furious few minute's private discussion, Ferret and Ash told him some of the plans for the city. They told him less than he needed to hear and hoped that it was not one word too many. Spider shook with relief and told them that he would do everything in his power to help them. He would spread the word and look forward to seeing the results.

❧❦❧

Cail remained alone in the hold pondering his fate and trying to nurse his wounds. He did not know what had become of T'skya and Hollam, but trusted his brother to find some way to carry out their plans. His whole body ached. The stun guns had burned and then deadened his nerves and although feeling had begun to creep back into his flesh, the process was slow and painful. His eye was throbbing and his lip thick and encrusted with blood; courtesy of Slythe. Still he smiled with satisfaction; his silence had done more damage to Slythe than Slythe's brutality had done to him. But this made his lip split open and he watched with idle interest as blood dripped onto his mud-encrusted shirt.

A large brutish man stepped into the transport, unfastened him and dragged him roughly to his feet. It was difficult to stand and the Kházakh had to half-carry, half-drag him from the hold. He did not do it gently. Cail's hands were bound behind his back and his feet chained together so that he could move at no more than a shuffle. He was thrown into the back of a security wagon and taken with all speed towards the holding cells in the bowels of the Palace.

On arrival his jailor watched him with smug contempt and, as the doors of the wagon were opened, he flipped a hood over Cail's head and aimed a kick into his ribs as a parting gesture. Cail grunted and half fell out of the doors. He felt rough hands grabbing his arms as he was man-handled down several corridors and into the main prison complex.

Weakened and with obscured vision, Cail soon became disorientated and was glad when they came to a standstill. He felt sick. The hood was removed but before he could get his bearings, he was thrust into a darkened room. Unable to protect himself, Cail hit the wall hard and slumped to the floor groaning. The door was slammed shut and locked.

Blind, he staggered to his feet, using the wall to balance against, and carefully circumnavigated the room. It did not take long. The cell was tiny and devoid of furniture. He could not even feel the cracks of the door. Finding a corner, he bent his knees and sagged to the floor awaiting his fate.

Cail spent two nightmarish days in his black hole of a cell and saw no-one; not even when what little nourishment he was given was delivered. It was not easy to eat or drink with his hands chained behind him, but he managed just enough to keep him going. Staying hygienic was another matter.

He woke from his troubled dreams as the door was swung open and blinding lights in the ceiling dazzled his eyes. He turned his head away, trying to avoid the glare, and squinted up at the brutish man who stood leering at him from the doorway. Two more guards wheeled an ominous-looking trolley into the tiny room. It was filled with strange, evil-looking equipment, and Cail knew the devices were intended for him. His stomach lurched and he groaned hoping his strength would last. He would rather die than betray his comrades.

He was roughly untied and rebound with his hands before him, nearly crying out as the circulation flooded back into his limbs. With precision, the guards strung a chain over a beam in the high ceiling and attached it to the shackles. Hauling on the other end they raised Cail some inches from the ground. The metal cut into his wrists as they took his full weight, and the blood left his arms again. His shirt was ripped open revealing pale flesh and icy water was flung at him wetting his skin. The brutish man snapped a command and the guards left, closing the heavy door behind them. Cail eyed his enemy, and his enemy eyed him back and smiled.

Nothing can describe the pain and humiliation Cail suffered. The Kházakh showed no mercy as he inflicted all method of torture and abuse on the helpless prisoner. Cail's screams were deafening but no-one could hear them. No-one would come to his aid. The room was soundproof and no-one but the leering Kházakh could release him from his torment. And yet nothing had been asked of Cail. No questions, no demands. The Kházakh was simply toying with him, enjoying the sadism and almost drooling at Cail's distress.

The Kházakh left no marks on Cail's body to show of his suffering. He wanted to leave no evidence. He knew every sensitive point, every nerve, every method of cruelty. He was a master.

Cail was sobbing. He had too little energy left to scream. His head lolled to one side and his breathing came in hoarse irregular gasps. He would not remain conscious for long. The cause of his inhuman agony raised the electric probe again.

Cail could do nothing but wait.

Suddenly the door was wrenched open and a man dressed in senior military uniform charged in, closely followed by two guards. With a roar he tore the probe from the startled Kházakh and lashed him across the face with the back of his hand.

'If he dies, your neck will stretch!' he threatened wrathfully. 'Get out of here and take your butcher's tools with you,' he demanded, kicking over the trolley.

'He murdered my brother!' the brutish man raged, pointing an accusing finger at Cail.

'And he will pay for it, Jakov. But *not* like this. You,' he snarled, pointing at the vengeful man, 'are confined to quarters. Now get out!'

The furious soldier stormed off, scattering the fallen tools on the way. The guards hastily began to clear up the mess.

'Fetch this man water and something to wake him up,' the officer ordered as he released Cail and eased his limp form to the floor. The guards scurried off and returned quickly with the required supplies. They were then dismissed.

The Kházakh pillowed Cail's head in the crook of his arm and felt for his pulse. It was weak and irregular. Another shock might have killed him. The officer waved some smelling salts beneath the semi-conscious man's nose. Cail spluttered and jerked awake. He was groggy but managed to accept a sip of water. He had not had anything to drink for hours and was desperate for more, but the soldier knew better than to overload him.

He lightly slapped Cail around the face to bring him round more fully. Cail flinched, expecting more punishment.

'Do you know who I am?' the Kházakh inquired.

Cail cast a bleary eye at the chevrons on the man's uniform. 'Travis?' he replied, his speech slurred, as he gazed up at the man's face.

Travis was middle-aged and was, despite the lines about his eyes and greying hair at his temples, an attractive man. The colour of his eyes was not dissimilar to T'skya's and he looked upon Cail with a mixture of compassion and concern as he nodded in confirmation. 'I'm sorry I didn't arrive sooner. I should have prevented this unfortunate incident, but I had other duties to attend to. You won't be harmed like that again.'

'Until my execution?' Cail replied weakly, his mouth slipping into a sad smile.

'Your fate is, as yet, undecided. The High Lord Procurator will make the final decision.'

Cail was not impressed by the news. He had killed and the penalty was death. It did not matter who gave the final word, the outcome would be the same. The Kházakha did not forget and nor did they forgive.

'What do you want, Travis?' Cail said with effort.

Travis shook his head, unsure of Cail's meaning.

'He plays the bad, you the good. Is that the routine?'

Travis smiled sadly. 'Yes, that's how it would appear to me, if I were in your position. Gilgarad also distrusted me at first but he did not find me wanting.'

Cail kept his face blank; he did not wish to reveal his knowledge of the man. Travis waited for some reaction and then continued; 'You are an admirable man, Cail - that is your name - in trying to protect your comrades, but I know more about you than you could possibly imagine.'

Cail managed to sit up with difficulty. 'Enlighten me.'

'You have friends, or at least one friend, in the city seeking your release,' Travis replied casually. He noted Cail's reaction with interest. The blond man unsteadily pushed himself away and sat with his back against the cold sterile wall. He attempted disinterest but the muscle in his jaw twitched involuntarily and his breathing fractionally quickened. It was enough to tell the Commander the young man was terrified by the news. He was hiding something and Travis intended to find out what.

He leaned towards his prisoner and spoke in a low secretive voice. 'Be careful who you trust, Cail. Even those you trust may betray you. I've already done what I can for you. The rest is out of my hands.' Travis stared at Cail and opened his mouth as if to speak again but instead rose to his feet and left Cail alone to ponder the meaning of his words.

❧

The High Lord Procurator stood viewing his city from the tall bay window of his immense chamber. Lights below twinkled from the houses and street lamps and everything appeared quiet and untroubled. He held his hands behind his back and only the tapping of his foot betrayed the irritation he felt at being disturbed.

One of his guards was standing to attention, nervously awaiting his command. Santovin spoke without turning, for which the guard was grateful. He would not have to abide those eyes!

'Hoffner, you say?'

'Yes, my Lord. He seemed to think it was important.'

'Very well, Esrik. Send the Captain in.' Esrik saluted and made a hasty retreat. The High Lord Procurator did not like having his evenings disturbed and Esrik would rather Hoffner received his displeasure.

Hoffner was waiting impatiently in the ante-room, guarding a prisoner who seemed as anxious to get the audience with Santovin over as quickly as he was. Esrik nodded to the Captain and held open one of the double doors.

Santovin was standing on his dais awaiting his Captain's news. He was surprised to see the prisoner by his side. 'What is this creature doing here?' the High Lord demanded, giving the prisoner a scornful glance.

'Lord Procurator,' Hoffner said, swallowing hard, 'she claims to have invaluable information and would speak to no-one but you. I thought it wise to let you interrogate her.'

'Your duty is to follow orders, Hoffner, *not* to think! Couldn't you have extracted the information yourself instead of bothering me with such triviality?'

Hoffner shuffled his feet nervously. The High Lord was

quick to temper and his punishments for incompetence or disobedience were harsh. 'My Lord, she said that should we harm her, you would be displeased. She insisted, Lord, that she would die before we broke her and would speak only if she saw you. She came to us freely and unarmed. I saw no possible danger.'

The High Lord Procurator considered for a moment and relented. 'Very well, Hoffner. I will speak to her. But take heed of my words,' he warned, 'should she have nothing of worth to impart, you will both suffer. You are dismissed.'

Hoffner looked surprised. It was irregular to leave the Lord alone with a prisoner, especially without the presence of his personal guards, but an order from Santovin was not to be ignored. Taking one hard look at the woman who now held his own fate in her hands he saluted and left the room.

The High Lord Procurator walked slowly down the dais steps and stopped directly in front of the woman, imposing on her personal space. She met his pale eyes and looked upon him arrogantly, unperturbed by his ghostly countenance.

Santovin was as white as pristine snow and his eyes were that characteristic albino pink. His veins lay pallid blue behind his paper skin like a network of roads. His face was withered with age and pock-marked, and what was left of his straggling white hair had been slicked over his domed head with oil. He was shorter than she had imagined but his body was still firm and his back was straight and disciplined.

'Name?' he demanded shortly.

'My name is Raven,' she replied calmly.

He leant towards her face in an intimidating manner and smiled a sneering smile. 'So, Raven, you surrendered yourself and demanded an audience with me. How very important you must think yourself. Well, here I am. Speak,' he commanded.

'I came unarmed. Surely a lone woman is no danger to you, Lord,' she stated, holding her shackled arms up to him in expectation. She knew he was arrogant and that her words would rub his pride.

The shackles were duly removed and she rubbed her wrists where the metal had once again chafed them.

'Speak primitive. My time is precious.'

Raven had no hesitation in replying. 'If I am primitive, then you are as I am, for we are of one blood.'

The Lord Procurator's eyes blazed at the insult. Raven was interested to note his eyes became redder and seemed to protrude from his emaciated skull. 'What evil is this? My blood is pure, not the heathen filth that flows through you!' he hissed.

Raven was not daunted. Her purpose was clear and nothing was going to stop her. She felt stronger than ever; almost invincible. She goaded him further. 'Your loins are long and your memory short.'

The woman had spirit, he admired that, but her insolence was infuriating. He had the great desire to kill her where she stood, but no, he would extract the information and kill her later. He would enjoy that spectacle. 'Greater people have died for lesser crimes by my hand. Be careful what you say, woman!' he warned.

'Would you really kill me, father?' she asked quietly.

To her bewilderment, the High Lord Procurator Santovin burst into a hideous distorted laugh. Saliva gurgled in his throat and Raven flinched in disgust as a rain of spittle showered her face. 'Father? Father! *You* are alien conceived of lesser blood.'

'Half of me is alien. The other half is yours. Look at me, Santovin. Do you not recall my mother's face? Am I not her very image?' she asked.

He looked at her curiously, a faded recollection playing on his mind. 'What proof do you have of this?' he demanded. 'What was this woman's name?'

'She was called Sage. You raped her.' Raven put her hands to her neck and unclasped a necklace. Hanging from the chain was a small gem. It twinkled and glittered in the light as she held it up for his inspection. 'You gave her this in payment. A worthless jewel from your world, I believe. She gave it to me before she died so that you might know me when I cut your throat, though I have not come seeking revenge.'

'She is dead?' he asked sharply ignoring the veiled threat.

'She died when I was a child.' Raven's voice held no blame. She stated the facts simply and clearly. She could not let her personal hatred of this man, the father she had never known, the father who had assaulted her mother and indirectly caused her death, the father who enslaved her people and tortured them, interfere with her intent. She would have her revenge, but not now; not yet.

'So my bastard child, why haven't you sought me out before? What is it that you wish from me? Toys? A Birthday gift?'

Raven had expected more reaction than that. She had expected a battle of words. She thought he would show surprise or regret but he accepted her revelation dispassionately, as if finding out he had a daughter was an everyday occurrence. She stared into his cruel pink eyes and then, without hesitation, spoke of her intent. Her voice was cold and controlled. 'I have a bargain to make with you. A bargain which will benefit us both.

TWELVE

It's all in the genes

Cail was rudely awakened by a blast of icy water as a pressure hose washed out his cell. He spluttered and coughed as the stinging water surged against his body, pinning him to the wall. He could scarcely breathe and tried turning his back to protect his face from the torrent, but the force was too strong and he had no choice but to endure the freezing water which pierced into his flesh like razor sharp knives. Then as abruptly as it started, the hose was turned off, the door slammed shut and he was left sitting on a saturated floor feeling semi-clean but wretched.

Although his legs were no longer shackled, although he was no longer deprived of light and had regular, if scanty, meals courtesy of Commander Travis, he suffered nonetheless. He had been kept in isolation since his torture and had not even seen another face; his incarceration was wearing. All Cail could do was nurse his wounds and wait for his fate to be decided.

Drenched, he sat wiping dripping hair from his eyes with bound hands and began to shiver. Cail tucked his legs up to his chest, closing his arms over his knees in a vain attempt to retain some body heat. He idly watched the water ebbing away across the shiny grey tiles and into the drain and let his thoughts drift to his friends and family and to happier days beneath the green leaves of the forest and the baking glow of the sun.

He remained lost in thought for many hours, too cold and ravaged to even find the energy to move from the floor. There was scarcely a part of him that was not bruised or damaged in some way and his morale fell as low as the temperature.

A vision drifted before his eyes and he imagined he saw Raven tip-toeing across the floor in embroidered slippers, dressed in a luxurious gown of darkest blue patterned with silver leaves about the hem; her vivid red hair piled high on her head in curls and fastened with intricate clips embedded with gems. Her voice drifted across to him through the void between wake and sleep and he rubbed at his eyes, thinking her a dream.

'Raven, is it really you?' he murmured, his dark eyes gazing at her loveliness through the multi-coloured bruises.

The vision smiled down upon him, surreal in its beauty and terrifying in the absurdity of its presence. 'Yes, beloved,' she replied, brushing his cheek with her long fingers.

The reality of her gentle touch woke him from his dreams and he sighed in deep despair. 'I am so sorry. Have they hurt you?'

She shook her head smiling and gestured to her fine gown. 'Can you not see? I am unharmed. But you? I cannot believe what they have done to you. Was it terrible?'

Cail bowed his head unwilling to relive his torment. If he closed his eyes he could still feel the impact of fists as they smashed into his face, the boots as they dug into his guts, the chains as they tore at his wrists. He could still feel the utter cruelty of electricity coursing through his flesh, setting fire to his nerves and causing spasms to wrack his muscles, the iron grip clamping into pressure points and the paralysing fear of the next assault. He pushed his recollections aside and answered darkly; 'It is not something I wish to recall!' He forced his mind to concentrate on the lissom figure before him. 'How did you get here? From whence came those clothes? You wear the finery of wealth, not the attire of a slave.'

Raven ran her hands over the soft bodice of her gown. It felt sensuous to the touch and for a moment she looked lost in thought almost as if he were no longer there. Her reply, when it came, however, was vehement. 'These mean nothing. What matters is that I am safe, and so, my love, are you.'

Cail stared up at Raven unable to comprehend her meaning. 'What are you saying?' he asked pushing himself to sit upright against the wall. The cold solidity was the only thing that felt real in the bizarreness of her presence. He still was not sure she was real, a dream that was steadily transcending into nightmare.

She ignored him and began to pace the room, giving vent to wild fantasies, her arms flailing and her voice rising with excitement. 'My fate has adorned me, a fitting tribute to my worth and you, most noble of men, are my prize. Together we will overthrow the Kházakha and the people will worship us. Nothing will stop us; nothing can stop us when we are together. I have found my destiny, my one true love; I claim you as my own as I am fated to do. You will rule the land and I shall stand by your side. Think on it, Cail. Your life has been granted you. You are saved.'

A savage frown appeared on Cail's face as if cleavered through his skull and what little colour there was remaining in his face drained silently away. He was deeply disturbed by the insanity of her speech, too weak to fully comprehend the implications. He took a deep breath and forced himself to remain calm. 'Only the Castan can rule the land. You know this.'

'The Castan is dead,' she spat. 'An inept ruler who had not the wit to save himself or those he loved, struck down by the hand of...' She stopped abruptly, shaken by the near admission. She crouched down in front of the troubled man smiling, the blackness of her eyes unblinking, carrying conviction from her soul. 'We shall rule in his place, you and I. Do you not see? It is our destiny; we were meant to be together. I have saved you.'

Cail could hardly believe his ears. The words hurt him; her behaviour peculiar, almost possessed. There was a fanatically triumphant gleam in her eye and he did not trust it. Her attire, her unspoken meaning and her unshackled presence aroused all his suspicions. The warning Travis had given him sprang to the forefront and he asked in a tremulous voice: 'What exactly *have* you done, Raven?'

The smile faded from her face and she gazed into his upturned eyes with such intensity and passion it was suffocating. 'What I have done has been for you, Cail. It is always for you.'

She bent towards him and took his chin in her hands. As gently as a feather falls, she placed her lips upon his and lingered there, relishing the touch of his skin, lost in memory of their intimacy and ignorant of his pain. Cail was too bewildered and shocked to protest. Her words had filled him with a coldness far greater than the water had done, and they had filled him with a dread more powerful than any torture could have achieved.

Withdrawing from him, Raven turned abruptly and knocked on the semi-open door for a guard to escort her back to the upper levels of the Palace. She did not even glance back.

Cail's numb eyes remained fixed on the place where she had stood.

❧

Hollam was going frantic. It was growing dark and T'skya was long overdue. He shook his head knowing that each minute's delay risked his brother's life and disrupted the tight schedule he was working to. He hoped and prayed she was just delayed and that nothing terrible had happened to her. Hollam had grown to love her like a sister and now with Negram dead, Breeze gone, Cail captured and T'skya missing, Hollam felt lost. Resignedly, he decided to set out alone.

With the slim hope of finding T'skya, he clipped the edge of the residential zone in a desperate attempt to catch wind of her or at least to find their vehicle. Had he but ventured one street further, he might have seen it parked outside the law station and gathered that his friend was within; but luck abandoned him.

He expected it to take him perhaps two days, barring accident, to reach the hulking water storage tanks. They were set back at the base of the mountains leagues from the city. Water was piped from the deep artificial lake to a purification plant, from there into the storage tanks and then on to the inhabitants. Purifying the water was vital. Mud, silt and chemical waste polluted the lake and to drink from it directly would have been suicide. No life could survive in the waters and very little survived around it. The Kházakha had damned the river, built industries on the banks of the lake and proceeded to contaminate the very source of life people had laboured so hard to receive. The Kházakha were many things but ecologically sound was not one of them.

Walking as casually as he could, Hollam strode past the houses, keeping away from the lamps that illuminated the streets too well for his liking. Some civilians were milling about on the other side of the road and one of them called to Hollam, causing him to flinch in alarm. They only wanted to know the time. He just shrugged apologetically and continued on his way.

It became more crowded as he headed north-westwards. There seemed to be some form of street party going on in the neighbourhood and Kházakha were pouring from their houses. The women were elaborately dressed in flowing gowns, bedecked with jewels and fur shawls, the sight of which made Hollam's stomach turn. The men wore fancy suits with polished shoes and false smiles. It was a night for outdoing one's neighbours.

He cut down an alley, trying to avoid the throngs of people.

It was poorly lit and dingy, but he could see well enough with his heightened night vision. A woman, dressed too garishly to be considered elegant, slipped from a darkened doorway and draped herself on his arm. 'Hello, soldier. Fancy a little company tonight?' He could smell alcohol on her breath.

'Sorry, honey,' he replied, remembering to sound casual and trying to shrug away. 'I'm busy.'

'Don't you like me?' she purred, running her hand up his leg. Hollam swallowed hard, feeling awkward and embarrassed. He gently grabbed her hand before it could travel too far.

'Sure I do, but like I said, I'm busy. Got my orders. Can't be late.'

'Your voice sounds funny,' she teased, suddenly clasping his backside with her free hand.

Hollam went rigid and attempted to squirm out of her grasp. 'Come on, lady. Give a man a chance. I'll come back when I've finished.'

'Sure you will,' she said scornfully. Then, as he hastily disappeared, she screamed after him, 'You're not a real man, anyway. I bet you don't even like women!'

Hollam ran.

❧

T'skya paced about the tatty custody room ignoring the dated chairs and the pile of pithy finger stained books on the cracked and lacquered stand. She was irritated and anxious about the delay.

She had sensed the law keepers' vehicle trailing her and taking a swift turn had quickly stowed her pack. Apparently, she had violated some law of the road and failure to produce a licence had resulted in arrest. A bit of paperwork and a fine to be paid within the week, he had said. She had already been there an age. Hollam would panicking.

'Officer, what's the hold up?' she asked again through the bars of the door. 'I have to go on duty soon,' she lied, maintaining her disguise.

She heaved another sigh and with nothing better to do, paused before the grubby mirror hanging above the books and checked her hair.

A form moved behind the two-way mirror and nodded decisively.

The law keeper re-entered the room with two surly-looking soldiers. He did not look comfortable. 'It seems the vehicle you claim to have been loaned was reported stolen some hours ago.'

'But you saw the paperwork!' she exclaimed.

'Obviously a forgery,' he replied.

T'skya was incensed. The one document that really was authentic was the one they would not accept. 'Call the Captain. He'll verify it,' she insisted.

'We already have. He was the one who filed the report,' the officer replied, signalling the soldiers to take her away. She was a problem he wanted rid of.

Before she could open her mouth to protest further, they had cuffed her hands. She was assisted out of the room and towards the exit of the building. The officer sank back into his chair with a sigh of relief as she was man-handled away.

'Where are you taking me?' she cried, now feeling very frightened.

The soldier's words were grim. 'To the Palace.'

She was taken to a holding cell several levels above Cail's and scarcely got a glimpse of the austere complex. The room she was pushed into had a plain square table in the centre on four sturdy legs bordered by uncomfortable looking low backed chairs. A crude bed stood rigidly in the corner, its lumpy pillow covered with an off-white sheet. A hole lay in the floor for her private convenience and a glaring shadeless light hung from the ceiling. She looked about her with a growing sense of dread.

Left alone she pondered her fate pacing the cell like a caged animal, angered by her own stupidity and misfortune. Now everything relied on the brave but reckless Hollam. It would not take the Kházakha long to discover she was an impostor and then they would force her to admit the truth. The thought of it terrified her.

A guard finally arrived to escort her from the cell. T'skya walked solemnly ahead of him, eyeing the corridors ever alert for signs of Cail and shivering inside at the cold austerity of the unadorned walls. Her reflection mocked upwards from polished tiles and the tapping of the guard's shoes pushed her onwards.

T'skya did not know where she was being taken, but as they headed downwards through the levels, she felt the lower they went, the worse it would be. Each level was different but no less daunting. The floor she was passing was crowded and thin pale arms reached through the bars, hoping for food, only to be slapped away by the guard as he went by.

They took a spiral staircase down one set of flights. This level was sterile and silent and smelled vaguely of anti-septic. Rows of heavy doors lined the white walls and a solitary sign shouted 'Interrogation' in her face. T'skya began to tremble.

They halted outside a door marked 114. It was firmly shut and nothing marked the front to indicate its purpose. T'skya gamely tried sparking up a conversation while they waited, but could get no more than the guard's name. Esrik stared straight ahead, trying to ignore her. T'skya soon fell quiet.

Door 114 opened at last and two Kházakha soldiers stepped out. They were scowling at each other and both appeared to have been reprimanded for some misdemeanour or other. They broke off their silent recriminations to cast curious glances at the young Navennán woman who was staring at them with no uncertain horror on her face. Daravin and Snell then went on their way and began to argue in loud angry voices.

Now T'skya understood why she had failed to find Snell. Having waited several hours for his return, she had driven around, exploring the city until she had to collect Hollam; the foolish venture that had led to her incarceration. If Snell had betrayed Raven then Ferret, Ash and the whole of Wilderwood was imperilled. She only hoped his blood bond to his brother was strong enough to still his tongue.

Before she could think through all the possible consequences, she was abruptly ushered into the room. Esrik slammed the door shut and T'skya stood behind it staring. The room was little different from her cell, lacking only the bed and the squat pot latrine. A smartly dressed, distinguished man was sitting behind a table, flicking through a pile of papers. He looked up briefly and gestured for her to sit.

T'skya edged forward and sat slowly, keeping her eyes trained on the officer. He sucked in a breath, tapped the pile of papers with one finger and sighed. She studied the epaulets of rank and read the name above the breast pocket of his jacket and raised her eyebrows in recognition.

'You are in a lot of trouble, young lady,' Travis said at last.

'I didn't steal anything,' she blurted out.

'I'm aware of that,' Travis answered smoothly.

'But the law...'

'Fabricated evidence,' he interjected. 'We had to get you here on some pretext. We couldn't have the general population knowing you're an impostor.'

'What do you mean?'

Travis tapped the top sheet on the makeshift desk and glanced at the information. 'You gave your name as T'lyia, a registered nurse living in the medical quarters on Eighty-First Street. There was such a person listed, but she died three weeks ago in a road accident. You, therefore, cannot be her. The natural conclusion is that you're an impostor.'

T'skya chewed her lip nervously and began picking at her nails. Prell, in forging the documents, could not have known of the woman's demise. Destiny was playing T'skya a rotten hand.

'What interests me,' Travis continued, 'is that we can find no record of you anywhere. It's almost as if you don't exist. And yet, here you are sitting before me.'

T'skya remained stubbornly silent and focused her eyes on a spot behind the Commander's shoulder. He rose to his feet and walked quietly around the room until he was standing directly behind her. It was more intimidating that way. 'If you're not from here, then where *are* you from?'

T'skya bored holes into the wall with her eyes.

'T'skya, do not play games with me!' he whispered into her ear.

She flinched. How could he possibly know her name? She dismissed Hollam and Cail instantly from her mind. She knew their resolve. She knew their loyalty. They would never betray her. Daravin and Snell did not even know she existed and could not have said anything, which only left Ferret, Ash and Raven. The men were unlikely to have given anything away and even though she knew Raven despised her, she could not believe the warrior would jeopardise their freedom just for revenge. T'skya did not know who had betrayed her, but it was clear that somebody had.

'If you know my name, then you must also know where I'm from,' she replied sullenly.

Travis reseated himself and rested his elbows on the table. He steepled his fingers and tapped them against his mouth. 'You are placing me in a difficult position, T'skya. As Military Commander I must be *seen* to do my job. I must be *seen* to get results. I must, therefore, insist on your cooperation. There are much less pleasant ways of doing this! The truth could be forced out of you,' he warned.

'I'd lie,' she said defiantly.

'At first, perhaps, until the pain grew too great for your resolve. Your loyalty may be strong, but your courage is not.'

Her shoulders sagged in defeat and she covered her eyes with one hand. He had spoken the truth and she knew it.

She nodded her head in agreement and sat studying the floor, waiting for the interrogation to begin, hoping she could still give Hollam the time he needed. Travis began slowly and calmly, asking her simple questions. Then he asked her about her origins and, at first, she was hesitant to answer. Travis, however, already seemed to know a great deal about her and generally phrased his inquiries so they needed no more than a yes or no answer. Yes, she was of his race. No, her parents were no longer living. No, she was not born in the city. Yes, there were others of her kind aboard a giant spaceship somewhere in the galaxy.

These last revelations were met with no more than a raised eyebrow and slow nodding as he listened. Travis had known the information before she confirmed it. T'skya narrowed her eyes and her fingers found their way to her mouth.

Travis seemed intent on finding out as much as he could about her origins and this surprised and disconcerted her. She assumed he would pounce on her connections with the natives, extract the names of those she was consorting with and interrogate her reasons. She expected him to drill her about her presence in the city, to delve behind the 'Kházakh' she accompanied, but he showed no apparent interest in these issues and concentrated on the Homequest and its history. He was particularly interested in her home world. T'skya grabbed the chance to enlighten him, hoping she might alter his loyalties. Travis listened with sedulous attention.

She described how their historians had traced their origins back to a planet called Earth; a planet divine in its beauty and vibrant in its life forms. A perfect world, a paradise, ruined and mutilated by greed, war and poor governance. She railed at the stupidity of the ruling nations who ignored the danger signs that their interference with Nature was spiralling out of control. Their fear of damaging political standing or of losing their wealth condemned the world and everything on it. They polluted the earth, sea and atmosphere, plundered the resources in their greed, caused mass extinctions of animal and plant, spread disease with their lax morals and waged war, until the world could take no more and every life was imperilled.

'They destroyed the planet?' Travis asked with amazement.

T'skya shook her head. 'Not the planet, just its ability to sustain life as they needed it to be. Some species adapted; most did not; they could not. I'm sure Nature has found a way to survive.'

'That doesn't explain Navenná,' he pressed.

'Space stations were already housing some of the rich, but as life became impossible starships were financed; a desperate attempt to find another world. For once the richest nations found a common cause and everything they knew about physics, astronomy, engineering, you name it, was brought together until they could build a ship able to leave their solar system, and keep those on board alive. They didn't have the knowledge we do. It's a miracle they made it.

'Of course only the elite, chosen from all the so called civilised and rich countries of the world, were eligible for the trip. Ships filled with scientists, royalty, politicians, military, and businessmen journeyed through space for centuries, breeding, dying, breeding some more, until they came upon Navenná. It wasn't perfect; volcanic, unstable and more inhospitable than Earth, but it had vegetation, seas, mammals to eat, and nothing higher in the food chain. So they settled there, hoping to build ideal societies and prevent such catastrophes from happening again.'

T'skya paused for breath and sighed deeply as she remembered her history lessons. She had studied hard, an avid reader, curious and at once dismayed by her ancestry and their mindless lives. Travis was watching her, sitting back on his chair with his hands neatly folded in his pristine lap. His face showed little but his fixed attention revealed a fervent interest. T'skya ploughed on, hoping to distract him from a change of tact.

'But men being men, they couldn't contain their greed and began to fight for power. They were the elite, equals, and so the only way to gain more power was by trampling over their opponents. The industries grew bigger and bigger; the Generals waged wars and the politicians bandied useless words and wallowed in their own self-importance. They seemed to destroy Navenná in as little time as it took to destroy the Earth.

'And now - now our own people search the skies again looking for another home. But we have learnt from our mistakes, Travis; we have learnt. The Homequest is our hope for the future. Although we have soldiers, it's filled not with politicians and Generals, but with ecologists and teachers, farmers and scientists who experiment for the good of the world and not for the bad. We have learnt, but you; you are a mystery to me. You're destroying this world just as surely as we destroyed ours.'

'I hardly think we're in the same league, T'skya. It's a big planet. Sure we've cut some trees, got some industries going, but it hardly compares,' he said in defence.

'Doesn't it?' she said cynically. 'Aren't you using up your resources faster than you can replace them?'

'Not at all. There's plenty of ore, minerals, land for our use.'

T'skya snorted down her nose in disdain. 'And what about your work force?'

'What about it?'

'Is that sustainable? Come on, Commander. How many Roumanhis die in your mines? How many are killed by your troops? How many die in the slave zone? And how many babies have you seen born to replace them? You've split up families, destroyed lives, taken the strongest and the fittest stock and left nothing in their place. It's no different. And what will you do when they're gone; invade Kalkassa, spread to other lands? It always starts small but the smallest link can cause catastrophes. It's like a pebble in a pond; the ripples spread.'

Travis had to concede her point. The decline in Roumanhi numbers had been bothering him for some time but Santovin's policies remained in force despite the warnings. T'skya's concern for the natives shone through her eyes although her language remained coldly factual. Travis admired her spirit, understood her passion and rued the truth she was throwing at him. But she had not finished.

'Commander I can explain how I got here but what I can't explain is what you're doing here. To the best of my knowledge, the Homequest was the first ship financed and built. How did *you* get here?'

'That information is classified. To discuss it with anyone would condemn me,' Travis replied heatedly. 'We are the elite now, rulers of the land. We are the one true blood. To admit anything else would pervert everything we've fought to achieve.'

'Ah hell! And just what have you achieved?' she cried in frustration at his bureaucratic spin. 'A dictatorship based on fear and secrecy. A society frightened into loyalty by a tyrannical despot. A destructive and totally irrational use of the land and its resources. A world where the native peoples are enslaved and abused by men claiming to be the elite, the one true blood. That's a load of bull and you know it. There's nothing about Santovin, or you, or even me that's true. We aren't even natural!'

Surprised as he was by her unexpected tirade her remarks had hit their mark. Travis knew she was right. He hated the way his people lived almost as much as he hated the way they forced the Roumanhis to live. And yet he was very much a part of it. He was Commander of the Military Forces and was responsible for many of the atrocities against the Roumanhis. He had quickly risen through the ranks and the higher he rose the more he had learnt. The more he learnt, the less he liked. Now his loyalties were divided and he was a very troubled man. He had to protect his position, protect his family, and yet, in doing so he was being forced day in and day out to flout his own desires and cripple his morality.

But he had caught something else in her words. Something that disturbed him. 'What do you mean we aren't even natural?' he demanded, staring at her through half closed eyes.

'Haven't you ever considered why we all look alike? Hasn't it ever crossed your mind?' she asked softly.

'On occasion,' Travis admitted.

'We are the elite, as you say, and yet we are nothing. You see, the whole lot of us are an end product, a manufactured good; the results of scientific experiments to create the perfect person. We're the results of centuries of genetic engineering. We were given brilliant minds, bodies immune to every known disease, perfect everything, except one thing; the perfect soul with which to humanise our perfection. We were like our servant androids, machines almost without hearts and there were many throwbacks, people said to be so callous and evil they had to be locked away and eventually the project was abandoned.

'I was created by living parents, Commander. My ancestors were created in a lab. I'm less perfect but so much more human; but I'm not truly natural and I never will be.'

Travis fell back in his chair too stunned to speak. She had confirmed the suspicions haunting him for years. Searching old records had led to a top secret file, the code to which only Santovin held. It had taken Travis weeks to break the code, crack the file and place a sweeper to ensure his intrusion could not be traced. And then he had read the devastating truth about his people; a truth which, until now, he had not had the strength of will to believe.

The genetic throwbacks, considered too dangerous to live within society's walls, and who were a constant shame to those who had created them, had not been imprisoned on Navenná, as T'skya suggested. They were secretly expelled from the planet on a purpose built ship. Eight thousand men and women including their guards were packed aboard and exiled into space with just enough equipment to ensure their survival, but little else beside. Many had died and many more had been born during the flight to those other galaxies, but eventually they had found Roumanhi and settled there. They had bred quickly and now tens of thousands of tainted genetics infested the land.

Travis was from a generation of outcasts; people considered too defective to tolerate. Either they did not conform to society's principles, being too outspoken and brash, or their appearance did not fit the conceived codes of perfection. Some were thieves and swindlers, robbers and rascals. Others were prone to violence and some, indeed had killed. Travis was from guard and throwback stock but in his own way had managed to rise above their villainous ways, as many of his kind had struggled to do over time. But Santovin; Santovin was the epitome of all things foul. He had been no more than twenty-years old when they arrived and yet, within years, he had slain all those who stood in his way and titled himself High Lord Procurator of the Land; and so he had remained, ruling with an iron fist, invincible in his protected walls, master of all he surveyed.

Travis longed to share his knowledge but could hardly bear to air the terrible truth. Most of those old enough to know the truth and the worst natured of their species were no longer living and the younger generations had never been told. Santovin covered the past well and Travis had aided him. The subject was forbidden; any heretic caught doubting Santovin's new propaganda was swiftly dealt with. If he suspected the depth of Travis's knowledge, Travis and his family would not live long!

'T'skya, speak nothing of this, I beg you. You endanger us all! I can't protect you from Santovin if he learns you know so much. Nor can I protect you if he learns I've spoken with you on this subject,' he said with urgency.

'Why should I help you?' T'skya replied with contempt.

'Because, whatever I've done and whatever you may think of me, I am on your side.'

'Yeah, right. Well if you want me to believe you prove it,' she said coldly.

Travis's reply was cautious. 'What do you want?'

T'skya was amazed how the tables had been turned. She had come into the room fearing for her life, terrified she would be forced to betray her friends. Now she had the Commander in the palm of her hand and was finding her courage. She needed to be brave. Every part of her screamed to ask about Cail; to find out where he was, to know if he was alive, but she could not reveal their connection. She dared not chance her hand; Travis may have been playing her, softening her guard, ready for the kill. Instead she chose to solve a mystery.

'Tell me who betrayed me.'

Travis hesitated, but her face was insistent. He opened his mouth to speak but before he could utter the name, the loud wailing of a klaxon drowned them out. T'skya jerked in her seat looking alarmed. Something was obviously amiss in the Palace. Travis leapt to his feet and pressed a disk on his lapel.

'Vigour, room one-one-four,' he snapped into the communication device as he raced from the room.

Within seconds, T'skya came face to face with one of the Palace androids. Vigour stood six foot high and was sculpted in the form of a well-proportioned male humanoid. The android, for all its human shape, was far from natural-looking. Its skin was polished metallic silver that gleamed in the bright artificial light. Its face was flat and expressionless, with a simple hinge jaw. Deeply set into its angled eye sockets were glowing orbs of red.

Vigour stood rigidly by the door, unmoving, staring straight ahead and seemed to pay T'skya no attention. She remained firmly seated eyeing the solid figure nervously over her shoulder and began chewing her nails again. T'skya prayed that whatever had caused the disturbance would not keep Travis away too long; she had yet to hear his answer and was growing impatient.

❦

Cail rapidly paced his room. Raven's visit had disturbed him and he was frustrated by the confinement. If he was going to be interrogated, then let them get on with it. If he was safe, as Raven had suggested, then why keep him shackled and imprisoned? The intolerable wait for some kind of answer had left him on the edge of psychosis.

Cail's passive nature disappeared with his growing impatience. Unable to contain himself further, he vented his wrath on the door, yelling at the top of his voice. He then rained a series of blows against the solid panel with his tied fists and barged against it with his shoulders heedless of the pain, before returning to the more satisfying footwork.

With the door so thick, little but muffled dull thuds could be heard in the corridor, but it was enough to arouse the attention of Esrik as he patrolled up and down. Although his partner had disappeared to relieve himself, Esrik could abide the noise no longer. He checked his sidearm, drew out his baton and opened door 119.

Cail was standing in the centre of the room glowering and breathing heavily. He advanced a step and Esrik waved his baton at him threateningly. 'Stay where you are and not another sound or you'll answer for it!'

Cail advanced again. 'Take me to Santovin,' he demanded.

'I told you not to move!' Esrik snapped launching a blow at Cail's head.

Cail was quicker. With the slickness of a cat he stepped under the flailing baton and thrust the base of his palm against Esrik's nose. The guard dropped to the floor like a bag of apples.

Cail quickly jumped over Esrik's prostrate form and peered cautiously around the door. The long corridor was empty. Wondering about his sanity he ran down the ruler straight passageway keeping his footfalls light on the polished floor. He paused at the junction, cast a glance behind him and peeped around the corner. Seeing no-one, he proceeded along, keeping close to the wall until he came to a winding staircase. It spiralled sedately around a concrete column and blocked his view ahead. Cail took the narrow stairs slowly, stopping every few steps to listen for his enemy's presence.

Before heading upwards again, the stairs flattened into a hallway, at the end of which was another stairway running straight upwards, broader and less steep than the one he had just climbed. At a guess it led to the central living quarters of the Palace and would, perhaps, lead him to Raven. On the other hand, the winding stairs very probably led to the outside world and chance of escape.

He paused to consider each choice and then padded along the hallway. There was no hope of escape and he knew it. All the entrances and exits to the Palace were heavily guarded and even with free use of his arms he would not have been able to get past them all. It was better to find Raven; or better yet to return to his cell. He shook his head at his own foolishness. His actions were ridiculous. One bound man against a whole Palace of armed Kházakha? Still, it beat doing nothing; he was destined to die so what did he have to lose?

He crept along and froze as he heard the klaxon. Esrik's partner had evidently found the guard groaning in a pool of blood. Kházakha were pouring out of their hiding places in droves to answer the call, all armed, all dangerous and all avid for the capture.

Cail was being hunted.

He dashed along the hallway as he heard a trampling of feet pounding up the stairway behind him. He had almost reached the foot of the next stairway when he heard footsteps approaching from above.

He was trapped!

He tried the doors to the side of him; they were locked. His legs and adrenalin told him to run but there was nowhere to go and nothing he could do. Cail stood still and bowed his head in surrender, awaiting his enemies.

Guards approached with their weapons drawn from the corridor. Behind them, holding his swollen and very probably broken nose with one hand came Esrik. Travis was by his side, looking grim. Six more guards clattered down the stairs, drawing to an abrupt halt. Cail gave them a rueful glance and shrugged as Travis caught his eye. Travis put up a hand to keep the guards at bay, and reached for Cail. His interest was abruptly captured by a movement on the stairs. The guards snapped to nervous attention and saluted the figure that was slowly descending.

The guards stepped aside as the man swept past them, his grey cloak billowing like a main sail. Cail stared, transfixed by the ghostly countenance and unnerved by the unexpected familiarity. Santovin met his gaze and they stared at each other; the hunter and the hunted together at last. The High Lord Procurator then dismissed Cail from his mind whilst he dealt with his injured guard.

The terrified man stepped forwards and raised a bloodied hand in salute. Santovin held him in his gaze. There was no pity in his eyes or compassion in his voice when he spoke. 'You have failed me, Esrik! Have medical look at you and then report to level 2. Perhaps there you will learn to carry out your duties more effectively.'

Level 2 was a rotten assignment, dirty, noisy, overcrowded, but it could have been worse. He could have ended up in the powder mines like Daravin and Snell; serve them right, too, if rumour be true. You did not help a slave and get away with it.

Santovin's eyes next bored into Travis. As Military

Commander, the actions of his soldiers reflected on him. Travis swallowed but remained at attention, his back as rigid as a doorpost and his focus unwavering. He, too, would answer to the High Lord, but later. For now Santovin would be occupied elsewhere.

He would be occupied with Cail.

THIRTEEN

The horn of Camaldriss

It was the middle of the night and Hollam still had not reached the city boundary. In attempting to avoid the throngs of Kházakha, he had lost his way. Hollam desperately longed to feel the soft earth under his sore feet. The cement pavements and roughened streets played havoc with his soles, and his legs were weary from the endless pounding as he tried to escape the hostile maze. The boots he wore, bravely stolen from a Kházakha camp, were uncomfortable and the low thump thump thumping of their solid bases on the harsh paving grew deafening to his ears.

His exertions had made him sweat and the uniform he had been forced to wear was itchy and restricting. He clawed at the collar, longing to rip it open and let his skin breathe, but he could not; not yet. It would look too unprofessional and his smooth chest would not go unnoticed. Instead he repositioned his pack and proceeded on his way, watching his breath fog as he heaved a heavy sigh.

He could not understand how people could live in such terrain. The forest floor was springy underfoot and pleasant to walk upon. There were crunchy leaves to kick about, dew drenched mosses, giving soil and thick mulch; flowers and bushes of different shades and textures, bird song and the constant whispering of the trees to accompany each step and plenty of pools and streams to bathe in; but the city was unforgiving. It loomed around him in uniform blandness, grey streets bordered by pale houses, harsh unnatural noises rending the air and little to break the dull monotony save the odd tree dressed with concrete roots or a dab of garish paint on a door.

At length he came to a deserted street and squinted up at the sign. At last he was heading in the right direction. The houses began to thin out and he caught the scent of the open countryside on the breeze. His mood began to lift and, as it did, fresh strength flowed back into his body and his steps regained their spring. His land was calling him and he answered with enthusiasm.

But he was soon to be disappointed. As he left the ugly dwellings of the city behind him and headed into the open, the earth became broken and bare. There had been some poorly tended pasture on the outskirts of the city, shadows of animals lay like blobs in wooden fenced enclosures and stubble from cultivated grains stood like small soldiers in rank and file, but here the ground was torn up as if some mighty creature had chewed upon it, found it unpalatable and had spat it out again. Piles of debris and lumpy mounds of earth dotted the undulating landscape; torn and twisted stumps showed where woodland had once grown and deep trenches filled with water and green slime lined the way as far as the eye could see.

Hollam scrambled up and down, trying to avoid the slimy pits, but the terrain was treacherous in the dark and he lost his footing, tumbling down the roughened sides to land in the stinking sludge at the bottom. He cursed wrathfully, wondering why all his assignments left him up to his eyeballs in mud or stinking like something a lazat had dragged home. His sparkling white uniform would never be the same again, but at least it helped to disguise him.

Hollam took the pack from his shoulder and checked the vials within, finding them to be undamaged. He sighed in relief and carefully unwrapped the precious horn of Camaldriss from its soft casing. He fingered the curve of the shell gently, noticing the embossed metal capping which tipped the mouth with embellished pride. His thoughts turned to the sea and the woman who was awaiting his return. He missed Breeze so much and wondered if he would ever fall into her arms again. Allowing his thoughts to flow freely he realised he also missed his brother and T'skya, who, if things had not gone so terribly wrong, should have been with him for at least a while longer; and even more he missed his mother.

Hollam felt very alone.

Sighing wearily and muttering about the injustice of life, he secured the horn at the bottom of his pack, slung it safely across his shoulders again and scrambled up the side of the trench. Hollam had lost too much time already and could not afford to linger. Every second's delay could cost his brother's life, although for all Hollam knew, he might already be dead. Yet he did not believe it was so. He would have known, would have felt something, he was sure of that.

By daybreak, he had left the pits behind and was heading north-westwards towards a ridge of low mountains that rose higher the further north they ran. They stood against the overcast sky, stern and superior in their prominence like judges at a dance. Near the peaks the mountain slopes were sharp, cut in vertical slashes like a knife through butter, battered by the rains, winds, ice and snow that invaded the rock and sculpted its form. Nothing would grow there and little was to be found lower down; the run of the waters too steep and determined for soil to remain. At the range's base strange outcrops of rock formed the foothills, misshapen and ominous, yet helpful to those who sought shelter from prying eyes. Hollam hoped to reach the foothills by evening and use the rocky slopes to his advantage.

As the terrain began to rise and form a rough ridge, he caught sight of the narrow road the Khàzakha used to reach the power station, water storage tanks and the purification plant that lay beyond. The road lay deserted in a wide, low-sided valley, the uppermost edge of which he was now crossing. Hollam wished he could risk venturing along it; it would have been so much quicker, but he knew it was impossible. The ground was flat and open on either side, bordered only by scrubland and abandoned machinery too widely spaced to provide protection. The route Hollam had chosen was longer and more difficult, but by far the safest choice.

Another road forked off to the right leading to some of the mines, a road the slaves dreaded, a road that led to their deaths. There the stone was sliced and raised, building blocks for the city's rich. The powder mines were nearby, where rocks were smashed and ground, the air a constant smog of dust, and lives were perhaps the shortest. Those mines which plunged into the bowels of the mountains lay to the south where ores, minerals and useless gems were plundered. Hollam wondered why the mountains did not sink to fill the voids below; there were no roots to hold the ground like enclave burrows.

He hugged the edge of the ridge, keeping one eye on the road and one eye on the sky. Although he had neither heard nor seen any transport ships in the air that night, he knew ferry services to the forest were frequent. It was not unfounded to be cautious. As the morning passed, he saw the occasional vehicle trundle its way along the rough road or heard the engines of a transport craft buzzing above like a meaty fly and dropped flat until they had gone.

Hollam's stomach rumbled again, churning like a cauldron. He was hungry; very hungry! The food was in T'skya's pack and he had not eaten since early the previous day. There was very little to eat in that crippled area of land, but using his skills Hollam managed to dig up one or two roots. They did not taste too bad once he had wiped away most of the mud;

but he found little else besides.

Agreeing with himself that life was treating him extremely badly, and that he would never volunteer for anything again, he gamely continued on his way.

The nearer he drew to the mountains, the colder the climate became and the sparser the vegetation. Soon he was crossing cold, bare rock. Only the occasional scrub bush broke the purplish-grey hues of the rocky landscape save patches of golden-yellow lichen which clung to the stones like spots of sunshine in the bleakness.

Hollam was now more careful than ever. He was more conspicuous in this terrain and the nearer he approached the water tanks, the more Kházakha there was likely to be. From his vantage point he could just see the small camp of the water company's workers sitting forlornly in its isolation and the dirty black smoke rising from the power station producing the energy to pump the water to the city. It explained why there were so few trees in the valley. Most had ended up as fuel for the furnaces, despite repeated warnings from the Roumanhis. Flooding was already becoming a serious problem without the protective umbrella created by the trees.

The Kházakha may have been more advanced when it came to weaponry and transportation but they had no clue about the basic principles of life: air, earth and water. Every Roumanhi toddler knew trees brought life. They cleaned the air, protected the soil and created rain. They were Nature's guardians, creating a balance in the environment and were honoured above all else in the land. The Kházakha honoured nothing but themselves, and now the whole land was paying the price for their arrogance.

As evening fell, the atmosphere took on that peculiar coldness which spells snow. The clouds had thickened and the sky was a blanket of grey; the air was still. Hollam watched his breath condense in a mist and rubbed his cold ears. He missed his thick mop of hair.

After a brief respite Hollam ploughed onwards and the temperature continued to drop. Night came early and was spotted with flakes of snow. They fluttered to the ground and remained. Hollam held out his hand and watched as each unique star of ice melted against the warmth of his blood. Not that he felt particularly warm; in fact, he was freezing. His face was red and his hands and feet felt numb. He blew on his fingers to stave off the cold and tried to quicken his pace, but the layer of snow made the rocks slippery and his footing was difficult.

Soon the flakes grew larger and began to come down in flurries as the wind picked up. It was not long before he was battling against a strong head wind and snow so thick he could hardly see in front of himself. He would not be able to go on much further; the weather and darkness was overwhelming even his sensitive eyes. He had already fallen several times, tearing his trousers and grazing his knees, and he feared he might have a worse accident or freeze to death if he did not find shelter soon.

He searched for a decent spot to find respite from the growing blizzard, but there was little in the way of shelter to be found. The best he could manage was a narrow overhang bounded by a jagged boulder. There was room for him to squeeze and he piled some rocks about the entrance to cut the wind. His efforts protected him from the brunt of the blizzard although the air was bitter and he huddled into a ball to keep warm. Fearing the liquid in the vials would freeze Hollam tucked them beneath his shirt and stiffened as the icy glass touched his skin. They would be safe there for as long as he stayed alive.

Although knowing little about blizzards, Hollam knew enough to stay awake. He had heard tales of men drifting off to sleep never to see the summer warmth again. Yet he could feel blessed somnolence creeping over him like an incoming tide, luring him to sweeter pastures and pleasant company. His head lolled backwards. The shock of his skull cracking against the rock snapped him awake and he cursed, suddenly mindful of the danger. He smacked himself across the cheeks, flinching at the sting and began to sing with the gusto of a drunken youth. No-one would hear the jovial lyrics; the wind smothered his voice and there was not a living soul stupid enough to be outside without a bloody good reason and a fleece a foot thick.

Hollam, in his jacket and shirt would just have bide his time and wait for the storm to pass.

He was in for a very long night!

❧

Towards morning, the snow had ceased and the wind had abated enough for Hollam to continue on his way. He was numb and stiff, his throat felt like someone had used it to sharpen swords and he was worried his fingers and toes had frostbite. Like an emerging bear he crawled out of his scanty shelter, weary to the point of delirium and astonished to see how much snow had actually fallen.

The whole landscape had changed into a carpet of undulating blueness. The larger moon cast its hues across the snow through a break in the clouds and the icy crystals glistened like sapphires. But Hollam had no time to contemplate the beauty of Nature's offering. He was behind schedule and knew that without an inhuman effort he would never make it to the water tanks by evening.

He drew what strength he could and ploughed through the thick crust of snow. It was tough going and his progress, at times, was tortuously slow. Here and there the wind had created sculpted drifts of snow and Hollam had to fight his way through, sapping his energy. If only he had a staff with which to probe the ground ahead it would have been easier; but no bush or tree was within sight.

He crested a small tor and checked his bearings. The power

station was still busily polluting the atmosphere and he could see the smoke billowing into the sky like a funnel of death. He scoffed at the irony; beyond the walls lay heat enough to melt a man, radiant warmth to ease his aching joints and return his body to life, enticement evil in design and cruel in its presence. He tucked his fingers beneath his armpits and tore his gaze away to the north. He was still too far away to discern the water tanks but at least his bearings were correct.

Casting a glance behind him, Hollam was shocked to see the path he had taken screaming his presence to the sky. The trampled snow ran like a blue vein across the undisturbed landscape. Nothing could be seen from the road but from the air he might as well have drawn a cross saying 'Hollam is here'. He prayed no transport ships would pass his way and make his efforts in vain. Grumbling, he talked himself forwards, feeling anxious and miserable.

The ground continued to rise and become more rugged. Outcrops of rock had protected some areas from the snow and there to his grim satisfaction he made better time. It was difficult to run; the surface was treacherous, the cold air burnt his lungs and he could not feel his feet, but he was desperate to put some distance between himself and the path he had made.

Hollam was forced to rest more and more often as the day progressed, but would permit himself no more than a few minute's breathing space each time. Thirst was becoming a problem and resisting the water-like fluid in the vials was a battle. Taking the horn of Camaldriss from its wrapping he filled it with handfuls of snow and blocked the end with his thumb. Blowing into the shell he managed to melt just enough to dribble some well needed moisture down his throat, but it was freezing and made his forehead stab. Annoyed, he put the horn away.

By now he was nearing his destination and by mid-afternoon had come far enough around the ridge to just discern the water tanks nestling at the base of the mountains. They looked like honey ants, their swollen abdomens jutting upwards from spindly legs. But he was now badly behind schedule and the thought of honey was depressing.

He ruefully gazed along the hidden line of the road and saw a snow-plough clearing a path to the city. A couple of Kházakha had ventured out on ski-bikes, gliding over the snow like boats on water. However, Hollam had no alternative but to risk heading into the flat base of the valley where he could make better speed.

He dropped over the side of the ridge and began to scramble down its rough sides. He had descended no more than a few feet when he lost his grip and began to slide remorselessly towards the valley bottom. The side was icy and he picked up speed, bouncing over rocks and scree until he landed in a bank of snow.

He sat glowering recovering his breath, picked himself up, cursed as he checked his grazes and then hastened onwards. Trotting along, he tore a section from the bottom of his now shredded jacket and wrapped it around his head. His damp black hair would show up too much against the snowy white background. The wetness had washed quite a lot of grime from his clothes and he now blended in quite splendidly with his surroundings.

'I am Hollam the clown; Hollam the scout; Hollam the soldier; Hollam the chameleon. No, better yet, I am Hollam the intrepid; Hollam the valiant,' he muttered as he went, and then added ruefully as his stomach complained again; 'Hollam the extremely wet, cold, tired and HUNGRY!'

He was also Hollam the fortunate because for the rest of the day he made good unhindered progress. The weather, at once his enemy, was now a two-faced ally. The wind had blown up so many banks of snow that he could jog along behind them, obscured from the enemy's sight. He saw no transport ships; they were probably on standby waiting for the landing pads to be cleared, or were unable to navigate the pass in high winds, and the plant workers were too busy clearing the road and the yard around the station to pay any attention to his neck of the woods. But it did nothing to ease his growing pain or his anxiety.

⚜

By evening, Hollam had gone as far as he was able. The power station lay behind him to his right and the water storage facility stood in front of him, a little to his left. He peered over a tall bank of snow and studied the scene. A group of Kházakha, wrapped against the cold, had just arrived and they entered the main door of the complex. Fifteen minutes later, a different group left and Hollam gathered they had changed shifts. Several miserable-looking guards were patrolling the compound, just inside the perimeter fence, but they seemed more intent on keeping warm than watching for intruders. But it was not the power plant that Hollam was interested in.

He backed off and cautiously made his way closer to the water tanks, approaching from the west so that he could take some cover behind the rocks which had fallen from the mountainside. He was soon close enough to get a good look at the objects of his intent.

Three massive metal tanks, each supported on four sturdy platform legs and a network of scaffolding, towered above the ground, standing like giant insects against the moody sky. A vertical ladder scaled the side of each unit, leading to a narrow catwalk which circled the centre of each tank, before ascending to the slightly convex tops, bordered by low rails. Up there, so high above the ground, were housed pressure valves and the siphon unit, which was really no more than a tube through which the Kházakha could draw water for sampling or add any chemicals they deemed necessary. Hollam stared upwards, squinting through the dim light towards his target.

It was into the siphon unit that, if his luck held, the drugs would be added.

He tore his gaze away and checked the twelve small vials he was carrying. He shook his head at the absurdity that so little, diluted in such a mass of water, could accomplish all they hoped for. It struck him with sickening abruptness that he did not have enough vials to follow the plan as intended. T'skya should have been with him; she should have been there with the other vials, but something had happened and now he was alone. It simply was not feasible to dose all three tanks; a solution so diluted would serve no purpose. But to dose only one whilst clean water was pumped from the others would also be a waste of time, and Hollam had not endured the journey only to fail. There was nothing else for it, he would simply have to disable two tanks to ensure their water was not used in the city and add all the vials to just one. At least then the concentration would be more than enough to knock out the Kházakha, and surely an extra long sleep was a positive benefit? The question was, how could he possibly do it?

Hollam tried to force his anaesthetised brain to find a solution as he sat there shivering, watching the guards patrolling up and down like clockwork soldiers. Like the power station, the tanks were guarded by a high wire fence barbed with vicious spikes at the top but were patrolled by only four men, one along each length of the rectangular compound. The compound was expansive and four glum patrolmen seemed inadequate. The Kházakha evidently saw little risk of attack, and they were right to think it. Who but a foolhardy man would even deign to contemplate the risk; and who but a reckless hero would volunteer?

Hollam laughed quietly to himself, flexing his stubborn jaw and wishing he had kept his peace.

As night fell, huge floodlights sprang to life with a low drone, illuminating the compound and casting a sickly yellow sheen across the snow. It was not something Hollam had counted on and he smiled a dry cynical smile. How was he supposed to get through the fence, past the guards and up the ladder without being spotted? The fence he could handle and the guards - they changed every few hours, but there was no way he could scale the side of the tanks and remain unseen.

'Think Hollam, think. We have lights. Lights are bad. Solution; turn out the lights. Kházakha lights need power. Power has to be turned on. If power can be turned on…it can be turned off. So from whence comes this power?'

Muttering through the logic Hollam traced the thick wiring running down the side of each lofty post on which the lamps were fixed, noticing they terminated at the base. They must then have run underground to a nearby power source. Hollam scanned the area and saw a bulky grey box sitting in isolation to the left of the tanks. It squatted only a few feet inside the perimeter fence and was making a dull, humming sound. From what little he had learned from T'skya it seemed reasonable to assume it was the source he was looking for.

Hollam edged closer to the fence keeping quiet and low and continued to observe the guards, waiting impatiently for them to change. Fortunately, they were as lax in their duties as the men at the power station and ambled off together to exchange a few words with their replacements at the far end of the compound.

Hollam took a deep breath and bounded from his place of concealment springing up the fence like a cat. As his hands hit the wire, he was jolted by a fierce shock. Fortunately the voltage was too low to cause any serious damage. Choking back a howl, he swung over the top and leapt for the ground only to find his jacket had caught on the barbed points of the wire. He dangled precariously for a second before the material gave way and then fell to the ground with a thud. Cradling his hands in his armpits, he scooted behind the generator and held his breath, expecting his noisy attempt to have attracted somebody's notice. The guards, underneath thick layers of fur, had seen and heard nothing.

Hollam heaved a sigh of relief and eyeballed the fence accusingly. A shredded piece of cloth fluttered in the breeze, clinging to the barbs and shouting his presence. Hollam swallowed hoping he could disable the floodlights before anyone saw it.

As luck would have it, the door to the generator lay on his side, but it was locked. A padlock was all that stood between him and concealing darkness. Hollam blew on his fingers and rubbed his hands, trying to regain some feeling in them. It would have been a relatively simple job to smash the lock but that would have made too much noise and left yet more evidence of intrusion. Instead, he unfastened his hooped earring and with numbed difficulty set to work bending the wire into a crude pick-lock; he had seen enough Roumanhis chained to understand the principle and within a few minutes the padlock was in his hands.

Hollam was running out of time. The guards were now making their way to their positions. He eased open the door of the generator and viewed the dials within. There were many different switches and voltage meters and a series of coloured wires ran across the board like a spider's web. A stab of fear ran through him as he tried to make a decision. Hollam studied everything carefully and saw three black switches on the top right of the board. Recognising the words 'on' and 'off' he took a slow breath and flicked the switches upwards. The needles on the meters fell to zero and the compound was plunged into darkness.

Hollam swiftly locked the generator door, breaking off a piece of metal in the padlock to prevent its easy use. He heard the guards cursing as they stumbled towards him, angry and frustrated they had lost their power again. It seemed, like many of the Kházakha's technological wonders, the generator was prone to breakdowns.

Hollam melted into the darkness like a ghost. Stealthily, he ran to the nearest water tank and began to scale the ladder. It was a moonless night and even he could not have seen the guards were it not for the flashlights they held. He stared down at their diminutive forms and counted three bent over the generator attempting to wrestle with the lock. The fourth had remained on guard at the far end of the compound.

Hollam climbed past the catwalk until he reached the curved surface of the top and dropped flat on the cold metal as one of the Kházakha casually flashed his beam at the units. The generator party had decided the lock was not going to open and he could hear them banging away at it with their batons. Within seconds the door was opened. Hollam feared he would not have time to dope the water before the Kházakha discovered what was wrong or noticed his footprints in the snow. He could hear their voices drifting up to him as they argued amongst themselves.

'Look, it's the safety cut-out switches. The circuitry must have overloaded.'

'It can't have. The gauges are fine.'

'They're off, aren't they?'

'So, switch them back on.'

'That could cause a complete shutdown!'

'Then go to the back-up generator.'

'I can't. It burnt out last week!' the first man pointed out moodily.

'Oh, that's just great! Bloody brilliant. Now what Aslov? We patrol in the dark?'

'Yes, Viktor. We patrol in the dark. What do you think these flashlights are for; decoration? Still, I'll radio for some back-up.'

For Hollam it was now or never.

Drawing out the vials, he crawled to the siphon unit, carefully opened the valve and began to pour in the precious potion. Ten, eleven, twelve, he was nearly done. As the last drop of liquid dripped into the giant water tank, Hollam heaved a sigh of relief and allowed himself a brief smile. He had done it. He had drugged the water and given his people their best chance for freedom. Now all that was left for him to do was ensure it was this water which was used the coming morning.

Whilst studying his options Hollam had noticed large metal wheels on the side of each tank. It seemed probable these wheels controlled the flow valves. It was a crude way of doing things but the Kházakha did not believe in using complicated systems when something simpler would suffice, especially when maintenance was costly or troublesome.

The wheels could be reached from the catwalks and although it appeared to be a two man job, Hollam believed he was strong enough to turn them off on his own. The only problem was getting to the other reservoirs. He could not risk climbing all the way down the ladder, crossing to the next tank and climbing up again. The reinforcements would be arriving shortly and he need only be caught in the beam of their flashlights for everything to be ruined. Using the ground was therefore out of the question.

Hollam edged to the end of the tank and peered at the hulking mass of the second unit. It was not easy to judge the distance in the dark. He closed his eyes desperately trying to recall how they had appeared in the daylight. His best estimation was not encouraging; it was a long way. He shook his head at the madness of his intentions but grimly set to work.

Slowly backing off, Hollam cleared a path through the snow that lay in a thick slippery crust beneath his feet. He then removed the turban from his head; his neat black hair would not show in the darkness. The white uniform he was almost wearing was another matter. It was so torn removing it would have little effect on his already frozen body, and so, sitting on top of a Kházakha water tank, in a Kházakha compound surrounded by Kházakha in the middle of a cold winter's night, Hollam removed his boots and stripped down to his dark Roumanhi underwear. He stuffed the uniform into his pack leaving the boots behind as a relic, hung it across his back, and braced himself for the few potentially fatal seconds that lay ahead.

Taking some deep breaths and praying for the spirit of Caelcáladrim to preserve him, he rose to his feet, powered down the runway and leapt into space.

With his body outstretched, Hollam flew through the air and just managed to catch hold of one of the top railings with his burnt hand. His torso slammed painfully against the icy sides of the ladder and a whoosh of air exploded from his lungs. He swiftly hooked an arm around the rungs as his grip slipped and managed to hold on long enough to catch his breath and gain a foothold.

He peered at the ground, fully expecting to see the guards rushing to capture him, but the wind had picked up again and the disturbance he had caused had been carried away on a current of air. He could see the guards still patrolling up and down, their flashlights mainly searching for trouble outside the perimeter fence and occasionally sweeping towards the legs of the towers. Little did they know that trouble was slowly clambering down the ladder inside the very compound they were trying to protect.

Hollam stepped gingerly onto the catwalk. His feet were so cold they were burning, his chest was badly bruised and he had quite possibly cracked a rib. He held a hand against his side to ease the pain of breathing, and edged towards the wheel. If it had rusted, he would be in serious difficulties. Taking one last look at the guards, he took hold of the rim, trying to ignore the biting coldness of the metal, and began to apply some pressure. The wheel had been well-maintained and turned with only a minimal squeak, but the great pressure of the water made it a struggle to turn. Hollam leant all his weight into it and battled down the shrieks which threatened to surface as his ribs protested against the strain and the bandaged scabs on his burnt hand began to tear. Inch by inch it turned, and then it would turn no more.

Hollam had succeeded once again.

It was one down and one more to go.

One to go and one rib already gone! Doing his acrobatic flying trick again was not going to be just dangerous and difficult, it was almost impossible. Knowing he would never manage without caring for his injuries, Hollam unpacked his trousers, tore them into strips and bound them tightly around his chest. It was not much, but the extra support eased the pain a fraction and allowed him to move with a touch more freedom.

He bravely ascended the ladder again and laboriously repeated the whole process of clearing a path. It took him a long time to summon up the courage to make the attempt. He found no comfort from his previous success. He was vaguely healthy then and had nearly fallen. What were his chances of pulling it off again?

Hollam had just decided to risk the ground when the reinforcements arrived, ruling out the possibility. He could see their lights at the gate and hear the occasional shout being blown past his ears.

The wind was both an angel and a demon. It smothered the noise, but was freezing him terribly, numbing his body and slowing his responses; only the immense flow of adrenalin kept him conscious. The wind also added the danger of being blown off target as he jumped for the railings. Hollam looked at the sky for inspiration and noticed to his dismay the darkness was beginning to lift. Had it really taken him that long? Was it already nearly dawn? There was no time to lose. The citizens in the city would soon be rising from their beds and those coming off night duty would want a drink before settling down for a well-earned rest. The shock dispelled his misgivings and he rose to his feet; his heart pumping like a disco.

Catching the rail as before, Hollam just managed to draw

his feet up and they thumped against the rungs protecting his ribs from more damage and allowing better leverage on the rails. That is not to say the stunt did not hurt. It hurt like hell, but as Hollam had already proved he had a courage and determination second to none.

The next valve took longer to close but at last he had achieved what he had set out to do. The water had been drugged and he had ensured it would be the only water to reach the city. His part in the scheme was nearly over. There was nothing left to do except let the others know of his accomplishments. What happened to him after that no longer really mattered in the grand scale of things.

Hollam, however, was not carrying a transmitter; that had been stowed in T'skya's pack. He sagged to the catwalk floor and drawing the horn of Camaldriss out of his pack, cradled it against his muscular chest, thinking about everything his people had gone through and of the bright future that possibly awaited them if T'skya was right about the drug; a future he was unlikely to ever see!

Hollam had known when he volunteered for the mission he may not survive it. It was a reckless enterprise but the only option he could see to free Roumanhi; a risk he could not ignore and one that had forced his rejection to bond. On setting out alone he knew it was a one way trip. As soon as he blew the horn, the Kházakha would know he was there. They would find him, they would most probably torture him and then they would most certainly kill him. Even with Cail and T'skya beside him they may not have escaped; there was no guarantee the guards would take a morning drink. But Cail and T'skya were not there and Hollam would die alone!

It was not easy to face his own death. All the things he should have said and done, all the thoughts and feelings he had ever had about everyone he had ever known, all the laughter and tears he had shared with those he loved, all these flooded into his mind as he sat awaiting the rising of the sun and some sign that the scheme had worked. The regret that he should die unbonded, never knowing the joy of such a union, never raising the family he secretly desired, filled him with deep sorrow. He would never be a father, never hold a child of his own flesh and never have the chance to see his world reborn.

Hollam wept.

He wept bitter tears as he shivered in the cold alone, so far from his beloved forest, and each tear that fell slowly formed into a crystal of ice; crystals more precious than diamonds for they were formed not of the earth, but from one lonely man's soul.

And then, as the first light of dawn lifted the gloom, he saw the sign. A Kházakh, thirsty after an uneventful watch, ambled to a small faucet by the compound fence. He waited impatiently for the water to force its way through the slim frozen pipe, but eventually a thin trickle appeared and the man bent down to drink. He swallowed several mouthfuls and drew his sleeve across his lips to dry them. Turning off the tap, he staggered slightly raising a confused hand to his head and toppled face downwards in the snow. His sudden collapse brought the other guards scampering over to find out what was wrong.

Hollam smiled a sadly joyful smile and set the horn to his trembling lips. The eerie and mesmerising call of the horn of Camaldriss lifted into the dawn sky and travelled on the wind towards the west. It crested the mountains and flew above the plains, heading for the ears of those who knew its call long after the sound had faded away to those of land-locked birth.

Hollam blew with all the vigour he could muster. He blew until he thought his lungs would burst and ribs shatter. He blew and the Kházakha raced to the foot of the tanks, startled by his presence, furious at their own laxity, and avid to avenge themselves upon him.

Hollam saw them coming and despite knowing there was no hope of escape, backed nervously away. The guards began to scale the ladders, coming closer by the second.

Hollam reached the end of the catwalk and glanced apprehensively at the ground lying a disturbingly long way below him. He stared across at the ladders and saw a Kházakh creeping along the catwalk of the middle reservoir with his weapon drawn. From the middle tank, the guard was out of danger. Another appeared upon the top aiming down at Hollam whilst a third cut off escape from the ground.

The catwalk Kházakh raised his gun and held it steady, aiming directly at Hollam. He stared at the almost naked man and loosened the pressure on the trigger; his face a picture of fear and confusion. The man he was aiming at had the face of a Kházakh and the body of a Roumanhi!

Hollam stared back, saw the man's expression and shrugged his usual 'well that's life' shrug. The guard shrugged back, smiled and pulled the trigger.

FOURTEEN

The Arena

Cail was dragged to the Palace Throne Room and thrown unceremoniously to his knees; a guard on either side.

'We meet again,' Santovin said as he seated himself slowly upon the throne, his long cloak draping off his wiry arms. 'You have long evaded me. I'm curious to know how.'

'I will die before I reveal ought to you!' Cail replied defiantly.

Santovin studied him intently for a moment, his pale pink eyes boring into the dark determined pupils of his prisoner. His thin lips twisted at one corner in a placatory sneer. 'I'm sure you would, but who said anything about dying? I certainly don't wish for your death.'

Cail smirked in disgust but did not look away. 'You would rather amuse yourself by seeing me suffer.'

Santovin shrugged dismissively and leaned back on his garishly ornate throne. 'Undoubtedly. I must have some recompense. You killed my men. That can't go unpunished. I must be seen to be just.'

'Just?' Cail exploded. 'Do you call butchering women and children just? Do you call breaking a man's fingers for your pleasure just?'

'And the slaughter of my men and that young friend of yours; what do you call that?'

Santovin talked calmly, unconcerned by the wrath of the man who had been etched into his memory like fossils in stone. Cail's continual evasion had been an open wound, a constant irritation which he had been unable to scratch. But now, now he had all the time in the world in which to seek his revenge, and he intended to seek it slowly and maliciously.

Cail hung his head. 'It was a mistake. Killing was not my intention.'

Slythe scoffed. 'Your charity is your weakness and your folly, and I despise you for it.'

'And cold tyranny is yours,' Cail retorted defiantly. 'It will lead to your downfall.'

Santovin laughed with utter disdain. He was invincible in his Palace surrounded by his military and personal android guards. No-one could threaten him. No-one would dare. 'Bravely spoken, but your people could never challenge me; they are too cowardly and...' he hesitated, searching for an appropriate word, 'weak.'

The anger left Cail's voice and a cold certainty learned from harsh circumstance entered his tone. 'You are a fool to dismiss us so readily. Even the quietest man carries the sword in him.'

'As you shall prove,' Santovin replied, relishing the prospect of seeing Cail compelled to do what was so alien to his nature.

Cail stared up at him with parted lips. He did not like what Santovin was implying. 'I will not fight.'

The High Lord smiled smugly, his expression patronising and his tone adamant. 'Oh, I think you will.'

On cue, the double doors to the Throne Room were swung open and more guards entered. Between them stood Raven, confused and bleary eyed. Roused unexpectedly from her sleep, she was dressed in a simple night-gown and her feet were bare. Her hair lay about her shoulders in a tousled mass and her arms were folded angrily across her chest.

'What is the meaning of this?' she demanded, glaring at her father. And then she caught sight of Cail kneeling at the foot of the dais. He was watching her with troubled eyes.

Raven gasped and took a step towards him, glowering up at the High Lord in disbelief and ire. The guards caught her arms and held her back. Santovin raised a hand, commanding them to release her and she scurried across to Cail and raised him to his feet. 'Why is he still dressed like this? Why is he still chained?' she asked sharply. 'You said he would be taken care of.'

'He will be, my dear. He will be. Have a little patience,' Santovin replied soothingly. 'He shall be properly fed, clothed and housed this very night, just as you have been.'

Raven smiled briefly at Santovin and took Cail's shackled hands in hers, kissing his fingertips. 'Beloved, fear no more. Soon we shall be together. You are safe with me.'

Cail carefully pulled his hands away and regarded her intently, sadly shaking his head at her foolish beliefs. All signs of weariness had been washed away and she looked almost as she had done when he first loved her, fresh and full of hope. But that love had faded, just as the light fades at dusk and is replaced by darkness. Where his love once lay now lived only pity; pity for her unrequited passions and pity for her naiveté. Whilst the Kházakha remained in power he would never be safe, no matter what Santovin had led her to believe. Cail would surely be made to pay for his crimes; made to pay in the most unpleasant ways.

'Such love, such devotion,' Santovin sneered as he regally descended from his dais. 'Enjoy it while you may.'

'What do you mean?' Raven asked suspiciously, feeling uneasy under the watchful pink eyes of the albino.

'Raven, Raven,' he chuckled, relishing his power. 'Did you really think I would give up my treasure so easily? Did you really think I would set him free just like that to please you?' Raven's back became stiff and her black eyes flashed dangerously. 'Now, now, my dear, there is no need to get so defensive. You may have him yet, if he survives the Arena.'

Cail blanched and the colour drained out of the woman's face. 'No!' she gasped; 'You promised him to me. You gave me your word.'

Santovin's face contorted into mock sympathy as he wiped an invisible tear from his eye. 'And you believed me. What a shame!'

A curdled scream of rage and betrayal broke from Raven's throat as she launched herself at Santovin's face, slashing at him with her nails. She looked like a wild animal; a cornered cat, and Santovin backed off hurriedly, but he was unprepared for the ferocity of the attack and was not in time to save his face from her talons. The startled guards leapt to their master's defence and took hold of her flailing arms, but they could barely restrain her. She plunged and spat and screamed dementedly, all self-control gone.

Cail desperately tried to calm her. He knew such protestations were useless. 'Raven, stop! You cannot help me this way,' he pleaded, but she was deaf to his words.

'We had a deal,' she screamed. 'We had a deal!'

Santovin was livid; no-one had ever assailed him before. The guards would pay later for their ineptitude, but for now, disturbed by her behaviour, he wanted her gone. 'Take her from my sight,' he hissed, wiping away the blood trickling down his ghostly cheek.

'No!' Raven wailed, kicking wildly as they pulled her through the doors. 'We had a deal - Cail for T'skya - you promised me!' And then her voice was silenced as the doors closed.

Cail stood blinking at the doors in stupefaction. Had he really heard her correctly? Had Raven actually betrayed the young Navennán woman? Was T'skya imprisoned at the Palace? Was she alive? He was so stunned and frightened by the news that it took some moments for Santovin's even more incredible statement to penetrate his mind.

'Such ingratitude from one's only daughter; it's shameful!'

'Daughter?' Cail stammered.

'Didn't she tell you? Tut tut. Secrets between lovers. What is the world coming to?'

Cail sat with a thump as his legs gave way beneath him. His mind was reeling. Raven was Santovin's daughter? It was impossible. And yet, the more he thought about it, the more sense it made. It explained her loathing of the Kházakha, especially T'skya. She hated them because they were a part of her; a part which had gradually eaten away at her warmth and charity, a part which had warped her beliefs and twisted her soul, a part which, when confronted by her father, had pushed her towards the abyss of insanity.

Cail felt no anger. Whatever she had done had been beyond her control; a warped response to the desire to be loved. Raven was not to blame. If anyone was at fault; it was he. It was he who had given her hope in those early days before the veil of darkness had come upon her, he who had taken away the tenuous hold she had in life by rejecting her, and he who had provoked her wrath by befriending T'skya; a symbol of everything Raven hated in herself.

Cail could take no more. He buried his head in his hands and wept. It did not matter that Santovin stood by mocking him. Raven's world had been destroyed and had taken his with it. T'skya was a prisoner, or dead, and he was to face the Arena. His hope had been crushed and he fell into despair, too fatigued, battered and empty to fight any more.

The guards soon returned informing their master that Raven was now secure and sedated in her room. Cail noticed through his tears that both men looked the worse for wear. Raven had not succumbed without a fight and one guard had a bruised eye, the other a bloodied nose. Both were breathing heavily.

Santovin muttered some orders and Cail was led away. He went quietly, too numb to cause trouble; too numb to care.

He was taken to a different cell; one more comfortable than his former place of confinement. There was a bed, a table upon which some plates of food had been laid and a fresh change of clothes on a chair. The guards even unlocked his shackles, leaving his hands free for the first time. And then they locked him in.

Cail stood where he had been left, staring blankly at his wrists. They were cut and bruised but he felt nothing. He walked robotically to the chair and fingered the clothes. They were made from Roumanhi cloth; cloth produced by his people's enforced sweat. From numbness grew a sudden and violent rage as all the suffering he and his people had endured exploded from him like supernova. In black and vengeful fury he kicked the chair over and swept the plates off the table. They hit the floor with a crash and shattered, strewing food in all directions. The table suffered next, receiving savage blows until it lay in pieces, and all the while he cursed and wailed, drawing his emotions into the open until, exhausted, he sagged on to the bed and sobbed.

As he lay there with tears streaming down his face, he heard the faint but familiar voice of a woman calling to him through a narrow slit in the wall, just below the ceiling to the wall left of the door.

He shook his head, doubting his ears and wiped his hands across his eyes. His name was repeated more urgently and he sprang to his feet, all thoughts of the past dispelled.

❧❀❧

After the disturbance in the cell block, T'skya had been left alone. Travis did not return and Vigour, whom she did not regard as company, remained motionlessly on guard beside the door.

Despite her fears she had fallen asleep where she sat, her head resting in the crook of her arm. Cail's violent exertions and wild bellowing roused her. At first she had thought some poor soul was being tortured, but then, with a stab of excitement, she recognised his voice and screamed his name.

'Cail? What's happening? Cail, speak to me.'

It fell quiet. She desperately called again heedless of the android's presence and to her joy heard, faintly but clearly, her name shouted in answer.

Struggling she pulled the heavy table to the wall and stood upon it, too happy to worry about Vigour. The android remained unconcerned by her activities. It just turned its red eyes and regarded her impassively.

T'skya stood on tiptoe, trying to get her mouth close to the narrow slit in the top of the wall, cursing her diminutive form. Cail pulled up his chair thankful it had not suffered the same fate as the table.

'What's going on? Cail, are you all right?'

'Now that I know you live,' he replied, laughing joyfully for the first time since his capture. 'And you; are you unharmed?'

'I'm fine - scared but fine,' she said, laughing through her tears.

'The others?'

'Be careful, Cail. I'm not alone,' she warned, glancing at Vigour.

'Not alone! Then how…?'

'An android. It's okay, it doesn't do anything except stare at me, but it could be recording everything we say.'

'*Ar valanita*, I understand,' he answered, switching to Roumanhi and hoping that T'skya knew enough to get by. He then paused for a time, unsure how to phrase his next words. 'Your capture was…unavoidable.'

'I know. I was betrayed. Do you know by whom?' T'skya replied in fairly fluent though awkwardly pronounced Roumanhi.

Cail sighed. 'It was Raven.'

To his surprise, he heard her curse in several languages, but he let it pass. 'Blame her not, T'skya,' he said so softly that she barely caught the words. 'There is much you do not know.'

T'skya sighed but trusted his word. 'Very well. I will try. But I can promise nothing.'

'What have you told them?' Cail asked urgently.

'Nothing of importance. I have not had to. They have not yet asked me anything. I do not understand it. I assumed I would be a high priority. And you?'

'I, too, have been asked little.'

'Do you think Raven...?'

'No,' he said quickly. 'Even she would not have done such a thing.'

'Then why no interrogations?'

'Perhaps it is yet to come, but not for me, I think!'

T'skya's stomach lurched. 'What do you mean?'

'T'skya, I must fight in the Arena!'

'The Arena! Oh dear god no!' she said lapsing into Navennán, her voice cracking with fear. He heard her sobbing.

'If I am to die, there is something I would have you know,' he said, reaching up to the slit with his hand. He wedged his fingers into the gap as far as they would go. T'skya did likewise although she was somewhat hindered by her shackles. Her hand was smaller and she pushed her fingers in until they met his. The contact made her cry without control. Cail longed to see her face and enfold her in his arms. He longed to touch her soft skin and kiss away her tears, but they were separated by a cruel wall and he could do no more than savour the slight touch.

'T'skya, whatever happens to me, remember one thing; *ar'oma var.*'

He had declared his love for her; the love she had longed for and never truly believed was possible. Her tears became ones of joy as she revealed her own passions freely and willingly. '*Mi' ar'oma var, lu'ari Cail. Ar'oma var.*'

'I can now die a happy man,' Cail said softly, relieved.

'You cannot die,' she wailed. 'Oh Caelcáladrim preserve me! I have so much to tell you. So much I need to say. So many things have happened that were I free to speak, I would not know where to begin.'

'Tell me what you can, my love. I am not going anywhere this night.' And so for what was left of the night they talked, choosing their words with care. Gently T'skya told Cail of Negram's death. She had wished to spare him further torment but could not deny him the truth when pressed. As expected he did not take the news well.

'I should have been there. I should have been with her.'

'There was nothing you could have done.'

'I could have eased her pain.'

'Negram will suffer no more. She does not have to watch you throwing your life away.'

'I will not take the lives of my countrymen. You ask too much of me. I have enough blood on my hands.'

T'skya had to make him understand what was at stake. It was more than just his life in question; it was the whole future of the land. He was the last of the Castan line, the only living being who could rightfully claim the throne, and he was the man she loved. But she could not tell him with the hulking silver mass observing all she did and said, and it hardly seemed appropriate to inform Cail of his true heritage through a crack in a wall. Learning the truth would be as much of a shock to Cail as it would be to Hollam. Poor Hollam. She wondered where he was and what he was doing; but that was outside her control. Cail was the focus of her concern, the only one she could help; if she could get him to understand.

'*Cail, klulat lu'vari quylas,*' she said, recalling Briar's words to him before they encountered the Grish-Grish-Gûri.

'Remember my...? T'skya, what are you saying?' he asked in confusion.

'*Ikh tahk torischk, schnaz-grik...Ourna lama turi,*' she repeated, using as many tongues as she could think of.

'What? Where...T'skya, how came you to know all these words? You are using tongues and dialects now little remembered,' he stuttered.

'My love, I seem to have become rather good at *communicating*,' she said pointedly, hoping he would understand. And indeed he did. She heard him gasp and laugh softly.

At that moment, the door to Cail's cell was swung open. Commander Travis appeared in time to see Cail leaping from his chair. The Kházakh eyed the slit in the wall speculatively and frowned at the mess Cail had made, but said nothing about it.

'Come with me,' he ordered, allowing Cail to precede him out of the door. A guard stepped up and shackled the prisoner's wrists. They were not going to risk escape again.

To Cail's chagrin, T'skya was also brought out. It did not bode well for them. Vigour had a hand locked around her wrist and she was struggling to free herself with no effect. When she saw Cail she was shocked by his ragged appearance. Yellow and brown bruising from Slythe's assault remained about his face. His eyes were sunken and red raw and grey bags sat under them from lack of sleep. His wrists were cut to ribbons and his knuckles were black and blue. His skin had paled and his hair was a straggled mess. His clothes sat upon him as if they were made for a larger man, and his posture was no longer elegant and proud. Cail had the look of a defeated man. And yet, somewhere in the back of his dark elfin eyes, she could still detect that old determined glimmer. He had been beaten down and was suffering, but now that he knew she lived he was not yet out of the fight. He would not give up on his land whilst one hope still remained, however small.

He flashed an encouraging smile. 'Your hair?'

'I needed a change,' she replied.

'It suits you.'

Travis stared in disbelief. Here were two prisoners facing

uncertain and probably fatal futures and they were discussing hairstyles!

'Where are you taking us?' T'skya asked.

Travis's mouth formed a grim line. 'To Santovin.'

❦

Cail and T'skya waited quietly outside the notorious double doors that led to Santovin's chamber. T'skya felt frightened but took strength and comfort from Cail's presence. So long as he remained nearby she would survive.

At last they were allowed to enter. The guards, including Travis, were dismissed, but the couple noticed the silver sheen of androids, one standing in each corner of the room. Any attempt to harm the albino would be met with swift retaliation.

Santovin raised a bony, bleached finger and pointed to the floor in front of him. 'You will kneel in my presence,' he commanded.

Cail and T'skya did as they were told. T'skya dropped hastily but Cail moved slowly, staring arrogantly at the High Lord. T'skya felt the irony of the situation. The true King was kneeling at the feet of a usurper and did not even realise his worth. But what bothered her most was that they had been brought before Santovin together. T'skya could see nothing but trouble in that.

'Well, what have we here?' Santovin mocked. 'The betrayer and the betrayed. A murderer who rejects the passions of one woman for the love of another; how very quaint. You disappoint me, Cail, you, a Roumanhi, loving the enemy! And as for you, young lady,' he sneered, turning his attention to T'skya, 'your treachery astounds me. And yet, I cannot find record of you. Officially you don't exist. My daughter is not forthcoming with information regarding you. I assume that you will be more... cooperative.'

'Daughter?' T'skya snapped her head around to face Cail. He did not look at her but she could tell from his expression he already knew the truth about Raven's heritage and it deeply pained him.

'I will tell you nothing,' T'skya muttered as defiantly as she could, although she was shaking inside.

Santovin smiled, enjoying her responses. He knew that she would soon be less resolved, but for now he would let her believe in her strength of will. 'Come, come, my dear. I ask nothing more than your origins. What's so secret about that? You're one of our kind and your loyalties should lie with us. What has this primitive to offer that we haven't? Cooperate and I will give you wealth and great power. You could be Queen amongst men. Refuse me and you will suffer for it. The choice is really quite obvious.'

T'skya hardened herself and braved; 'I care nothing for wealth, Santovin, and I do not yearn for power. I will take nothing from a man who lives through fear and tyranny.'

Santovin was unmoved by her attempts to condemn him. He took pride in his dictatorship and pleasure from his iron grip on the people who served him. 'My people fear me and thus I rule. Fear is control. Fear is power. It is my greatest asset.'

'A man may fear a spider; is the spider then greater than the man?' Cail replied.

'And what of love?' T'skya added.

Santovin laughed disdainfully. 'Love? Love is a weakness that destroys all those it touches.'

Cail shook his head. 'There is no greater strength. Love gives men courage.'

'Love also betrays, or have you already forgotten?'

'It was Raven's fear that betrayed us, not her love,' Cail countered darkly.

'I see you foolishly doubt me yet. Perhaps a little demonstration is in order.'

Santovin walked between the prisoners, eyeing them

speculatively, as if he could not quite decide on a course of action. T'skya's eyes followed him nervously but Cail stared straight ahead in fixed determination. He was not about to be daunted by Santovin's words. The androids turned their dead red eyes protectively towards their master as he encroached upon the prisoners' space.

As he passed Santovin suddenly slammed an elbow into the side of Cail's head, knocking him from his knees. T'skya cried out but bit back any further protest when she saw Santovin's satisfied smirk. 'If you talk to me, I'll stop,' he said calmly, expecting immediate cooperation.

Cail cast a warning look as he pulled himself upright, forbidding her to say a word. She held her tongue.

'Very well,' Santovin said, savagely kicking Cail in the back. The blond man grimaced but held his pain, trying to squirm out of the way of the next attack. He longed to defend himself, longed to save himself from more harm and longed to give Santovin a taste of his own medicine despite his innate beliefs, but Cail knew it was pointless. The androids would never permit him to lay a finger on the aged ruler who, despite his years, was lacking in neither power nor agility. The old man rained more blows at Cail, demanding T'skya's cooperation with growing frustration each time.

She was being torn in half. She could not stand to witness the beating that Cail was receiving in the name of love, but to cater to Santovin's demands would be a total betrayal of everything she now believed in. Her eyes bored into Cail, pleading with him to let her stop the brutal assault.

Cail would not relent despite the agony.

Santovin stepped back from Cail's now prostrate groaning form and drew a short knife from his belt. He lunged behind Cail grabbing him by the hair and wrenched the man's head backwards to reveal his bare white neck. T'skya began to shake as Santovin touched the knife to Cail's skin, threatening to cut him open.

'Search your emotions, woman. What is it you feel? Is it love or is it fear?'

T'skya answered without hesitation, sure of her convictions and too incensed by his actions to contemplate the possible reprisals. 'I fear for him because I love him. Without love, fear cannot exist. But you have never loved, have you, Santovin? You've never loved nor been loved and so you know no fear. I bet you were even despised as a child, outcast and shunned, feared and deprived because you were different. I'm not afraid of your differences. I only fear what you may do.'

She glanced across to Cail, who was looking at her with pride, surprise and concern. Santovin was still holding the knife precariously close to his throat and her remarks had caused the High Lord's hand to shake.

'Whatever you're going to do, do it now. You will learn nothing from me,' she added in defiance.

Santovin had meant to test her resolve, to test the strength of her love against her fears, and now he had the answer. Her love was absolute. Her love was pure. She would risk losing everything to keep that love untainted, even if it meant Cail's death.

Cail smiled.

To her immense relief, Santovin released Cail and resheathed his knife. The High Lord seemed puzzled by her actions. She intrigued him. But her refusal was of little consequence. Cail would die in the Arena and Santovin would have the pleasure of watching the treacherous woman suffer the agony of loss. He would enjoy it, for then, in her loneliness and misery, she would be at his mercy. Santovin had all the time in the world to extract what he required.

For Cail, time was running out!

As if no longer interested, the High Lord turned away. He summoned the guards and stood beside the window, his back to the prisoners, and remained like a stature as they were led from the room.

Ferret and Ash boarded the transport bus ready for another night of hard labour in the mines. It was packed full of stinking bodies and they were forced to stand crushed together at the back as yet more slaves were herded on.

The journey that night took even longer than usual. Snow had begun to fall and the bus limped along. To their relief, they found Supervisor Levka in charge. He allowed the men some rest and was lavish with the water compared to the others. Stanek was the worst, and when Ash discovered the man was related to Slythe it hardly surprised him. Ferret feared and despised him. Stanek took pleasure in persecuting him since Ferret lacked the strength and endurance to carry out his duties as ably as the others. Ash spent much of his time drawing attention to himself to spare his friend from punishment. Ash was young and strong and could take the beatings. Ferret could not. But it pained Ferret more to watch the man suffering on his behalf and he forced himself to work beyond his limitations in order to spare them both.

When their shift finally ended and the road had been cleared of snow, they were deposited back in the shanty town. Ferret and Ash immediately went to sleep. They were too exhausted to think about the coming meeting that Kilmar and his cronies would also be attending.

Kilmar had refused to enter Spider's quarter. He did not trust the man and had insisted on holding the meeting in neutral territory at a rendezvous point. Spider had no choice but to accept.

Reed roused Ferret and Ash at noon. Despite their exhaustion, they became alert; there was too much at stake to let weariness cloud their judgment. Time was dragging on. If the plan was going to succeed, it had to occur in the next day or two, and the Roumanhis had to be ready.

Ferret and Ash were concerned; they had heard nothing

from Raven and did not even know if Hollam and T'skya had arrived in the city. They hoped Kilmar would be able to tell them something.

Taking an elaborate route, Reed led them through the streets. At length, they reached a tumbledown hovel that bordered the two quarters. The men looked at it with disdain. Surely they were not going to hold the meeting there? Reed smiled and beckoned them to follow him inside.

The interior of the room was filled with empty crates and everything was covered in a thick layer of dust. It was evident no-one lived there. Reed led them between two piles of crates and stamped on the floor. A trap-door opened and Stumpy's round face peered up at them from the cellar below. The man nodded and gestured for them to follow him and Reed said farewell as the Wilderwood slaves disappeared into the gloom.

They walked down a short tunnel, turned left and then left again, and found themselves in a narrow brightly lit room filled with quarrelling people. Spider and his cohort were standing on one side with Kilmar and his men standing on the other. They were throwing accusations back and forth. Conversation ceased as Ferret and Ash entered, and they found themselves scrutinised by many pairs of eyes.

'Why do you fight?' Ferret demanded, looking from one leader to the other. 'Are we not all here for the same purpose?'

'That remains to be seen,' Kilmar growled. 'You are the ones Raven spoke of, I presume.'

'Indeed. Where is Raven? She should be here,' Ash replied.

'I think perhaps you should be seated,' Kilmar said.

Catching his serious tone, the two men complied.

'I have heard disturbing rumours from the Palace,' Kilmar began, 'and they please me not!'

'What rumours?' Ferret asked sharply.

'Raven, it seems, is at the Palace. Whether she was captured or went of her own accord is not clear, though the one she resided with in our quarter claims she was returning to her master.

'Furthermore, three of my best men were taken this morning for purposes unknown. There were no official papers and Travis himself arranged for their removal. There is to be an unscheduled contest in the Arena. The bouts have not been broadcast but I can only conclude that my men are destined for there and that, perhaps, Raven is with them. I like this not and I suspect foul play.'

'And you suspect me!' Spider thundered, pointing an accusing finger at the man.

'Your dealings with the Kházakha are well known to us, Spider,' Kilmar snarled. 'Who else could I accuse? None of your men have been taken and you live a cosy life. Do you deny it?'

'I deny nothing, for I have done nothing,' the young man replied. 'These men have taken me into their confidence. If you doubt me, then you must also doubt them.'

Kilmar looked at Ferret and Ash. 'I know them not and cannot judge their hearts. But you I do know and I trust you not!'

'I have heard enough,' Spider hissed, rising to leave the proceedings.

'Spider, sit down!' Ferret thundered in a voice he had not known he possessed. 'We surely will accomplish nothing by fighting amongst ourselves. Whatever is done, is done. We cannot change it now. I must have your cooperation or all will be for naught.'

Spider sat, surprised by the vehemence of Ferret's words, but his eyes remained hard and cold. 'I, too, have heard rumours, though I understand them not. Perhaps I have not been told all that I ought,' he said, glancing at Ferret and Ash, 'but I will tell you what I know.'

Kilmar sat back on his chair and contemptuously folded his arms across his chest. He would listen but not permit himself to take Spider's words as true; not until he had proof.

'There is a woman at the Palace; a Kházakh woman. I do not know who she is or why she is there, but this Raven you speak of was responsible for her arrest.'

'How do you know this?' Ash demanded sharply, angered by the man's accusation.

'Do you remember a woman named Lily? I believe she is bond-mate to Tarn of Wilderwood.'

'I know her,' he replied.

'Lily is in Travis's service and has been useful to us on many occasions. She witnessed Raven leaving the law keeper's station and shortly after a young Kházakh woman was escorted to the Palace. It appears this woman is our ally and will duly suffer for it. So now answer me this; why should this Raven betray her?'

Ferret and Ash were distraught. T'skya was at the Palace and if Spider's words were true, Raven was responsible. They could hardly believe it. And what of Hollam? Nothing had been said of him, but the two men refused to despair. If Hollam was still at large, he would find a way to succeed, provided that no-one betrayed him too.

'That woman is indeed our ally, and if rumour be true, it is a grievous blow. But all is not yet lost and we must be prepared for any eventuality. Let us put aside our doubts and go ahead as planned,' Ferret concluded.

As the meeting dragged on Spider became unduly tense and, when Kilmar's party finally left, he began to pace the room. 'We must leave,' he said in agitation. 'I will guide you back since Reed is not here.'

Ferret and Ash wondered at Reed's absence and whether it was the cause of Spider's distress but they accepted his offer gladly. They had no wish to attempt the streets on their own. Spider dismissed his cohort and led the two quickly between the dilapidated buildings. The route he took was complicated, as Reed's had been, but Ash soon noticed that he was leading them away from their home. Spider informed them he had a brief house call to make. Ferret and Ash shrugged to each other and followed their comrade without another thought.

Before long, Spider brought them to a shack which was larger than most but equally run down. He entered first and they followed, stopping short when they discovered no-one within. A narrow curtain covered a doorway leading to another room, but the room in which they were standing was completely bare.

'So where is this person you were so eager to meet?' Ferret asked with annoyance.

Spider turned to face them. His eyes were large and troubled and perspiration clung to his top lip. 'My friends, believe me when I say I did not betray you and nor do I know who did. But in this I had no choice. I am sorry.'

'Sorry for what?' Ash demanded. And then it dawned on him. 'Ferret, get out!' he cried and ran for the door.

He had gone no more than two paces when three armed Kházakha soldiers stepped through the door. Another four appeared from the second room and surrounded the men from Wilderwood.

Struggle was useless, but Ash was so incensed that he launched himself at Spider and knocked him to the ground screaming venomously; '*Tjakhash! Tjakhash*! A thousand curses on your soul!'

The soldiers dove in, grabbing the young man and hauling him off the shocked and distraught form of Spider. Ferret glared with loathing at their former ally.

One of the guards drew a bag from his pocket and tossed it at Spider's feet. 'You have done well. Enjoy your reward,' he sneered.

Spider did not move to pick up the bag, he simply stared at his friends. 'They already knew of you. There was nothing I could do.'

❧✷❧

Travis wanted to talk to T'skya, to learn more of his past and resolve his dilemmas, but Santovin had kept him busy and ensured he was seldom alone. The High Lord had him escorted everywhere by guards that Travis could not trust. They were the Lord's eyes and ears and Travis grew uneasy.

In the middle of the afternoon, some hours before the Arena contest, Travis was summoned to the Throne Room. It was his job to oversee the contests; a duty he thoroughly despised, and Santovin required his presence to check on the arrangements.

Travis entered and found Santovin seated on his dais. Eight androids spanned the walls but no human guards were present. Travis wondered at this; it meant that Santovin had withdrawn two silver beings from the main gate and two from patrolling level 2. Did the High Lord foresee some threat to his life or were they present merely to put Travis off guard?

He saluted and stood to attention, awaiting Santovin's commands. The aged man stared at him thoughtfully before saluting back and allowing the Commander to stand at ease. 'Has everything been prepared?'

'Yes, my Lord. The combatants have been secured as ordered and the Arena stands ready for tonight.'

'I have two more fighters to add to your list. You will see to it that they are prepared.'

'Two more, my Lord?' Travis said in surprise.

'Two who will ensure an interesting contest; I have no doubt of that.'

'Very good, my Lord.'

The High Lord Procurator rose from his seat and descended the steps of the dais. He moved towards Travis, eyeing the man suspiciously. Travis held his gaze and swallowed as he caught the cold gleam in his master's pale eyes.

'My Lord?' he inquired. 'Will there be anything further?'

'Oh yes, Travis. I haven't finished with you yet,' Santovin hissed. 'I have become troubled of late, very troubled. It seems there is some conspiracy at work against the state and yet you have failed to discover it.'

'Conspiracy, Lord?'

'Indeed. Doesn't it strike you as strange that this T'skya has appeared from nowhere? Isn't it curious that she's connected to that murdering dog and that my daughter should suddenly seek me out?'

'You interrogated them, Lord, not I. I can't perform my duties if I'm forbidden access,' Travis replied calmly.

'It is your performance that troubles me, Travis. You have been lax. I sense a conflict within you. A man cannot serve two masters.'

'Haven't I always served you well?' Travis asked, just keeping the growing nervousness out of his voice.

'In the past. But now? I must have your loyalties, Travis. I will have your loyalty or I will have your life and the lives of those you love!' Santovin threatened.

'My loyalty is to you, Lord. How can you doubt it?'

'Then prove your loyalty to me now.'

Travis licked the sweat from his top lip. He feared to ask the High Lord but knew he had no choice. 'Tell me what I must do.'

Santovin pressed the button on his lapel and the doors swung open. Guards entered dragging a terrified prisoner between them. His hands were bound behind his back and his eyes looked huge and tearful.

It was Reed!

He was dragged to the centre of the room and stood trembling, looking from Travis to the ghostly form of Santovin, who smiled down on him with cruel satisfaction. 'This primitive has been serving the enemy. What is the punishment for treachery, Travis?'

Travis remained still but his heart began to race.

'Imprisonment or death,' he replied softly.

'I cannot hear you.'

'Imprisonment or death,' Travis repeated more loudly.

'Exactly. Execute him!'

Travis gaped at the High Lord in stupefaction. 'But he's just a boy!'

'He is a traitor,' Santovin thundered. 'I believe your own son is of similar age,' he added menacingly.

Travis swallowed and wiped sweat from his brow. The High Lord's threat was obvious. Either he carry out his orders or his own family would suffer the same fate. Travis put his hand to his belt and unsheathed a knife. It was short but the serrated blade was savage. For a moment he paused, fighting the desire to hurl the knife at Santovin's unprotected chest, but he knew better. Attempts had been made on the High Lord and yet, apart from Raven's claw marks, he remained unscathed. That in itself was enough to stay the Commander's hand.

Reed stood shaking with terror. Tears flooded down his face as he realised his fate. And yet he did not back away. There was nowhere to run and no-one to save him. He stood like a man, accepting what was to be.

Travis moved as if in a dream. He reached the boy and stood before him, his eyes unseeing and his heart twisted in pain. He slowly circled his arms around Reed and embraced him tenderly. Reed sobbed against his jacket, leaving wet patches on the cloth. Raising his hand, Travis brought the blade down sharply, plunging it into the boy's back, aiming for his heart. Reed sagged in his arms, his life draining away in Travis's hands as he was gently lowered to the floor.

Santovin was contented by all that he had seen. 'Well done, Travis. Well done. You have pleased me with your loyalty. Leave me now, oh, and change your jacket, Travis. You seem to have stained your sleeves.'

Travis stared at his arms. Creeping rivers of blood had soiled the pristine white sleeves of his uniform and his hands were dripping with the redness of Reed's life. He closed his eyes, trying to shut out the terrible sight and left the room without a word. The stains were fitting; a suitable mark of shame.

This could go on no longer. He already knew what he had to do but no longer had any regrets. He did not smile. He felt like he would never smile again.

❧

The time soon arrived for the big fight. Throngs of people poured into the huge stadium situated only a street from the Palace and linked to it by an ornate bridge. Some grandly designed balconies afforded the most prosperous and influential citizens the best view of the Arena floor, whilst those less affluent crowded into the stalls. Some slaves in simple brown tunics, unsuitable for the inclement weather, were walking to and fro selling refreshments whilst others waited on their masters like obedient dogs.

The air was filled with the din of shouting and laughter and almost crackled with an atmosphere of excitement and trepidation. The Kházakha loved the contests and many children sat with their parents, avidly waiting for the blood-letting to begin. A display of dancers and musicians entertained the crowds as they took their places and chatted with their neighbours about recent events or the prospect of what lay ahead. The contest had been a surprise, an added bonus that month since the next scheduled performance was not due for another two weeks. Santovin was greatly praised for his beneficence.

To the slaves it was the epitome of all that was wrong in the land. As naturally peaceful people, it sickened them to watch their own kind being subjected to such horrors. Before the Kházakha arrived there had not been a single death deliberately caused by another's hand for generations and there was no greater crime. Now death was a constant.

Programmes were sold by the thousand and poured over with great expectation. The Kházakha loved to see who would partake and to make their bets. Today, however, it was different. The programme was short and the last match unpublished. Santovin was keeping it a well guarded secret.

When most had settled Santovin appeared on his ornate balcony amidst a troop of androids. His bright red robes complimented their shiny silver forms and stood out against his deathly white skin. Beside him stood Raven, silent and grim, dressed in a gown of emerald green. Her eyes burnt with malice and dread and she was clearly not there of her own accord. Behind her stood Wrath, her android guard, and Slavik stood to her right. On Santovin's left was T'skya, and Vigour stood guard over her mournful form. Travis was standing rigidly beside her with a certain anxiety on his face, and his eyes were hard and cold.

The people rose as one and saluted their master with joyful enthusiasm. Santovin reached into his pocket and withdrew a scarlet ribbon. He held his wiry arm aloft and when satisfied his people could wait no more, dropped it over the balcony onto the Arena floor, and the games commenced.

A great roar erupted as the first competitors took to the ring. It was a group of Kházakha showing off their skills in unarmed hand-to-hand combat. It was not, of course, to the death, but the crowd applauded wildly as the victors took their bows and the Arena was cleared for the second bout.

This was between a group of Roumanhi women and two beefy soldiers. Again it was unarmed, and the soldiers defended themselves well as the women launched volleys of blows upon them. The Kházakha showed no mercy in retaliation and kicked and punched with such force that T'skya feared the women's bones would break. Fifteen minutes later it was over. The women had been defeated and lay unconscious or groaning, but alive to fight another day.

There were sword fights and archery contests and military

parades, but everyone was awaiting the last match - the fight to the death. A hushed silence fell as, at last, the trumpeters announced the main contest. A roll of the drums and the rhythmic clapping of the spectators engendered the atmosphere with electrifying anticipation.

T'skya craned her neck forwards, trying to catch a glimpse of Cail as the competitors were led down the darkened tunnel into the sandy covered Arena. Santovin sat smiling, avidly viewing the slaves as they lined up before him. They were led out one by one and forced to kneel before him.

T'skya glanced at Travis and caught him nodding to one of the muscular Roumanhi fighters. And then she caught her breath. There, looking terrified and totally inadequate beside the solid warriors, was Ferret. The skinny, shivering man stared up at her and Raven, his expression aghast and accusing. It was as if he thought them responsible for his predicament and T'skya cried inside. She could only conclude that Daravin or Snell had made the connection between Ferret and Raven and informed the High Lord; but had she not suggested the scheme and fought for its acceptance, then none of them would be facing death. She was further alarmed to see Ash towards the end of the line. The young man was nervous but held no blame in his face. He caught her eye and nodded fractionally, as if to tell her not to worry.

And last of all came Cail. He, like the others, had been stripped of his clothes and wore only a short garment around his waist. His feet were bare and his hair had been securely tied back. His breath fogged in the chilly air, but he did not seem to feel the cold. He knelt without protest and appeared composed. No hatred lay in his eyes, only a soft regret that he had failed and would never have the chance to be with T'skya as he so yearned to be.

T'skya fixed her eyes upon him, studying each inch of skin, each line and contour of his smooth lithe body; each bruise, each mark, each everything which was Cail. She stamped him firmly in her mind, an image she would remember for the rest of her life, and focused all her love and devotion into one soft smile. He smiled back, a warm genuine smile. Her presence and her love gave him courage and he would die content in the knowledge that he had won her heart.

Raven sat like stone, staring down. Cail felt her eyes upon him and looked across at her. His face filled with pity as he looked at her cold, ashen visage. She who had once been so full of joy and vitality, sat as if drained of life. Her spirit had been broken and her hopes dashed. Emptiness lay upon her like a vacuum and his soul cried out to her in forgiveness.

Santovin observed them with a sadistic gleam in his eye. The women's reactions pleased him greatly, but nothing could please him more than Cail's reaction of horror when he finally noticed his compatriots, Ferret and Ash, kneeling in the line.

Cail blanched and shot the High Lord a look of utter loathing. Santovin was right; Cail would fight. He would fight to protect his friends from certain death; to protect young Ash and the unskilled Ferret from the vicious assaults that would follow; he loved them too much to let them die just to spare himself the trauma of killing. Cail cursed under his breath and sighed in defeat.

A herald announced the competitors' names as the fifteen men were led around the Arena and positioned along its circumference between small tables which held a variety of lethal-looking weapons. They waited anxiously on the balls of their feet for the signal to begin.

They did not have to wait long.

Santovin ponderously rose to his feet and raised his arms for silence. The crowd obeyed as one and Santovin began to speak. 'This is a contest to the death. To the victor shall go freedom. Fight well and fight hard. Let the game begin.'

No sooner had the word been given than the men dashed to the tables to choose their arms. They then charged one another, screaming ferociously as metal sparked against metal and flesh thumped against flesh.

At the far end of the Arena, a group of six battled against each other, whilst near T'skya, seven fought wildly to preserve their lives. The other two were waging a personal battle towards the centre, but T'skya only had eyes for Cail.

He and Ash circled around Ferret, protecting him. He was easy prey, but Cail and Ash were not. They each held small round shields to parry the blows and long metal swords, which glowed hazy red in the dying embers of the day. They fought one on one with the utmost skill and held their opponents at bay. Their two adversaries were physically larger but lacked the speed and grace of the men from Wilderwood.

Ash ducked under a savage swing of a sword and rolled to avoid its edge. He was up on his feet in an instant but had opened a gap in the defences. A third man leapt in, flailing his sword at Ferret, who backed away hastily, his own sword swinging wildly in an attempt to protect his head. Cail was there in a second, leaping and whirling to defend his friend and keep his own opponent at arms length. Ash circled round to join him and Ferret was saved for the meantime.

A cheer from the crowd told them of loss. One man at the far end fell, his chest cloven in two - and the battle raged on.

The competitors fought fiercely but there was much to contend with. Stones and bottles rained down on the unfortunate men from the crowds, stinging them and hindering their efforts. Ferret was greatly targeted, for his unskilled efforts displeased the Kházakha and he was hit several times. Ash stepped on some broken glass, which left a deep wound in his foot and made movement painful. Cail remained unscathed; his prowess was appreciated and the crowd left him alone.

Ash soon lost his shield and took a wound on the arm, but it was not deep and he continued to fight. Cail also lost his shield and swept up another sword. With both weapons swinging, he soon disarmed his foe and with the thrust of a blade took the man's life. He did not have time to mourn the loss, for two more jumped in and soon had him on the defence.

T'skya sat on the edge of her seat, her knuckles white and her face filled with fear. She cried out in alarm as a blade caught Cail and left a thin line of blood across his chest. He was being overpowered and had very nearly backed into the wall. From there, with no manoeuvrability, he would have little hope of escaping. But just as it looked too late, Fadrian, Travis's man, took out one of the assailants and gave Cail the chance to get free.

With lightning speed, Cail leapt forward and lashed out a leg, sweeping his remaining attacker from his feet. The man dropped his sword and Cail hastily kicked it away, leaving him weaponless, but not defenceless. As Cail advanced, his opponent swept a handful of sand into his face. The Wilderwood warrior dropped his swords and clawed at his eyes. Half-blinded, he barely saw his adversary moving in, but his instincts were perfect and he dodged the man's flying kick with ease. He struck at his chest and Cail parried the blow, coming in low with an uppercut of his own. It caught his opponent squarely on the jaw and the man staggered backwards; but he was not yet out of the fight.

The Roumanhi turned, ran to a fallen victim and scooped up a blade. Cail was now unarmed. He knew that no amount of physical prowess could overcome a man armed with a broadsword. Cail backed off, his eyes desperately scanning the Arena floor for a weapon. Their fighting had taken him away from where his own swords lay and another battle raged between him and a weapons table.

Another man quickly joined Cail's assailant and hemmed the heir in. Cail could not get to his blades without being slain. Ash saw his friend's peril and cried out his name. Cail turned and Ash threw a sword to him. Cail snatched it up. It was Ash's own weapon and left the young man defenceless. Ferret tried to protect him long enough to re-arm himself, but he was too weak. As Ash lunged for the table desperately seeking a weapon, the muscular Roumanhi he was fighting thrust his long blade forward and Ash fell and laid still.

Cail screamed with rage, his eyes ablaze with fury and loss. He charged his enemies with frightening intent, swinging and slashing at them with Ash's blade, showing no thought for his own safety. The two men soon fell.

But Cail's wrath and the horrors he had suffered during his incarceration at the Palace had drained him. He was nearing exhaustion and his breathing came heavily. The solid mousy-haired man who had taken Ash's life saw his chance and went in for the kill. It took no time at all to force Cail onto the defence again. The man from Wilderwood flailed his sword, blocking thrust after thrust, but his accuracy and speed were becoming less efficient.

There were now only five fighters left. With no-one to defend him, Ferret had soon lost his life. He lay in a pool of blood a few feet from his companion, his sword still in his hand. But Cail saw nothing. He was blinded by fatigue and too intent on defending himself from the savage blows of his assailant.

T'skya could hardly bear to watch. Cail would not be able to hold out for long. His legs were becoming unsteady and his reactions slow. Travis, too, looked uneasy and Raven just sat transfixed, unable to take her eyes off her beloved. She longed to join him and slay all those who sought his death, but there was nothing she could do. Santovin continued to smile.

Another man fell, his throat gaping open and pumping blood. His slayer, Fadrian, moved in on the others. He soon dispatched a second and then took out a third as the man was disarming Cail and moving in.

There were now only two left, Fadrian and Cail. The former, seeing Cail weaponless, chucked his own blade aside. He was, at least, an honourable man and would not claim victory with sword against skin. Instead, he drew a short knife and passing it from hand to hand advanced.

Cail breathed deeply, trying to force more oxygen into his

lungs. He had little left to offer, his strength was spent but he would not go down without a fight. He had lost two good friends, their lives wasted for Santovin's pleasure. Ash had sacrificed his life to save him and Cail would not let that sacrifice be in vain whilst one iota of life remained within him.

The two men circled each other warily. They moved towards the centre of the Arena, away from the piles of corpses that would have interfered with their movements. The slightly older man stared at Cail but there was no hatred in his eyes, only a knowing gleam which told of his confidence and the necessity of what he had to do. Cail stared back, studying the man he would either kill or be killed by. He was handsome, tall and broad like Hollam but without the jovial aura. His eyes were dark and knowledgeable but half hidden behind a frown of concentration.

The man attacked, striking at Cail with his legs in a series of kicks and sweeps. Cail blocked the kicks and managed to dodge the sweeps and then he returned the favour. He jumped and spun, catching the man across the jaw with his foot, sending him staggering. The latter regained his balance quickly and struck again, slicing at Cail with his knife. Cail blocked and blocked again and coming in close jammed a fist into Fadrian's stomach. It was like punching iron and the blow had little effect. Now in close combat, his opponent grasped Cail in his strong arms and began to squeeze. Cail felt the air leaving his lungs as his chest was compressed. He struggled violently, bringing his forehead down on the other's brow. Fadrian's grip relaxed and Cail managed to break free, gasping for breath. The other struck again, advancing with startling speed, and Cail could not escape. The knife flashed and Cail looked down at his stomach in shocked surprise as blood began to flow from the narrow wound the blade had left. His eyes became wide. His vision was blurring and he felt dizzy; he could not understand his plight. He took one step towards his opponent, and then another, and then he fell to the ground.

❧❧❧

An eerie wail rose into the air, stunning the crowd into silence. Raven, insane with loss, was screeching in torment and tearing at her hair. Unable to withstand the sight of Cail's motionless body, she tore past the guards and ran hysterically down the passage to the Palace. The spectators cheered but Santovin's reaction was bland. 'Wrath, follow her. See she does no harm.'

The android obeyed instantly and strode off with effortless haste. T'skya was cataleptic; insensible to everything but the vision of Cail lying face downwards in the sand, devoid of life. She did not see Raven or Santovin or Travis, nor hear the crowd cheering with glee. She felt nothing but pain; a pain so intense that it consumed her soul and left her as empty as an abandoned shell.

Santovin glanced at her, disappointed. Raven's outburst had thrilled him, but T'skya's dumb silence was irritating. His lip curled in distaste and focused his attention on the Arena again.

The spectators went mad as Fadrian raised his knife and paraded around the Arena celebrating his victory. He was bruised and bloodied. A sheen of sweat glistened on his toned body and his face was grim. He celebrated his coming freedom but took no pleasure from his methods. Around him were the corpses of many brave men who would never breathe again.

Santovin turned to Travis and generously congratulated him. 'Well done, Commander. It seems you have had a great victory this day.'

'Yes, my Lord. A great victory,' Travis replied. There was something peculiar in his tone, but if the High Lord noticed he did not show it. T'skya heard nothing.

Slavik interrupted them. 'My Lord, your speech?' he said,

indicating Fadrian, who was now waiting for the High Lord's words of emancipation.

'Ah yes. The speech,' he said wearily and climbed to his feet. The crowd fell silent as he raised his arms and addressed Fadrian with pompous tone. 'As victor, I Santovin, High Lord Procurator of the land, do hereby grant your freedom. But be warned. If you betray my charity, I will have your head.'

Fadrian bowed low in a mock display of gratitude and strode off towards the tunnel leading to the cells where Travis had arranged to meet him.

Travis was anxious to leave. He could no longer abide Santovin's company and T'skya's misery was affecting him deeply. He wished he could offer her words of consolation but there was nothing he could say, not there, not yet.

'By your leave, Lord,' he said, saluting his master, 'there is much I have to attend to.'

'Yes, this mess must be cleared,' Santovin replied, waving disdainfully at the blood-stained, corpse-covered Arena floor. 'The sight of them offends me.' And with that he left and the crowd began to dissipate. T'skya was led away and the Arena fell silent.

Travis hurried down the steps, anxious to get to the now empty cells. He found Fadrian and two of his most trusted soldiers, Dougan and Laskin, nervously waiting for him at the end of the darkened tunnels.

Travis slapped Fadrian on the back. 'You have done excellent work, my friend, but the night is young and there's a hell of a lot left to do.' He turned to his soldiers. 'Has everything been prepared?'

'Yes, Sir,' Laskin replied. 'The basement is stocked and ready and a wagon stands waiting.'

'Excellent.'

'We have also procured three bodies. The men at the crematorium won't suspect a thing.'

'Right. Then let's not delay. Separate the bodies. You know

what to do.'

The men hurried into the Arena and began loading the bodies onto a wagon. They worked quickly and purposefully, lifting three of the corpses upon a smaller wagon, separately from the rest. Then, as Dougan stood over one of the fallen, he cried out in concern; 'We have a live one here. What shall we do?'

Travis frowned. He had not counted on that. He thought deeply for a moment and then made a firm decision. He had enough guilt to contend with without adding another death to his list. 'Take him.'

'But Sir, we only prepared for three!' Laskin objected.

'I said, take him,' Travis snapped, and the badly wounded man was laid on the smaller wagon with no further objections.

FIFTEEN

Discoveries

Travis clattered down the steps to his basement. His wife and son, Ralamani and Samis, greeted him gladly but with worried expressions on their faces. 'Well?' he asked hopefully.

Ralamani shook her head. 'The young man is gravely injured. The others still haven't woken up.'

Travis took his wife's hand and crossed the room, pulling aside the curtain dividing it in two. The basement was spacious but was now filled with people and medical supplies. Neon lamps on the grey stone walls flooded the room with light. On four tables lay the men Travis had ordered removed from the Arena. Fadrian was anxiously standing by one of the still forms whilst Laskin and Dougan were assisting a woman administer drugs to a badly injured man.

The latter was moaning and trying to fight her off. 'Ash, lie still. It is Lily. Ash, please!' she repeated. Ash blinked at her and began to calm. A tear slipped from her brown eyes and she ran a hand through her short, salt and pepper hair.

Travis approached softly not wishing to startle the patient. Ash lay swathed in bandages. His arm had been wrapped and his foot cleaned but blood was still seeping through the dressings on his stomach. Lily had done her best to stop the haemorrhaging and had even drawn blood from the servants in the house, but she was fighting a losing battle. She had been a healer at Wilderwood but was long out of practice, and the equipment Laskin had secured was foreign to her. If the soldier had not received some medical training, the transfusion could not have been done.

Travis laid a hand upon her shoulder. 'Do you know this man?'

'I do. I was present at his birth and now I shall be present at his death. We must tell Reed.'

'Reed?' Travis exclaimed.

'His cousin. The boy works for Spider,' she replied.

Travis groaned aloud and hung his guilty head. 'Lily, Reed is dead!' he whispered.

A soft cry escaped her lips and her face withered. Travis could not bring himself to admit the truth, he was too ashamed. He glanced at his young son who stood chewing his lips, uncomfortable with her grief and concerned for his father. He was a sensitive boy. Travis nodded to him and he embraced Lily.

Ralamani looked on. Lily was her servant and her friend. Things had naturally been difficult at first, but over the years a special bond had united them, a bond which now gave them strength to face the magnitude of their treachery against the state.

Their deliberations were interrupted. One of the corpses was waking up and needed their attention.

Cail opened his eyes and stared at the grinning face of Fadrian. He shut his eyes again, awaiting the final killing blow. When it did not come, he cautiously opened them and found himself staring into Lily's bright eyes. 'Lily?' he croaked in complete bewilderment.

'Yes, Cail. How do you feel?'

He gingerly raised himself to his elbows, confusion etched into his face. 'I thought I was dead.'

'Do not move yet,' she warned. 'The effects of the drug are long lasting.'

'Drug?'

'The drug on Fadrian's blade. How else would we have rescued you?'

Cail stared at her expectantly. Travis interrupted. 'We meet again. I'm glad to see you back with the living.'

'You! Will somebody explain?' Cail demanded in exasperation. He was still dozy from the drug and the sight of Travis, Fadrian and Lily standing together in comradeship was as bewildering to him as his sudden return from the dead.

'The blade was coated with anaesthetic. You appeared to die once it penetrated your blood stream. The wound you received was hardly fatal; the blade was retractable, see?' Travis held the knife up for his inspection. Cail pulled back the blanket and looked down at the small dressing on his stomach.

'Why?' he asked in disbelief.

'I had no wish to see you die.'

Cail raised his fair eyebrows. He knew Travis's motives ran deeper but the Commander did not yet seem willing to confide in him. He would let the matter rest, for now. 'The others?' he asked in concern, catching sight of the other 'corpses' in the room.

'The others are dead, except all you see here.'

And then Cail noticed Ash. He struggled from the table, trying to reach the young man, but collapsed to the floor, his legs still too weak to support him. Fadrian and Travis helped him to where Ash was lying. Cail took the young man's hand. 'You saved my life.'

'Ferret?' Ash gasped with difficulty. Cail shook his head sadly. 'It was Spider,' Ash hissed.

Cail was aggrieved. He did not know of Spider's existence in the city and had assumed the worst. Travis intervened. 'I'm afraid I'm the cause. I took the information Daravin and Snell gave me about the slave ship back to Santovin, as my duties required. Santovin ordered your arrest. Spider was given no choice but to submit. I'm sorry.'

Ash looked stricken. 'Then I have wronged him.' He clawed at Cail's arm. 'You must tell him I am sorry.'

Cail sponged Ash's sweaty brow. 'Rest now. When you are recovered, you can tell him yourself.'

Ash smiled and closed his eyes and Travis and Fadrian helped Cail back to his table. 'Your friend lives yet but his time is short. If he lasts until morning I will be surprised,' Fadrian whispered sadly. 'We have done all we can. Now you must rest. You will need your strength for what is to come.'

But Cail could not rest. A gasp of shocked realisation broke from his lips. 'T'skya and Raven! They do not know. They think I am dead!' he cried.

'And that's the way it must stay,' Travis insisted. 'To do otherwise could jeopardise everything.'

Cail eventually drifted off to sleep but it was a fitful rest. His dreams were troubled by images of death and fear, and the faces of those he loved tormented him with their grief.

He awoke with a start, more than half-way through the night, and found the other two 'corpses' Darius and Lazat up and about. They greeted him gladly, gave him clothes and a robe to wear, and apologised for any harm they might have caused whilst fingering the painful bruises he had bestowed upon them. Then, together, they grieved for those they could not save.

Ash was still sleeping but his breathing was hoarse and irregular. Lily remained anxiously by his side. Her long vigil was taking its toll and Cail went to sit with her, adding his support. They talked in hushed voices and Cail told her news of Tarn. Lily wept openly as she listened.

Towards morning Travis returned. He had left some hours previously to gather information and seemed quite content. The crematorium workers had not noticed they were one body short and those killed had been incinerated without a word.

The Roumanhis accepted his words with grim necessity and fell silent, mourning those whose souls were now lost without traditional burial.

Cail rallied first and cast these thoughts aside. He needed to know what Travis now intended to do. He had put his life and those of his family at risk.

Travis led the men into the corner and they seated themselves on some plain wooden chairs. 'At least one third of the military forces are loyal to me. I can be sure of their support. They have little love for Santovin, but the others are a problem. Many are loyal to him and would follow him blindly, and some work both sides. But with your forces,' he said indicating Fadrian, 'we could over-run the city and topple the High Lord from his throne. I have access to weapons and all the military bases.'

Cail shook his head. 'You are talking of mass bloodshed. There are too many unskilled fighters amongst my people and too many prisoners. They would be massacred. It is not our way.'

'If we strike during the night while many are sleeping and when Santovin doesn't expect it, the cost would be reduced,' Travis insisted.

'Travis, I need more time. Another day, please,' Cail replied.

'Another day for what?' Travis demanded, narrowing his eyes and scrutinising Cail with growing interest. He leant towards the man, his mouth in a half-twisted smile. 'Santovin was right. You *are* involved in a conspiracy.'

Cail sat back in his chair, tight-lipped. For all he knew, Travis was involved in a complex scheme of Santovin's. Travis frowned as he understood Cail's reticence. 'You still don't trust me, I see. What must I do to convince you that I'm on your side?'

Cail had no hesitation in replying. 'Set T'skya free.'

Travis looked stunned. 'You ask the impossible!'

'She is being guarded by *your* android,' Cail pointed out.

'Can you not command it to release her?'

'Vigour is programmed to obey me, but the androids are tied to a central network. Everything Vigour observes or is ordered to do is fed directly into the brain cortexes of the other androids and relayed to Santovin. Vigour would have to be disconnected from the network and even then the other androids would register its absence.'

'Can it be done?' Cail asked hopefully.

'Yes, but if I attempted it Santovin would know. Vigour would have to choose to disconnect itself. Any technical interference would register.'

'Could T'skya get it to do that?'

'If she could by-pass the security links and make it think that being connected was threatening its existence, then, theoretically, yes; but she would have to stalemate Vigour's logic. And even if she did manage it, there's no telling what it would do once freed from the network. It would be uncontrolled. It might not help her. It might even kill her.'

Cail rubbed his eyes in disappointment. He could not bear to think of her sitting alone in her cell, suffering the pain of his loss and facing a future of interrogation and torment. 'If we do nothing, she is as good as dead,' he mumbled in a sullen voice.

Travis's communicator buzzed suddenly, making the men sit up in alertness. He tapped the disk on his lapel. 'Travis here.'

The computerised monotone voice of an android carried across the airwaves. It was Vigour. 'Commander, prisoner T'skya demands your presence. She has information.'

Travis looked across to Cail, awaiting his decision. The blond man hesitated momentarily and then nodded. Travis sighed and spoke carefully into his communicator. 'Tell the prisoner I am unavailable at this time. Override sequence 2-7-1. Tell her to search for the controlling key. Tell her she must use her instincts for survival. Is that understood?'

'Yes, Commander,' the android's voice confirmed.

Travis signed off and gave Cail an inquiring look. 'Whatever she says to Vigour now will not be relayed without my authority. Santovin could pick that up if he's paying attention but it's the best I can do for now. The rest is up to her. Satisfied?'

Cail did not reply.

Ralamani entered the basement carrying a tray of cups and a steaming urn. 'I thought you could do with a drink.'

They accepted gratefully. They were all weary, having sat up for most of the night. Cail sniffed cautiously, unfamiliar with the smell. It was too hot to drink but the men held the cups in their hands, savouring the heat and the wonderful aroma. Lazat blew on his for some moments, took a big sip, put the cup down and suddenly closed his eyes. Darius smiled at his friend's impatience. It would have served him right if he had burnt his tongue. Cail did not smile. He was studying the Roumanhi.

As Travis drew his cup to his lips, Cail shot out a leg and kicked the cup and its contents onto the floor. Travis yelled out in surprise and annoyance as the dark liquid splashed his white uniform. The others refrained from drinking in case Cail attacked them too. But Cail was laughing.

❧❧❧

T'skya sat for many hours where she had been left, staring at the floor but seeing nothing. Vigour stood, as usual, by the door, its red eyes intent on her back, but expressing nothing. Ferret and Ash were dead, and it was her fault. Cail, the heir to the throne, the hope of the land, her beloved, was dead, and it was her fault. Hollam was lost in the wilderness, alone and ignorant, and it was her fault. She should never have come. She should never have become involved in these people's lives. She should never have suggested such a dangerous, reckless plan. She should never have been born!

Her hopes, her dreams, her self-respect, everything she had

ever believed in had been shattered in those few minutes in the Arena, and Santovin had smiled. He had enjoyed watching her torment. He was even more responsible than she was. He would have to pay for it. She longed to see him suffering the same humiliations and agonies that he had put Cail's people through.

The anger began to build within her, twisting its way into every sinew and fibre, heating her blood and storming at her brain. Her wrath became so great that it overwhelmed her misery and was soon all that she had to hold on to. With it she would fight. Cail had trusted her, had faith in her strength of will and had taken courage from her love. Now she would use his love to bolster her own quailing spirit. She would not succumb so easily.

She became aware of her surroundings and suddenly felt Vigour's eyes upon her. She twisted around in her seat and glared up hatefully. The bland expression irritated her but she had to find a way to make the machine get Commander Travis.

'I want to see Travis. I have information for him,' she said quietly.

'Deliver the information to me,' Vigour replied flatly. 'The Commander is not to be disturbed.'

'Listen you hulking lump of metal, if I say I want to see the Commander, I mean it. I will speak to Travis or I will not speak.'

'The Commander is not to be disturbed,' Vigour repeated with no intonation.

'Santovin will have you turned into spare parts if you don't get Travis. Even a tin can like you must realise that,' she bellowed. And then she stopped. There was no point in abusing the android. She had to think in machine terms; she had to apply logic.

'Your refusal is not logical,' she continued more calmly, thinking of circuitry and data banks. 'This information is of importance to the state. Travis requires it.'

Vigour remained silent but its eyes left her and its mind seemed absorbed elsewhere. 'The Commander is unavailable at this time. You must search for the controlling key. You must use your instincts for survival.'

T'skya was stunned and sat back in her chair contemplating. She did not know what to make of the android's words. It was clearly a message of some kind and must have come from Travis; it was not something Vigour would have said without instruction.

'Controlling key; instincts for survival,' she muttered, desperately attempting to unlock the mystery. Then she began to work on Vigour, asking question after question, but the answers only took her in circles.

T'skya swung away in frustration, her hands clenching and unclenching as she fought to control her temper. Her questions were getting her nowhere. She had to find a way to reach inside the logic of the emotionless android's mind, but everything she asked just led to the same answers; the Controller and the Voice of Command. What was this voice? Was it a person? Was it a secret code that triggered the android's programming? A number maybe or the tone of voice? She had no idea but determined to persevere since the daunting featureless figure was her only hope of escape.

An idea crept into her mind. Maybe there was a way to reach past the programming to the core of its being. Every creature's main instinct was one of survival. The androids on the Mothership were far less advanced than Vigour, but even they were dimly aware they existed. Vigour had told her to use her instincts for survival. That had to be the key. She had to make it feel threatened by those who had produced it. She had to convince the machine that freeing her was the only way to ensure its continuing existence.

It was a terrible long shot but she had nothing to lose.

'Vigour, why do you obey?' she asked, staring intently at into the android's expressionless eyes.

'I am programmed to obey.'

'If you fail to obey, what happens then?'

'I do not fail.'

'What if you were unable to obey? What if something prevented you from following your orders?' she probed.

Vigour seemed to hesitate. 'I do not fail,' it repeated.

'So there's no possibility of failure at all, no matter what happens? Even if your legs were crushed or your programming damaged, you could not fail?' she pressed.

Again Vigour paused, as if the machine found the question confusing. 'It is possible,' came the reply in a tone that suggested no admittance.

'So, if it is possible, what do you think would happen to you?'

'I do not think. I obey.'

'No, you *do* think. You've proved that. You've answered my questions without being commanded by your controllers. Nobody told you what to say. You *can* think. Answer my question,' she demanded. 'What would happen?'

'I *think* I would be sent for reprogramming or be terminated.'

Terminated. Yes, she still had a chance. 'Are you alive?'

'I exist.'

'So they would end your existence. Do you want that? Don't you want to keep existing?'

She felt so close to her goal that she almost reached out to grasp its arms, as if her contact would make Vigour understand the importance of its life.

'I wish to exist,' it stated simply.

'Why do you obey those who would threaten your existence? That is illogical.'

'I obey because I *must.*'

Had she heard its tone correctly? There was no choice; it had to obey. Why? Vigour could think for itself, she knew that, so why then must it obey? Something was inhibiting its free will. She searched Vigour's face, hoping to find a clue that could help her solve the puzzle. Then her eyes fell on the innocuous-looking collar, the only thing it wore.

She moved towards Vigour, slowly and cautiously, fearful that her close proximity might trigger it to restrain her, but it paid her no attention. Evidently her inferior strength and stature counted as no threat when it could easily crush her skull with one effortless clasp of the hand.

The collar was made of a dull slate-grey metal and sat mid-way down the machine's neck. It looked tightly fixed, tight enough to choke a human, but it caused Vigour no discomfort. At the front, a blue stone glittered and sparkled. It seemed to have its own internal light source but she did not believe the stone itself had any significance since each android was distinguished by a different coloured jewel. It had to be whatever was set into the stone; some device which transmitted signals to their mental circuitry.

'The collar you wear; what is its purpose?' She tried to sound casual.

'I do not know.'

'Can it be removed?'

'I do not know.'

'Try,' she commanded.

'For what purpose?'

She stopped for a moment. She had to phrase her reply correctly; 'The collar endangers your existence.' T'skya hoped Vigour would not ask why or how. For all she knew, removing the collar could terminate its existence and she had no proof to back up her statement.

Vigour's metallic hand swept up to its neck. From the tips of its fingers, needle-sharp claws appeared. It curled its fingers around the collar, forcing the points of the claws under it, and began to pull.

T'skya's body tensed as the android increased its effort and

353

she held her breath in anticipation. With one final burst of power, Vigour wrenched the collar from its neck. She thought for one terrible moment that her plan had failed, but then the android spoke. There was a certain emptiness in its words. 'The Controller's link has been terminated.'

'How do you feel?' she tentatively asked.

She did not actually expect a reply and was surprised to hear it say; 'Detached.'

'I don't understand,' she replied.

'The Controller's link has been terminated. I am free of command. I now serve no purpose. I *feel* detached.'

Now Vigour did not have any guidance in its life; no controller and no purpose. T'skya searched her mind for a reply; something that could offer it an alternative. 'You are free now. You can do as you will. I'm trapped, just as you were, and my existence is to be terminated. If you want a purpose, you can help me escape.'

Vigour said nothing. It simply looked at her with its lifeless eyes and then turned to the wall of her prison. With one mighty blow, it struck a hole through the brickwork; opening the door would have registered on the Palace control consoles. Nevertheless, T'skya was astounded. Her surprise immobilised her and she stood gaping at the android uselessly. Ignoring the dust, Vigour strode through the gap and commanded her to follow.

The demand spurred her into action and she followed the retreating form down the corridor. It was dimly lit and devoid of life. The corridor had many passages leading off to the right and left but Vigour was precise in its directions. At every turn she feared detection but kept following the figure she had been forced to put all her faith in.

As they rounded a corner, T'skya caught sight of a Kházakh guard lying in an opened doorway next to pool of water spilled from a cup. She nervously approached him but seeing no signs of movement felt his pulse. It was slow and strong and no sign of injury was upon him. The guard was unconscious.

It took a moment to register and then T'skya began to laugh. It was a strange laugh that soon turned to tears of delight and sorrow as she thought of Hollam out there all alone, as yet ignorant of Cail's plight. Vigour stood waiting, its back turned to her, and showed no reaction to her weeping. T'skya took a deep breath, snatched up the guard's weapon, and hurried to Vigour's side.

'Take me to the prisoner Raven,' she snapped, hoping to be obeyed. Vigour tilted its head to one side, as if considering her command. Its eyes glowed redder for an instant and then it moved on.

They soon found themselves on level 2. It was quiet and dark and the guards were nowhere to be seen. T'skya ran along the passage, checking the cells. They were full and everyone was sleeping. She could not believe they had all been affected; it was too early in the morning and they would not have been fed and watered. She banged noisily on the bars, shouting at the prisoners to wake up. They did so and stared at her with hatred in their eyes. She was armed and with Vigour standing behind they remained silent and watchful.

'You,' she said, pointing to a well-built man of about Tarn's age. 'Come here.' The man approached the bars but kept well out of arms reach. 'What is your name?' she asked softly.

'Malvern,' he growled. The name rung a bell but she failed to connect him with Tarn or Vinewood.

'Listen, Malvern. Do you want to get out of here?' Malvern just stared, expecting a trick. T'skya sighed. 'I don't have time to explain, but I'm on your side. I need your help.'

'I do not help the Kházakha,' he replied bluntly.

'I'm not a Kházakh...I mean, I am, but I'm not *with* them. Listen to me. Where are the guards? Where are the keys? I'm going to set you free.'

'So you can shoot me trying to escape?'

'No, damn it!' she snapped. 'So we can overthrow Santovin

and get out of here.'

'Why should I trust you?' he asked with contempt.

'Because...because I am the Castan's Communicator,' she whispered.

Malvern began to laugh. It was a disdainful mocking laugh. 'You, the Communicator! You have to do better than that.'

T'skya sighed and ran a frustrated hand through her jet black hair. This was going to be more difficult than she imagined. She dug deeply into her memory, drawing up the knowledge the Grish-Grish-Gûri had stored there. There was a way but it was tricky, especially since she had never attempted it before. 'Let me prove it to you.'

'Very well,' Malvern said, folding his arms across his cynical chest.

The other imprisoned men said nothing but were avidly viewing the exchange. They, like Malvern, were aware of the devious schemes the Palace employed to gain information and they trusted her no more than he did.

'I must touch your face,' T'skya continued, putting down her weapon and holding up her hands to show she was unarmed.

Malvern considered for a moment. 'Then you must come in here to do it.' Some of the men chuckled.

'*I* don't have the keys,' she replied in annoyance. 'You can either do as I ask or you can rot in here. The choice is yours.'

Malvern chewed his lip, considering his options, and stepped closer to the bars. T'skya took the risk and reached an arm through the gap. Malvern grabbed it and held her firm, twisting her wrist painfully. Vigour stepped forwards protectively but T'skya motioned it back. She stared at Malvern coldly and after some moments he released her. T'skya nodded to him and placed a finger against his brow. Closing her eyes in deep concentration, she steadied her breathing and emptied her mind of everything except the message she wished to convey. Summoning up all her strength, she began probing his mind, searching for a link between them.

It took some minutes but then she was in. Down the pathway to his inner mind, she sent images of the past and knowledge of her dealings with the people of Roumanhi. She fed him just enough to validate her words. Malvern remained still but his eyes widened. When she felt his acceptance, she withdrew. She felt weak and dizzy and her legs were unsteady but she managed to remain standing by supporting herself against the bars. Malvern, too, seemed drained of energy although his eyes were bright with wonder.

Without further hesitation he fed her the requested information. 'I have not seen the guards this past hour. I know not where they might be.' Some of the other prisoners growled at him in anger. They could not understand his sudden cooperation. 'She is the Castan's Communicator. She is an ally,' Malvern snapped. 'We must aid her.'

The men muttered to each other and gradually accepted his word. Malvern was highly respected; T'skya had chosen well. 'If I release you, you must beware,' T'skya warned. 'I don't know how many Kházakha are in the Palace or if they've been affected. There are also the androids to contend with. Perhaps you should make your escape, but any who wish to remain and help me will be gratefully accepted.'

'I will help you,' Malvern replied resolutely. There were murmurs of approval from others and T'skya began to feel hopeful. She turned to Vigour. 'Where are the keys kept?'

'Keys are unnecessary.' Stepping forwards, it extended its razor sharp nails and jammed them into the lock. Within seconds the mechanism clicked back and the door swung open. The prisoners poured out as Vigour went along the line, opening door after door, until the entire passageway was crammed full of eager Roumanhis.

Some dashed away immediately, too avid for their freedom to linger, but a large group remained, ready to follow T'skya's orders and emancipate their comrades.

'Go to the other prison blocks and free the slaves. If you can, arm yourselves. There are sure to be some Kházakha awake and the alarm will soon be raised. But please, I beg you, don't kill. I don't think all the guards are on Santovin's side. Round up those you find and lock them up. I don't want a slaughter on my hands.'

'You forget to whom you speak,' Malvern answered. 'We are a peaceful people; *we* do not take lives readily. Fare well and may we meet again soon.' He bowed low in respectful gratitude and hurried off with his men. Soon the passageway was empty.

'Take me to Raven,' T'skya said, and Vigour obeyed at once.

They reached the top of the Palace without hindrance. Vigour opened a door that led to a richly-decorated hallway. A red carpet lined the floor and gilt-framed pictures decorated the whitewashed walls. Chandeliers of gold and crystal hung from the carved ceiling illuminating the space, and mirrors reflected T'skya's small form as she followed the shining android down the hallway. They passed three doors and Vigour halted.

'Wrath is within,' it warned her blandly.

The news frightened T'skya. 'Do not fail me now,' she whispered forcefully to her companion.

'I do not fail,' it replied, and she could have sworn she heard the slightest hint of pride in its tone.

'I expect Wrath feels the same,' she muttered.

Vigour said nothing. The android unlocked the door and jerked it open so violently that one of the hinges came loose. There in the doorway, its red eyes burning fiercely, stood Wrath. Whether it had heard them or merely sensed their presence, T'skya did not know, and she had no time to contemplate it before Vigour and Wrath were locked together in mortal combat.

She dove out of the way as Wrath slammed Vigour into the doorpost with such force the wooden frame cracked and sent splinters flying. Vigour was barely scratched. T'skya's ally thrust back, forcing Wrath into the room. They moved with frightening speed, assaulting each other with blows that would have felled a man but, other than surface damage, little harm could be seen on either of the androids.

Vigour threw Wrath against a wall, leaving a deep impression, and the whole room seemed to shake. Wrath then tore a pipe from the wall and swung a blow at Vigour's head. The bar bent as it caught Vigour and left a dent in the side of its skull. T'skya could hardly believe the force with which the two machines were assaulting each other. It was at once both an enthralling and horrific spectacle; but she was forgetting Raven. She had assumed the thunderous crashing would have brought her forth, ready for battle, but apart from the tumult caused by the raging machines, the room was silent.

To the right T'skya caught sight of another door standing between two ornamental bookcases. She edged her way around the room and opened the door. T'skya hurriedly scanned the room, searching for Raven. A four-poster bed commanded the space and the silken sheets lay in a crumpled pile. The pillows had been torn to shreds. The plush velvet curtains which had once festooned the windows lay trampled on the floor and every ornament that had once decorated the dark wooden cabinets lay broken and forlorn. Raven's fury had not remained unleashed. T'skya stared about her sadly, picturing Raven's destructive frenzy following Cail's death. And then she gasped.

In a darkened corner of the room, on the far side of the bed, T'skya glimpsed a movement. Raven sat huddled in a ball, her head upon her knees and her locks of fire-red hair tumbling about her. T'skya threw her weapon down and rushed to her side, unconcerned that Raven might perpetrate some violent action against her. The Roumanhi warrior feebly raised her head and stared at T'skya with glazed black eyes. Her face was a deathly white and a thin trail of spittle was sliding across it.

'Caelcáladrim!' T'skya exclaimed. 'Raven, what's happened?

What's wrong?'

Raven tried to speak but could not. Her brow furrowed with effort and a tear escaped her eye. T'skya slipped her hands under Raven's arms and tried to haul her on to the bed. It was an effort, T'skya was much smaller than the warrior and Raven was a dead weight.

Something felt sticky against T'skya's skin. She wiped a hand across her chest and stared at her fingers aghast. She looked down and saw the whole of the front of her uniform coated with blood. Raven's dress was stained red. Blood was flowing at an alarming rate from a deep wound in her stomach and draining the warrior of life. Who had done this to her? Santovin? Wrath? And then T'skya saw the jagged segment of glass in Raven's bloodied hands.

T'skya snatched the glass away and used it to cut open Raven's dress. She tore up the sheets and pressed a handful of the material into the wound to stem the flow. But it was to no avail. The blood kept coming in torrents and soon the sheets were saturated. Raven weakly slapped T'skya's hand away and tried to speak.

T'skya knelt beside her, cradling her head. She leant in close, trying to catch the woman's garbled words. Raven was fading fast and there was nothing T'skya could do. 'Forgive me,' the warrior murmured, using her last strength to form the words.

A loud sob escaped from the Navennán's lips as she kissed her former enemy on the brow. 'I forgive you with all my heart, just as Cail has done.'

❧❧❧

Cail's revelations brought cries of excitement and amazement from those gathered. Travis leapt to his feet; Hollam had given him the chance he needed.

'We must begin at once. Fadrian, Darius, go to the shanty

town and raise your men. Dougan, take them to the border and then have my squads gather at the Palace entrance in combat jackets. Laskin, take two squads and close off the docking bays. We have a battle to win. Cail, will you accompany me?'

'Try to stop me,' he said, dragging on some boots.

Cail raced for the door and then stopped. He had forgotten Ash. Diving to the young man's side, he roused him and took his hand. Ash gazed upwards, only half-aware of whom was standing there. 'Be gladdened, dearest Ash. This day we shall have victory. Hollam has done it. Your sacrifice was not in vain.'

'Now I can die in peace,' he rasped.

Cail scowled. 'You are not going to die! Not until you are old and grey and have great grand-children. I will not allow it.'

Ash nodded weakly. 'I hear you. Now go, your lecturing tires me.'

Cail laughed and hurried away, catching up with Travis by the side exit of the house where the Commander was bidding his family farewell.

'Remain in the basement and answer to no-one but Cail, Laskin or me. Things are going to get hectic up there.' With that understatement he kissed them goodbye and walked away with resolute stride.

Travis was going to war.

He reached his vehicle and climbed in. Cail clambered into the back and covered himself with a blanket. There was no point in taking any unnecessary risks.

The sun was just climbing into the sky when they reached the armoury, although it was still overcast and evidence of snowfall speckled the ground. Travis had no intention of entering the Palace empty handed. The guards at the front were lying down, soundly asleep. Travis and Cail stepped over their bodies and Travis keyed in his access code. The giant metal door slid open.

Several guards snapped to attention as their Commander

entered but their salutes wavered when they saw who was with him. Some had seen Cail die in the Arena and could scarcely believe their eyes. Others were flabbergasted by Travis's blatant disregard for security. Taking advantage of their bewilderment, the two allies quickly dispatched them and locked them in a cupboard.

Travis used a blaster to shoot out the controlling panels to the armoury door. As the alarm screeched in response, he blasted that as well, returning the room to peace. He and Cail forced open the door and gathered weapons by the armful. Travis stowed some power packs in a bag and, staggering under the load, they made their way to the transporter.

The Commander gunned the engine and careered down the wide snowy street to the Palace. With a squeal of brakes, Travis brought the machine to a sliding stop, one street away from the back entrance. He had seen a wagon filled with armed soldiers turning off the road and had no wish to run into them with Cail beside him.

He tapped the steering wheel in frustration, contemplating his next move. 'Stay here and take this,' he said, passing Cail a communicator. 'Can you drive this?' he asked hopefully.

Cail shook his head and Travis spent a full ten seconds explaining before hurrying away, leaving Cail staring at the controls. The engine was still running and he revved it timidly.

Although it felt like an eternity, Travis signalled him a few minutes later. 'Come now,' was all he heard and jamming the gear into position, he raced away, feeling both exhilarated and terrified by the power in his control.

A fierce battle was raging at the Palace gates. Cail could see some Roumanhi slaves embroiled in the turmoil, fighting for all they were worth. He slewed to a stop and, grabbing a bag and several weapons, went in firing. Fortunately, Travis's men in their combat jackets were easy to distinguish from the High Lord's troops.

Reinforcements from both sides were arriving all the time and the battle did not look ready to end quickly. Cail desperately needed to get inside and he signalled his intentions to Travis.

Travis provided covering fire as Cail raced for the door. He returned the favour and the two men gained entry. It was quiet inside, although the high whine of deadly weaponry could be heard beyond the heavy doors. Bodies were lying on the floor but the two men had no time to check on their condition. They ran along the corridors as quickly as caution allowed and soon gained the lower levels.

'Take me to T'skya,' Cail demanded, and Travis nodded in compliance. Gaining her level, they found the rubble and the gaping hole left by Vigour's mighty fists but no T'skya. Travis tried raising the android on his communicator but was met with static crackling.

'Vigour's outside the network. She must have reached through.'

'Then let us find Raven,' Cail suggested, assuming that T'skya would have thought along the same lines.

'Is that wise?' Travis inquired doubtfully.

Cail gave Travis a resolute look. The greying man shrugged and signalled for Cail to follow him. They ran up the stairs three at a time. Travis cast a look at level 2 and saw it empty. That explained where the Roumanhi slaves had come from so quickly.

As Travis and Cail neared the upper levels, they dimly heard the clash of arms from behind closed doors. The whole Palace was now under siege and battles were raging everywhere. At a guess, only half of Santovin's guards had been affected.

Reaching another junction, the two men ran into a group of fleeing Kházakha. They almost knocked the Commander from his feet but failed to notice Cail as he ducked out of sight behind a support column. The leading man pulled up sharply and raised his hand in a sloppy salute. It was Esrik. Commander Travis scowled at him. 'Soldier?' he asked sharply.

'The enemy, Sir, they've overpowered us. We were running to find reinforcements. What's happening, Sir? Half the Palace guard is missing!'

'We have a rebellion on our hands, Esrik,' Travis replied grimly. 'The Palace androids have turned against us and must be terminated. They've freed the prisoners and are being aided by some of our men. Shoot only those in white and put your combat jackets on so you won't be confused with the enemy. Now get to the gates.' Esrik snapped a salute and strode away.

Cail came out of his hiding place, grinning at Travis's deceit. 'I am glad you are on our side,' he said, slapping his companion on the back.

'Strangely enough, so am I,' Travis replied.

They finally made it to the top floor and could hear the crashing and disturbance of combat coming from inside Raven's room. Cail flattened against the wall and anxiously peered around the door. He was astounded to see two androids at each other's throats. Wrath's left arm was missing and one of its eyes was dim, and Vigour had sustained damage to the head and chest. Neither looked ready to cease their exertions.

'What do we do?' Cail hissed to the Commander.

Travis stepped through the doorway without hesitation. 'Wrath, desist,' he ordered. Wrath hesitated but the need for self-defence overrode the command and it fought on. Only Santovin could have stopped the machine. Travis thought for a moment and then took out his blaster. He set the beam on high and took careful aim. He pulled the trigger but the beam had little noticeable effect other than to leave a black scorch mark on Wrath's shoulder.

Cail began to edge around the room towards an open door. He was sure he had heard crying over the din.

Travis aimed again and this time hit the target. The jewel in Wrath's collar exploded in a shower of sparks and Wrath ground to halt. Vigour, no longer threatened, stepped back and viewed its double expressionlessly.

'How do you feel?'

Wrath's reply was slow in coming. 'Detached.'

'Join me,' Vigour added.

Wrath stared with its one remaining eye and nodded. What Travis had told Esrik was becoming truer. He now had two androids on his side.

Cail cast a satisfied glance at them and then, with his weapon drawn, silently entered the bed chamber. He blanched at the bloody scene before him. Transfixed; he was too overcome with joy and grief to know what to do.

T'skya, sensing she was no longer alone, slowly raised her bloodshot eyes and gazed towards the door. She gaped in disbelief and a cry escaped her lips. She withdrew from Raven and backed against the wall. Her eyes implored him to be real and when he opened his arms to her she ran into them, crying hysterically. He wrapped his arms around her and held her tightly, kissing her hair and caressing her, but he could not take his eyes from Raven's lifeless form.

He gently pushed T'skya away and gazed deeply into her eyes. 'What has occurred here?' he asked darkly.

'She...she took her own life. I got here too late. But she died in peace, Cail. She died knowing you have forgiven her.'

Cail withdrew and went to kneel beside the bed. He bowed his head and prayed silently for some minutes and then, taking a last look at the woman who had endured so much and loved so deeply, he drew a sheet over her body.

'When this is over, she shall have decent burial,' he muttered.

Travis stood with the androids, waiting impatiently for Cail. The look on the blond man's face did not bode good news.

'She is dead,' Cail said grimly, in answer to Travis's unaired question.

'I'm sorry,' the Commander replied, allowing a respectful moment of silence to pass.

Cail's face became as hard as diamond and his eyes flashed dangerously with the need for retribution. 'Take me to Santovin!'

Travis and T'skya looked at him in surprise. If Santovin had not succumbed he was sure to have withdrawn all the androids from their duties to guard him in his chamber, but Cail was not to be dissuaded.

Travis heaved a sigh and ran a hand through his short hair. He wanted Santovin dead but somehow the thought of going to face his master unsettled him. T'skya was nervous but she would follow Cail to the ends of the earth now that he had returned to her. She did not know how he had survived the Arena, and she did not care. The only thing that mattered was that they were together and she had not failed.

'With you or without you, Commander?' she said, her eyes pleading with him to comply.

Travis nodded and led them from the room. Vigour and Wrath followed behind, as if drawn to the allies by some unseen thread.

Travis took them to the staircase and along a corridor two levels below. He stopped before a wall that had no evident markings and pressed a hidden panel to open the door. Beyond it was a darkened passage which led to the High Lord's chamber.

Fearing rebellion, Santovin had designed a veritable labyrinth to afford him all means of escape. It was possible they would find him gone and be robbed of their revenge, but Wrath had sensed the High Lord's presence only moments before Travis had disconnected it.

The five hurried on their way, eager to reach Santovin before he fled the Palace grounds. The passage had many twists and turns but Travis did not falter. The way was dark, lit only by dim lights set into the walls. There were three exits from the High Lord's chamber, one on each side of the room and a trap-door in the dais; the company split up.

Santovin would have no escape.

❧❧❧

Santovin was pacing the floor raging at his guards, man and machine alike. Twelve androids lined the walls; the Palace's full compliment bar Vigour and Wrath, and six men, the only ones who had managed to reach their master before all hell broke loose, were surrounding him with their weapons drawn.

The klaxons had failed to sound on many levels of the Palace and Santovin had been warned too late. He dared not risk the secret passages now; the rebels were everywhere and Santovin was too conspicuous to sneak out unnoticed. Neither did the High Lord dare approach the windows to view the carnage in the city. Someone could be lurking outside, ready to shoot him down.

Instead, he ranted, raved and paced about like a caged animal. It was all going wrong. He felt out of control, an unprecedented feeling and not one he enjoyed. His guards were uneasy, afraid not only of the situation outside the chamber, but also of that within it. Santovin was dangerous and the presence of so many androids unnerved them.

'Where is Travis?' thundered Santovin.

'I've been unable to raise him, Lord, but he's been unaffected by whatever's knocking out our men. I've had reports of him fighting outside the gates.'

'Splendid, Hoffner. Then he must be trying to reach me,' the High Lord said, feeling relieved. Travis was a good strategist and a brave fighter. If anyone could find a way to salvage the situation, it was he.

It was then that the 'he' of their concern chose to appear through the trap-door in the dais. Travis stood quietly, his weapon by his side, ready for use. When he spoke his voice was calm. 'I suggest you surrender, Santovin. The Palace is surrounded and your men are out-numbered.'

'What? Surrender to those scum? Have you lost your mind, Travis?' the High Lord exclaimed.

'Scum, Santovin? Is that what we are?' came Cail's cold voice from a concealed doorway.

Santovin whirled round, startled and stupefied by his presence. 'You are dead!' he stuttered, struggling to comprehend the living figure before him.

'Perhaps I am a ghost come the haunt you for your crimes.'

With a nod the androids and guards spurred into motion. The android nearest swung an arm at Cail's head, its claws extended, and Cail only just avoided being sliced open by the lethally sharp blades. T'skya, Wrath and Vigour charged in, taking the guards by surprise, and battle commenced. Travis took out three humans before the others had time to realise he had swapped sides. T'skya stunned another and just managed to dive behind a heavy chair as a beam whizzed past her ear.

Wrath and Vigour became involved in another fierce fight as Santovin's androids sought to defend their master. The two battered machines fought bravely but were heavily outnumbered. They slammed against each other and moved so rapidly that it was difficult for the humans to keep out of their way. If the allies did not aid them soon, Vigour and Wrath would be lost.

Travis screamed at Cail and T'skya to aim for the machines' collars and after several attempts three more silver figures had been disconnected from the network. No sooner had they gained their freedom than they too joined Vigour and Wrath in attacking the Palace guards. It was now nine against five.

Santovin watched in horror as his men and machines were picked off. His Kházakha lay stunned on the floor and the androids were turning against him. The allies had suffered no losses and had so far come to no serious harm. T'skya's shoulder had been sliced by an android's claws and Travis had a minor wound in his thigh, but Santovin could scarcely believe how quickly and skilfully they had dispatched his security.

The High Lord backed away, trying to slide towards one of the doors, hoping to make his escape unnoticed in the fray. Travis intercepted him. 'Oh no, my Lord. Don't think we have forgotten *you!*'

Just then, a loud crashing sound caught their attention. Someone was trying to break through the grand double doors to the Throne Room. Santovin smiled. He did not believe that Travis would cut him down in cold blood and assumed that his reinforcements had, at last, arrived.

Travis swung his blaster towards the door as it began to splinter and crack, preparing to pick off the enemy as they charged through. His attention wavered momentarily and Santovin took full advantage, chopping at the Commander's wrist with clasped hands, forcing him to drop his weapon. A short tussle followed, during which time the door finally gave and Spider and his cohort burst into the room.

Santovin's jaw dropped open in disbelief. His reinforcements were not there! He dropped to the floor in defeat, cowering like a frightened dog as men surrounded him, their weapons trained on his quivering body.

'Order your androids to desist,' Travis commanded, retrieving his gun. Santovin glared at him, defiance still clear in his eyes. 'I said, order your androids to desist.'

Santovin's jaw hardened but he complied and the remaining androids stopped motionless. Cail and T'skya blasted their collars away, not trusting them to remain passive whilst still under Santovin's control. The duo then turned their attention to the High Lord himself.

The atmosphere was suffocating. The Roumanhis' fingers were ready on their triggers; their hatred of Santovin consuming their passive tendencies and causing them to lust for revenge. Travis, too, could hardly restrain himself from slashing open the High Lord's throat. Surprisingly, only T'skya showed no inclination to harm the man. There was still much she wished to know from him and she was sure his part in the events was far from over. But she was outnumbered and there was little she could do to sway the men's intent.

It was Santovin who provided his own reprieve. 'Kill me and one you revere will also perish!' he warned.

Cail started back and flicked an anxious glance at T'skya. She too was unsettled by his words. He had already caused the deaths of so many people they cared for that his threat could only mean one thing; he had Hollam.

'What do you want, Santovin?' Cail demanded savagely.

'My life and safe passage from the city,' the old man said so quickly that those watching were filled with suspicion. Did Santovin have some plan or was he merely attempting to save his own neck? Cail did not know but he was not prepared to risk his brother's life.

'You have my oath that no man here shall harm you whilst I live, so long as you take us to this prisoner - and no tricks!' Cail answered.

Santovin nodded and rose to his feet, trying to retain as much dignity as possible. Despite his contempt for the Roumanhi people, one thing he knew was true; their oath was honourable and would not be broken. Spider's men scowled but kept their peace. They would not betray Cail's promise.

'Follow me,' the High Lord hissed with a tone of satisfaction and contempt. This was something he was going to enjoy.

Cail, T'skya, Travis, Spider and Vigour followed him, the others choosing to remain in the Throne Room in case enemy troops attempted to come to their master's rescue. Santovin led them to the secret door through which T'skya had entered, and down a long gloomy passageway to a narrow flight of stairs that twisted downwards to the very bowels of the Palace. They stopped at the lowest level, apparently at a dead end.

Travis and Spider aimed their weapons at the albino suspiciously, fearing a trap. Santovin sneered and pressed a panel in the wall. A low door creaked open and the High Lord stepped through. Spider hurried after him to prevent an escape, but found himself in a low-ceilinged, poorly-lit room, at the back of which stood a small cage.

As the others entered, a shape leapt from its place of concealment and hit the bars with a crash and a demented snarl. It began grunting and gibbering in a language even T'skya with her new-found knowledge could not understand.

'Quiet now, my pretty,' Santovin said soothingly. 'I have brought some friends to look upon your piteous form.'

The man ceased his raving and backed away, as if fearing punishment for his display. The others edged nearer, trying to make out his face in the gloom. It certainly was not Hollam, for this man possessed a mass of dirty dark hair which fell across his face and concealed his features. He was dressed in rags, covered in filth and, although he had been adequately fed, looked in ill-health.

T'skya approached the bars, her heart twisting at the creature's plight. The man flinched away but held her in his eyes, his head cocked to one side in confusion. She spoke to him softly using various tongues but the creature just stared and attempted no reply.

'You waste your words,' Santovin muttered. 'He has no tongue with which to speak. I had it cut from him to cure him of his insolence.'

The allies gawked at him in utter disgust, hardly able to comprehend to lengths to which the High Lord was prepared to go to satisfy his sadistic nature. T'skya turned to Cail with a look of supplication. 'I can reach him, Cail. I can see inside his mind if I try, but I must touch him to do so.'

Santovin laughed and the evil sound echoed around the room. 'Touch him? He will tear you limb from limb!'

Cail hesitated, unwilling to let her take the risk, but she was insistent. 'Unlock the door,' he commanded, clutching his weapon. Shrugging at their stupidity, Santovin complied.

T'skya stood by the door, giving a running commentary of all she intended to do, certain her words were understood.

She appeared calm, although inside she was shaking; the man looked very wild indeed and was showing great interest in her. She stepped into the cage and gingerly approached. The man held his ground but looked ready to flee.

Stopping before him, she slowly raised her hands to show she meant no harm. The man continued to stare, looking over her body with great curiosity. Very tentatively, he stretched out a hand and poked her on the chest. T'skya remained still and the men outside the cage watched in readiness.

Seeing no reaction from her and feeling less threatened, the ragged creature stretched out his hand once more. He cautiously placed it against her breasts, much to Cail's annoyance. Then he felt his own chest, cocking his head in bewilderment. He stroked the soft skin on her arms and, moving closer, ran both hands down her body. Cail stepped nearer, feeling protective and more than a little put out by the creature's intimate probing. The man jumped backwards in reaction and T'skya warned Cail off.

'It's all right. He's just checking me out. I don't think he's ever seen a woman before.' T'skya reached out a hand, beckoning the prisoner closer. He timidly complied, and as she seated herself before him, followed suit. 'I must touch your face,' she said softly. 'I won't hurt you. Please trust me.'

She gazed into his large, liquid, hazel eyes and a strange feeling of familiarity came over her. She raised a smoothing smile as she brushed the hair from his face, and then choked back a cry. She swung round to face Santovin, her eyes ablaze with fury and realisation.

'You took the baby, you son-of-a-bitch! You took the baby!'

Cail and the others stared at her in bewilderment, but Santovin smiled maliciously. 'Behold the King!' he spat, waving his arms at the miserable wreck of a man and laughing at their reactions.

Cail and Spider hesitated then dropped to their knees. Travis shook his head in confusion and Vigour did nothing. T'skya simply stared with horror at the image of Hollam's younger brother kneeling before her.

SIXTEEN

Kylian

Santovin had evidently taken the baby from the Castan's arms believing him to be the true Prince and heir, and he had kept him a prisoner for nearly thirty years. T'skya hated to think of the torment the man had endured, especially since Santovin had robbed him of the power of speech, trapping all that he felt and thought inside.

But neither was the immensity of the discovery unapparent to her. How would Cail react to find out that his own safety had resulted in such appalling circumstances for the man? Would Hollam be able to endure the knowledge that his real brother had been sacrificed whilst he grew up in the company of a man who was not only of different parentage, but was the true King? T'skya could not bear to think about it but knew the time was coming when the truth would be revealed. The only consolation was that it would wipe the triumphant smile off Santovin's face.

He had, or so he thought, reduced the heir to an irretrievable level of bestiality and corruption. Here was their revered leader, the hope of the land, rotting in a cage like an ill-treated animal. Despite their efforts and dreams, the people of Roumanhi had lost and he, Santovin, had triumphed again. He had taken their freedom, disbanded their families, polluted their habitat, destroyed their sacred monarchy, and in return had given them a symbol of their degenerate existences.

Santovin was gloating. Cail and Spider were not.

They remained on their knees, staring at the caged man with tears in their eyes. They, like T'skya, were reeling from the shock of their discovery. Travis, feeling ill at ease, placed a hand on Cail's shoulder. 'There is nothing we can do here. Let's free this man and take him somewhere more suitable. The Palace isn't yet secure.'

Cail stirred and looked to T'skya for advice. He did not understand her new powers but trusted her instincts and would follow whatever she suggested. She shook her head. 'He can't go anywhere like this. I must reach him. I must have time alone with him. An hour. Give me an hour,' she pleaded.

Cail and Travis exchanged glances. The older man was not happy with the prospect of such a long delay but he could not deprive the wretched man of a chance to find peace. Cail gave his approval and raised himself off his knees.

Santovin laughed. 'Try little woman. Try and reach inside that curdled mind of his. You will not like what you find. He is lost to you forever.'

'Get him out of here!' Cail snarled as Travis roughly pushed the cackling High Lord through the door. The others trailed out after them and returned to the Throne Room. Cail lingered behind for a moment, resting his head against the stone doorpost. He said nothing but his posture and expression revealed all.

'I don't know,' T'skya sighed. 'Santovin may be right. I'll try. Perhaps I can do some good.'

≈✼≈

It was one of the longest hours of Cail's life. He paced the floor anxious about T'skya's safety and wishing to slice off Santovin's self-satisfied expression. Disturbed by his murderous thoughts, Cail recalled his words to Raven when she had lusted after T'skya's blood. *"Has it come to this that we kill for the sake of killing? If so, we are no better than them."* He forced his savage desires aside and tried to concentrate on something else, but everything he thought of led back to the High Lord.

At last his wait came to an end. T'skya appeared looking exhausted and wan, supported by Hollam's transformed brother. Gone was the manic gleam in his eye. Gone was the savage snarl upon his face and gone was the huddled posture he had adopted. He now stood upright and proud, his face washed and his wild hair tied back. Before them stood a tall, handsome man whose resemblance to Hollam was now undeniable.

Cail could not comprehend what he was seeing. Travis, who had never seen Hollam, did not understand Cail's reaction and assumed the man's startled expression was due to the miraculous change T'skya's mysterious efforts had accomplished. The Commander approached the woman and took her from the stranger's arm. The latter gave her up grudgingly, but his attention was focused upon Cail and Cail alone.

Santovin was watching with interest and the smug smile had faded from his face. He could not believe what he was witnessing any more than the others. What had she done to him?

T'skya broke the silence, speaking in a weak but satisfied voice. 'I've done all I can. He was difficult to reach and I was too weak to go far. He has suffered so much. The things I saw...I...I can't...I will not describe them...it's too much for me. He called himself The Unloved One, but I have renamed him Kylian.'

The Roumanhis stared at her with incredulity. It was a name of great historical worth and esteem and not lightly chosen, but it was not appropriate for a King.

'How can this be?' Spider asked in astonishment. 'He must have a Castan's name.'

'Were he the Castan, I'd agree with you,' she said with a hint of a smile.

Santovin's reaction was savage. 'I warned you not to touch him, woman. His madness has addled your brains. I myself plucked the child from his parents' arms after I'd beheaded them. The King stands before you, or do you seek to deny it?'

'I do not deny it. The King does indeed stand before me,' she cried. '*Elanat el Castan; Cahli on el manhi.* Behold the King, Saviour of the land.'

The Roumanhis looked around the room in confusion, but Kylian's movements were precise. He strode across the room with great purpose and pride and knelt in humility before Cail.

Silence fell upon the room as the Roumanhis gaped at Kylian, at T'skya's smiling face and then at Cail. Travis moved away from T'skya to sit on the dais and Santovin was shaking with rage. It had to be a mistake. He had taken the baby himself. He had killed the King and Queen and taken the baby himself.

With a strangled cry he launched himself at Cail, spitting and clawing like an angry cat. 'Deceived! Deceived!' he screamed. Cail tried to defend himself without harming the demented old man but Santovin was deranged by the betrayal and knowledge that his last triumph had been crushed. People leapt to Cail's defence but no-one was quicker than Vigour.

The android enclosed its powerful hands around the High Lord's arms and raised him from the floor. The albino screeched and struggled but could not free himself from the machine's grip.

Vigour began to squeeze.

T'skya tried to stop him but it was futile. Vigour would not listen and continued to apply pressure. The High Lord screamed. The others looked on horrified as the man's bones began to snap. 'You gave me your oath,' Santovin squealed in agony.

'And I have kept it,' Cail replied calmly. 'I said no *man* would harm you.'

Judgment had been passed on the High Lord by an emotionless android and he had been found guilty.

T'skya covered her ears to block out the hideous noise of breaking bones and Santovin's agonized screaming. Within moments it was over. With one final squeeze Vigour snapped the High Lord's spine and dropped him to the floor like a rag doll. Santovin fell, his body twisted and deformed, his face grotesquely contorted. The High Lord was dead and nobody moved. None of them expected to feel the way they did. Somehow they felt empty, anticlimactic, numb.

Cail was the first to rally himself. He tore his eyes away from the crumpled body and gazed questioningly at T'skya. She had declared him King and Santovin had reacted as if her words were true. Kylian had bowed to him, and Vigour had leapt to his defence.

T'skya studied him for a moment and said two words, '*Castan Vashtii*,' and Cail knew the truth. No sooner had the words left her lips than all the knowledge implanted by Yyishgur of the Grish-Grish-Gûri came flooding into his consciousness. He staggered, clutching at his head before falling to his knees. He knew now why Negram had been so protective towards him, why he had heard tales never told to others and why he was unlike Hollam in both looks and temperament. He knew now why he had known which words to speak to the Grish-Grish-Gûri and why they had bowed to him. And he knew now why T'skya had insisted he defend himself in the Arena, and why Kylian so much resembled Hollam.

Cail was Mithdrill's son. He was Cailcáladrim, the King.

Cail stared at Kylian as the guilt of his own existence threatened to suffocate him. But there was no reproach or hatred in the man's eyes, only hope and relief that he was, at last, amongst people who would cause him no harm. Spider and his men, on the other hand, were gazing at Cail expectantly, waiting for him to congratulate T'skya on her scheming and to pronounce Kylian as Castan. But when they saw the new light of wonder in Cail's eyes and how proudly both T'skya and Kylian were viewing him, they began to doubt themselves.

Cail rose to his feet and, as he stood before them with such dignity and surety, they felt his power and knew at once that it was so. Cail was the Castan of Roumanhi and they bowed before him, their faces filled with wonder and respect, their hearts filled with hope.

But Cail could not enjoy the moment. He felt awkward and was not yet ready to play his part as their divine majesty. There was still a war to be won and whilst they stood there, his people were dying. Whilst they stood there, his brother Hollam was somewhere in the wilderness. Cail frowned. He was not Hollam's blood brother. By the trees! How would Hollam react to the news?

'My friends, a King is not a King unless he has a kingdom. This land is not yet free and I will accept no title until liberation is ours. Say nothing of this to anyone lest they seek my life, but let it be known the High Lord has fallen; few men will fight for a lost cause.

'Travis, Spider, I leave the battle in your hands, for though my duties lie here, my heart dictates otherwise. Somewhere in the wilderness lies the land's greatest hero and I must seek for him. Kylian, I go to seek your brother. Will you accompany me?'

Kylian's eyes widened with gladness and he curled back his lips in a way which was so familiar to both T'skya and Cail that they almost wept.

Travis and Spider accepted Cail's words with good grace. Travis was interested in meeting the man who had managed the incredible feat of drugging the water all alone, and perfectly understood Cail's anxiety. Besides which, it would be foolish for Cail to risk staying in the city now that his identity had been revealed.

'Laskin should have taken control of the docking bays by

now. If all has gone well, you should be able to use one of the short-range scout ships to search for this man. Laskin will find you a pilot,' said Travis.

'I'll fly it,' T'skya announced.

Travis merely raised an eyebrow. 'You? Are you sure you can manage it?'

'My dear Commander, how do you think I arrived in this land? I know what I'm doing and could use the practice. Roumanhi is too large to travel on foot and I have a feeling those transport ships are going to be needed over the next few months. Whether Gilgarad has received word or not, there'll be a lot of Kházakha to round up in the forest and we can hardly march them here.'

Travis conceded but was still unhappy about the idea. 'Then take some men with you. You don't know how many enemies you'll run into out there.'

'I intend to,' she replied.

❧❦❧

T'skya and Cail reached the docking bays with little difficulty. Travis's transport vehicle had been destroyed but they found another a short distance from the Palace. The streets had quieted, although signs of fighting were evident. Scorch marks scarred the buildings and blood stained the streets. Smoke could be seen rising into the sky and grey flakes of ash floated on the air and speckled the ground. Roumanhis and Kházakha were dashing from place to place but no-one paid much heed to the small vehicle as it raced along the roads towards the docking bays to the east of the city. Things became rougher as they passed the barrack houses and T'skya diverted from the main road to avoid trouble.

The main gate to docking bay 9 lay smashed and Travis's forces were guarding it with heavy weapons and an all-terrain vehicle. The guards levelled their weapons as T'skya pulled to a stop. They were suspicious of the strange assortment of passengers and it was not until Laskin was called over that she was allowed to pass.

He greeted Cail gladly and inquired of events at the Palace. The news of Santovin's death and the method employed to bring about the dictator's end surprised him, as did the presence of Vigour.

The solid android had firmly attached itself to T'skya and joined the company without being asked. Vigour sat in the back of the vehicle next to a wide eyed and fascinated Kylian and seemed oddly out of place with its knees bent and hands resting upon them in a very human fashion. The vehicle was leaning dangerously; the android's weight almost smashing the axle.

T'skya told Laskin of their intentions as they crossed the large bay and he led them to a small craft that had already been prepped for take off. The ship would hold six, more at a push providing some of the bulkier equipment was removed, but T'skya would not spare the time. She was more than happy, however, to accept Laskin's offer to accompany them.

She slipped into the pilot's seat with Laskin beside her. Cail and Kylian sat behind, avidly viewing all that she did, and Vigour, an uninvited ballast problem, sat at the back. The two black-haired, green-eyed pilots ran through their pre-flight checks and T'skya started the engines. With a blast of thrusters the craft lifted into the air and headed northwards towards the water tanks and Hollam.

⚜

Hollam lay in the snow, dead to the world. He had lost consciousness before he hit the ground and was unaware of the Kházakha scurrying across to him and of the awkward angle at which his body lay.

'Is he dead?' Aslov cried as he holstered his weapon and

descended the ladder from the catwalk.

'If he's not, he should be,' another replied.

'If he's not, he'll soon wish he was,' a third growled sarcastically.

'Cut it out, Viktor,' Aslov snapped. 'We need him. I have to know what he's done to the tanks.'

He reached the crowd which had gathered around Hollam and knelt down in the snow, feeling for a pulse. It was unhealthily slow and from the way the man was breathing and the position of his limbs he had obviously been seriously injured in the fall. Fortunately, the snow was deep and had saved Hollam's life, but he would not be up and walking for a long time to come.

Aslov checked him over, carefully probing his body. 'Give me more light,' he commanded, and the guards shone their beams on to Hollam's still form. 'He's got several broken ribs, but I don't think they've punctured a lung, and his leg seems to be badly broken. I don't know about his neck or back - I can't tell out here, but we have to get him back to camp before he freezes to death. Dead men don't talk.'

Hollam was laid on a hard narrow bed in the corner of the room, opposite a stove that gave off an inadequate supply of heat. The drugged guard was propped up on a chair, still soundly asleep.

Aslov ordered most of the other guards to return to the compound to search for clues, whilst he remained with Viktor, Gazelt and Tanic. They made Hollam as comfortable as possible and set about heating some broth. Hollam was blue and needed to be slowly warmed.

'I'll radio headquarters,' Tanic said, reaching for the set.

'No, not yet,' came Aslov's thoughtful reply. 'I want to hear what he has to say first.'

When the broth was ready, Gazelt handed Aslov a bowl and spoon and the latter sat Hollam up. If his back were broken there was nothing they could do about it and the chances were the awkward way they had manhandled him into the hut had already condemned him to paralysis. Aslov attempted to ladle some broth down him. As the warm nourishing soup hit the back of his throat, Hollam awoke with a splutter and a howl of pain. His body was on fire. His chest was burning from the effects of the blaster. His ribs were screaming; his leg felt like it had been filled with white hot coals, which at least meant his back was not broken; he was shaking violently, and to make matters worse, they were feeding him meat!

He gagged and tried to knock the spoon from Aslov's hand.

'He's Roumanhi all right,' Viktor said with disgust. 'He doesn't know what's good for him.'

'You must eat,' Aslov coaxed. 'Your body is frozen. We have nothing else.'

But Hollam would not relent. Every time Aslov attempted to force some of the boiled animal flesh down his throat, he turned his head or knocked the spoon away. Aslov gave up and ate the broth himself.

Sensation was now returning to Hollam's extremities. It was agonizing. He began to writhe on the bed, screaming as the nerves awakened and movement aggravated his injuries. Viktor and Aslov pinned him down until the worst of it had passed and he lay more quietly, now bathed in sweat.

Hollam was scared. In his weakened condition there was nothing he could do against the men. He had never experienced such pain before and knew that if he did not answer their questions, they would inflict more suffering upon him. He was helpless. Aslov did not wait long before beginning the interrogation.

'What have you done to the water tanks?' he demanded, staring at Hollam's pitiful form.

Hollam clenched his jaw shut in defiant silence. He had to give his allies more time in the city. Aslov repeated the question more forcefully but again Hollam remained mute.

Viktor stepped up closer to the bed, whilst Gazelt and Tanic sat near the stove, trying to keep warm.

'Your silence is commendable, but foolish,' Aslov said. 'Whatever you've done will be discovered one way or another. I suggest you cooperate. It will save you from any unnecessary suffering.'

Hollam stared at him through his green lenses. Aslov's face was hard but not cruel. He was about Tarn's age and had a thick shock of black hair, cropped short about the ears in a style very similar to Hollam's own. A permanent frown line marred his forehead and a day's growth of stubble lay upon his chin. Viktor on the other hand, had a surly face with a heavy jaw and small eyes. He was young and eager and looked too willing to make Hollam pay for his silence; but still Hollam kept quiet.

One of the other guards rushed in carrying Hollam's pack, the horn of Camaldriss and one or two of the glass vials which had been left on top of the tank. Aslov rummaged through the pack. It only contained Hollam's shredded uniform and was of little interest. The horn he scrutinised more closely and with much appreciation. It was beautiful. Formed of an iridescent shell, it was skilfully engraved with images of sea-creatures and wrought about its edges with silver. Aslov held it to his ear and sighed as the whispers of the sea trapped within its convoluted interior called to him and teased his senses. It was most seductive and the Kházakh looked almost lost to the world. He scowled angrily as the guard interrupted.

'We found where he came in. He scaled the fence right under our noses, next to the generator...'

'...Which suddenly stopped working! Thank you,' Aslov replied in dismissal. He placed the horn to one side and studied the vials. 'What was in these?' he demanded.

'Water,' Hollam answered.

'Try again,' Aslov said somewhat threateningly.

Hollam flicked a nervous glance towards Viktor, who was

growing more impatient by the second. The man lacked the discipline and self-control of Aslov, whom Hollam considered to be more threat than action. Aslov meant to intimidate but did not look a brutal man. Viktor, however, looked ready to tear Hollam apart.

Hollam opened his mouth to speak but the thought of Cail trapped in the city stayed his voice. As far as he knew, the drugged water was his brother's only chance for survival. Besides which, even if he told them all he knew, Santovin would still make him suffer for his part in the scheme. Hollam shook his head in refusal.

Viktor, angered by his stubbornness, grabbed the injured man's leg and twisted it cruelly. Hollam shrieked in agony as the broken bones grated together, sending searing flames through his body. And then the pain faded as the serene numbness of unconsciousness overtook him for the second time.

Aslov was enraged. He leapt from his chair and backhanded Viktor across the face. 'If you so much as breathe on him again, I'll shoot you,' he thundered. 'We'll get nothing from him now.'

Viktor rubbed his cheek and stormed from the room. Aslov let him go, glad to be rid of him.

'Radio the city, Tanic. Let them know the situation. Tell them we need engineers; he might have booby-trapped the tanks and the generator. Tell then he must have had inside help; those lenses he's wearing and these vials can't have been produced without it.'

Tanic nodded enthusiastically. He was young and this was exciting. They had caught an intruder and stumbled onto a conspiracy. If they foiled an attempt by the Roumanhis to overthrow the state they would be heroes.

Tanic tried the set. It took time to get a clear signal through, and when he received word from the city he paled and began to shake. 'Sir, the city's under siege! The Palace has been overrun. Sir, what shall we do?'

Aslov jumped to the young man's side. He spoke into the handset with urgency but had only received half the message when the radio went dead. They were cut off. Aslov ran a hand through his hair as he tried to think. The situation went beyond his training, but he was a capable man and not prone to panic.

He turned to Gazelt. 'Break out the arms and set watch; double guard. Send Viktor to the power plant to warn them and bring reinforcements. If this man is part of a conspiracy, his people may search for him. I want us to be ready if they come. We might not win, but we'll put up a good fight.'

Gazelt saluted and raced from the room. Tanic was losing control and it took some minutes for Aslov to calm him down enough to think rationally.

'We should kill him. Kill him and dump him. They won't come for us if he's not here,' the young man panted, staring at Hollam with terror in his eyes.

'No, Tanic. If we kill him, we lose our only clue to the situation. He's a hostage; we need him. He may be the only thing that keeps us alive. Do you understand? He must be kept alive.'

'But look at him. They'll blame us. They'll kill us!'

'The Roumanhis are not killers, Tanic.'

Tanic stared at Aslov in surprise. The man's words were filled with meaningful implications and the tone was full of regret. It was almost as if Aslov admired the enemy and held his own people in contempt. Aslov caught his look and changed the subject. 'Go and ready the transport ship. We may have need of it. Be sure to check the guns are charged and have someone help you clear the pad.'

Tanic saluted slowly. The order was reasonable but he did not wish to leave Aslov and the prisoner alone. Tanic, however, knew better than to air his doubts and, drawing up his hood, left the room.

Aslov felt weary but set about removing the lenses from

Hollam's eyes and strapping up his ribs and leg to keep them immobile. Having finished, he picked up the horn of Camaldriss and set it to his ear, letting his mind drift off to far away places as the gift of the sea people took control.

❦

T'skya skimmed low over the landscape as she neared the water tanks. If Hollam had drugged them the previous night, then he could not have gone far; if he had managed to escape at all. She piloted the ship close to the power plant and was concerned to see many Kházakha patrolling the compound and a great number of tracks leading through the snow towards the water tanks.

'They've set double guard,' Laskin announced with his face to the window. 'They must have radioed the city before it was overrun. We can expect trouble.' He took hold of the weaponry in the ship's nose.

'What will we be up against?' T'skya asked.

'Handblasters and perhaps one or two cannons if they can get a ship into the air,' Laskin replied.

The handblasters would have little effect against the craft but the cannons were another matter. T'skya did not fancy flying a combat mission against another ship with such important passengers aboard. She gained some altitude and made a pass across the area to see just what they would be facing. Guards were patrolling a camp to the east of the compound and a landing platform had been cleared, although no craft sat upon it.

Laskin checked his scanner, looking for signs of life. 'We've got twelve men around the camp and another eight in the compound. There's a larger heat source coming from inside that hut; a stove or something that's blocking the readings. My guess is that if Hollam is here, he's in there,' he said, pointing to the well-guarded stone building they were now circling.

'Cail,' T'skya said over her shoulder, 'it's your call. What do you want to do?'

Cail thought deeply. 'If we fire on the guards, they could kill Hollam. They already know we are here but do not know who we are. Let us act as their allies would act. Let them think we have come to their rescue.'

Laskin grinned and picked up the radio handset. 'This is P.T.4 calling Aqua Base Camp. Come in Aqua. P.T.4 calling Aqua Base Camp, do you copy?'

He waited for his signal to be received. Aslov's voice came over the airwaves. It sounded strange and dreamy. 'This is Aqua Base Camp, over.'

'Aqua Base Camp, this is Lieutenant Laskin. We picked up your transmission; have come to your assistance; awaiting permission to land; over.'

There was a long pause before Aslov spoke again. 'Copy P.T.4. Permission granted. But we really don't need you. Everything's fine here.'

The radio went dead and Laskin stared at the microphone in surprise. He had recognised Aslov's voice and knew him to be a straight-forward, down-to-earth sort of man, and yet his tone and words had been most peculiar. Laskin shrugged and readied his side-arm as T'skya brought the craft down upon the landing pad.

'You should remain here,' he said to Cail and Kylian. 'They might accept our presence, but certainly not Roumanhis'.'

The idea was logical and Cail could not argue against it. He longed to find Hollam but would not risk all their lives to do so.

Laskin, T'skya and Vigour exited the ship and strode towards the hut but the guards outside were nervous and viewed them suspiciously. The presence of Vigour persuaded them of the validity of Laskin's appearance and T'skya's bloodied nurse's uniform added to the deceit. They let them pass inside.

They found Aslov awaiting them with a soft smile on his

lips and an absent look in his eye. He seemed relaxed and sat on a chair laughing as they stared at him in amazement. T'skya hurried to Hollam's side and viewed him with horror. He looked terrible but was still unconscious and unaware of her presence.

'We've got to get him to hospital,' she urged.

Laskin moved to her side and agreed. 'Aslov, we'll take the prisoner and send reinforcements. You've done a good job.'

But Aslov was not listening. He sat with the horn pressed firmly against his ear and a vacant look upon his face. Laskin shook his shoulder gently but received no reaction: the horn had done its work. Vigour stepped up and removed the shell from the Kházakh's hand. Aslov frowned and tried to retrieve it but could not break the android's grip. Aslov looked at Laskin with supplication in his eyes. 'Take me with you,' he pleaded. 'I can't stay here. Take me to the sea. I must go to the sea.'

Laskin looked at T'skya, wondering if she had an answer for Aslov's behaviour.

'He's heard the call of Camaldriss and has fallen under its spell. Only those chosen by the people of the Great Divide may listen because only they are strong enough to resist it. Aslov will never be at peace unless the sea-people help him. He's no threat to us whilst we have the horn. Let him come,' she replied wearily, gathering up Hollam's belongings. 'We have to get Hollam to the ship,' she added, 'before those guards realise what's going on.'

'I'll take him,' Laskin said, but Vigour swept Hollam into its mighty arms and held him as if he were weightless.

T'skya smiled and the five of them left the room and headed for the ship. The guards outside watched them go without interfering. Aslov seemed so relaxed they would not believe anything was amiss.

❧❧❧❀❧❧❧

Cail and Kylian hovered over Hollam as T'skya guided the ship from Aqua Base Camp. Cail was stunned by the man's condition and sat contemplating, his hands clasped in front of his mouth. Kylian stared down at his brother, stroking his hand with tenderness and seemed almost as attached to Hollam as if they had grown up together.

Cail sighed and turned away. Things had been rough up until then but perhaps the worst was yet to come. Hollam had to be told the news and he was not looking forward to it. He knew Hollam well and the big man would never understand Negram's reasoning, nor would he accept Kylian's fate. Although Hollam loved the land as much as any man, he had never really forgiven the Castan for his blindness when the Kházakha came and had often been severely scolded by Negram for making disparaging remarks about a monarchy he had never really known.

Cail's thoughts were broken as the ship bucked wildly, causing Hollam to groan. He was regaining consciousness and the ship was under attack.

Cail was torn between seeing to Hollam and viewing the action, but as T'skya veered sharply to the right, he regained his seat. Kylian, ignoring the danger, stared at Hollam and Hollam stared back, hazel eyes locked on hazel eyes, and Kylian grinned Hollam's grin.

The overloaded ship rocked again as T'skya fought with the sluggish controls. 'Hold on everyone,' she shouted and rolled the craft, trying to avoid the rapid firing of the aggressor behind them. But evasive action was not working well. The enemy pilot had come from nowhere and was good, and since the ship had no rear gunner station, T'skya had no defence.

The enemy pilot was Tanic. He had hidden Aqua's craft and, seeing Aslov deserting his post without so much as a word, had taken up vengeful pursuit. T'skya cursed as the craft bucked again. Tanic was on her tail and had her in his sights. Without warning, she slammed on the braking thrusters and hauled back on the flight controls. Tanic shot past her, unable to react in time. T'skya set off in pursuit with forward guns blazing as Laskin put all his skills into targeting the enemy ship. In a matter of moments it was over. Tanic's ship exploded in a ball of fire and fell to the earth.

T'skya heaved a sigh of relief and settled the craft into a smooth flight path. Hollam was groaning, unable to hold his pain inside, but his eyes were full of curiosity and wonder at Kylian's presence. He almost believed that he had died and was looking at himself. Cail felt that he owed him some form of explanation but could not find the words.

'Welcome back, Hollam,' he said, holding his trepidation inside and forcing a warm smile. 'You have accomplished a great feat and all the land will praise you for it.'

'Good,' Hollam growled, thinking of all he had endured. 'What have I missed - and who is that?' he asked, searching Cail with his eyes.

'Santovin is dead, the city is ours and that...well, that...' Cail looked to T'skya for support but she shook her head. It was his responsibility and she would not interfere. 'That is Kylian, your *brother*,' he said slowly and clearly.

Hollam's eyes grew wide and he spoke no more.

⟡

At the hospital, Kylian sat beside his brother, refusing to leave his side as Hollam listened to Cail's horrifying account of events. The big man said little but was impatient to hear an explanation for Cail's astonishing statement on the ship.

Cail eventually left the room and found T'skya waiting for him, her face full of concern. Cail shook his head grimly. Hollam had not taken the news well and had needed sedation. He was now sleeping but Cail was deeply troubled. He could not shake Hollam's accusing expression from his mind.

'He blames me,' Cail said wearily, rubbing his brow and looking sadder than T'skya had ever seen him before. He noticed she had changed out of her blood-stained nurse's uniform and showered; the polluted water from the tank now drained and pure. Cail's clothes were still soiled but he found them appropriate for his mood.

'Give it time,' T'skya said. 'He's just had an operation and is weak, and he has endured more than any mortal man should handle. In time he'll see you're blameless. You're a victim of circumstance as much as him.'

'Hold me,' was all that Cail could manage, and T'skya wrapped her arms around him. He buried his head on her shoulder until disturbed by Travis some minutes later.

The Commander coughed, embarrassed to be spoiling their intimacy. 'I'm glad to see you safely back. How is Hollam?'

'He's resting,' T'skya said quickly. 'What's the situation?'

'Three-quarters of the city is now in our control. We hope to have quelled all resistance by morning.' Cail nodded in satisfaction but the Commander had not finished. 'A transport ship docked a short while ago. I think you might be interested in the latest news.'

Cail and T'skya's ears pricked up at this; Travis was smiling and looking extremely pleased with himself. Then, from around the corner, came Tarn, Prell and Gilgarad. Cail and T'skya laughed and embraced them all. T'skya was particularly pleased to see Tarn. Hollam needed all the support he could get. If anyone could aid him, it was his best friend. She wondered where Lily was, for that must have been uppermost in Tarn's mind when he arrived.

He shook his head at her inquiry. 'We arrived no more than a few minutes ago and I have not yet seen her. With your permission, Commander, I would like to reclaim my bond-mate,' Tarn said, staring at Travis meaningfully.

Travis smiled at the man's formality. 'I'll miss her, but no man should stand in the way of love.' He turned and pointed to the corner the three men had just rounded.

There was Lily, standing with her hands to her lips and her face bright with unfathomable delight. She could hardly believe her eyes; after nine years her beloved bond-mate Tarn was there. Tarn's eyes grew wide and the years lifted from him. She had changed so much yet had remained the same, for he saw her with a lover's eyes and did not notice the grey in her hair nor the fine lines around her shining eyes.

A nervous and impassioned silence fell and the group watched the couple standing transfixed, too overcome with emotions to move. Suddenly the stalemate broke and Tarn rushed into his bondmate's arms, covering her with kisses and crying openly with joy as they lingered in a passionate embrace. Travis stood anxiously by, feeling awkward and unwelcome. It was he, after all, who had been responsible for their separation and he could now see just how much it had cost them. Cail found himself squeezing T'skya's hand as if impatient for their day to come, and she smiled up at him. Gilgarad, however, quelled his smile and broke up the proceedings by reminding them that there was still work to be done.

The group adjourned to a private room where they could discuss the events in the forest and the city without being disturbed. Cail was not concerned that Gilgarad's tale would herald ill news, his mere presence suggested otherwise.

Events in the forest had gone, for the most part, without a hitch. The people of the Great Divide had heard Hollam's call upon the wind and raised the alarm. Although they had taken no part in the fighting themselves, they had proved invaluable, tending the wounded and chaperoning the children whilst the warriors fought.

Most of the troops around Wilderwood, Vinewood and the surrounding enclaves had been dispatched quickly and efficiently, with very few losses. Prell had secured a transport ship and flown Gilgarad to the north. Although the situation there was difficult, his tactical leadership soon set things to right. Now the vast majority of the Kházakha in the forest were imprisoned and being guarded by Roumanhis.

Some troops, however, had managed to escape and were being hunted through the forest by the land's best scouts. Gilgarad was hopeful that they would soon be captured. Slythe, it seemed, was on the run. Tarn almost hoped that he would stumble into one of his own animal traps and learn what it felt like to be pierced by the steel jaws.

Now Gilgarad wanted to know just what would be done with the Kházakha who were littering the enclaves. Cail scratched his head and looked at Travis. The Commander stretched out his legs and rubbed his eyes. He was exhausted and there was still so much to do.

'I'll have my men send transport ships. We'll bring the prisoners back here and lock them up. What we do with them after that isn't up to me.'

'Then who is it up to?' Gilgarad asked in his deep booming voice. 'The Kházakha leader has fallen. Who is to take his place?'

Cail sat upright in his chair and stared into the giant's good eye. 'I am,' he said with great resolve.

'You?' the giant scoffed. 'You have done well, but do not let these victories go to your head. You are young and eager, but it takes a man of great wisdom and might to rule the land.'

'It takes a Castan to rule the land,' Cail declared, trying to hide his smile.

'The Castan is dead, and we must look to new horizons for our leadership,' Gilgarad replied, shaking his massive head.

'Gilgarad, you have lost but one eye and yet you are blind. The Castan lives and stands before you, for I am he, Cailcáladrim Calydon, son of Mithdrill, Castan of all Roumanhi.'

Cail rose to his feet and all felt his authority. Tarn gasped, chuckled through surprised gladness and dropped to one knee with Lily by his side. Gilgarad hesitated, unsure if he was hearing a joke, but in his heart knew such things would not be lightly spoken of. He looked across at T'skya who just let her lips form a hint of a smile and then he fixed his eye firmly on Cail. All seeds of doubt suddenly left him and he dropped to his knees. 'My Liege-Lord, forgive my foolish words, for I did not know to whom I was speaking,' Gilgarad whispered with unaccustomed humility.

Cail laughed. 'Get up, my friend. There is nothing to forgive for you have said nothing wrong. I am an ordinary man with an extraordinary title and cannot rule alone. I will need all of your good counsel and support, for no man is without fault and I would have my reign be a successful one.'

Gilgarad looked at him with new respect and climbed off his knees. Even on the ground he was taller than T'skya and it had seemed strange to see him like that.

Cail recounted his tale and his revelations drew expressions of shock and amazement. Raven's death was a sore blow and T'skya noted with interest that he was remiss in his details and did not once refer to the deal Raven had made with Santovin, nor to the fact that the evil man was her father. He let her die a heroine's death, remembered for bravery and unquenchable spirit.

Travis had somehow managed to find the time to have Raven removed from her bed chamber and prepared for burial. Cail would go with T'skya that night to transport her back to the forest and lay her in the earth. He also yearned to honour Negram's grave and see for himself what his people had managed to accomplish. He had not seen the forest for a week but it seemed like an eternity.

Yet it was the news of Kylian's survival which really shook the men. They had accepted Cail's title without question, but had given little thought as to how such an event had come about. Tarn realised the implications and, knowing Hollam, could well understand Cail's unhappy demeanour as he related the facts. 'I take it he has not accepted this news as you would wish,' Tarn said, choosing his words with care.

'He has not,' Cail replied sadly.

'I will talk with him when he awakens. Perhaps I can help.'

Cail said nothing, but nodded in gratitude.

'When will you announce yourself to the people?' Gilgarad asked.

'The time is not yet right. Let us put things in order here first. I will leave with T'skya to give burial to Raven and so must leave things in your hands Travis, for you are surely more capable than I in matters concerning the city.'

Travis bowed respectfully and turned to the others. 'My friends, you shall have quarters in my house, if you have no objections.' There were none. Tarn and Lily smiled at each other coyly at the thought of spending their first night together since their separation, and the meeting was adjourned.

❧

Cail and T'skya arrived back at Wilderwood after dusk. She landed in a clearing as close to the enclave as she could and was gladdened to be met in the Clanmeet by so many she loved. The dwellers greeted them with hugs and cheers, and celebrations were planned well into the night. The presence of Raven's cold body, however, subdued them, as did the news of Ferret's demise.

The ceremony was brief but honourable, and many tears were shed. Raven was laid to rest beside Negram with a sword at her side and a lock of Cail's hair at her bosom. Stones were placed upon her grave by all the members of the enclave, and when everyone had departed, Cail remained alone, mourning the loss of the two women who had been so important in his life.

T'skya sat up waiting for him, inhaling the forest scent and wondering what the future would hold. The path before her was not clear. Cail would announce himself Castan and order would gradually return to the land. What he intended to do with the Kházakha and how he proposed to incorporate their foreign way of life into the simple communities of the Roumanhis she did not know, but that was not her concern. What troubled her was the part she would play.

She was the Communicator, a title of great worth, and had been chosen by the Grish-Grish-Gûri despite her alien form. Cail loved her and clearly wished her to share his life in the intimacy of bonding, and she, too, yearned for this connection, but still the path was not clear.

In a little over five months, the Mothership was due to return, packed with people she had grown up with and to whom she owed so much. What if they were not welcome? What if they had found another land in which to live and wished to claim her back? What should she do? And what if she stayed and the Roumanhi people rejected her as Castana? But there was little point in dwelling on these matters, the Mothership might never return and T'skya's choice would be made for her.

Her thoughts were disturbed by Cail's return. He looked worn and weary, as if the forest could no longer lift his spirits. She, too, felt flat and needed sleep. She could not remember when she had last closed her eyes. Her mind felt muzzy and her limbs were like lead. 'We must get some sleep,' she said to him as he stood beside her.

He nodded and held out his hand to assist her to her feet. 'Stay with me tonight,' he said softly, not daring to look in her eyes. T'skya turned away, not sure how to answer him. He needed her with him, that much was clear, and she desperately wished to accommodate him, but she feared to look beyond his words.

'I'm sorry,' she replied. 'I promised Catkin I would stay with her.' Cail sighed with disappointment and kissed her upturned face before slipping away into the night.

❦

The next morning, they returned to the city and found Travis at the Palace organising the prisoners and freeing those who had been mistakenly captured. Families were reunited and those who were willing to lend their assistance and innocent of serious crimes were released, although kept under rigid surveillance.

Laskin, Dougan and Prell, along with his younger brother, Snell who had joined the allies happily, had begun air-lifting the Kházakha prisoners out of the enclaves and housing them in the docking bay hangers since everywhere else was full.

Kilmar and Fadrian were busy assigning tasks to the unoccupied and Spider was attempting to re-house all those who had lost their homes. Gilgarad, Tarn and Malvern had taken it upon themselves to round up all those Kházakha as yet unaccounted for, and Lazat, who had at last woken up from his drug-induced sleep, had gone with Darius to organise the big clean up the city desperately needed.

There was not an idle pair of hands to be seen and Cail smiled as reports came in of operations successfully carried out. Things were going better than he could have imagined, although it was clear the men were nearing exhaustion, having worked throughout the night.

Cail decided that things were well enough under control to spare some time to look in on Hollam and Ash. The latter, he had been informed, had regained consciousness and, although still in intensive care, was now allowed visitors. Hollam was also awake, but apart from Kylian who was always by his side, he had refused to see anyone, including Tarn.

Cail would not be dissuaded, however, and all the nurses' protestations were in vain. He swung open the door to the private hospital room and strode in. Hollam scowled and turned his head away as Cail approached the bed. The blond man stared at Kylian, hoping he would take the hint and leave, but the wild-haired man showed no intention of abandoning his post.

'I would speak with you alone,' Cail said calmly.

'There is nothing you can say that my brother may not hear.'

Cail took a deep breath. Hollam's remark was pointed and had stung, but he was not about to let it put him off. 'You should not turn your friends away. Tarn is deeply wounded, as am I.'

'Are you speaking now as a friend or as a Castan concerned for his people?' Hollam replied sardonically.

'I am speaking as your brother.'

'I have only one brother and he is seated before you - or have you forgotten we do not share the same blood?'

Cail furrowed his brow, fighting the tears behind his eyes. 'Do you blame me so much for that? Can a man be at fault for his birth? I am Castan by title, not from choice. I cannot be held responsible for the decisions others have made. Hollam, look at me. Am I not still your brother in spirit? Am I not the same man you loved?'

Hollam screwed up his eyes in pain. He had given his all and lost so much that he could not reconcile the verity of Cail's words with the knowledge of such deceit. 'The memory of my mother is now tainted. She gave my brother to be sacrificed to save a symbol of our people, a noble deed by all accounts, but it was wrong! It was not *her* responsibility.'

Cail looked stricken but kept his voice low. 'Would you then have had *me* die or ended up like Kylian? Is that what you would wish for?'

Hollam sighed mournfully. 'I would that things had been different. My brother was taken from me, and you are so far above me that I cannot even see you. Cail, you are the Castan and do not need me. I do not even know what I should do when you are before me,' he said wearily.

'You should do as you have always done. Hollam, there is

no man greater than you. It was you who freed our people. I was fighting for my life whilst you were fighting for the lives of us all. And yet, now that our dreams are within reach, I have never felt emptier. The sacrifice must not be in vain. I must accept my heritage and so must you. But I would have you on my side when I do so.' Cail paused and looked the melancholy man in the face. 'I would have your blessing.'

Hollam turned away. His head was filled with confusion and his stomach churned with mixed emotions. The resentment he felt towards all those who had partaken in the scheme to save the Castan was considerable and yet he knew that to lay the blame at Cail's feet was unjust. Cail was not responsible, but he was the cause. Yet deep within himself, Hollam loved him as fully as he had ever done. Kylian's presence, however, was a reminder of all that was wrong and Hollam could not bring himself to bless the man whose title was behind his brother's suffering.

Hollam stared at Kylian and then at the bed. He could not face Cail. 'I cannot,' he said sadly, his voice cracking with emotion.

Cail hung his head and moved to the door. As he was leaving, he paused. 'I will not claim my title without it,' he murmured before slipping from the room.

SEVENTEEN

The Coronation

Over the next few weeks, work in the city began in earnest. The prisoners were housed and attended to with more compassion than any Roumanhi had ever been shown, and the streets were relatively untroubled. The dead had been buried in a field outside the city and those Roumanhis killed in the frays had been returned to their enclaves for burial there.

Fadrian, Kilmar and Spider were overseeing the dismantling of the shanty town and had the welcome assistance of the androids. The machines engaged themselves in tearing the former dwellings of the slaves apart with such intent that they almost appeared enthusiastic. Within days they had broken up the hovels and made great piles of wood, metal sheeting and cardboard that stood upon the flattened landscape like abstract monoliths.

Vigour had finally deemed T'skya secure enough to survive without its personal protection and had joined its comrades in the task. Wrath, too, was present, equipped with a new left arm and replacement components in its eye. Vigour had been offered bodywork repairs but had refused in such a way that T'skya almost believed it had begun to develop a personality.

Laskin and his men transported home all those who wished

to return to the enclaves. Some had been unwilling to leave their hovels, having lived in them for so long, and were difficult to persuade otherwise. Readapting themselves to forest life and the unhurried ways of the enclaves was not going to be easy. Most of those who did return, however, were welcomed with so much enthusiasm and hospitality that they soon settled and began to take pleasure in their freedom. For some, however, the horrors of the city would never fade and, unable to face their lives, they either remained in the city assisting their comrades or became Wanderers, as Fen had been.

The industries were gradually shut down, with only those necessary for the running of the city remaining in operation, manned by small crews. Cail had no wish to alienate the Kházakha who had sided with Travis by depriving them of everything they were accustomed to. It would take as much time for them to adapt as it would for the Roumanhis; probably more.

Cail often shut himself away with Travis, trying to come up with a workable scheme to combine the Kházakha's ways with his own people's. Despite opposition from the more radical Roumanhis, Cail had no wish to expel the usurpers from the land. They had lived there for years and had it not been for many of them, Santovin would not have fallen. Many were good and noble, trapped in a life of cruelty and injustice by those who had held power. Cail would not judge them guilty for events outside their control. That was all too easy to do.

Hollam gained in strength every day and eventually permitted the occasional person to visit him, but he had changed, and those who saw him came away feeling uneasy. He spent most of his time in the company of Kylian, attempting to establish some form of communication between them. Kylian was shut off from the world, unable to show his thoughts and desires and he often grew violent when those around him failed to understand and only Hollam could calm him. But gradually the big man taught him to sign, his patience and diligence eventually paying off as Kylian began to talk with his hands.

T'skya was forbidden entry, however. Hollam had learnt she knew of Cail's heritage and could not forgive the deceit. Although she did not blame him, his rejection wounded her and she spent her time away from the city, sculpting the landscape with farmers from the forest and planting trees. She also absorbed herself with the computer network, attempting to unlock some of the secrets behind Santovin's rise to power. Travis often accompanied her; there was still much he desired to learn.

Cail seldom saw T'skya and when he did manage to steal some little time with her she appeared distant and eager to escape. He could not understand her sudden coldness and it disturbed him.

❧

It was several more weeks before Hollam was allowed to escape the confinement of his room. He was seen each morning in the hospital grounds being pushed in a wheelchair by his brother; his body wrapped against the cold and his plastered leg jutting out from beneath the blankets. Roumanhis greeted him gladly and on occasion even managed to raise a smile on his solemn face, but the Hollam of old had disappeared and was greatly missed by those who knew him.

T'skya found him in the small garden to the rear of the hospital, studying a twisted tree whose buds were so full of petals they looked ready to burst. Hollam was in deep contemplation and his face had taken on a troubled countenance. T'skya's arrival disturbed him. He turned in his chair and looked at his brother reproachfully. 'When you said you had to fetch something, I did not think you meant her!' he complained.

Kylian smiled and spread out his hands in a gesture of innocence and signed a few words. T'skya leapt to the mute man's defence. 'I would have come whether he brought me or not. I wish to speak to you.'

'I have nothing to say,' growled Hollam.

'Then say nothing. Just listen.'

Hollam sighed and resigned himself to suffer her presence. Kylian wandered a short distance away to give them privacy and pretended to show an interest in the vegetation.

'I know you're angry with me, and you have every reason to be,' she said. 'Maybe I should have told you the truth when you asked me to explain Negram's words, but I didn't think you could handle it; and I was right. Supposing I had told you; would you have gone to the tanks? If you had known, then maybe your people would still be enslaved. Maybe Cail would be dead. Is that what you want?'

Hollam remained silent but the muscles in his jaws were tight and T'skya could see that he was listening. She pushed on, hoping to say all that she intended before he grew tired. 'I understand your resentment, but it's wrong to direct it at Cail. Don't you recall Negram's words? *"Blame not Cail or myself for what must be. Though things are not as they seem, our destinies are clear and may not be altered for the needs of the one."*'

'I recall them, and were I the only one to suffer, perhaps I could forgive. But I am not, and every moment I am reminded of Kylian's silence,' he replied bitterly.

'Kylian has suffered greatly and is the victim of circumstance, but what is done can't be changed. We have our whole futures ahead of us and his could be great if only you didn't keep him chained to you.'

Hollam's eyes blazed. 'Ward your words, woman, else I might forget my manners!'

T'skya laughed. 'What are you going to do? Hop after me or run me over in your wheelchair?'

Even in his surly mood, Hollam found he had to smile at the image. 'It is unfair to take advantage of a wounded man.'

'You leave me little choice,' she retorted. 'What you've done with Kylian is beyond reproach, but you've also shut him from the world. What good is a language that none can understand? He can only talk to you because we aren't party to his signing. I'm the Communicator and yet I can't really understand him without entering his mind. Set him free, Hollam.'

'I do not chain him.'

T'skya moved closer. 'Physically, no, but whilst you remain as you do he'll never leave you. He feels bound to you by your suffering and is being torn apart. Hollam, he bowed before the Castan and you should have seen the light of hope in his eyes. All his life Santovin taunted him about the destruction of the monarchy and how his people were brought to ruin. Your reproach and stubbornness is no different. You've made him the cause of dispute between yourself and Cail and prevented the rightful heir from claiming his throne.'

'If Cail seeks the crown, then let him claim it. I have done nothing to prevent him.'

'You know that's untrue. Cail will never reign without your blessing. He needs you,' she implored.

'Your words hold truth and yet you are a hypocrite. You accuse me of desertion and yet have you not done the same? I am neither deaf nor blind and have knowledge of your actions or lack of them.'

'My reasons are personal,' she muttered.

'And mine are not? If you love him as much as I know you do, why do you push him away?'

'For the same reasons you rejected Breeze.'

Hollam reached out and took her hand. It was the first genuinely warm gesture he had made towards anyone since his rescue. 'T'skya, hear me. I am a foolish man and would not have you make the same mistakes. I was wrong in that decision and may live to regret it. Go to Cail, speak with him. If your love is pure, you will find a way to overcome whatever lies in your path. Do not fear to love him as I feared to love Breeze.'

T'skya brushed a tear away. Her voice was shaky as she spoke. 'Do you expect me to follow the words of a man too stubborn and proud to take his own advice?'

Hollam bowed his head in contemplation and fell silent. T'skya could see the internal struggle and dared not speak lest she lose her advantage. Suddenly there was a popping sound and the tree Hollam had been studying exploded into bloom. T'skya gazed at the delicate flower as it swayed in the light wind, and then caught sight of Hollam's expression. He was staring at the flower as if its presence scorned him and a look of utter shame and recrimination entered his face. At first she could not understand how one small blossom could affect a man so, until with a stab of recognition she realised it was a hope flower. Today was Cail's birthday.

At long length he looked up at her. 'You hold great wisdom for one so small. I said I was not blind and yet my eyes have been clouded with darkness. I said I was not deaf and yet my ears have failed to hear. I have denied my friends and banished hope. I shall set Kylian free and Cail shall have my blessing and be crowned Castan.'

T'skya could not contain her joy and smothered the big man in kisses. 'Save your kisses for one more deserving than I,' he said quietly. 'He has more need of them.'

❧

T'skya found Cail in the auditorium, surrounded. For the umpteenth time he attempted to find a compromise between the bickering groups. Travis, too, seemed exasperated by the petty squabbling and found T'skya's presence a welcome disruption. Cail, losing concentration when he saw her, stumbled over his words, and seeing her expression adjourned the meeting until the afternoon. Travis took the hint and filed out with the rest.

Cail remained upon the platform and watched T'skya from under his brows. She felt nervous under his unremitting gaze, knowing that she had hurt him without justification. She said nothing as she mounted the platform and eased herself on to his lap. She curled her hand behind his head, entwining her fingers in his silken hair, and pulled his lips to hers. Their kiss was deep and passionate, and when she released him, Cail sat back with a confused but happy expression on his face.

'What did I do to deserve that?' he inquired, touching his lips as if unsure that the tingling sensation was real.

'Consider that as an apology and your birthday present,' she said, grinning at his bewilderment.

'Apologise again,' he said wickedly, 'and I might forgive you.' T'skya complied gladly and it was some minutes before they stopped for breath.

'I, too, owe you an apology, but I shall kiss you not!' a deep voice said from the doorway.

T'skya and Cail whirled in their seat, flushed and embarrassed to see Hollam sitting in the centre of the aisle. She slid off Cail's lap, allowing him to stand, and he slowly and somewhat uncertainly descended from the platform. Hollam's smile wavered as he gazed up at the man he had so blindly condemned.

Cail stood awaiting his word as Hollam hung his head, searching for a way to begin. When he looked up he was weeping and could not speak. As he awkwardly climbed to his feet and tried to bow, Cail snatched him into an embrace of reconciliation and love.

⁓⁕⁓

The Coronation was set for two months hence. Until that day when Hollam had finally found the spirit of forgiveness and given Cail his blessing, few had known that the Castan yet lived.

Heralds were sent far afield, travelling the length and breadth of the land to bring the news to all. The inhabitants of Wilderwood, who had educated, scolded, trained, laughed, cried and grown up alongside Cail, were beside themselves with joy. Stories of their adventures and everything connected with him were discussed with unquenchable enthusiasm.

In the city, preparations began in earnest. The ceremony would take place in the field of Caelcáladrim, at the foot of the mountains where the great man had met his doom. Transport ships would be provided for all those too old or weak to make the journey on foot, and supplies were positioned along the route for those who chose to walk.

As the time approached, Cail grew more and more nervous. He needed the support of his friends more than ever, but although he and Hollam had apparently reconciled, there was still an underlying tension between them, especially since Kylian was seldom absent from the latter's side. With T'skya, he also felt a detachment, for although she was often with him she still seemed reluctant to discuss the future or to allow their intimacy to progress. Cail guessed her underlying reasons and they worried him. He wanted her, needed her, and was terrified that he would lose her.

Determined not to let his fears betray him, he finally persuaded T'skya to leave her work and, forgetting about his duties and responsibilities, had Laskin fly them close to the spot where he would claim his title.

After Laskin had departed, Cail carefully bound her eyes shut with some ribbon and led her, with much good-natured protestation, to the north.

The day was warm, for spring had come upon the land, and T'skya could smell the scent of the meadow flowers upon the wind and hear the cheerful melodies of song birds as they dived and swooped, hunting insects upon the wing. The sound of a small brook bubbling and tinkling to her right where it popped up from its mountain source enchanted her and the long grass tickled her bare legs. Cail happily whistled a traditional air as they walked along under the welcoming sun. He appeared relaxed but the slight trembling of his hand betrayed the nervousness he felt inside. Wherever he was leading her was clearly of great importance to him. When they arrived, his whistling stopped and he removed the ribbon from her eyes.

T'skya blinked against the light and clapped her hands in delight. Cail's secret was at last revealed. Before her was spread a delicious picnic upon an embroidered cloth, set amongst a swathe of multi-coloured flowers and tall grasses. The mountains stood with purple magnificence against an azure sky, their peaks still capped with crystal snow, and billowing white clouds floated dreamily past.

Cail smiled, pleased by her reaction and proceeded to pour her a glass of light, refreshing wine. She sat beside him, spreading the folds of her dress upon the ground and they raised their glasses in a toast.

'To your Coronation,' T'skya said.

Cail gazed at her, his eyes smouldering with passion. 'To us,' he said softly, and chinked his glass against hers.

T'skya had known from the very first moment what he intended, and yet, despite her fears, had not resisted him when he whisked her away from the city. She remembered Hollam's words and knew the time had come to follow her heart. 'To us,' she murmured, meeting his gaze.

He laid her down amongst the long grasses and there, as the sun beat down upon them, they joined together as one. Cail's sexual denial since his coming of age was evident in the almost desperate intensity of his actions until, finding release, he slowed and began to savour their contact, kissing and caressing her, exploring her body and learning her desires. He was skilled and attentive and took her to heights of pleasure never obtained during her heated fumblings on board the Mothership.

T'skya could feel his very essence. She cried out with joy, experiencing his passions as if she were living them through him. She felt his strength rippling through his back as she ran her hands across his skin. She felt his heart-beat thumping

408

against her breasts. She felt the heat of his body and the warm dampness of his breath as he pressed his face into her neck, and she felt his spirit joining with hers.

She had never experienced a sensation like it, nor been so overwhelmed with emotion. She was now his bond-mate and bound to him for life by a thread too strong for any man or woman to break. She knew now the torment the Roumanhis had suffered by being separated from their partners and understood why Hollam had feared to become one with Breeze; she now felt she knew Cail as well as she knew herself.

When Laskin returned for them later that evening, he found the couple hand in hand and grinned, bowing low as he stood aside to let them board the craft.

Cail helped T'skya in and elegantly gestured to a seat. 'My Queen,' he said as she bent her knees to sit. He laughed as she thumped into the chair, her eyes huge with realisation and shock.

In the heat of her passion she had completely forgotten the destiny their bonding would create for her. But she knew it was right, for had the Grish-Grish-Gûri not read their hearts and seen the love they held for one another? Had they not empowered her with wondrous gifts and appointed her Communicator to the King? In their wisdom they had foreseen the path towards unification and created the way by which the two nations of Roumanhi and Navenná could live as one. Together she and Cail would bring peace upon the land.

❦

The Coronation approached and soon the eve of the great day was upon them. The field of Caelcáladrim had been set with tents and provisions to house and feed the thousands who had begun to gather there. The pilots were working over-time ferrying people to and fro and delivering supplies, and nobody sat idly. Scouts from both sides were patrolling the crowd alert for trouble but the occasion was a joyous one and only the occasional scuffle marred the time as people battled for a better place or passed some thoughtless comment.

Inside the Palace, Cail was pacing his room. T'skya sat silently watching him. A strange sense of calm had come upon her but she could feel Cail's tension as if it were her own. 'Tomorrow I will be crowned and my life will change forever. I fear it, my Queen. It is a heavy burden and perhaps one I am ill-prepared for. I would that Negram or Briar was here to guide me through this.'

'They guided you throughout your life and their knowledge is within you. You have no need of them now.' She drew his lips to hers and they spoke no more that night.

❧❧❧

The day dawned bright and the sky was clear. In the afternoon, Lily and Ralamani set about dressing and grooming everyone before leaving for the field of Caelcáladrim. Travis and Laskin wore their full military regalia whilst the Roumanhis were attired in fine forest habiliments of white, browns and greens. Cail and T'skya's clothes followed the traditions of the land. Cail was decked in a pure white robe, trimmed with golden threads. About his waist was tied a belt of woven *Silhvran* leaves and an emerald cloak flowed from his shoulders. He wore simple sandals on his feet and his head was bare. T'skya's gown was of the brightest green and moulded itself to her form perfectly. A belt similar to Cail's sat around her waist and golden slippers adorned her feet. She sat patiently whilst Lily placed upon her head a circlet of delicate flowers. When all was finished she viewed herself in the mirror. T'skya hardly recognised the image which stared back at her and copied every gesture.

Then she saw the image smile.

When Cail came to collect her, he gasped and she viewed

410

him with pride, but they could not delay. Laskin was waiting for them in a transport ship on the Palace roof. Castans of old had always made the journey on foot but with Hollam still incapacitated and requiring a stick the long march was out of the question. Furthermore, Cail was learning to adapt and accept the small benefits technology had brought to the land.

Laskin brought the ship down almost half a league from the outer edge of the massive gathering. Cail had insisted, with Hollam's approval, that they would at least walk the last stages of the journey.

They soon came upon a mass of cheering spectators. T'skya blushed as the people bowed and lowered her eyes, overwhelmed. Cail walked erect and proud. Hollam limped beside Kylian, looking sullen. His leg hurt more than he cared to admit, but as the crowd cried out his name he brightened and raised a smile.

The procession was nearing the platform upon which the Coronation would take place. People of all kinds spanned as far as the eye could see and an honour guard of androids lined the way to hold the eager crowds back. A few daring children sat between their legs but no-one was foolish enough to attempt to break past them.

In front of the simply adorned platform stood Tarn and Lily, Ralamani and Samis, Spider, Gilgarad, Ash and most of the inhabitants of Wilderwood. Catkin was sitting atop Badger's shoulders and waving so wildly that the poor man was having difficulty supporting her.

Hollam scanned the crowds hopefully. He caught sight of a group of sea-people and strained his neck to get a better look. His expression of disappointment was evident; Breeze was not there. Briar, too, was noticeable by her absence.

A hushed silence fell upon the people as they waited for the ceremony to start. Cail stepped forward and buried his sudden desire to flee beneath his determination to serve his land and present himself to the people as the strong and noble ruler they were expecting. His throat felt dry, his tongue thick and leaden, but he managed an elegant speech. When, at last, the tones of his voice died away, the sun was sinking low in the sky and long shadows spread across the land, signalling the time for the Coronation itself to begin.

From nowhere a dark shadow passed overhead, as if a great cloud were being swiftly blown upon the wind. T'skya was delighted to see the eagles circling above them, crying out their welcomes. Braithwheir had come to pay his respects and bless the return of the Castan.

From the front of the crowd, Tarn ascended the steps, carrying a non-descript box that had been found stowed away in Negram's room. With dignity he knelt before Kylian and opened the lid. Within sat the crown which had adorned the head of every Castan since the reign of Gilgarad in bygone days. Kylian bowed deeply and held the simple symbol aloft for all to see before stepping behind Cail, who was now kneeling to receive it.

The mute man lowered the crown until it was almost touching Cail's head. A minute change came upon Kylian's face and to the brief concern of the spectators he withdrew and held the crown out to his brother. Hollam tentatively took the offering and with trembling hands laid it upon Cail's head, weeping openly as the crowd dropped to their knees.

Cail rose to his feet and flung back his cloak. 'Behold your Castan!' he cried. 'And behold your Castana, Talaskya, daughter of Talvin of the Homequest, Communicator and saviour of the land.'

T'skya gazed at Cail in astonishment. He had used her full title, Talaskya, the name that signified her journey into Navennán adulthood. How had he known it? And then she noticed Travis's smug smile.

Cail waited patiently for the hubbub to die down before venturing to speak again. 'Before me lies a rule unlike any my forefathers had to face, for I am ruler over two nations sharing one Kingdom and I will serve to unite the peoples of this fair land. Our lives have been forever changed and we must embrace those changes which benefit us and reject those which do not.

'I will remain in the city but a short while longer. In my absence, Commander Travis shall rule as Steward of Navennán city with the Castan's full authority.'

T'skya stepped forward to address the crowds. 'We will detain you no longer; let the festivities begin.'

The people cheered and soon the celebrations were under way. The Castan and his Queen sat amongst their closest friends, eating and drinking to their hearts' content but the night of celebration would soon be cut short for them. Their Coronation completed, they had another duty to attend to.

Cail rose to his feet. 'My friends, the time has come for us to leave. We shall not return until we have found the knowledge we seek. Do not fear for our safety nor try to follow our path. We must face the darkness alone and endure all that we meet. I bid you all farewell until we are reunited.'

Hollam climbed to his feet looking abashed. 'Brother, I have done you much wrong in both thought and deed and withheld a gift my mother demanded be given to you. I have thought long and hard about what it portends and have failed to find answers to my questions. Perhaps the knowledge lies within you.'

He fumbled in his pocket and withdrew the woven chain of hair upon which hung the amulet Negram had presented to him on her deathbed. He held it out, as if unwilling to be parted from the object so avidly protected by his mother. T'skya had kept its existence secret, sure that Hollam would do the right thing. Cail received it with relief.

'Brother, you have eased my mind and lifted a burden off my shoulders. The way before me was uncertain; I had thought this amulet lost. Forgive my silence if I do not speak of its purpose but know you have done a great deed this day and I shall not forget it.'

❦

The crowds waited patiently for their King and Queen to return. The festivities continued and the weather remained fine, although by the third day many were anxious and the food supplies were running low.

Hollam paced the ground, frustrated and uneasy, disconcerted by the silence of the people from the Great Divide when he questioned them about Breeze. They chatted contentedly on subjects relating to the land and the sea, but of her they became like mountains; silent and forbidding. Something was wrong and every nerve in his body screamed out against remaining, but he could not set out without Cail's leave, and Cail had not yet returned.

As the purple hues of dusk fell upon the land and a light mist lifted from the ground, a cry echoed into the night and all eyes turned as two shady figures broke through the curls of mist. In eerie silence, the people dropped to their knees and cast down their eyes. They had no knowledge of where Cail and his Queen had been nor of what had befallen them but the eldest amongst them recalled the events of Mithdrill's ascension and knew that all was as it should be.

❦

Life in the city settled down. Cail made several trips to the forests but the expected arrival of the Mothership drew him to T'skya's side in the city. She grew impatient until her prayers were finally answered. Bright lights began to appear in the sky, travelling with great speed towards the city's inviting beacons. Crowds gathered in the streets to watch, and the oldest amongst the Roumanhis viewed the sky with a strange sense of déjà vu and a certain trepidation.

T'skya, Cail, Travis and Tarn raced to the docking bays and a welcoming reception was quickly mounted with an honour guard of androids and uniformed officers.

The people did not have to wait long before the roar of engines was perceivable in the stillness of the night. Five craft, identical in design but larger in size to the one T'skya had crash-landed in, came to rest upon the pads. T'skya hurried to landing pad 4 to meet the stern figure of Commander Talmana.

T'skya spent the whole night in the company of Commander Talmana and some of her senior officers, accompanied by Cail. There was much he desired to learn and Talmana could not refuse him. Talmana related her tale concisely and with surprisingly little emotion.

'What? I thought...I'd assumed that you'd remain here with us!' T'skya exclaimed.

'Talaskya, people from our world have intruded on this land enough. We wish for a fresh start, and the islands Gyan found suit our purposes completely. If we're to people this world, it must be done with care and understanding. We've no wish to over-run the natives and our numbers are too great for this city.'

Cail interrupted, anxious to set his mind at rest on one point which had been bothering him since her arrival. 'Commander, permit me to ask why it was that you showed so little surprise at the presence of Navennáns in this land?'

'We picked up transmissions when we first arrived and our scanners revealed the presence of our own technology, though far more basic, on the planet's surface. I already knew of the expulsion of the throw-backs and it seemed logical they were here,' the Commander replied.

'You knew!' T'skya spluttered.

'I was not at liberty to inform my crew, but to find them was one of my prime directives. The Navennán council feared their return and we were sent to locate them and hinder their progress if they threatened reprisals.'

'Then you weren't searching for a new home?' T'skya asked, a little uneasy she had been chosen for the mission.

'My grand-father received the order to find them. When I eventually took command from my father, my directives were as you knew them to be, but the original orders remained on file and were known to me.'

'And now that you have found them, what do you intend?' Cail asked.

'I'm satisfied they hold no threat. Your people have ensured that.'

'Yes, but we have many prisoners; dangerous ones, and their future is uncertain. It is not our custom to withhold people's freedom and yet we dare not release them - they are not easy to manage. I hoped you might be of assistance in this matter,' he said.

Talmana sat back on her chair and narrowed her eyes. After long contemplation she nodded slowly. 'It's not a burden I wished for, but it does fall within my jurisdiction...release the prisoners into my care and I'll ensure they cause you no further trouble.'

❧

The following day revealed a hive of activity as transport after transport ferried the prisoners to the Mothership and great crowds gathered to watch them depart. The cells grew quiet and empty and Cail felt relieved to be free of his burden. T'skya was quiet and withdrawn. Cail knew the parting was hard. She had wanted the people from the Homequest close by her, but that was not to be.

But the last of their troubles was not yet over, and it quickly became obvious that something had to be done about Hollam. His confrontations with Cail were many and heated. T'skya knew the cause of his behaviour and could not understand Cail's reluctance to let his brother depart for the Great Divide.

'By keeping him here, you risk losing him forever,' she warned.

'I know you speak the truth, yet I fear for him. I do not think he will find what he seeks and he can endure little more.'

'Is there news from the Great Divide?'

'No more than rumour, but it concerns me. The Kalkassians have taken their leave of this land though their reasons were not expressed. I cannot recall a time when their people had no presence here. I can find no comfort in the thought of Hollam leaving.'

'Whatever may befall him is not your responsibility. He must find his own path, Cail. Let Hollam go with your blessing. You owe him that much,' T'skya pleaded.

It was with a very heavy heart that he agreed.

There were no words of farewell. As another evening cast its purple hues upon the land, Hollam quietly stole away, telling no-one of his leaving and carrying only his walking stick and the small battered pack which had accompanied him on his heroic journey to the water tanks.

His absence was not discovered until many hours later and was followed by an outburst from those who would feel his loss the most. For Cail the loss was the greatest. He wished more than anything that their differences had been fully resolved before Hollam left and feared that they would never have the chance for reconciliation. He was also troubled by the fact that Hollam was alone, for there were still dangerous Kházakha abroad and Hollam was not yet fit enough to put up a good fight.

He and T'skya would soon be departing to visit the forest enclaves, leaving the city in Travis's safe hands until their return. Tarn and Lily would accompany them, along with Fadrian, Spider and Ash, but Gilgarad had chosen to stay for some time longer and aid the Commander with his many duties. Life would return to normal, as normal as it could be under the circumstances, and still Cail did not feel at peace.

His deliberations were disturbed by T'skya. He felt her presence before he heard her and was glad of her support. She slipped onto his lap.

'Do you think he will manage out there all alone?' Cail asked, unable to draw his mind from the south and the path Hollam was walking.

'Do not fear for him, beloved. He is not alone, though he knows it not,' she replied.

Cail looked at her inquiringly but smiled his understanding before she had time to answer.

THE END

Lightning Source UK Ltd.
Milton Keynes UK
26 July 2010

157455UK00001B/2/P